NIGHT CROSSING, the third in The
Trilogy of Remembrance.

Mary E Martin has done a brilliant job of developing her
cast of characters, not just over the book, but over the
trilogy. I'm sorry to see the end of this trilogy: it's been
intriguing and the characters have stayed with me long
after I've turned the final page.

Sue Magee for thebookbag.co.uk

THE DRAWING LESSON the first in
The Trilogy of Remembrance.

Mary E. Martin understands the craft of writing engrossing
novels peopled with credible and fascinating characters...
storylines that are propulsive and challenging in content
and technique of development...an exceptional book...She
is a fine writer.

Grady Harp, Review from Amazon Reviewer
GRADY HARP, Hall of Fame Reviewer
[#28] from 2006 to and including 2011

Two fascinating and intertwined stories. Mary Martin
handles a large cast of characters with great narrative skill.
Each has a compelling story to tell and a past—sometimes
shocking—to come to terms with.

Robert Adams, author of "A Love of Reading;
Reviews of Contemporary Fiction.

The Drawing Lesson by author, Mary E. Martin, stands among the best of literary fiction... A compelling and moving story to be savored on the palate like fine wine.

Vonnie Faroqui Ink Slinger's Whimsy.

An ending you will not expect and a final twist that will surprise you. Mary E. Martin has created her own masterpiece or work of art in this outstanding novel. "

Fran Lewis, Goodreads.

THE FATE OF PRYDE, the second in
The Trilogy of Remembrance.

Martin continues to teach the reader about contemporary art and the working of the minds involved in the changes that occur in the arts while weaving a terrifically interesting story. She is a writer to heed!

Grady Harp, Review from Amazon Reviewer
GRADY HARP, Hall of Fame Reviewer
[#28] from 2006 to and including 2011

With incredible depth of empathy, Mary E. Martin once again captivates our imaginations and transports us into the heart of artistry...The artistic vision which infuses her work is pure genius.

Vonnie Faroqui, Inkslinger's Whimsy

NIGHT CROSSING

THE THIRD IN THE TRILOGY OF REMEMBRANCE

Mary E. Martin

NIGHT CROSSING
THE THIRD IN THE TRILOGY OF REMEMBRANCE

iUniverse books may be ordered through booksellers or by contacting:

iUniverse LLC
1663 Liberty Drive
Bloomington, IN 47403
www.iuniverse.com
1-800-Authors (1-800-288-4677)

ISBN: 978-1-4917-3715-6 (sc)
ISBN: 978-1-4917-3717-0 (hc)
ISBN: 978-1-4917-3716-3 (e)

Library of Congress Control Number: 2014910430

Printed in the United States of America.

iUniverse rev. date: 06/10/2014

To my family, David, Stephen, Timothy, Susan, Harrison and Victoria and to my muse.

Yarmouth, from near the Harbour's Mouth
Joseph Mallord William Turner 1775-1851

Only recently have I realized that Alexander Wainwright, Britain's finest landscape painter, whom you are about to meet, shares with the painter J.M.W. Turner a passion for light in his paintings.

Alexander has spent his life searching for his light and ways to express it in his art. For him, as with Turner, light has a deep spiritual significance.

In the first novel in The Trilogy of Remembrance, The Drawing Lesson, Alexander wins the Turner Prize from the Tate Modern. This prize is most frequently won by conceptual artists and in The Drawing Lesson Rinaldo, a conceptual artist, is driven to seek revenge upon Alex for his winning the prize with his representational painting "The Hay Wagon." Consequently, it seems appropriate to place one of Turner's water colours, "Yarmouth from near the harbour's mouth" on the front cover.

To me, this painting evokes a sense of yearning for that light and the unknown potentials in life.

That is what Night Crossing is all about as well as— a love so profound it transcends life and death. Please join the search and enjoy. Mary E. Martin

Cover Art
Yarmouth, from near the Harbour's Mouth
Joseph Mallord William Turner 1775-1851
Tate Images
©Tate, London 2014

LONDON

CHAPTER 1

Sharp rays of sun illuminated tubes of paints set out in orderly rows. Brushes stood upright in tins like sentries organized by size and rank. A dirty rag, smelling of turpentine, dropped to the floor and a stony-faced artist gazed at his half-finished canvas. Suddenly, with an anguished cry, he flung his palette at the canvas.

What he then saw froze and silenced him. The palette did not strike the canvas but veered willfully off in a wild arc of its own creation.

The spinning palette appeared to take aim at the long, elegant neck of a mannequin he sometimes used for still-life drawing. It struck it with full force. At first, the mannequin seemed suspended in time and space but then it clattered downward onto a tin of bright red paint. The tin spilled over dripping paint from the table to the floor where it congealed in a massive red pool. The mannequin lay face-up with a bloodied nose.

Witnessing such absurdities unfolding before his eyes, the artist gave an angry bark of laughter. Surely some unseen hand had mysteriously directed the cascade of events! How could one tin of paint flood an entire studio floor? Astonished to witness such unnatural events, the artist glanced warily about his studio. Shaking his head, he rushed to sop up the mess with a rag.

Even inanimate objects seemed to mock him. Although there was nothing to do but laugh, he did not. Throwing aside the rag, Alexander Wainwright, Britain's finest landscape painter, glared at his canvas and shouted, "Disgusting! Stupid and trite!"

Scowling, he stared out the high windows of his studio. Beyond them, twilight crept over the Thames dotting it with tiny pinpoints of light. A ferry churned across the river just beyond Tower Bridge and shadows fell softly across his studio. His foot tapped out a staccato rhythm.

As if doomed to repeat his work forever, he had painted a dilapidated farmhouse with a horse in a distant meadow. He sighed. At least he had the beginnings of a human figure—a farmer with a hostile gaze. *Where is something new?*

Alexander rubbed his grizzled beard and whispered, "I've struggled with painting this bucolic stuff for years. Why can't I free myself?" Lost in thought, he gazed down the Thames at Big Ben.

For some months, he had felt a stirring within, a questioning of his old habits of thought and feeling. If only a new, clean and cool wind could sweep into his life and cleanse his weary spirit!

Alexander fumbled for his pipe and lit it. He gazed again at Tower Bridge spanning the steel-coloured waters of the Thames. Bathed in pale light, the bridge seemed to beckon him to some far off mythical land where inspiration might lie. He slumped down on a stool.

His art was renowned for its *light.* A magical sense of the *beyond* enthralled his viewers. Surely some marvellous secret of life must lie just on the other side of his fields and streams. With his brushstrokes, he transported viewers into the *beyond* where they could imagine eternity upon eternity. Quickly, he painted over the farmer who seemed angry at being awakened into existence. Satisfied with his handiwork, Alexander thought, *Can the light shine through something new—not physical objects or people?*

In his tiny kitchen, he put on a pot of coffee. From the corner of his eye, he caught some movement—a shadow or shifting shape dancing on the wall. As he turned toward the shadows, his mouth grew slack. His breath deepened and a blissful, innocent smile spread across his face. His legs grew weak and he staggered toward his vision as if drawn by irresistible but unknown forces.

Against the tall windows, now blackened in the night, a golden egg rose up, shimmering with beautiful gems— diamonds, rubies, sapphires and emeralds which sparkled like the purest sunlight. Turning slowly, this marvellous object throbbed with life as if it contained all the energy in the world. His lips parted and he spoke three words—"the cosmic egg."

It was perhaps three feet in height and, at its widest point, two feet in breadth. It rotated majestically several times and then drifted upward toward the ceiling. Although stunning, it was as insubstantial as a rainbow and began to dissipate before his eyes.

Awe struck, he stood motionless. The cosmic egg was the seed heralding new creation. Everything necessary was at hand

and contained within that egg. For eons, it had tantalized humankind with the secret mystery of creation, life and death and the promise of immortality.

Every so often, Alexander experienced a vision. Sometimes he wondered if he hadn't really slipped into a dream-like state where anything could be imagined. It usually happened without any warning and certainly could never be commanded. Over the years, he had grown to cherish these dreamy, extraordinarily beautiful fantasies.

He sank to a stool and made a note. *Golden egg studded with every sort of gem appearing after my fit of frustration with painting. The most beautiful vision ever sent!*

He took another deep breath and smiled. *But what is it telling me? Why has it appeared now?* He hoped it promised that his period of stultified creativity was at an end. He swore to keep the image close to his heart as a guide.

Within moments, he felt *ready*—a sense, impossible to describe to anyone who did not create. A fullness within his mind, spirit and body infused him right down to his fingertips. He might overflow, he thought, or even burst if he did not begin at once.

Without thinking, he reached for a pad of drawing paper and his coloured pastel sticks. He began to doodle in an absent-minded fashion. After several moments he stopped and held his work up to the light. *Where did those lyrical shapes come from?*

In a minute or two, he had drawn three soft shapes in yellow, blue and green—one was a wildly free form shape. The second was oddly angular and yet fit into the free form in such a way, it appeared to give it newly conceived dimensions. Amazing! The two seemed to move together on the page, first closer together and then farther apart. He smiled again. *Perhaps they are making love! Something new may be born.*

After several moments of intense concentration, he filled in the third triangular shape with shadow giving it surprising depth. These strange shapes communicated in some universal language he had never heard. If he stared at them long enough, his eye was taken into more delicious fantasies of light and colour.

Over the next hour, he filled pages and pages with lines, angles, circles—such undulating shapes which had never flowed from his hand before. Anyone watching him work would be amazed. His entire visage swiftly changed from the serenity of a Buddhist monk to the despair of a distressed captain lost at sea and then to joyousness of a child at the circus.

At last, he was spent. He set down his pastels and spread out his drawings from one end of the workbench to the other. Rubbing his jaw and smiling, he studied the colours and shapes he had created. He laughed out loud. *Abstract art! I am painting my own personal interior world.*

His *friend* Rinaldo, the conceptual artist, whose performance events Alex privately regarded as silly grandstanding, was always quick with a sarcastic comment. But every now and then the thin and wiry little man struck home with a point.

Parading about his garret only a few weeks ago, Rinaldo had flung out his arms dramatically and declared, "Your so-called *real* world, Alex, which you paint in such tiresome detail, is but an illusion." Arms akimbo, he stood over him and fixed him with his stare. "Everything we see, touch, taste or smell is made of atoms." He pirouetted away. "And those atoms, which are as innumerable as stars in the sky, are only tiny packets of energy with no substance whatsoever." He spun back on

Alex, stabbing his finger almost under his nose. "And that cow in your pretty pictures is made entirely of such insubstantial stuff." He sighed deeply. "I grant you that somehow you see past these illusions and into that great *beyond* which your fans love. But when you go further and deeper, you will see that this world is simply shifting shapes and shadows of energy. Your famous *beyond* is not mysteriously tucked *behind* your fields and streams. It is *within* you."

Alex got up from his stool. Annoying as Rinaldo could be with his smirks and taunts, he had to admit there was some truth buried in his histrionics. *How can I find new forms of expression?* He shook his head. *But what do I want to express?*

He frowned when his cell phone rang. "Hello?"

"Hi, it's me."

Alex massaged the back of his neck. "Hi Daphne. How are…?"

"I thought we might have dinner tonight. What do you say?"

Good, he thought. *I need someone to talk to.* But then he glanced down at his drawings.

"How about tomorrow night? I'm working on something right now."

There was a pause and then she said, "All right. Tomorrow then. I'll come to your studio around seven so think of a place to eat."

He did not miss the forced cheeriness in her tone. "Sounds good. I look forward to it." They hung up.

Alex sighed. They didn't sound like lovers. Or at least he didn't. He knew he wasn't giving her what she wanted—what she needed and deserved. He really should for who else cared about him? Why should he be so chary of his love and time?

He looked again at the drawing. *Why did I think this scribbling is so terribly important?* But he knew it was.

He remembered when he first met Daphne on a train to Venice —a woman with unfathomable regret in her brilliant, blue eyes. Her loveliness and vulnerability drew him to her with a force someone else might have mistaken for naked passion. But she had inspired him to draw and paint again and so, she became his muse. And—he told himself he loved her, something which he had not felt for many years. He thought of calling her back, but did not. Instead he pinned the drawings to his workbench and opened his pad of paper.

CHAPTER 2

Perhaps, by now, you are wondering who is speaking to you? If we happened to meet, my pin-striped suit and briefcase might make you think I'm a drab and dreary soul—a civil servant at Whitehall lost in reams of facts and figures. I do like to foster this impression. It creates anonymity and anonymity confers a certain degree of freedom. But to the observant, the twinkle in my eye will dispel any sense of ennui common to government functionaries.

My name is James Helmsworth and I am greatly honoured to count myself as friend and art dealer of Britain's finest landscape painter, Alexander Wainwright. As such, I straddle two separate worlds—art and commerce. Such a dual perspective has helped me keep my feet on the ground to relate this extraordinary tale.

But first a word about the *light* in Alex's paintings. If you've ever been awestruck by the soft and serene light in a Monet painting of lily pads or the luminous twinkle in the eye of

Rembrandt's Laughing Cavalier, you will love Alex's work. He is the true master of light.

In his landscapes, you see beyond the rivers and rocks, the trees and the hills into an eternity of time and space of an entirely different world. His brush can capture a shaft of light from another dimension to illuminate the darkness of our world.

Aside from me, Alex has just a few close friends. The comely, Daphne Bersault, seems torn. He claimed her as his muse when he met her on a trip to Venice on the Orient Express. Although such a role might flatter any woman, she appears more puzzled than pleased. Perhaps she simply craves real love in this *here* and *now* world. But she knows that she can never come between him and his muse, whomever or whatever that may be. While my opinion is of no great significance, I believe Daphne provides an excellent balance to his creative flights and keeps him securely fastened to our so-called real world.

Alex also has his own personal nemesis, Rinaldo, the conceptual artist—scarcely a friend as you and I might understand the term. He is still a person of some strange and improbable influence upon Alex. Both men are very different, not only in their artistry, but in their fundamental temperaments and views of the world.

Rinaldo believes that existence is just a meaningless dance of molecules. Alex, always on the lookout for *signs*, is convinced that the world is filled with marvellous, secret forces which teem with with personal significance for us. It's useless to debate who is right and who is wrong especially when the *appearances* of life hide much more than they reveal and no one *really* knows.

If you are like me, you may find that some of the events in this story strain your credulity. Don't worry. As I, first and foremost a businessman, wrote it, I had considerable trouble believing that such *happenstances* could actually occur. But I assure you they did. Alex often felt as if some mad puppeteer was chuckling above as he pulled strings to make him do his bidding. I assure you it is worth the effort, as they say in the literary world, to suspend your disbelief.

But I get ahead of myself! Think of me as a dedicated biographer, who has pieced together this account of several months in Alex's life in which he brought his art to further greatness.

Much rose up from the darkest regions of Alex's passionate, hungry spirit on his journey from London to Paris and then St. Petersburg where he delved into some very murky places which you are now about to explore. But despite these kinds of events, don't forget that this is also a tale of mystery and great romance!

CHAPTER 3

Let me begin with our lunch at the
Savoy where I first heard of Alex's latest *vision*.

When I called him that morning, he said, "Jamie, I don't
really have time for lunch today." He sounded almost breathless.
"I think I've had a breakthrough."

"Surely, you can take an hour, Alex?" I said. "I have
something very special to show you in Jonathan Pryde's estate."

Alex groaned, "Does it have to be today? You know how
upsetting that whole business is!"

"It's a very intriguing piece in the collection." Alex was
silent and so I pressed on. "I've taken a photograph of a painting
which I *know* you'll want to see." The inventory in the Pryde's
private collection would make the British Museum or the
National Gallery drool!

He sighed but there was a faint note of interest in his voice.
"All right. Where shall we meet?"

"The Savoy," I said grandly. "This painting alone justifies
the extravagance." I knew I had him hooked.

I had copied out the inscription on the back of the original painting which read: *To Henri Dumont—Parisian pianist and fine composer. May you step from the shadows and into the sunlight you so richly deserve!* However, there was no signature by the artist. I hoped Alex might have some ideas.

Savoy Court is a very short street leading up to a very grand hotel. Today it was clogged with cabs and scores of people chattering and jockeying about. As I approached, the doorman gave a cheery smile and tipped his top hat. Through the revolving doors, I was swept into another gleaming world of black and white marble tile, rich oak paneling and elegant furnishings. A superb combination! Edwardian style mixed with touches of Art Deco. Despite the large groups of people in the lobby, sound seemed softened and so it was delightfully quiet.

Alexander was seated at a table in the Thames Foyer next to the glass and wrought iron gazebo which housed a grand piano. A blonde haired woman in a sleeveless dress played the piano. Soft melodies of Brahms cascaded from the keyboard and filled the room. As I approached, Alex pulled on his goatee as if ruminating over a deeply perplexing problem.

Standing before him, I said, "Alex! You look lost in a fog. What are you thinking about?"

As if startled him from sleep, he jerked his head upward. He had that dreamy, bleary look I knew so well. Usually it meant that he had experienced some kind of revelation. "You look like you haven't slept for nights."

He motioned me to sit down. The waiter handed me a menu and opened the napkin in my lap.

"Listen Alex! I've made an exciting discovery."

Alex pulled on his goatee again. I'm always concerned when he grows a beard or moustache. With him, it heralds a period of withdrawal as if he wants to hide some part of himself for reasons unknown to me.

We each ordered a sherry and settled back to examine the menu. When the waiter returned, I ordered the chicken pot pie and salad. Alex had to be roused from his reverie to order smoked salmon and scrambled eggs.

Alex nodded at the envelope on the table. "So what have you there?"

I took the photograph out and held it up for him. "This is the painting." I looked up at my friend. "My God, Alex! What is it?"

All colour had drained from his face, which was twisted in a strange expression of something akin to terror or awe. His breathing was sharp and shallow. I stared at him as he took the photograph.

"What is it?" I asked. "Do you know this work?"

He gave me no answer but continued to gaze open-mouthed at it. His hands shook when, reverentially, he held up the photograph as if he were, at last, touching the Holy Grail.

"Alex! Please! What is it?"

At first, my friend groaned. Then he threw back his head and gave a delighted laugh. When he finally focused on me again, I could see tears were ready to spill down his cheeks. He took his napkin and dabbed his eyes. He returned to the photograph.

In a hoarse whisper, Alex said, "Dear God, Jamie! It's incredible! Absolutely unbelievable!"

I sat opened mouthed. The waiter set our meals in front of us.

Alex said, "I've seen this very egg before with its jewels encrusted on gold!" He laughed again and nearly jumped from his chair. The waiter gave us an inquiring look from the servery. We both ignored him.

Alex's excitement was puzzling. "So you've seen the painting before?"

"No…no, Jamie. I saw *it* in my studio last night! The very egg which some person has painted."

"Pardon? What do you mean?"

He shook his head and looked at me as if I were rather slow.

"No…you know…sometimes I see things…" His voice trailed off.

"Oh… I see!" Alexander experiences visions. He is one of those very creative people whose mind and spirit work in a unique and special way. "You mean you've had a vision?"

Alex motioned me in hopes I would keep my voice to a whisper.

"You saw something like this work?"

Alex broke into a grin and shook his head violently. "No!" Trembling with excitement, he said, "I saw *that* very egg from my kitchen rising up in mid-air just in front of my workbench."

I looked at the photograph again. "What sort of egg is it?"

"It's the cosmic egg! Actually, I've seen it twice. Once last night and once a few years ago when I was painting *The River of Remembrance.*"

With that painting Alex had achieved his goal of making his *divine* light shine through the human form—one dozen figures for that matter.

He raced on. "It, too, was incredibly beautiful...almost more than I can find words for..." His voice trailed off. Then he said, "The first time, I was looking down upon it like in a dream. It began to float up slowly right past me to the ceiling where it disappeared. It was covered in gold and the most beautiful gems—rubies, emeralds diamonds—were all glittering. Then it came back last night even more beautiful than the first time."

"What happened last night?"

"It disappeared—quickly, both times." His eyes took on a faraway look as he said, softly. "My poor brain can't comprehend how this happens. I only know that it does and that it fills me with sublime pleasure." He grinned sheepishly and said, "It's like being stabbed through the heart—but tenderly. Arrested, you can't breathe. You can't keep looking and you can't tear yourself away."

With Alex, there are times when you are absolutely stunned with his work and the thoughts behind them. You yearn to experience the world the way he does.

We both began to eat lunch as it had been growing cold. When he finished, Alex set down his knife and fork. "But don't you see, Jamie? This is a truly spectacular event."

"I'm sure! But exactly what meaning do you take from it?"

Eye's filled with excitement, he hunched forward. "Whenever I've envisioned this cosmic egg, it preceded a breakthrough in my art. *But this time it's different*—the very next day, I see this painting of exactly the same cosmic egg."

"Yes?"

"It means *two* things. That someone else has seen what I've seen. It's not just a product of my imagination. *And*—well, some might call it a coincidence, but I would call it a very significant, meaningful event occurring…"

I knew that Alex was a great believer in synchronicity. No, that's not fair. He has experienced such *coincidences* many times before and has always taken them seriously as a signs of powers in the universe operating outside space and time—somewhere beyond causality. *And that he must pay the greatest attention to them.*

"Who's the artist?" he asked.

"That's the trouble, Alex. I don't know. It isn't signed but there's an inscription." I withdrew another paper where I had written the artist's words. It read: *To: Henri Dumont—Parisian pianist and fine composer. May you step from the shadows and into the sunlight you so richly deserve!*

Alex frowned deeply but remained silent as the waiter cleared the table and I ordered coffee for us.

Suddenly, he slapped the table. "Then I must go to Paris and find this Henri Dumont. That shouldn't be too hard, should it?"

I shrugged. "You should look at the original, Alex, and see if you can glean anything more from it."

This time he rapped on the table sharply and said, "Done, my friend. I'll drop in tonight."

As I paid the bill, Alex tapped his foot as if off to the races.

"What were you working on last night when you had the vision?" I asked.

"That's just it Jamie. It appeared right before the breakthrough came."

"What sort of breakthrough?" I asked carefully. Alex has gone off on tangents with his work before and found his share of dead ends.

Alex gave a short laugh. "I can see from your expression, my friend, that you will be displeased if I depart from my usual landscapes."

"Oh…no, Alex. I know you have to set new challenges for yourself. Every artist must." Clearly, my tone was not sufficiently convincing.

Leaning across the table, he said hoarsely, "I *must* move on from my fields, streams and clouds. If I don't, I'm dead as a creative artist."

"Of course," I said soothingly. "What have you come up with?"

"Interior landscapes."

"Pardon?"

"Abstract art expressive of my very soul." He gave me a wink and stood up ready to leave.

As we left the restaurant, the maître d' approached us. "Mr. Wainwright?"

"Yes?"

"The front desk has left an envelope for you."

"For me? But how did they know I'm here?"

"I don't know, sir. But this *is* your name, isn't it?" He held out the envelope.

Alex took it and sat down on a nearby chair. When he opened it, he frowned deeply and then a look of absolute confusion passed over his face. He held the letter up to me. "This makes no sense whatsoever, Jamie."

It was a very brief communication from a company called Channel Hopper which booked passages on ferries crossing the English Channel.

It read—*Dear Mr. Wainwright, We are pleased to confirm the booking of your first class cabin [1B] on the Iliad on October 24th 2010, leaving from Portsmouth at 5pm and arriving in Caen at 8 am.*

Alex stared into space with a look of consternation on his face. "How can this be? I never booked a ferry berth."

Looking at the letter again, I smiled. "Here's your answer. It's addressed to an Arthur G. Wainwright. Not you."

Not comprehending, he continued to stare up at me. "But how…?" Then a hint of a smile appeared. "Ah…yes, perhaps that's it." He stood up. "Just a minute, Jamie. I'll return this to the front desk."

True to form, Alex seemed to draw some great significance from the mistaken delivery of the letter. That he is alive to *signs* was the most likely explanation.

"How odd!" Alex muttered.

"What?"

"Do you see that old lady seated over near the elevators?"

"The one with the ridiculous hat?"

"Yes. You can't make out her face."

"So? What about her?"

"I would have sworn she smiled and nodded at me."

"You handsome devil…" I laughed. "Always attracting the ladies!"

Alex chuckled and shook his head. "That's not what I meant. I just wondered if I knew her from somewhere. She looks familiar."

I shrugged. "If she knew you, she'd probably come over and invite you for tea."

Alex laughed. "I suppose…"

But as we walked to the lobby, he stopped several times and, frowning, glanced over his shoulder. "Oh well, she seems to have disappeared. I wonder where she went?"

In the foyer, we shook hands. "Come around tonight." I said. "I'll show you the original."

"Excellent!" He grinned at me. "Can't wait to see it." Then he became more serious. "If we can't find the artist, I'm still going to Paris to find this Henri Dumont."

He set off across the lobby but then stopped abruptly at a potted palm. Snapping his fingers, he turned on his heel and headed back to me, "Do you think Daphne might like to come?"

"To Paris? Why not?" With Alex, I've found it wise to refrain from expressing opinions on personal matters too enthusiastically one way or the other.

He grasped my forearm. "Of course! I'll ask her the next time I see her." Looking rather absent-minded, he suddenly smiled and said. "I'll see you around seven?" He started off but stopped yet again and slapped his forehead. Looking crestfallen, he said, "Damn! I'm getting forgetful. I didn't call Daphne back." He glanced at his watch. "I should have hours ago." He grimaced and headed out the revolving doors.

I shook my head. Alex gave the impression he was only *really* here with us part time. With his mind floating about in *other* realms, I was scarcely surprised he forgot such mundane matters as returning phone calls.

CHAPTER 4

In my study that evening, Alex appeared nothing short of awe struck. "Jamie, this painting is a miracle!"

He stood before the cosmic egg slack jawed for long moments. Then he moved in silence about the room to examine it from a variety of angles. He shook his head and gave a delighted laugh. "It's *exactly* what I saw in my vision!"

"Interesting! And what do you conclude from that, Alex?" I asked.

He resumed his examination of the painting close-up. "If I saw this in a vision and others have seen it too, then it must *really* exist somewhere and not be just a creation of my fantasies. And, of course personally, that my work is headed in the right direction."

I frowned and did not reply immediately.

He resumed his seat. "Now, I *really* must find the artist who painted it!"

"But there's no signature," I said.

As we sat in silent contemplation for some moments, his eyes took on a dreamy, unfocused look suggesting that he was travelling *elsewhere*.

I found Alex's trips into what he called the *beyond* a little unsettling. I do know that science says—at least in its present state of knowledge—that everything is connected and that everything we see or touch is composed of atoms—those insubstantial little bits of *nothing*. Since Alex was caught up in his philosophic ponderings about what was *real* and *unreal*, the question was vital to him.

Without hesitation, I preferred to limit my concerns to my *real* world. I snapped on the desk lamp and gazed about my study. There were the shelves of art, philosophy and history books I so greatly loved. The wall was painted a rich dark green with all my nautical prints displayed on it. The Edwardian library chairs covered in leather nearly glistened in the light. This was the reality I loved and clung to.

I have always been sceptical of people who claim to have visions, except, of course, Alex. I had no doubt that, because of his great creative spirit, he *really* did have visions. I, on the other hand, am a man primarily of commerce and do not have such insight. But now, a new thought swept over me like an epiphany. Maybe Alex was right!

If other people see exactly the same visions, doesn't that mean there's a whole, other world, perhaps observable by only a few creative sorts, existing somewhere just as surely as my books, chairs and study exist for me right here? But why was my world illusory and his, filled with visions, real?

At last Alex said, "Tell me again. What's the inscription on the back of the painting?"

"To Henri Dumont—Parisian pianist and fine composer. May you step from the shadows and into the sunlight you so richly deserve," I said.

Alex noted it down. "There are a few clues there. We have the last name and an initial. A name, a place. But it sounds like something has held this pianist back from fame and fortune either as a pianist or composer or both." Alex frowned. "When do you think it might have been painted?"

"It's not that old," I said. "Perhaps in the seventies."

"Then I may have a chance of finding the pianist and the painter still alive."

Daphne left her hotel in Bow Street, Covent Garden to meet Alexander at his studio for dinner as previously arranged. She passed The Royal Opera House with its Grecian columns lit up and The Drury Lane, where she could see the swirl of people inside lining up for tickets for the bar. The wind picked up as she started down toward the Embankment past Somerset House, gloriously lit up with its courtyards and galleries.

Walking freed her mind, which wandered back to her first meeting with Alex on the Orient Express. By chance, he had been seated at her breakfast table. His gaze upon her had been so intense that she had resented the intrusion. But his eyes reflected a rare kindness and attentiveness. A peculiar restlessness stirred within and she became attentive.

Later, on the train, he brought his drawings of her to her cabin and made a curious confession. She was his *muse*.

Although greatly flattered, she was unsure just what such a relationship entailed. *Was it love or something more complicated?*

But now, she was afraid she had been supplanted by another. No longer was she an inspiration to him—or so it seemed. In his studio, Alex showed her beautiful drawings of a willowy, young woman lifeless like a store mannequin wearing a stupid floral hat! His eye was cool, critical and professional in assessing his own work. Never once did he express any emotion about the woman—this new muse. *And* he seemed oblivious to the pain he was causing her, the rejected muse. At first, she felt jealous fury boiling up inside, but then felt foolish. She tried to reason. *You can't expect an artist like Alex to limit his talent to one source of inspiration.* But it hurt. She slowed her pace, realizing that it had become an angry march of clacking heels.

Memories came flooding back. Days later, when they made love in Venice she realized that his art was his true mistress. He had already made love to her with his drawings made in his cabin after dinner. Could such a man ever lie—flesh and blood—beside her as her lover? She had no answer and suspected neither did he. After that, they parted for a time.

In her own right, Daphne considered herself a creative person. Without that ability, she would never have built her own highly successful advertising agency. Just how did this muse relationship work? If she inspired such creativity, why could she not have a part in the expression of it? Did a muse always have to be passive without any say?

For the past ten days, she had been in London on business. In New York she was known as the *queen of the ad world* with her company *Lorena*. She had one partner, Bradley Franks, a man with whom she had a solid working relationship. Both of them agreed that now was the time to expand into the

European markets with the United Kingdom as the base. Consequently, she and Alex had looked at office space for the company the other day. Next she hoped they might find an apartment together. That had not yet happened. Some invisible, nameless impediment loomed up and the empty space between them widened day by day.

Now at the Embankment, she hurried to his building. Only one of his lights was on. She rushed up the steps and rang. Alex did not answer—not then nor after five minutes of sporadic ringing. She found her cell phone and called him. No answer.

"Alex? Where are you? We were to have dinner tonight. Call me please." She crossed the roadway and looked out on the Thames. *This is ridiculous! Why does he have to be so thoughtless?*

She waited ten minutes and called again. "Damn it, Alex! What's happened?" Then she softened her tone which became vaguely seductive. "I want to see you. You can't stand your date up like this." She hung up. After ten more minutes she caught a cab back to her hotel.

At my place, Alex reached inside his jacket. When he took out his mobile, his face drained of all colour.

"What on earth's wrong?" I asked.

Alex groaned. "Good God! There's a message from Daphne. She was coming to my studio to go out for dinner." Again he slapped his forehead, a gesture becoming all too frequent. "And I completely forgot! What an *idiot* I am!"

Rapidly he called her number. No answer. He left his message. "Daphne! Forgive me! I'm so stupid. I'm at Jamie's looking at a fantastic painting...no...no that doesn't matter. I should have remembered. Please call me back and I'll meet you wherever you are right now."

He rang off and looked at me like he'd been kicked in the gut by a horse. "Let's talk about the painting later, Jamie. I'll call you in the morning."

As I showed him out, I patted his shoulder. "I'm sure she'll understand. People get wrapped up in what they're doing."

He shook his head and spoke sadly, "It's not the first time, Jamie." He put on his coat and turned back to me in the hallway. "She deserves someone much better than me." He waved goodbye and stepped out into the street. Once again, he turned back and said rather sadly, "I get so wrapped up in this world of mine that I forget the most important people." Although he called her back several times that evening at her hotel, she did not answer.

CHAPTER 5

It was just past eight o'clock when Alex left my house. I decided to take a walk to clear my mind. If one cannot find a moment to stroll about London, what is the point of living amid such glorious history, replete with tales of spooks and apparitions? I really have no firm convictions about any kind of afterlife. As a gallery owner and Alex's dealer, I find this world quite enough to cope with. But I've always been intrigued with the huge number of stories of haunted places in my city—London.

On any day, you may find a ghost beside you, ordering a pint in the Nell Gwynne Pub or a spectre floating through walls and down alleyways near the Adelphi Theatre close to the Savoy. That theatre boasts a romantic tale of the famous actor, William Terris, stabbed by a jealous bit-player, Richard Prince, only to die in the arms of his leading lady, Jessica Milward. His last breath was—*I shall be back!* Since Terris and his love, Jessica, died their intimate whispers can still be heard from behind curtains and drifting down cramped and draughty corridors. Since then, he's been seen hanging about that stage door with his lady love probably looking for Mr. Prince. I suppose I'm a romantic at heart!

I, for one, marvel at the power of a love strong enough to span the generations and—amazingly— survive beyond death. I guess I'm just old fashioned. Why does one love last a lifetime and another can't make it past a year or two? But truth be told, nobody really knows. I guess the magic's there or it isn't.

That evening, with romantic tales on my mind, I decided to stroll through Sloane Square in Chelsea, the part of London where my wife and I live. Freezing raindrops slid from the branches of barren trees in the Square and smacked onto my head and down my neck. I passed the Venus Fountain where there is a sculpted relief depicting King Charles II and his mistress, the actress Nell Gwynne at the Thames in the 1680's. Perhaps it was the dark shadows and the glaring red and yellow lights flashing in the puddles or my increasing weariness after a long day, but my imagination visualized people from centuries ago crowding into the Square.

Is this the way Alex experiences the world? Mine was not an actual vision but at least it contained the possibility of one—rather like a dream or an imagining.

Although some people criticize Alex for being *elsewhere*, I think they may be just a little bit jealous of his original way of seeing the world.

Again I thought that appearances so often deceive. One lifetime is brief in time and space, but is that really true? We are all actors on a stage until the final curtain call but we do not and cannot know that it is really *final*. Who knows? Maybe we all experience myriad lives.

Putting my umbrella up, I plodded on my way. Actually, I was pleased with the direction of my thoughts—and myself. I am not usually given to philosophic pondering and this, for me, this was quite a dissertation.

I began thinking more about Alex and Daphne. When they first met on his trip to Venice, Alex was enchanted. His muse –he called her! After meeting her, he produced that stunningly evocative painting, *The River of Remembrance*, in which he painted twelve human figures resplendent in his numinous light. Each one of them represented a person he had met on his travels—including Daphne, who was at the very centre of the composition. On his canvas, Alex was creating the human being as a portal for his divine light. Just think how difficult that might be! Human being? Divine light? No wonder he had trouble!

About a week ago, I dropped in on Alex at his studio. Although he was expecting me sometime that afternoon, I felt as if I had stumbled into one of those awkward moments where a great gulf between two people had frozen in time and space. It was no one's fault and everyone's fault.

Daphne had some floor plans spread out. She said, "But Alex, it's perfect. I don't need a lot of space…not to start." She turned when she heard me come in. "Hello, James…"

"Excuse me… I just need a word with Alex." Everyone has experienced that sense of barging into a situation.

Alex stepped forward. "What's up, Jamie? Is it more about Pryde?"

"Yes, I'm afraid so."

Alex took a deep breath and shook his head. "That business is taking far too much time."

I glanced from one to the other of them. "Listen, I'll come back another time…"

"Don't be silly, James." Daphne smiled warmly and touched my sleeve. "Alex and I were just discussing where I should open up the new branch office." She picked up one of the floor plans. "This one's perfect. What do you think?"

I shrugged. "I didn't know you were thinking of a branch office." I glanced at Alex who was staring out the window.

"It's an excellent location," she continued. "Right in the building next door. One floor down."

"You mean right here?" I tried not to sound too surprised. Alex turned from us and began a slow walk to the far end of his studio.

"Alex is concerned about the cost…"

"Really?"

She turned to me with a brilliant smile. "Listen, Jamie, stay for coffee. It'll be good for him to talk to you." She headed for the kitchen. "I'll put it on right now. Won't take a moment."

The clouds shifted over the Thames and a gray, glaring light filled the studio. Alexander turned and, smoothing his hand along his workbench, traced the work surface from one end to the other.

Watching him, I wondered—how many ideas had been born right here? Immediately, I could see Alex, at the window, his eyes scanning up and down the river. For him—and I expect for almost all real artists—creation is the loneliest act imaginable. For his work, he required solitude and time—and of course, inspiration. I don't pretend to understand where an artist like Alex finds his muse.

Daphne had returned and set out the coffee mugs. "I've always been fascinated by Picasso."

"Picasso? Twentieth century's finest artist! The one creating human beings in the form of cubes."

"Yes. But I was thinking more about his relationships with women…his muses."

"Rather hard being Picasso's muse or lover, I expect," I said.

She handed me a cup and nodded in Alex's direction as he approached. "It's hard enough to understand the greatness of an artist…much less the man!"

I remember the first time Daphne really looked at *The River of Remembrance*, a sense of longing, perhaps even envy, seemed to sweep through her. The relationship an artist might have with his muse might be far more complicated than originally thought. Was a muse ever jealous of the creative power she inspired? Did she lust for it herself?

Alex had left some of his drawings spread out on the workbench in what appeared to be a casual fashion. Daphne had sorted through them and placed them in several neat piles. She called to him. "Alex? Come get your coffee. I've sorted through your work from this morning."

Only the almost imperceptible tug at the corner of his lips gave Alex's distress away. He stepped forward to the bench and examined each drawing with care. Then he carried them to another work space and put them in a drawer. Without further word, he took his coffee and sat down.

"So Jamie!" began Alex. "What's this about the Pryde Estate? Yet another work of incalculable value?"

When I left the two of them that afternoon, unease crept over me although I could not have said precisely *why*. Alex is not the sort of man who expresses anger or frustration readily. At worst, a chilliness creeps over the scene and he retires into himself. Although I do not know Daphne nearly as well, I would guess she is similar in temperament which, I suppose, is fortunate around Alex.

CHAPTER 6

How shall I put this? Improbably, the conceptual artist, Rinaldo, has considerable influence on Alex, a traditional landscape artist. I say *improbably* because both their forms of art and their views of the world are as different as fire and ice. That opposites attract to form the whole is perhaps an explanation. You will understand me when I tell you about the Piccadilly episode and how Alex eventually came to Rinaldo's rescue—again. Although many are tempted to laugh at Rinaldo's performances, this time I had a vague sense that he was onto something quite original. But it was hard to say exactly *what*.

At four o'clock that morning, Piccadilly Circus was deserted except for Rinaldo and his crew. Glittering neon signs, still flashing in a curious rhythm, danced their reflections in the puddles and wet pavement of the plaza. *Anteros,* the statue in the centre of the fountain soared up like a naked, winged god in flight. Because of its name, Rinaldo—and to be fair, many others—incorrectly believed the creation was in the celebratory spirit of all imaginable sexual acts and fantasies. In fact, the statue was erected in honour of Lord Shaftsbury for his charitable works.

They parked their white lorry at the corner of Piccadilly Circus and Regent Street. No wardens were in sight. Under the *Anteros* statue, they uncrated many painted cardboard cut-outs of animals and arranged them in a circular fashion around the statue. There stood a horse, a cow a sheep and a pig, each with its mate, perhaps in homage to Noah's ark. The male of each pair was posed, vigorously mounting the female, or otherwise engaged in highly imaginative sexual acts.

Rinaldo said to his workmen, "You have contributed to twenty-first century art! This is a great conceptual art project as significant as Picasso's *Guernica*."

One of them shrugged. "When do we get paid mister?"

"Oh yes…that little matter. When you pick up the figures tomorrow after ten."

Shooting uneasy glances at one another, they left.

Rinaldo placed a sign at the statue which read in stark white letters on black *THE RUTTING FIELDS*. With his mobile phone, he activated hidden speakers which broadcast the braying and snorting of farm animals in Piccadilly Circus.

At eight o'clock that morning, like industrious ants, workers scurried across the plaza with unified intent to find their cubicles. They filed up the stairs and escalators of the Tube station and into their buildings for their daily labours. Despite the presence of large cut-outs of farm animals, few pedestrians slowed or even glanced at Rinaldo's display or the signage.

Shock was Rinaldo's entire purpose. The animals began to bray when pedestrians, trucks and buses jammed the circle. When a horse's whinny could be heard above the din, some people looked about in confusion. The braying of donkeys and the snuffling, oinking pig sounds made some laugh at the commotion.

From the van, four men and four women, all wearing black cloaks, strode in lock step like a cortege of bishops to the fountain where the animal shapes awaited them. Rinaldo leapt to the fountain and began his video recording of the scene.

One of the eight stood apart from the group and produced from underneath his robe a brass candlestick and candle. The remaining seven bowed and addressed him as master. With a match, the master lit the candle which flickered uncertainly in the breeze. Holding it aloft, he bowed to the group which began a Gregorian-sounding chant. Pedestrians, purposefully striding by, faltered in their step and gawked in confusion.

Standing alone, the robed figure muttered dark incantations. Then the first of the seven remaining people stepped forward and bent to the knee. The master, laying his hand on the bowed head, gave some secret signal and the supplicant rose and let his robe fall to the ground. Then, completely naked, he turned and faced the crowd which had gathered. The assembly gasped. Only a few gave a momentary giggle. The chant continued throughout the performance and created an atmosphere of ancient ritual.

Over the next five minutes, one by one, each of the robed figures bowed down to the master and then disrobed. In the crisp fall morning, soon all seven figures were entirely naked, as they stood as still and solemn as guards at Buckingham Palace. As more people crowded about, the chanting peaked and then the master blew out the candle. A strange, but momentary hush fell over the crowd.

Then the crowing of roosters was heard throughout the plaza followed by all manner of rude barnyard noises. First, Rinaldo slowly panned across the naked performers and then he turned the camera on the gawking crowd to catch their stunned expressions. Oddly, no one laughed or tried to approach the performers. They, too, seemed frozen in place and unable to move. Performers and audience were one, *except* for the attire or lack thereof.

Police sirens filled the air. Ten policemen descended upon the crowd. Rinaldo caught them all on camera as they hurried to cover the motionless and somewhat *blue* coloured performers. By then, some in the crowd had begun to laugh, shake their heads and then move on. The police confiscated Rinaldo's camera and shoved him in back of a police car.

The policemen scratched their heads wondering just what should be done. Eventually, they shrugged their shoulders and ordered the performers from Piccadilly Circus. By eight thirty the plaza was cleared of performers and the cardboard cut-outs of farm animals. The tape recording was seized and marked as Exhibit "A".

In Rinaldo's You Tube video of the event, the robes, candles and chanting created the sense of a very strange, pagan ritual. The concept seemed to be that the humans were obeying the law of the herd by standing in a row like mummified creatures. The animals, on the other hand, exhibited the free spirit of humans by *rutting* about with abandon.

Rinaldo was taken to the station for questioning. What did he think he was doing stopping rush hour traffic in one of the busiest spots in all London on a workday morning?

In disdainful tones, he began, "The city, indeed the world, is my canvas, gentlemen. Art must remind us that we live far too much in our heads and not our skins. In my little performance, the animals were far more intelligent than the humans. They did not hesitate to follow their very natural natures to enjoy themselves and procreate. The humans just stood there like mummified creatures unaware of their bodily needs. The animals exhibited the free spirit of humans by *rutting* about with abandon. We mistreat our poor little bodies—those deliciously, sensuous, fleshy parts of us which can be oh so attractive!" Rinaldo grinned wickedly and squeezed his thighs together in excitement.

Then he tried to spring from his chair to continue his speechifying. One burly copper grabbed his shoulder and forced him down, but he was not to be so easily deterred.

"Please, gentlemen! I have an urgent message. People need *sex* of every kind and then more mindless *fucking*. Otherwise we will wither up and die. No one ever gets enough! But look! The animals do. There they are screwing their silly little brains out. The seven men and women, naked and lifeless, just stupidly stand there with the animals which are happily *rutting* and making all sorts of rude noises. The people are off somewhere else in their heads—thinking, always thinking. So who's smarter—and need I say happier—us or the barnyard animals?"

A guffaw or two came from the officers as they rubbed their jaws and smirked at one another.

Rinaldo threw out his meagre chest and pronounced, "Some of us think only of money and spend our days grubbing about for it. Some of us never stop going on about prayers or some *afterlife* where our bodies do not encumber us. God and Mammon! That's the problem!"

Rinaldo began feeling somewhat odd—not ill in anyway— but just as if some other person had crept under his skin. Someone he did not know. "But how do we get from the profane to the sacred? It's urgent we find the way!"

No one was more surprised than Rinaldo to hear himself. For a man who had always maintained the universe was simply a meaningless dance of molecules, his words seemed absurd to his own ear.

But with the zeal of a Sunday preacher, he continued, "Ritual of church and the creation of art transport us to that special place, sir, where the spirit floats free of earthly concerns. With all their rituals, the churches are the *real* experts— with their hymns and incantations, their baptisms, funerals and weddings. First you're rattling off some ancient, gloomy prayer. Next thing you know, you're in that weird, timeless place where time becomes *all time.*" He grinned maliciously. "And once you're done with the funeral you go out for a pint and a nice lunch at the pub or champagne at the Savoy."

The sergeant was an angry, impatient man who shook his head and scowled. The other coppers did their best to hide their smirks.

Rinaldo smiled beatifically at the sergeant. "Same thing happens in an art gallery. People with their sad, little lives, swoon in front of the Mona Lisa and gasp soulfully—*such beauty*! They are *saved* by art. Just as good as going to church! You see, art can take us to that same incredible place as the church. If we don't pay attention we're stuck in limbo between the profane and the sacred. It's the task of the artist to lead the way and cut the path ever upward so that the two may be joined."

At this point, Rinaldo pointed upward as if to the heavens. "In so doing, artists stop up that river of time so we can capture it and give meaning to our lives."

I'm sure it was entertaining to watch one side of a man at war with his other side. One moment he praised the church and art. Next, he maliciously gave it a very profane poke. He was like a clown repeatedly slapping one side of his face and then the other. This was the newly enlightened Rinaldo!

The sergeant, a red and beefy sort, tossed down his notepad in disgust. "What have we got here men?" He looked ready to explode. "This man is wrong in the head! Just a babbling fool!" Shoving back his chair, he stood up. "Listen! Stop your nonsense. We're charging you with…"

Waving his hands in protest, Rinaldo cried out, "But sir, the world needs its artist, visionaries and prophets and I am at the service of mankind." At the end of this pronouncement Rinaldo bowed deeply to his audience of greatly amused policemen.

The sergeant towered over Rinaldo and hissed, "Right at the height of rush hour, you set up these cardboard cut-out animals and then you blasted barnyard sounds into the air. That impedes the flow of traffic. *And* you've done all this nonsense without a permit of any kind!"

Rinaldo gave an impish grin. "Thank you, officer. I'm so glad you appreciate the intellectual concepts and the artistry of my project!"

"To say nothing of the acts of public indecency!"

"How so, officer? All they did was stand there hardly moving."

The sergeant growled, "They were naked—all of them!"

"But sir, the naked human form is not indecent. Have you *never* been to the National Gallery in Trafalgar Square? You'll find scads of naked people there on the walls."

"Those are paintings, not real people!"

The sergeant was sick of arguing with the fool. "We're charging you with obstructing the highway, creating a public nuisance and public indecency." He and the other men left slamming and locking the door behind them.

Rinaldo sank to a chair. He was proud of himself and his speech. Never had he spoken so eloquently in defence of his art. But he was at a loss to understand just who had spoken. Whose words had come from his mouth? Certainly not his! Fucking scary!

After ten minutes, Rinaldo banged on the door and shouted. "I need the loo! I gotta take a piss!"

Foolishly, the officers ignored him. Rinaldo kicked the door but no one came. The conceptual artist unzipped and relieved himself by spraying the wall behind him. *Such an imaginative, free form drawing!* When finished, he sat down to wait.

Of course, I was not present when Rinaldo made his pronouncements at the station. But after seeing his manifesto, which drew a lot of attention on You Tube, I was able to piece together much of the scene.

Alex and I have had little patience with Rinaldo's so-called performances. So many have seemed little more than *juvenile* antics. But I confess this one stuck in my mind.

Rinaldo has always been contemptuous of the spiritual dimension believing that existence is entirely random and meaningless. Consequently such comments on ritual, art and spirituality could scarcely have come from a more unlikely person. Later, I gathered that Rinaldo became somewhat embarrassed by his outburst and his new reputation as a spiritual guru for the arts.

Somehow, he was trying to combine two very separate worlds—the very human sensual and sexual parts of us with the spiritual. *And* that, in my opinion, is no small feat. Many artists argue that any form of art creates a much needed sense of permanence in a constantly flowing river of time. Like a resting place for the weary. But for an artist not only to combine the two spheres of the worldly and the spiritual, but *fix* it in our lives is, to me, quite an amazing accomplishment. Perhaps Rinaldo is, himself, from another time—the mediaeval where the distinction between the two worlds as separate was not so clear either in people's minds or in their art.

CHAPTER 7

Daphne had been speaking on a panel at the London School of Advertising and Media. The topic was *Fostering Creativity in Your Advertising Agency.* During the break she got a cup of coffee and looked about for colleagues.

"Daphne! How great to see you." A beaming young man approached to shake hands. "You were superb on the panel. I'm so impressed with your firm's work."

"Thanks very much!" She hesitated not remembering his name.

He introduced himself. "John Dylan. Media Circle in Toronto."

Behind him was a line of four or five people to greet her. Most of them were young and bursting with ambition. She was beginning to regard them, as "babies" in the industry— which made her feel old.

"I'd love to show you my work, Ms. Bersault," said a young woman. "Could I send you my portfolio?"

"Yes." She smiled briefly. "Contact my secretary. I'll give you my card…" She did not have the heart to tell the girl they were already over-staffed.

As she reached into her purse, she noticed a man at the end of the line staring belligerently at her. He had a vaguely disheveled look as he fiddled with a loose button on his tweed jacket. His raised eyebrows and pinched expression gave him an oddly sinister look of a comic book character.

He approached and took her hand, he said, "Ms. Bersault? Do you *really* think true creativity can thrive in a communal setting?" He moved within a few inches of her. "What makes you so sure?" He took her arm and ferried her off to a corner. "You *must* tell me."

Daphne replied, "That's the way it's done in my company and it seems to work well."

"What about the lone wolf?"

"Pardon?"

"The lone wolf… the truly creative person who listens to his inner self in the lonely quiet of his midnight hours." Breathing heavily, he moved even closer.

Daphne stepped away. "I'm sorry, but I don't remember your name Mr.…?"

When he grasped her elbow, she winced. "Dodsbury, Geoffrey Dodsbury from Baltimore."

Daphne frowned. She could only recollect one or two advertising firms in Baltimore and thought she knew all the members. She could not place the man. She said, "It's like producing a play or a movie. The talents of huge numbers of people have to be coordinated, so…yes, in that sense, creativity can be communal."

Dodsbury looked ready to pounce.

Daphne rushed on, "Everyone's involved right from the start. A variety of concepts have to be developed. The copywriters produce multiple versions of the text. The illustrators in the art department all have their input."

Dodsbury fixed her with a speculative look. "Really, Ms. Bersault!" A smirk crossed his face as hostility grew in his tone. "If it's to be any good at all, we must foster private time to delve deep into one's soul to seek out the muse. The outer world is a distraction." His lip curled contemptuously downward. "Nothing truly creative, new or brilliant *ever* resulted from a committee."

What is this man trying to prove? "I suppose you know Stephen Larson at Crommarty's?"

Dodsbury nodded sagely. "Oh yes, a fine ad man!"

Daphne edged away. She had just made up the names of the firm and the individual. *This guy is a fraud.* Suddenly she heard her thoughts pouring out of her. "It's a romantic notion, Mr. Dodsbury, to praise only your lone wolf. Lots of bright people do their best work in conjunction with others. They draw inspiration from *this* world—the one we can all see, touch and smell *together*. Collaboration gets the creative juices flowing and helps bring a project to fruition and for that we need to be with lots of people."

He smirked. "Perhaps in the mad advertising world people can get away with superficial efforts. But too many cooks in the kitchen will spoil the dish!"

Who the hell is he? Have I offended him in the past? Is this pay back for something else?

His eyes bulged. "The truly creative soul goes off alone into the forest through his own personal hell and brings something truly original back for society. He is the hero!"

Good grief! The man is unhinged. Daphne looked desperately around to find someone to rescue her.

"Mr. Dodsbury, of course your lone creative soul has his place but he can't hope to produce quality without assistance."

Surprisingly, Dodsbury gave a friendly shrug of his shoulders. "Now you've got it at last, my dear!"

Daphne turned away.

He stopped and took her arm. "Such an engrossing debate, Daphne. We really must have a drink sometime." He waved as he turned to go. "Oh! By the way, how's Alex these days?"

"Alex? Alex who?"

"The painter, of course, your good *friend* Alexander Wainwright." After giving her a lurid wink, he turned away and was lost in the crowd.

She called after him. "How do you know him?" But he was gone.

Never in my life have I seen this man.

She would call Alex for dinner tonight. Her annoyance at being stood up had, for the most part, subsided. Alex was a perfect example of a *great artist* unaware of his world and the people in it who cared about him! *Maybe he was off in his forest!* Immediately, she felt guilty at such a thought.

After the session, Daphne shouldered her way through the bustle of Oxford Street crammed with shoppers. Alex's face floated into her memory. In her cabin on the Orient Express, his eyes had smoldered with a strange passion she had never seen before. Under his arm were the sketches of her he'd drawn just after dinner. The words he spoke were etched upon her mind.

My art comes from deep within. Some places are comfortable, familiar rooms, which I have often visited in dreams and reveries.

Others are wonderfully fanciful and enchanting lands. Still others contain the terrifying stuff of nightmares. But all those places have their treasures and must be explored and intimately known if one is to create. Some quality, an essence, within the muse is like a candle flickering in the dark, illuminating everything in those rooms. That light leads the poor artist through his own private heaven and hell ever onward to his creation.

And so said Dodsbury! Alex—a lone wolf? Perhaps so! But Alex had captured her essence in those drawings after just a few meetings.

As she approached her hotel, the doorman tipped his hat and opened the door for her.

CHAPTER 8

In the lobby, there was Alex sitting in a corner next to a potted palm. Daphne almost laughed at his hang-dog expression. But when he saw her, he jumped to his feet and took her hands.

"Daphne, please forgive me for last night!" Gazing deeply into her eyes, he held his breath waiting for her response.

She smiled briefly at him. He breathed again.

"Yes…of course, Alex. There must have been some sort of mix-up. It can happen." She smiled more warmly.

Alex knew there was no mix-up. Guiltily, he reflected that he had simply become too caught up in his work—the beautiful abstract shapes which flowed from chalk to paper. "Shall we have dinner tonight?" he asked.

"Of course! Why not? Give me fifteen minutes to get ready. I've had the most ridiculous afternoon."

He cocked his eyebrow. "Really? What happened?"

"Wait here. I'll tell you at dinner." Then she was gone to the elevator.

Upstairs she changed and he read the newspaper in the lobby. In fifteen minutes, she was at his side ready to go. They walked over to Cindy's, an elegant restaurant where, seated at the window alcove, they had a fine view of Trafalgar Square.

Alexander gazed out the window. Around the perimeter of the Square, black cabs crawled and stood in thick lines. The Square took on the glow of an ancient, dream-like city bathed in a wonderfully magical light. He could see thousands of pigeons descending upon Nelson's Column and then, in unison, flock skyward above the crowds of humans. *How interesting,* he thought! *Both the humans and the birds seem to have similar patterns of synchronous flow in their movements. Just like the flow of shapes I drew the other night.*

Daphne, who had been concentrating on the menu, cleared her throat and asked, "What appeals to you, Alex?" *There he is again. Off in his own world.*

Blinking, he brought himself back into the room. He smiled at her, picked up the menu and became attentive. "Shall we order drinks?" He leaned forward on his elbows. "Tell me about your *ridiculous* day."

The memory of Dodsbury was fading—fortunately. She laughed. "I was on a panel at the London School of Advertising this afternoon. At break, this very strange man introduced himself to me as Geoffrey Dodsbury. Very argumentative! He wanted to know if I really thought creativity could be fostered in a communal setting. So, I said—*yes, of course. Just as in producing a play or a movie many minds contribute to the project.* But what was so odd and unpleasant was the hostility."

"Really? Do you know him?"

"No. I don't think so. He seemed determined to settle a score with me. And one other thing—he asked after you."

"Really? I've never heard of him."

The waiter came to take orders for drinks. When he was gone, Daphne continued, "A lot of nonsense about the true creative spirit being the one who went into the forest alone in the dead of night and brought back gifts."

Alex looked sceptical. "That's a bit overstated, I think."

"Overstated? He sounded unbalanced."

"Many people do believe that *real* creativity is a very lonely activity."

Daphne chuckled. "Really Alex! You mean to say that a number of people can't get an original idea together and execute it? Must we all become hermits and hunt for roots and berries in the forest?"

"No doubt, in larger projects, such as you say, a film or play, many have to be involved, but perhaps he meant that it should be one pure idea from one mind which launches the creation. Imagine if I tried to collaborate with another artist on a painting. Suppose the other painter says let's make the clouds in the sunset—green? And I say...but that's not what I had in mind..."Alex stopped.

Daphne sat back. What had she expected? Some support of her position? Certainly not an argument. She studied the menu. "I suppose..." Looking out onto the Square, she thought she would have liked him to laugh just a little at the absurd Mr. Dodsbury.

"No, Daphne. I see your point but..."

"Let's order dinner, Alex."

"All right." He waved for the waiter who hurried over. "We're ready now."

After they had placed their orders, Alex suddenly beamed at her and took her hands in his. "Listen Daphne. I've been wanting to ask you something. Would you come to Paris with me?"

She smiled. "Paris? When?"

"Why not as soon as you're finished your work here."

"That's on Friday."

"Yes, you could leave for New York from Paris." His eyes were filled with excitement. "We could stroll the Seine…find the best bistros…drink the best wines!"

She was delighted. "I could work it out with the office. Maybe three or four days?"

"Yes, exactly." Folding his arms across his chest, he leaned back in his chair.

She smiled broadly. "Sounds like fun! I'd love to."

The Chateau de Roquefort red wine was set upon the table and the sommelier poured out a glass for tasting. Alex took a sip and nodded.

Once the glasses were poured, Alex raised his. "To Paris!"

"To Paris." Smiling, she raised her glass.

What time can you fly out on Friday?"

She shrugged. "I'll set the day aside just for us! So any time, really."

His excitement was infectious. Except for the Orient Express and Venice they had never travelled anywhere together. As she gazed at him over the candlelight, she imagined a few carefree, intimate days. Maybe they could reach some sort of understanding.

Soon the spinach salads and tomato soup arrived. Hungry, they spoke little until the bowls and plates were cleared away.

His eyes sparkled. He reached for her hand. "I want to tell you something else…something I'm terribly excited about!"

"Really? What is it?"

"You won't think I'm crazy if I tell you?"

"No, but how can I say until you tell me. What is it?"

Still holding her hand, he looked down at the table. "You see, Daphne, I've seen something."

"Seen something? What do you mean?"

Smiling, he looked up into her eyes. "I've had a vision…a new one."

Daphne frowned only slightly. The main course was delivered. "What sort of vision?"

Alex began to eat hungrily. She thought he might be nervous. He set his fork down. "It came to me the other night."

"What? Where?"

"In my studio."

"What was it?" He had told her of other visions. Although she knew no one else who claimed to experience them, she conceded that a great artist might well be visited by visions. If they brought him inspiration—*why not?* She never once doubted his talent and the excellence of his art.

He grinned with the excitement of a schoolboy. "It was the cosmic egg!"

She folded her napkin in her lap. "The cosmic egg? What's that?"

A thrill coursed through him as he began. "Daphne, it was incredibly beautiful! It was gold and set with a myriad of coloured jewels and diamonds. It appeared right before me in my studio. And the most incredible part? It drifted about like a living being!" When he finished, he was almost breathless.

She smiled trying to mirror his excitement. "What does it mean?"

He waved his hands in the air. "No. Wait. I haven't told you everything yet! The very next day, I had lunch with Jamie.

He showed me a photograph of a painting he had found in the Jonathan Pryde estate. I was nearly overcome! It was a gorgeous painting of *exactly* the same cosmic egg I'd seen the night before." Again, he stopped to catch his breath. "You see how incredible that is?"

She frowned. "I'm not sure…"

"You know…all about amazing happenstance or what might be taken as chance. Since I'm convinced *chance* does not exist, I keep an eye out for signs and…" He shrugged. "Look for any special meanings they might have for me."

Daphne was confused. "And what would that be?"

He tried not to sound impatient. "Certain events occurring in time which seem highly significant but one not causing the other—you know—synchronicity."

Daphne was a very practical woman. She had never experienced *anything* even remotely like a vision or synchronicity. Oh yes, once she had been thinking of an old acquaintance and just then he called. But that happened to lots of people and was scarcely unusual.

If she had not known Alex well, she might have easily dismissed the event. Although she did not want to admit it, she sometimes wondered how his world could ever fit with hers.

She smiled and, looking at him closely, said, "Alex, I'm *very* happy for you. It's so exciting." She prayed she sounded genuine.

"Thank you, but that's still not all." He motioned to the waiter to clear the table. When he was done, he brought dessert menus. Alex said, "The painting isn't signed by the artist. But on the back of it there's an inscription— *to Henri Dumont— Parisian pianist and fine composer. May you step from the shadows and into the sunlight you so richly deserve!* I have to meet the artist who created this amazing painting!"

Alex did not notice Daphne's sharp intake of breath.

Slowly she opened her menu. "Let's have dessert and coffee, Alex. I'm going to the ladies room."

Alex was on his feet to assist her with her chair. Waiting for her, he stared out the window into the darkened street. Her face, when he first met her in the dining car of the Orient Express floated up before him. How intrigued he had been. *Although her polite smile made a bright facade,* he had thought at the time, *her deep blue eyes were tinged with unfathomable regret and vulnerability.* But now, he had just seen that very expression on her face as she left the table. *That closing in and regret.* Had he disappointed her in some way? He dismissed the thought. She would love the excitement of the hunt for Henri Dumont as much as he.

In the washroom, although she was not sure *why,* Daphne fought back a gloomy sense of disappointment as she reapplied her lipstick. She returned to the table.

Sitting down, she said, "Tell me more about the trip to Paris. Where shall we stay?"

He shrugged his shoulders. "Wherever you like…"

"It should be somewhere romantic, overlooking the Seine. It's wonderful that we can have this time together." She smiled warmly over her coffee which had just been set before her.

"Ah yes, the Seine! You'll be seeing a lot of the Seine. I have to see someone whom I believe lives on the Île de la Cité.

Daphne looked up sharply. "Who?"

"Henri Dumont, of course. The Parisian Pianist."

"But why?"

"I want to meet him so I can find out who painted the cosmic egg."

Daphne shoulders slumped. She twisted her napkin in her lap. "So, this is a business trip, Alex?"

"Only in part…"

"You didn't plan it to spend time with me."

"Of course, we'll be together all the time."

She looked out the window and spoke quietly to herself. "I'm such a romantic fool…"

"Daphne? What's the matter? I so sorry if I've disappointed you."

Smiling bravely, she looked up at him. "Alex, I really don't want dessert. Let's go back now. I'm very tired after today."

"Please Daphne. I'm sorry. What have I done to upset you?"

"Please just get the bill."

He found the waiter and gave him his credit card. Returning to the table, he found Daphne putting on her coat.

"If you're very tired, we'll get a cab and I'll take you back to the hotel."

"Yes, let's do that."

At the hotel, she reached over and gave him a quick kiss on the cheek. "Don't get out Alex. I'm very tired and want to get some sleep."

"Listen Daphne, why don't we have a drink or some coffee? Talk this over. If I've upset or offended you, I'm so sorry. I *really* do want you to come to Paris with me. If it sounded as if…"

She smiled briefly, waved and was gone. Alex told the driver to drop him off on the Embankment at his studio. Perhaps he could spend some time with his work. Oddly, it seemed all the more important to go to Paris to find Henri Dumont.

In her hotel room, Daphne cast her eye on the silver wine cooler and the bottle of Pinot Grigio ordered in hopes of a romantic conclusion to the evening.

She tried to decide if she were justified in her reaction. *Why in God's name must he be so thoughtless?*

She took off her red wool dress and flung it inside out on the chair. She kicked her heels across the room.

First he makes me think the trip is just for us when, really, it's for business. I'm just there to tag along—a convenient after thought!

She glared in the mirror at herself. *Why have I fallen in love with this man?* By the time she was running a bath, the thought occurred to her—*had he realized how he had hurt her and been sincerely trying to apologize?* She was tired of the same old questions and the same old struggle with him.

First she phoned the front desk to block her calls. Then she arranged a flight to New York for Saturday afternoon. She got into a hot bath and then went to bed. In the morning, she would call and tell him the change in plans. Business had called her back unexpectedly.

From his studio, Alex tried to call her without success. He got out his sketch pad and began to draw. Damn! Nothing was coming out right.

In the morning, he had a message from her on his phone. *I have to get back to New York on Saturday. Have a great time in Paris.*

He called her back but could only leave a message. "Daphne, please. Can we at least talk this over before you have to go?" But she did not respond.

CHAPTER 9

Later that day, Alexander held open the heavy wooden door of the Magistrate's Court. Grinning, Rinaldo skipped out.

"Alex! You are a true friend. Because of you, I am a free man."

"This is the second time I've bailed you out. How did you have the nerve to call me again?" Alex asked sourly.

Rinaldo took his arm. "Listen friend. I'm truly grateful. I could not have survived another night in that awful place."

Alex stopped up. "You didn't spend the night! It's only six o'clock in the evening now. They arrested you this morning."

Dancing beside Alex, Rinaldo pulled a face. "Don't be so testy, Alex. I lost track of time. It could have been *years* since they brought me in." He made an exaggerated, deep bow. "I am forever in your debt, friend. If it is in my power to assist you in any way, just call me."

"You're welcome." Alex kept walking. "Just don't run out on the bail bond."

"You wouldn't believe it, Alex! The police station is filled with Philistines."

"That surprises you?"

"Yes, of course it does! No concept of art or its importance to mankind! I tried so hard to make them see the brilliance of my project, but it was not to be!" He threw up his arms in dismay. "The magistrate was so grumpy, I was lucky to get out. Imagine a country where they jail artists!"

Suddenly, Rinaldo started patting his pockets. His mouth hung open in surprise. "Someone has filched my wallet. Can you believe it—right in the halls of justice where they wear those funny white wigs!"

"For God's sake, Rinaldo! Did you leave it behind? They take all your valuables when they arrest you."

He patted his breast pocket again. "Oh, I'm wrong. Here it is!" He pulled out his wallet and looked in it. "Shit...someone took my money!"

"That doesn't happen! I suppose you want me to buy you supper?"

Rinaldo's face softened. "Oh no, Alex. I couldn't presume to ask!"

Alex shook his head in disgust. "Oh yes you could!" Alex had been walking as far from Rinaldo as he decently could because he smelled strongly of wet dog, sweat and God knows what else. He looked around for a cheap restaurant—one in which Rinaldo could possibly be allowed to sit. Fortunately, he spotted one on the far side of the street.

"Let's get a bite over there." He hoped the cooking odours would cover Rinaldo's stench.

They sat in a booth near the door to get as much air as possible.

"So very kind of you Alex."

Alex handed him a menu.

"Would you like to hear about the *rutting performance*?"

"Not really…"

"But I want…I *need* your opinion, Alex. It means so much…"

Alex winced. "That's ridiculous. My opinion is of no use to you."

"Absolutely not true! You see…"

Alex knew there was no way of stopping the man. It would be easier just to listen. He held up his hand. "All right. Tell me."

"Are you a church-goer, Alex?"

"Me? No. Why do you ask?"

"But you *do* celebrate Christmas, don't you?"

"Yes. After a fashion."

"Put up a Christmas tree?"

"Yes, most years. Why do you ask?"

"I'm thinking about rituals and why we do them. When somebody dies, we all gather around the graveside and the minister says all sorts of mournful, solemn sounding words he's said a thousand times before. Then everyone goes out for a nice lunch."

"So?"

"We do it because we won't feel right if we don't. *And* I was thinking people are trying to get into that special place where time stops and we can think about the meaning of life."

"What? The *meaning* of life?" Alex was so astounded, he nearly broke into laughter. "You've always said there was none." When he saw that Rinaldo was deadly serious, he decided not to joke. "Go on. Tell me more."

"I want to see if we can affect time through performance art."

"I'm sorry?"

"Just like the churches do. Get us to that special *sacred* place."

Alex's alarm was growing. "What on earth have you been smoking, Rinaldo?"

Rinaldo looked as offended as anyone, who persistently mocked others, could. "They're always going through some sort of ritual whether it's for Sunday service, a wedding or a burial." The little man hunched forward, his eyes gleaming with excitement. "If they can do it, why can't artists with their art? Churches are the experts at it." He looked surprised as if struck by a new thought. "Maybe that's why they own so much of it."

"I still don't understand…unless you mean by preserving an image through painting."

"Watch someone at Mass. They get this stillness in them like they're off in some very special place where we'd all love to go."

"Where did you get all these ideas?" Alex frowned. "They don't sound like you at all."

Rinaldo began to build a tower with the packets of sugar. "That's just it, Alex. Neither do I. It just came to me when I was in the police station trying to educate the Philistines. The words…the ideas just started to come out in some weird way… like somebody else was speaking."

Alexander shook his head. "But I still don't understand…"

Rinaldo gave a bark of laughter. "Don't look so upset, Alex. You look absolutely desperate in your confusion! It's hard for a representational painter to understand and so, I'll switch to the much more down to earth part of the project. You know what *rutting* means?"

"Of course I do! Just because I didn't grow up on a farm like you…"

Rinaldo beamed and proceeded to ignore Alex's answer. "It's a fascinating concept—all about *sex*! First, I created cutouts of different farm animals and positioned them in sexual acts, around the statue of Eros in the fountain in Piccadilly Circus."

"It's not a statue of Eros…It's Anteros, the twin brother of Eros. Complete opposites."

Rinaldo waved off Alex's correction. "No matter, my friend!" He hunched forward.

Alex began breathing through his mouth. "What do you want to eat?"

Rinaldo wanted the roast beef sandwich and chips. Alex got up and placed their orders at the counter. He returned reluctantly to his seat.

"*Every* human being has sex on his or her mind—non-stop."

Alex raised h is eyebrows, but allowed him to continue.

"But why is that?" Rinaldo looked expectantly at Alex for an answer and then rushed on. "Sex is the *life force* of every human being. It is essential to our continued existence as a species. Animals don't have to think about it. They just do it— as often as they can." He paused as if to gather his thoughts. "So then I brought the men and women into the performance. When they disrobed, they were completely naked and just stood there as if they were *lost* with no idea what to do. Brilliant concept!"

"Brilliant? Why brilliant?"

Again, Rinaldo leaned forward in his excitement. Alex breathed through his mouth.

NIGHT CROSSING — 59
NIGHT CROSSING — 59

"It makes the point that animals fuck wildly, uninhibited by thought—any restraint! Human beings just stand there frozen in place not thinking of their bodily needs."

Alex stared at him for a moment. "I suppose they were too cold or embarrassed at being naked in the middle of Piccadilly Circus at rush hour in late autumn. Those circumstances create bodily needs too."

Rinaldo gave his cackle. "Don't be so literal, Alex. Please don't be anti-intellectual. Unless you have sex, and lots of it, you'll dry up!" Grabbing Alex's sleeve, Rinaldo said, "I can see—and I say this as a good *friend*—that you simply aren't getting *enough*!"

"Enough? What are you talking about?"

"You look as if your head's about to pop off. It's why you're always so testy and going on about your *beyond*! You're trying to protect yourself from your perfectly normal needs by keeping your head way up there in your clouds."

Nearly overcome by the stench, Alex moved back in the booth as far as possible. "That's ridiculous, Dr. Freud! Just like him, you think sex is the one and *only* motivation for human activity!" Alex began drumming his fingers on the table. "What about art, creativity, love, hunger, pleasure ...avoidance of pain? Human beings are more complex than what you suggest!"

When the food arrived, Rinaldo looked hungrily at his roast beef sandwich. Quickly, he began to munch on it. Small dribbles of gravy dripped down his chin. Suddenly he cackled, "Alex...Alex! When will you see that humans are no more than animals rutting in the field?"

Alex snorted. "Your remarks—your arguments—are so inane. Besides, you just said that humans also perform rituals to stop time. What about spiritual aspects...sensing something greater than yourself?"

"Moi? Something greater than moi? Impossible!"

Alex regarded the man who had been a painful thorn in his side for as long as he could remember. "There are matters other than just sex or as you say—*rutting*. We are far above the animals." He determined he would not say—*even you, Rinaldo.* "Take Daphne, for example. We have a relationship which transcends the usual ..." Suddenly overcome with unease, Alex stopped.

Rinaldo said, "Daphne? Oh yes! She is someone I would *take* in an instant, given half a chance!" He continued to grin as he chewed on the beef in his sandwich. "Absolutely gorgeous woman. Why? Doesn't she keep you happy?"

Alexander sighed. It seemed too much to explain that a man and a woman could have a relationship in which sex was not at the root of *everything*. Suddenly he was weary of the conversation, weary of Rinaldo. Without thinking he muttered, "But she's gone back to New York..."

"Really? I thought she was staying here with you."

"No... Something came up back home."

"You mean she left you?"

"It's not the way you make it sound!"

"Then how is it?" Rinaldo grinned one ear to the other." Did you have a lovers' spat. Something dramatic?"

"No, of course not."

"She didn't have time to go to Paris with me..."

"What?" Rinaldo's eyes bulged. "No woman would turn down a romantic interlude in Paris. C'est impossible! There is something very wrong here!"

Later, Alexander put his uncharacteristic confession to Rinaldo down to his complete weariness. "She was all set to go...seemed excited at the prospect, but then suddenly turned very cool and then cold."

"You must have said something."

"At first, we talked about an intimate hotel on the Left Bank and going for walks along the Seine. Just the two of us. Lots of bistros and wine and baguettes...you know. Then I told her that I had to see a pianist about a painting in the Pryde Estate. The painting is beautiful ...of a cosmic egg. And how I had just seen exactly that egg in a vision."

Rinaldo smashed his palm against his forehead in a gesture of despair. "So, first you invite that gorgeous woman to a *romantic* tryst in Paris. And then you tell her it's really for business *and—for God's sake—a spiritual* trip. I suppose you said it didn't really matter if she came?"

Alexander examined his hands. "It wasn't really like that."

"Ha! That's when she started to cool, wasn't it? That's when she decided to go back to New York. Alexander, you are an absolute *imbecile!*" Rinaldo sighed deeply. "You are so caught up with your *beyond*, your visions and creative inspiration that you don't even see what's right under your nose! The woman is in love with you...wants sex and lots of it with you...hopes to get you all to herself. And then, she learns she must share you with someone else and a cosmic egg!" Rinaldo shook his head "What is wrong with you, man! It's really easy. You just don't understand anything about people, much less beautiful women."

"Wait a minute, Daphne and I..." Alexander stopped. There was no use trying to explain himself or Daphne to a man who put on outlandish, tacky and pointless performances in Piccadilly Circus. *And* got arrested.

Rinaldo leaned in close. He grasped Alex's sleeve. "I tell you this for your own good. You are a complete idiot. Any man, worthy of the name, would go to the bottom of the sea just to get her back!"

When they parted, Alex took the tube home. *I don't need her trying to organize me and my work! And I don't need Rinaldo's advice.* He was shocked to catch his angry expression reflected in the window of the train. *If she's going to be that way, watch out! Soon she'll be telling me what to paint!* He looked at his reflection again. *But just look at the loneliness in your eyes.*

He turned away. There seemed to be no solution to his problem. His anger had dissipated by the time he had marched the two streets to his flat. At home, he undressed and got into bed. After half an hour of thrashing about with the pillow, he got up and made a cup of tea.

The tea burned his tongue as he gazed morosely at the black screen of the telly. He could see Rinaldo's annoying face grinning up at him and hear his words—*Any man, worthy of the name, would go to the bottom of the sea just to get her back!* He began drumming on the table with a paintbrush. Rinaldo was incapable of understanding a relationship that did not involve sex ninety-five percent of the time. He picked up and then set down his mobile phone three times. On the fourth, he called her hotel.

"Please connect me with Ms. Daphne Bersault's room."

"Ah…one moment sir…"

The voice disappeared for at least a minute.

"May I have your name, sir?"

"Wainwright. Alexander Wainwright."

"I'm terribly sorry, Mr. Wainwright, but Ms. Bersault has asked that she not be disturbed by *any* calls tonight."

The message was clear enough. She did not want to hear from him. Two hours later he was finally exhausted and fell into a deep and dreamless sleep.

Headed home, Rinaldo walked around Oxford Circus trying to decide if it would be as good a site as Piccadilly. *Poor Alex!* He chuckled. *He's so busy with his creativity and inspiration, he'd probably never see himself as the drowning man.*

CHAPTER 10

On her flight back to New York in business class, Daphne stretched out in her seat. Expelling thoughts of Alex from her mind was as hard as battling the tentacles of a savage octopus. She tried to concentrate on business in New York. This morning, she had spoken with her partner, Brad, and sensed an odd excitement in his voice.

"What's up?" she had asked.

"Just waiting for your return." He sounded as if some sort of surprise awaited her, which made her slightly uneasy. If anything, Brad was a straight forward and direct person and certainly not one for games.

Her anger with Alex had subsided to a low but persistent boil which sometimes threatened to spill over. *It cannot work,* she told herself. *Why would I want someone who's always lost in his own world? Not only that, but he looks down on my work like it's something inferior or tainted with commercialism.* She admitted that he had never actually said any such thing.

At the moment, she was determined to give up on him. But a life without Alexander left a looming space which looked frighteningly empty. Could anything else ever fill it? A vague but persistent hunger gnawed at her.

Alexander saw what few people ever saw or even knew existed. He seemed haunted by the notion that behind this *material* world lay the *real* world and he was obsessed with finding it. She knew she didn't have the imagination or perception to follow him there although she longed to. Consequently, she felt forever consigned to some lesser realm. But she *knew* creativity had many different forms. Just because the world of advertising sold *things,* the inspiration which fuelled it should not be trivialized.

She prized her rational side. Taking out a pad and pen, she began to list all the problems of her present situation. First and foremost, she doubted whether *love* in this world—with all the sensual pleasures—was really *that* important to Alex. She would always have to share him with his art—with his muse—whomever or whatever that might be. Not only was he living in the clouds, but she sensed she was no longer an inspiration to him.

But then she remembered those nights when he had truly given himself over to her. He would make love with such intense passion that his entire being seemed swept away. And when they were satisfied, he seemed as if he had died and then miraculously come back to life as if nothing had happened. Where had he been? Nothing was *usual* with Alex.

A woman, elegantly dressed in a dark navy suit and white silk blouse, sat next to her.

"Do you live in New York, dear?" the woman, who must have been in her sixties, asked.

Daphne was startled. Her seatmate's voice was so deep throated and gravelly she thought it came from a man.

"Yes, I do…"

"Do you like the city?"

Daphne nodded.

The woman turned sideways and looked straight into Daphne's eyes with such intensity that Daphne drew back slightly. "I'm originally from New York but I've been living in London for the past twenty years." The woman held out her hand. "I'm Freda Munster and you…?"

"Daphne Bersault."

"Well, Daphne Bersault." The woman leaned far back in her seat and studied the ceiling, "Shall I tell you why I'm going to New York?"

Daphne hesitated just a fraction of a second. "If you like…"

"I'm off to my sister's funeral."

"Oh!" Daphne looked over and saw that her jaw trembled slightly.

"She took her own life, you know."

"Good grief!" Daphne was immediately drawn in. "Why?"

"Over a man. After all, sweetie, what other reason is there?"

"Well I…" muttered Daphne.

"She always *was* a little fool! But at fifty-eight, I should think she'd be able to stand on her own two feet and not let some man destroy her!"

Daphne was at a loss for words. Finally she said, "How unfortunate! How did it happen?"

The woman gave her a sour look. "It's a very old but universal story of unbelievable cruelty in which a person's soul is stolen— erased. Woman thinks she loves man so much she abandons herself to him. He seduces her into giving up her very being.

Soon she has no sense of herself, because she only exists in his eyes. She becomes what she thinks he wants, but she's never sure that she's got it right. When he leaves, she's destroyed. The looking glass is smashed." The woman turned to her. Her eyes were filled with tears and her mascara was making ugly tracks down her cheeks. She asked, "Are you married, dear?"

"No."

"No, I didn't think so. You're too smart for that."

Daphne could think of nothing further to say and so she buzzed for another glass of Pinot Grigio and turned on her screen. Freda Munster's message resonated with her. Would Alex take her over body and soul? A man would never even think of such a question.

Fortunately, they were only an hour from LaGuardia. The woman spent the time either flipping through *Vogue* magazine or snoozing. Daphne dropped into a light sleep until they arrived. Later, headed to midtown in a cab, her mind returned to Freda Munster. *How bizarre! She seemed to be delivering a message just for me from Alex's world where everything contains a meaning!*

Rinaldo's workshop was formerly a factory for producing light fittings. Located on an industrial estate just outside London, the rent was much more affordable. Seated with his coffee and newspaper the following morning, he read the report of his disruption of Piccadilly Circus.

Fuck! Not a word about the artistic merit of the project! *And* he had tried so hard to educate the constabulary to no avail! He had been especially pleased with catching the *dead,* and *lifeless* nature of the human forms in contrast to the riot of animals beneath the statue. Playing with the ritual of stopping time was fantastic! He would upload his video onto You Tube and watch it go *viral.*

He was intrigued with the idea of human beings frozen in place. What did that mean, he wondered? *Simple! It means that people are lost in the world without the necessary life force to impel them to action. We are in danger of becoming statues! Even mummified!*

He giggled when he thought of Alex. He was the perfect *statute.* Dead to sex, his feelings and dead to the world. Disconnected from whatever was right under his nose. So weird for someone claiming to be an artist.

Building on that brilliant concept, he wanted to display women wrapped in papier-mache looking like mummies. Just imagine how hard it would be to move. His first female model would arrive at ten o'clock this morning and another one at noon. His musings were interrupted by a knock on the side door. It was only nine o'clock. Rinaldo sidled up the delivery ramp and opened the door.

Before him stood a small figure. He could not immediately tell if it were male or female, although he suspected the latter. Its head was covered with a hood and a baggy sort of jacket and pants hung over the slight frame.

"Yes?"

A pair of piercing blue eyes looked up at him. "Rinaldo? I'm Krysta."

Rinaldo nodded. Taken aback, he had not expected the eyes. It wasn't actually an aura which emanated from her, but there was definitely a sense of the *extraordinaire* about her.

Rinaldo grinned ear to ear. "Come in my lovely! Are you here for the sitting?"

She marched in and handed him her jacket which he hung up. She looked about suspiciously as if *something* were hidden in the vast, darkened space of the studio. "So what do you do here?"

Rinaldo was unused to women with such a direct approach. "It's my studio where I produce my performance pieces."

"Like what?"

"Did you hear about the one in Piccadilly Circus yesterday?"

She gave a nonchalant shrug. "No…don't think so."

Rinaldo expected a woman to be in awe of his work *and* of course— him. "You're answering the advert for the modelling job?"

She looked at him as if he were slow. "Of course. I wouldn't come all the way out here except for a good paying job."

Rinaldo struggled to gain control of the situation. "You're not hired yet, sweetie." He gave her a slow, appraising look. "This is an interview or rather a try-out. I've got another one coming at noon." He guided her toward a corner of the studio which contained a large sofa and a few armchairs. "Let's sit down and I'll tell you what I need."

Krysta casually removed her arm from his grasp. He motioned her to the sofa. She took an armchair.

"You've heard of me—no doubt."

"You're the guy who created the *ditch* down the centre of the Turbine Room at the Tate Modern for the Turner Prize years back.

"Just two years back…"

"Whatever…It was on You Tube. Somebody else won though." Looking puzzled for a moment, she then said, "That's

it! Alexander Wainwright won the prize with *The Hay Wagon*."
She smiled brilliantly at him.

It was painful to be reminded about not winning the Turner
Prize. It was ridiculous! Dear Alexander Wainwright had
walked off with the honours with his oil painting. How such
a precious work, entirely devoid of any intellectual concept,
could win was beyond him or any dedicated conceptual artist.

"So what am I supposed to do?" she asked.

Rinaldo grinned at her. "First, you have to disrobe."

She shrugged. "Turn the heat up, will you?"

"And then, you'll stand up on the stage over there while I
cover you in papier mache. Needless to say, you cannot move
at any point in time until it dries."

Krysta simply sat and stared at him for a long moment.
Then she took her bag and stood up. "That's dumb! I'm not
doing that!"

"What on earth do you mean, my dear? I thought you
wanted work?"

"I'm not *that* desperate! That'd be horrible. I'd be all itchy."

"It's not that bad. Others have done it," he lied. "All done
in say… five hours. Then after it's set, I take photos of you from
a variety of angles." From under lowered lids and in his most
seductive fashion, he said, "It pays very well."

"How well?"

"Ten pounds per hour."

She shrugged. "Make it twenty."

He laughed. "What a hard bargain you drive, my lovely! All
right, fifteen it is." He held out his hand to shake hers.

For the first time, she really smiled at him. Something
about the glimmer in her eye entranced him. It had been a long
time since he'd felt that way about a model—*anybody* in fact.

Maybe she was his needed inspiration for the project. Maybe she was his muse.

"So, when do we start?" she asked.

"Right now." He took her arm and guided her to the far reaches of the studio. There was a stage with an odd assortment of articles set out on it—a spinning wheel, a cash register, several old wooden armchairs and a grandfather clock. The general effect was that of a stage from the Vaudeville era. He glanced at the rumpled bed with pillows heaped upon it at the back of the stage. "This is where we'll be working. Shall we start now?"

She nodded. "While we work, I want you to tell me about your projects." Her intense blue eyes smiled up at him. "Will you do that?"

Rinaldo was easily flattered. "I'd be delighted to impart the secrets of my art to one so lovely." He ran his hand along the line of her shoulder.

"Where shall I change? Where's that robe?"

Rinaldo almost skipped to the cupboard for a robe. "You change and I'll get the materials ready, my dear. You and I will have a *very* good time."

Within a few minutes, Krysta was standing naked on the stage. Slowly, Rinaldo circled her, his hand cupped under his chin as if lost in study. Then, backing away, he cackled. "Rather skinny, aren't you? I may have to feed you to fatten you up!" He rubbed his hands together. "But, I think you'll do. Won't much matter when you're all pasted up!"

"Are you going to paint the paper?"

"Ha?"

"What good will newspaper be? Not very interesting."

"Hmmm…That's a rather stupid question, my dear. Whatever made you think a mere model could take part in the creative process?"

Krysta tossed on her robe and marched toward him. "Why not? Art liberates! You, Rinaldo, want to go beyond art on gallery walls. You scorn the artists stuck in the last century with their paints. My group wants to take the next step of liberation and move art into the hands the *people* who have every right to express themselves. It's *democracy* in action. *Everyone* has the ability to create."

At first, Rinaldo was stunned into silence by her manifesto— briefly. "So, my lovely, you have been following my work, my performances and my writings. The entire art world needs to be shaken up top to bottom."

She shrugged. "Yes and I really *do* admire your work and want you to be part of our movement."

"What movement?"

Her eyes shone. She raised a fist. "*The People's Art.*"

Rinaldo took her wrist and sauntered with her to the bed. "How very interesting, Krysta! Let's talk more about your plans right here." He tossed several pillows aside and guided her down to the bed. "I can tell you're a very *passionate* woman."

NIGHT CROSSING

CHAPTER 11

Alex was half way across his studio when he turned back to me. Rubbing his chin, he finally said, "Jamie? I think I'll take the ferry instead."

"The ferry? What ferry?"

"The one from Portsmouth to Caen."

"Why don't you fly or take the train?" Both were far simpler ways of travelling from London to Paris.

Alex hunched his shoulders. Pale morning sunlight spread over the Thames silhouetting him in the window where he appeared like an ominous, black hawk ready to take flight. Since I could not see his face, I could not read his expression.

"I don't know." He sighed. "I just feel as if I should…that it's important." He gave me a quizzical look. "Because I need time to think…"

"Whatever you like, Alex," I said somewhat doubtfully. Since I didn't want to pry, I didn't ask what he wanted time to think about.

"And," Alex continued more decisively, "It will be a night crossing as well."

I recalled the note about the ferry addressed to Arthur G. Wainwright that had been mistakenly delivered to him at the Savoy. I knew Alex would have taken that as some sort of *sign* which should be heeded.

Alex shook his head. "I have a funny feeling about this Dumont."

"Really? Why?"

He shrugged. "Hard to say..." He smiled sheepishly. "It's an adventure...a mystery."

The next day Alex started his journey to Paris via the train to Portsmouth and then, by ferry, to Caen on the north coast of France. From there, an hour's train ride would get him straight into Paris. Over the past few days, we had made various inquiries about our mysterious pianist and scoured the web to ascertain his whereabouts—without result. There was an R. Dumont living on Île de la Cité, the island in the middle of the Seine in the centre of Paris. That seemed like a place to begin but we had no address.

That area, steeped in history from before Roman times, is stunningly beautiful with ghostly, white-clad plane trees lining cobblestone streets. Ancient cottage-like residences hide behind stone walls along narrow alleyways. A perfect place for a romantic soul to live! R. Dumont's telephone was privately listed and so we could not obtain his number. Alex insisted he had enough information to set out, but to tell the truth, I think he simply wanted to get away and take in Paris again.

I knew something was troubling him. When he left, I didn't know what it might be, but I could see something was amiss with Daphne. Apparently she had turned down his offer of a trip to Paris and returned to New York rather abruptly. It was certainly not my place to inquire, but Alex did confide in me later that a disturbing question had simply popped into his head—*do I really love Daphne?* At that point, he resolved to find an answer during his trip.

Apparently, their last meeting had been disastrous. No outright accusations. No recriminations. Just a sudden and swift cooling covered over with brittle pleasantries. With all his heart, he tried to understand what she wanted and worried that it was not in his power or nature to give it.

Alex is not an easy man to understand especially when it comes to art and his creative process. When he is working full tilt, the world and all the people in it just fade away and he finds himself alone almost without physical form. Throughout this trip, the question would not leave him. *Must an artist live a life without love—other than the love of art?* He knew he was greedy about time for thought and work, but it was his muse who demanded it.

Alexander entered Waterloo Station through the Victory Arch just after four o'clock leaving almost an hour to board. In the concourse, he stopped before a statue of an impressive gentleman. At its foot, a sculpted mouse peeked out from underneath a book.

That mouse was the trademark of the artist Terence Cuneo who found considerable fame for his railway paintings. Alexander remembered him fondly from the Slade School of Art where he taught when Alex was a student struggling with criticism that he was far too traditional in his style. Cuneo, a kindly gentleman, made a point of speaking with him one day in the studio.

"Remember!" Cuneo said with a wink, "There's always a fine place for an artist who observes records and illustrates." The old man paused and then said thoughtfully, "But I think you, Alexander, see much more beyond the surface of things than most artists. And that is a very great gift."

Those words had echoed in his mind over the last few days as he debated abandoning landscape for his *inner* world of abstract art. As he stood before the statue, he took the question up again.

Why must I abandon anything either in style or subject matter? But if an artist does not challenge himself to create something new, he should pack up his paints and retire to a home for the creatively spent!

Gazing up at Cuneo's statue, he thought—*I saw the cosmic egg. Surely that means inspiration is within me and I'm on the right track.*

In search of washrooms, Alexander turned down a dark, tunnel-like passage. Up ahead, a woman walked hand in hand with her young daughter. The little girl, in play, skipped ahead of her mother. To Alex, her giggle was like a silver sprinkle of sheer delight.

The mother rushed to catch up with her. Alex smiled to see the child skip on ahead but as the corridor darkened in the distance, he frowned and hurried his pace. The dimly lit signs for the lavatories were far along the empty passageway. The child turned down a corner and her voice fell silent. Now the mother chased after her calling out—*Victoria! Wait for Mummy!*

The shrill and strident scream of the child ricocheted up and down the hallway. The mother ran. Alexander ran.

"Where are you, Victoria?"

They found the child trembling all over and crouched down on the cement floor with her hands covering her head.

"Victoria…my God! What's wrong?" The mother rushed to her and then she, too, screamed and covered her head.

A winged swirling noise with little high-pitched screeches came from above. Looking up, Alex saw the mindless, incessant circling and swooping of *bats* around the light.

He nearly laughed in relief. Bending over the mother and child, he said, "Come. There's nothing to fear. They're only bats." He tried to make light but, when he saw the child's face frozen in fear, he spoke gently to the mother. "Let me help you up. The bats won't hurt you but you should keep moving."

The little girl grasped her mother's hand tightly. Alexander touched the woman's elbow and directed her along the corridor.

Back in the light, the woman felt foolish. "Sorry to bother you Mister. I should have known! But it was so dark and…" Her fear was still plainly written on her face.

He spoke gently and smiled down at them. "My name is Alexander Wainwright. They're only bats and they don't harm people. In fact they help us by eating mosquitoes. Unfairly, they've got a bad reputation, but some think they bring good luck." He nodded goodbye.

The woman reached into her purse. "May I repay you for your help?"

Alexander shook his head and smiled. "You have a beautiful daughter. Take good care of her." Then he collected his bag and was off.

At the sink in the washroom, he shivered and examined his face in the mirror. *Those winged creatures belong to the world of dreams and nightmares. Not the sunny world of a child.* He checked his watch. Time to go. He made sure he had the envelope containing the cosmic egg safely tucked away in his pocket and headed off for Platform Number 5.

The train was already waiting. He boarded and, after walking through several carriages, found his seat. He tossed his bag on the rack above and folded his jacket on the empty seat beside him. It was only an hour or so to Portsmouth on the south coast.

Looking out the window, he saw the hands of the station clock creep toward five o'clock. The guard was about to remove the step to the carriage. At the far end of the platform, coming out of the darkness, was an elderly woman dressed in black. With great care, she carried a paper teacup which made it hard to manoeuvre her bag behind her. Although she called out, the guard did not seem to notice her and so he began closing the door. Getting up from his seat, Alex waved at the man and pointed down the platform at the woman. In her struggles, she nearly lost her balance, but held the cup upright with as much concentration as a devoted *alchemist* carrying the elixir of life.

Alex caught his breath. From somewhere in the upper reaches of the train station, a dozen huge, black crows descended upon the platform. Surrounding the old woman, they flapped noisily and marched about as if providing a convoy. The woman tried to shoo them away, but they only jumped a foot or so away and continued to follow her until she boarded the train. While the guard helped her with her bag, the crows stood themselves in a straight line along the platform and stared up at her. She boarded the train. Making her way slowly through several carriages at last she arrived where Alex was seated.

The train gave a jerk and began to creep from the platform out onto the tracks. Another jolt caused the old woman to topple directly onto the seat across from Alex. He hoped it was not her place, but the conductor came by and took both their tickets. Apparently, she was to be his companion for the trip.

His first impression was that she was ever so slightly unkempt. A hem hung down and a coat button was loose. Under her arm, she clutched a ragged, rolled up newspaper leading him to speculate that she was a reader of the more sensational tabloids. He opened his own newspaper and tried to concentrate.

"Sir?"

Unsuccessfully, he pretended to be hard of hearing but she was not so easily ignored.

"D'you go to Portsmouth often?"

He lowered his paper slightly and shook his head.

"My sister used to live in Portsmouth that is until her and Ronnie—that's her husband—died last year, both of the cancer. And so…" She gave him a quick glance. "They're in a better place now, I'm sure."

Alex nodded and made some sort of sympathetic noise.

"Cancer it was!"

"Hmmm…So you said."

"But her kids—she's got four of them—all live in London."

Alex hoped he could just let the old woman rattle on and simply ignore her.

"Are you taking the ferry too?"

Alex, being a polite man, finds it difficult to ignore persistent people. To do so is rude in his books.

He sighed, "Yes, Madam," he said as frostily as possible.
"Then to Paris?"

Alex nodded.

She beamed. "Oh yes! So am I. Nice to have a friendly companion along the way—don't you think?" She broke off from talking just enough to open a bag of licorice Allsorts. "Want some, Mister...?"

Alex pursed his lips and shook his head. He hadn't gotten much beyond the headlines of his paper.

"Tomorrow I'm taking the train right into Paris." She gave him a charming smile marred only by one chipped tooth. "I've been thinking about this trip for a long time. You see, I want to look up a very old friend who I haven't seen in *ages*." The focus of her eyes shifted suggesting she had retreated to her interior world of memory. She spoke as if only to herself. "I regret not keeping in touch with him and often wonder what our lives would have been like if we had."

She sighed deeply. "He was the first and last person I ever loved."

Although Alex still resented her intrusion, he was caught by the wistfulness in her tone about a love strong enough to span the decades even though they never saw each other. He was surprised to hear himself say, "So many choices in life. One can never be sure of their importance."

She shot him a canny look. "When you get to my age, young man, sometimes you want to tie up the loose ends in your life. You wouldn't likely know about that yet."

"I suppose not..." Alex muttered. He wondered about Daphne from whom he was apparently now parted.

"What's your name, sir, if I may be so bold to ask?"

Hoping to retreat, he spoke stiffly, "Wainwright, Alexander Wainwright."

"Pleased to meet you, Mr. Wainwright. I'm Miss Maureen Trump."

For several moments, she set about rearranging the contents of her purse. "I do *love* Paris! When I was a young girl, I used to go there once a year to visit father. Father and mother lived separate and apart, you see. Quite something in those days! Father had a mistress in Paris and so, I only got to visit once a year when he'd safely packed her off to the country. The mistress, that is."

Alex looked closely at her. "Your mother lived in London? When did your father leave?" He was surprised at his own questions.

"Oh, yes. Mother lived in the East End, I'm afraid. Not like Dad near the Arc de Triomphe. I was only five when he left."

"Your father lived near the Arc de Triomphe?"

"Oh yes, he had a *magnificent* apartment. He was quite rich and famous you see. Much better off than poor mother." She smiled in recollection. "It overlooked a promenade of very expensive shops. I used to watch all the shoppers—very smart they were—walking by. I'd dream of buying fabulous clothes one day."

Alex put down his paper and looked more closely at the old woman. She scarcely impressed him as a person who had lived in the finest *arrondisement* of Paris.

Wistfully she said, "I always hoped father would take me shopping for clothes, but I think he thought me much too plain to bother about." Then she smiled and popped a licorice in her mouth. "A few people thought him cruel, but I think he..."

She unrolled her newspaper. To Alex's surprise, it seemed to be about astronomy or maybe astrology.

"Where do you stay in the city, if I may ask, Mr. Wainwright?"

Alex was unaware he had been eyeing the bag of licorice Allsorts. She handed it to him and he took one.

"Usually on the Left Bank."

"Oh yes! Where all the *artists* live. Are you an artist, Mr. Wainwright?"

"I'm a painter." He took another candy—this one bright yellow and black. She set the bag on the seat beside him.

Sighing, she looked heavenward. "I just love art!"

Alex steeled himself against uninformed people whose remarks betrayed their ignorance of art.

"Do you ever wonder, Mr. Wainwright, what's in those empty spaces?"

"Pardon?"

"You know…in a painting, you think there's nothing but air between a horse in a meadow and the barn but is that *really* true? Is it really empty?"

Alex was taken aback by her description of *his* subject matter. "What else could there be?" he asked.

The woman shrugged. "There must be something but can't say what or why." She paused and then continued thoughtfully, "Maybe that's where all the *stuff* of creation can be found. You know where artists find their inspiration and their materials." Suddenly she blushed. "I confess that I have this passion for licorice."

He smiled slightly. "Surely an innocent pleasure…" Then he frowned as he puzzled over her question of empty spaces in painting which struck him as extremely intelligent.

"Oh yes...some would say, sir." She popped a pink and black Allsorts sweet into her mouth and smiled sweetly at him.

"But allsorts—they put me in a reminiscing mood. I hope you don't mind, Mr. Wainwright."

Alex had set his newspaper aside and found himself listening intently to her. "Reminiscing about what?"

"I know you'll find it hard to believe but once upon a time..." She looked about the car too embarrassed to meet his gaze. "I know, today, I don't look like someone who's had much of a life, but it did have its moments."

"My dear lady! Forgive me but I thought no such thing!"

"Then would you like to hear my story? By the time I'm finished, we'll be in Portsmouth." She looked out the window for a moment. When she turned back to him, he was struck by the calm dignity in her gaze. "Things are not always as they appear on the surface—as I'm sure you, a painter, are aware."

Alex drew closer and took another sweet. He spoke earnestly. "Please tell me, Miss Trump."

She looked sharply at him. "Do you believe in dreams, sir?"

"Believe in? Well ...of course..."

"Actually, I mean the *importance—the significance* of dreams."

Alex had experienced many dreams which did seem exceedingly significant. He sat forward and said eagerly. "Yes, in fact I do! Why do you ask?"

"Because the story I'm about to tell you is a dream or a sort of vision of mine."

To Alex, the woman's statement was extraordinary. Just as he was on a journey in search of his cosmic egg envisioned by him, here sat a woman who claimed visionary experience! Life for him was often punctuated by, sometimes, lovely *happenstance.* But he knew all too well that such events could come as *warnings.* Hard to interpret meaning in most cases!

Maureen Trump held out the package of licorice. He took one and sat back.

"Please go on, Miss Trump."

She smiled and began. "I can't be sure if it was a dream or a vision." She looked at him shrewdly. "Do you know what I mean?"

He nodded.

"Good. Let's just say, I was in a state of *altered consciousness.*"

Alex's eyebrows shot up. Before him a sat an elderly woman who some unkind souls might call frumpy. Apparently, by appearances, not terribly well educated nor, if one paid little heed, particularly worldly. But here she was speaking of *altered states of consciousness* and raising questions about empty spaces in art. She was right. Things were often not as they seemed.

She beamed at him. "You see, I was someone else in the dream. Definitely not the Maureen Trump of *this* world—not at least as I know her. I was *someone* else— a woman living in the seventeen eighties or nineties." Her eyes glazed over and her voice softened. "I'm somewhere out in the English countryside in the north." She folded her hands carefully in her lap and then closed her eyes.

"Someone has died. I think it's a child...someone I'm related to. It might even be my own child. I am sitting in a darkened cave or no! I think it's a barn because there is straw all around. A man—he's a doctor—is speaking to me in a very kindly fashion. His voice is soft and low. I am swept with a sorrow I have not known in this life."

Alex was mesmerized. He sat forward with his elbows resting on his knees.

"The doctor has wrapped this little child in a blanket like a small bundle. The words *swaddling clothes* come into my mind as he is about to take it away. He is trying to keep hope alive in me—not that this child will miraculously revive—but that it will live on in another time and place."

The woman was telling the story with such simplicity and directness that Alex was greatly moved. He held his breath waiting for her to continue.

"As the doctor is about to leave, he hands me something. It's a sort of talisman—something with magical properties about the size of a hairbrush." The woman broke off. "Do you know, Alex, children's sweet called twizzlers?"

He shook his head.

"They're made of long strands or strips of licorice all woven together. This object had a handle which was just like that! Strips of licorice woven together. But when I examined it carefully, I saw it was *hard* and *rough* and felt just like pumice stone—not at all like licorice. The doctor closes my hands around this strange object and tells me to keep it safe as it belongs to the child who has died."

Alex's eyes widened. "How very strange!"

"Then he took the child away, Mr. Wainwright."

Maureen Trump closed her eyes and sat in silence for long moments. Alex did not wish to break in on her reflections and so he sat perfectly still.

Then the old woman's eyes flew open. "Did you know that a plant gives us licorice? It's a perennial which means, at the end of the growing season, it dies but then after a time begins life again—as I'm sure you know, sir."

Surprised at the woman's range of knowledge, Alex nodded and smiled. "And so," Alex said quietly, "In this dream the licorice tells us that life continues after death. In fact it is a continuous process—perennial. I think our ideas of life after death come from our understanding, in ancient times, of agriculture."

Maureen Trump's eyes came alive with a twinkle. "Ah...Mr. Wainwright, I see that you are a skilled interpreter of dreams."

"Oh, not really…"

"And the pumice?" she asked.

"Pumice is an extremely hard stone formed by hot lava. Stone is the state of perfection—as in the *Philosopher's Stone.*"

"Again, sir, you are correct. You *are* wise in the ways..."

Alex shook his head. "No, I think not. But I do pay attention to such things."

She smiled sadly at him. "And so, from that experience, I think life is one continuous, unending stream. Departure and return." She looked out the window of the train and then said quietly, "You see, I was correct. My story is done and here's Portsmouth." The old woman began to collect her things.

Alexander rose and got his bag. "Thank you for telling me your dream. It's given me much to contemplate. Perhaps I'll see you on the ferry."

The guard helped the old woman down from the train. Alexander followed.

Reaching up, Maureen Trump placed her hand on Alex's sleeve. "Tell me, young man, what did you make of the ravens as I got onto the train?"

He shook his head. "Miss Trump, I don't know. But did you feel they were bringing any message? They're often thought to herald some news."

She nodded solemnly. "Yes, Mr. Wainwright. "Perhaps even a *warning*. That is why I spoke with you at such length about my dream."

"What do you mean?"

"I knew you would be alive to such things. I was interested in your thoughts. That's all." She waved goodbye. Within moments he had lost sight of her.

Lost in thought, Alex started out of the station as the sun was beginning to set. Furious looking clouds hung low on the horizon in the west. Just as he was getting into a cab for the ferry dock, he stopped and, in panic, searched his pockets one by one.

For God Sakes! I've left the cosmic egg on the train. He remembered setting it on the seat near him where it must have slipped onto the floor. He waved the cabbie off and rushed back. *The train will still be there. They'll be cleaning it up before turning it around.* At the gate, the guard remembered him and let him up to the platform. Rushing past the cleaners, he arrived just in time to see one of the men pitching his envelope into a garbage bin. Although his copy of the painting could certainly be replaced, it would be unsettling to lose such a *gift* through his own carelessness. The cosmic egg, he realized, was much more to him than he had thought. It was like a polestar for his art and perhaps a guide for his very being. He hurried back to the line of cabs.

In the back seat, he thought once more of the old woman. Miss Trump possessed a quality he could not immediately identify. Perhaps it was simply wisdom for he knew that such dreams did not come to everyone and her telling of it was greatly impressed on his memory.

"Gonna be tight, Mister," the driver said. "They're just about ready to set sail and we got traffic to get through."

Alex sighed. "Just do your best, please. If you can make it, I'll double the tip." He felt in his pocket to be sure he still had the cosmic egg. He had booked the best berth he could on the ferry. Years ago, he had taken the trip and enjoyed a cabin with bed, a sitting area and bath. Now he thought he would order dinner and some wine and put his feet up.

He smiled to himself. *I just need some quiet time to myself crossing the Channel—time to think. First I envision the cosmic egg which another artist has painted and next comes an old woman who offers up her dreams. What does it mean—if anything at all?* He shifted uncomfortably on his seat. *And I have to decide about Daphne. To have a future, we have to find a middle ground.*

They pulled up at the dock where the ramp hoisted the last vehicle upward. The heavy metal screech and crashing of equipment was deafening. Just in time, he was the last one up the gangplank.

From the deck, Alexander looked toward the southwest to see the sun slip to just above the horizon. Suddenly a light, warm breeze came up and caressed his face. Odd for a fall day, he thought. Turning back to the shore, he saw the last moments of fading sunlight bathe the buildings and spires of the city by the sea. Within moments, the ship had left the dock and was now edging out into the harbour.

Sudden jostling and angry cries broke out up ahead. Deck hands shouted to one another and motioned the last of the passengers into lines.

A red-haired man with a pale, pinched face shouted, "They've screwed up all the reservations, Gloria. Bunch of Goddamned morons!"

Gloria was standing directly in front of Alex. Waving her bag of crisps in the air, she stepped back onto Alex's foot and shouted, "Tell them we bloody well made those reservations a month ago—the bleeding idiots! I want that cabin we asked for!"

Screams came from behind Alexander. He was shoved sharply forward nearly losing his balance.

Someone up ahead shouted, "Watch it asshole! You're gonna…"

"Merde!" A man, at least six feet tall, pushed his way forward knocking a small boy to the deck as he tried to get to the counter. When a foot struck the child on the side of his head, he covered his ears and wailed.

A bearded man raised his fist. "Fick dich!"

"Watch out for the kid! Speak English why don't you, fucker?"

Alex steadied himself at the rail and then reached down to help the boy.

His father grabbed Alex's arm, shouting "Bastard! Leave my kid alone! You some kind of pervert?"

Alexander stepped back quickly. Other men were crowding about him. No point in trying to reason with a mob which was coming to a boil.

Another man shoved his face up close to him. "You trying to hurt a kid?" His mean eyes narrowed.

As quickly as possible, Alex moved off to one side. "Just trying to help him up, sir."

Suspicious, the man's eyes narrowed to slits. He raised his fist but then he was jostled forward in the crowd. Alex dropped back and out of sight.

It took at least half an hour for the staff at the desk to settle the crowd down and issue the keys to the cabins. Alex was the last in line. When the passenger immediately in front of him turned around, Alex saw his nose was bloodied. He was the one who had knocked the boy down.

The desk clerk was hostile. "Wainwright? We got no Wainwright in the system."

Alex spoke patiently. "My ticket's right here. It shows the cabin number."

"Still...you gotta be in the system for a cabin assignment, mate."

"Sir? I'd like to see the manager, please."

"Right then..." the man behind the desk seemed relieved. "Then you gotta wait over there sir by the manager's door."

Alex went to the manager's door and rapped on it. A ferret-like face poked out. "Ya? What is it?"

Alex took the manager through his documents, which clearly showed his payment for Cabin A-2 on the uppermost deck.

After consulting the computer, the man spoke brazenly. "Looks like there's been a double booking, mister."

"I'm sure another cabin on that deck will be fine."

The manager tapped more keys. "No luck. All full up." He gave a short, nervous laugh.

"Then give me any cabin you have." Alex's patience had thinned.

After a few more moments, the man said, "Well you can have Cabin F-5. Three decks down. No window 'cuz it's under water." Again, he laughed.

"For God's sake!" Alex glanced about. There were no comfortable looking chairs on the deck.

"You'll get a refund sir if you send a letter to head office at least that portion which…"

Alex sighed. A relaxing evening with dinner in his cabin was only a fantasy. "Give me the cabin then." Night had descended like a black, heavy curtain upon the water.

The manager handed Alex the keys and smiled. "Have a pleasant journey sir. Glad to have been of service."

Alex, shaking his head in amazement, collected his bag and found the lift down a dimly lit hallway crammed with other disgruntled passengers. He waited on the outer deck for the congestion to clear.

In late autumn, he had expected to feel a stiff, cold wind not the gentle spring-like gusts now teasing his face. Suddenly, the dense atmosphere cleared in the northeast and he could see the lights of Portsmouth drifting away.

He looked up at the sky and down to the sea. At first it seemed a mad artist had chanced a serpentine roll of the dice and spread his creation of fire and water helter-skelter across the universe. But in time, a subtle order began to emerge as patterns of light and dark coalesced before his eyes.

At the stern, the swirling wake broke away into beautiful, lacy patterns spreading out upon the sea. The stars above, so cold and clear in their intricate arrangements, shone down upon the swirling water. He remembered his drawing made just before the cosmic egg had appeared in his studio. The shapes had moved back and forth with one another in a rhythm unknown to him. *Perhaps they are making love,* he had thought. And so it seemed now with the sky and water before him.

Intuition burst upon him. Whether looking up or down, he saw patterns—similar and connected—forming, disappearing and then reforming before his eyes in a dance of all creation—eons ago, now and forever. All existence was like the finest gauze in which he was wrapped as one tiny particle.

Gazing upward in the vast firmament and then downward into the waters, he marvelled at the immeasurable extent of the empty space surrounding him. Just as Miss Trump had said.

In my paintings, I try to express the light and unity spread before me, but I know the light lies beyond it and holds it all together. I try to capture that light.

But what do I see when I look inside myself? And what is there when there seems to be nothing outside me between the stars and the waters— that empty space of which Miss Trump speaks?

He closed his eyes and— for just an instant— caught within himself, the same ebb and flow of patterns and shapes meshing and parting. *How similar,* he thought. Whatever is within me is patterned like all creation outside of me.

But then I see space—empty space—everywhere, between me and those stars and between me and that deck chair by the door. Is that space really empty? He stepped away from the railing and turned back inside to find his cabin.

Staring at their shoes in silence, only a few weary passengers waited for the lift which reluctantly wheezed open. When Alex stepped into the narrow cage, he drew his breath in sharply and tucked his elbows up into his ribs. Four other passengers squeezed to the back. The cracked ceiling tiles pressed in on the single light bulb, which cast a yellowish, green light upon the passengers. The walls of the carriage seemed to fold inwards upon them until Alex felt his brow dampen. The carpet was stained with something he hoped was not blood. A faintly vile smell, like a garbage bin, permeated the air.

Just before the doors closed, he heard a soft voice calling out from the hallway. "Wait. Please wait. I have a baby."

Alex grabbed the door and then a woman—she was somewhere in her thirties—entered, with a beautiful baby in her arms. The woman herself was dark haired and lovely. Alex breathed deeply.

She smiled but averted her eyes. "Thank you, sir. You're very kind."

"What a lovely child you have, madam! What is her name?"

The woman glanced at him with a hint of suspicion. She shifted the child protectively in her arms. "Celestine," she answered.

When they got off at the lowest level, the woman scurried along the corridor sheltering the child in her arms. Alex stopped and looked about for Cabin F-5. As he headed for the stern, the further he walked the narrower the corridor seemed to become. His breathing grew sharp and shallow. He retraced his steps and saw a bent figure—Miss Trump— struggling with her key. Then she opened her door and was gone. Just beyond her cabin, he found his own. So narrow was the door that he had to twist sideways to get in.

"Dear God!" he gasped. The odour—some combination of damp, animal hair and vomit—overtook him. He switched on the light—a little ceiling bulb. Alex was nauseated. The total length of the room must have been no more than six feet. Its width was perhaps four or five. On the left was a low-slung day bed covered with a filthy rug and an inch thick pillow. On the opposite wall hung a dirty, cracked sink with a scrap of soap in a dish. He tried the door next to the sink in hopes of finding the shower, but it was stuck. After he shook it, someone on the other side banged and swore. The shower and toilet must be down the hall—somewhere.

Nowhere to turn! The walls seemed to contract making the cabin even smaller. He flung his coat on the bed and spread it out for protection should he dare lie down. He hunted for his toothbrush and ran the water—only cold—and did his best to tidy himself up. Of course, there were no towels.

Because every muscle and sinew in his body ached, he tried to stretch out on the bed. If he could lose himself in his book, he might be able to pass the night. But the damp, fetid odour could not be ignored.

He decided to go up to the deck, find something to eat and sit in a chair. On his rush to the lift, he heard every imaginable human noise—laughter, angry cries and an odd snuffling— coming from the cabins. It was a full house.

The lift was not working. Two steps at a time, he started up the pale green stairwell. The stench of urine made him breathe only through his mouth in short, sharp draughts. The clanging of his boots on the iron steps pounded in his brain. Finally on the main deck, he leaned over the railing and took greedy gasps of air.

It was as sweet as a late summer evening. The stars were even more brilliant than before and the breeze caressed his cheek. He found a poorly lit cafeteria at the stern where he bought a container of stew and heated it in the microwave. When he took it out, crystals of ice still coated the surface. He tossed it in the garbage, drank his coffee and ate a stale bran muffin. *How shall I pass this night?*

Suddenly, he wondered if the series of events of the day might contain some meaning—perhaps some *warning* which eluded him. For the first time, he wondered about the wisdom of his trip. His thoughts returned uneasily to Miss Trump and her strange theory of empty spaces which, of course, needed filling.

Then he thought of Daphne whom he had not called. They were so different and yet there was something in her which inspired him…drew him inexorably to her. She was brilliant, creative and so focused in every way. He was quite the opposite. Scattered. Dreaming, always dreaming. But didn't opposites attract?

To pass time, he strolled about the deck. At mid-ship, at least thirty passengers had gathered around a large wooden table. A tarp, draped over four posters, created a sort of primitive roof.

A very large man was seated with the young woman and her baby. A brass candelabra sat on the table. The dripping candles flickered in the breeze and made shadows dance on the faces of the crowd. Some expressions were laughing. Some were bored or aloof. A few were twisted in astonishment or fear. No one spoke and the gathering held its collective breath. The Tarot card reader wore a shawl made of a loose, filmy fabric. Alex winced at the thinness of her shoulders which trembled slightly. At her feet, the little child slept soundly in a basket.

Alex edged closer. Tarot cards were spread upon the table in the form of the Celtic cross. He recognized the *Death* and *Tower* cards.

With a sudden roar of laughter, the large man, whose fortune had been read, smacked his hand on the table. "Well, little lady!" Directed at the card reader, his tone was good-natured. "So that's my fortune, is it? No sacks of gold anywhere?"

"But you got the Death card in the spread, Jack!" said the woman next to him.

He pushed himself upright. "For God's sake, Martha!" He threw his arm around her and grinned. "It's just a game. Just silliness...really."

He gave her a quick hug. "Hey! I'm not going anywhere. The Tarot lady," he said, gesturing to the young woman, "says her name, Lia, means *bringer of good news.*"

Alex saw, during the commotion, that an elderly woman had slipped into the chair previously occupied by the man.

Ah! Miss Trump, he thought. How deceiving appearances can be! Somehow, she had changed yet again. An ethereal calm emanated from her in the midst of the carousing vacationers. Alex moved closer to see the faces of both women.

When Lia met Miss Trump's gaze, a concentrated energy flowed from her to the old woman like an electrical current. Lia placed the Tarot deck on the table and asked her, the *querent,* to choose ten cards. Quickly, Miss Trump picked them out. The intensity of her manner demonstrated that it was, to her, no mere amusement. Drawn in by the energy of the two women, at least twenty people formed a circle around the table. With the Celtic Cross Spread, ten cards were placed face down.

When Lia turned over the card, which traditionally represented the *Self*—or one's innate essence, the lines of her mouth softened and her breath deepened. With shadows flickering across her face, her eyes shone with new recognition and respect for Miss Trump. The *Temperance* card was now face up.

Alex had a smattering of knowledge of the various cards. This Temperance card pictured an otherworldly creature—a winged angel in white—suspended against a rich green background of primeval forest. Her expression was of great patience. From one sparkling crystal beaker to another, she poured a golden liquid.

The angel so pictured was sometimes called *The Alchemist*—the one who laboured with creativity and imagination to make something *new* from *nothing*. Lia inclined her head respectfully to Miss Trump as if acknowledging the presence of a savant.

The temperature had dropped by several degrees. Hearing low rumbles of thunder, the onlookers glanced about. The once sparkling night sky had filled with dark clouds.

Lia flushed and said, "I can tell you little you do not already know."

"Please, my dear," said Miss Trump gently, "Please continue. You have much to offer, I'm sure."

The reader drew herself up and recovered some of her composure. She turned all the other cards over and spoke slowly. "It is as I thought. What shall I tell you?"

Alex looked over the cards. The most striking was the Tower card indicating *Opposing Forces* to the *Self* or that which stands in the way. In the picture, lightning illuminated a blood red tower crumbling against a black night sky. Human bodies flew in every direction. The *Outcome* card—was Death. When Alex saw it, his eyebrows shot up. On that card, a voluptuous woman, wearing an evening gown, was being stalked across a desolate plane, by a black, menacing abstract form—apparently representing some impersonal form of Death.

A sharp crack of lightning sliced the sky.

"Don't be afraid child. I welcome the spread," said Miss Trump.

"I'm sure you can interpret it better than I can." When her child stirred and cried out in her sleep, the mother bent to comfort her. The baby settled back lulled by the rocking of the ship. Lia continued. "As I'm sure you know, the Death card means many things—an end of something and a new beginning."

"As always, in life and the following next stages," said Miss Trump quietly. "But I have a mission I hope to complete first. Do you see anything in the spread to suggest success or failure?"

Alex drew closer to listen. The candle tipped over on the table but was quickly righted. Someone re-lit it.

Lia fingered the Temperance card. After a moment, she looked directly into Miss Trump's eyes. "This card tells me you have already accomplished much. But your present mission will be difficult, involving much travel. You and a helper will need great strength and determination." She leaned across the table and spoke urgently. "You must have faith in your helper and the success of your mission. You have already made the right choice."

The wind had picked up and the air was cooling quickly. Furrowing his brow, Alex wondered what Miss Trump's mission was.

Lia continued, "You have achieved that fine balance so hard to find in this world of clashing opposites." She touched the Tower Card. "But this one puzzles me, madam. It suggests you may have missed something or *someone* unnecessarily."

Miss Trump smiled slowly. "In life, that is entirely possible, my dear." She shook her head and bent over the basket where the child lay. "Enough about me, child. You have such a fine and strong daughter. Our future lies with them." Then she looked over her shoulder to see others waiting for a reading. She opened her purse. "And what do I pay you?"

Sheet lightning illuminated the sky and the frozen faces around the table.

"But I've not told you anything of use."

"You have confirmed much. I want to pay you."

"Five pounds, please."

The old woman handed her ten and then rose. "Thank you, my dear. You have more customers waiting." She spotted Alexander in the crowd and, approaching him, lightly touched his arm. When he looked into her eyes, he saw both determination and a momentary touch of fear. Then, without a word, she disappeared into the crowd.

At first, it looked as if he storm would move off. Thunder was a mere distant roll and rain only splattered lightly on the deck. Lia cradled her baby in her arms. From the railing, Alexander looked southward across the Channel. Expecting storms, most passengers had gone below. A long night lay ahead.

Alex said, "Your daughter is so beautiful! How old is she?"

The woman smiled warmly. "Almost six months."

"How lucky you are!" He hesitated and then said, "May I sit down?"

Alexander usually impressed women as a warm and kindly person. Lia motioned him to a chair. Very slowly, she laid the baby back into the basket and tucked the blanket around her.

"Would you like me to read your cards, sir?"

"Oh yes please..."

At that moment, the candle flame flickered and suddenly went out as if doused by an unseen hand. Alex found his matches and relit it.

"You watched me when I read the woman's cards."

Alex nodded. "Yes. A very interesting spread."

"Do you know the Tarot well?"

Alex shook his head. "No. Only that it's about our journey through life and what we may encounter."

She smiled and handed him the deck. "That is all you really need to know."

He chose ten cards and laid them out in the Celtic cross formation. He chuckled when he turned over the *Self-card—the Fool!*

"That is an excellent card, sir. It means you are open to life and learning."

Alex suddenly spotted a stringed instrument beside her chair. Smiling, he shook his head. "That maybe so, but instead of a reading, I'd be delighted if you'd play that instrument for me. Is it a lute?"

The full moon sailed from behind a bank of clouds.

"Yes, it's a very beautiful instrument." She picked it up. The sound box—almost a triangular shape—was made of intricately scrolled, ancient wood. Its highly polished surface gleamed in the moonlight.

Alex was attentive. Her strumming and low, melodious voice rose up to the sky. The child at her feet suddenly wakened and smiled.

It was an old Irish folk song lamenting the spurned love of an aristocratic gentleman for Barbara Allan—and the death of both of them. She sang.

> *He turned his face unto the wall*
> *And death was with him dealing*
> *Adieu, adieu, my dear friends*
> *Be kind to Barbara Alan*

The wind stiffened and the clouds raced back over the moon. The baby drifted back to sleep.

O mother, mother make my bed
O make it fast and narrow
Since my love died for me today
I die for him tomorrow.

The old folksong struck deep chords with Alex. Again, he thought of Daphne whose presence seemed to follow him no matter where he travelled. A guilty conscience, he thought. Now he was hearing a song about spurning love, of which he was no doubt guilty. The questions—*what do I really feel for her? Is she simply a muse?*—would not leave him. He thought of his art and his creativity, which at times had seemed more important to him than life itself. Yet he had a nagging perception that he had closed out the world and the people in it. Perhaps that made his art sterile. From the other night, the reflection of his face in the train window appeared in his mind's eye—*hollow and empty.*

A huge, rogue wave roared up like an angry tongue lashing the ferry broadside. For long moments, the vessel seemed suspended in a silent mid-air space, threatening to capsize. A deathly groaning and an eerie whistling came and they were flung downward. Water rushed onto the deck nearly sweeping the tables and chairs overboard. But then the ferry heaved upward finally righting itself.

Alexander and Lia were still seated in their chairs which were now lying flat on their sides on the deck. Miraculously the bassinette, wedged into a corner, had remained dry and had not moved. The little girl cried out but settled fretfully again at the touch of her mother's hand.

Sheet lightning whitened the sky and thunder grumbled in the distance. Alex and Lia struggled to stand up. Rain lashed down upon them. He carried the bassinette inside for the mother. As they stood in front of the lift, he caught the fear in her eyes.

"Whatever happens, sir, to me? Please keep Celestine safe... if you can."

"Of course! But we'll *all* be fine. Please don't worry yourself."

She gazed at him for a moment, but said nothing.

The ship began a gentle, rocking motion, but then it became strong enough to make them reach for the walls. The lift creaked and clanged slowly downward to the lower decks. At last, the doors opened and they stepped out. A groaning sound began deep in the belly of the ship. They did not speak. The lift jerked to a stop at the bottom and the doors wheezed open.

Alex smiled down at the tiny girl who stared up at him with great curiosity and then rewarded him with a grin which made her wriggle all over with pleasure.

Alex, who had little experience with babies, laughed aloud. "She is so precious. Does she smile like that often?"

"Yes. Celestine is a very happy child."

Alex continued to grin back and make what he hoped were funny faces. Celestine approved, gurgled happily and reached up to touch his face. At least the rocking had settled and they could walk to their cabins without difficulty.

In the darkened corridor Alex asked, "Do you take this ferry often?"

"It is my job. The Ship's Master pays me to entertain the passengers with cards and the lute."

"I see." He took another peek at the baby. "Good night..." He smiled again. "Such a lovely child."

As Alex unlocked his door, he hoped that his cabin was not as terrible as he remembered. He turned on the light. It was.

He rinsed his face in the sink and, since there were no towels, he dried it on his sleeve. After loosening his shirt and pants, he hunted down a sweater for a pillow. The rocking of the boat had started again. He lay down and drifted off.

A violent jolt and a strange rushing, hissing sound awoke him an hour later. Loud banging and shouting followed. The entire ship shuddered and shook. Springing from the bed, he wrenched open the cabin door.

Rivers of water raced along the corridor. Surging, black currents spilled over the bulkheads and into the cabin. He waded into the freezing water now at mid-calf. He banged on the doors on either side of him—for Miss Trump and Lia and her baby. The force of the water nearly swept him off his feet. Their frightened faces appeared immediately in the doorways. The water had risen to Alex's knees and had filled their compartments.

"Lia!" he shouted. "Give me Celestine! I'll take her up. You and Miss Trump try to reach the stairs. I'll come back for you."

He took the tiny bundle in his arms. She was still warm but he wrapped his sweater around her and waded out into mid-thigh water.

Lia followed. "Save her, sir, please if you can!" she cried out.

Trying to follow, Miss Trump slipped and fell backward into the water. She staggered upward.

The water roared up past Lia's waist fast enough to knock her over. But she grasped a door handle and held on tightly.

At the stairs, Alex shouted back to them. "Hang on to the handles! Try to get to the stairs! I'll get the baby up and come back for you."

He saw no other passengers on their level. *Everyone must be on the main deck!*

With the child held tightly to his chest, he grasped the railing and dragged himself upward one flight. His legs began to buckle. Looking down, he saw Celestine's face suffused with happiness as she gazed up at him with—he could find no other word to describe it—except *love*. Energy flowed into his arms and legs. He made it up the next flights. On the deck, he handed Celestine to a crewmember who was organizing the lifeboats.

"Promise you'll get her safely onto the lifeboat!"

"Yes sir!" The man took the child.

"I'm going back for her mother and another woman."

"Are you crazy? You can't go back down!" the man shouted. But Alexander was gone.

It was a harrowing descent down into the belly of the ship. In near darkness, Alex was tossed and pitched against the railings and walls of the stairwell. He stumbled on the last few stairs and fell into the rushing water. At the bottom, he saw that Lia was almost at the stairs. Further back Miss Trump clung to a fire extinguisher fixed to the wall. She was exhausted and nearly sinking under the water. He swam to her.

"Put your arms around my neck," he shouted, thinking she was frozen in panic.

"No, Alexander. I will not!"

"What? Why not?"

"Go! You must save yourself and the mother for the child and you have much work to do!"

Uncomprehendingly, he shook his head. "That's ridiculous!" He grabbed her arms to force her but she fought him off with manic strength. Drowning man's panic, he thought. He grasped her shoulders and tried to pull her from the fire extinguisher.

Again, she fought him off. "Let go of me! Stop it!" With her feet, she shoved herself back up the river of water now over her head. At first she thrashed but then seemed to calm herself. Alexander dove head first after her. Underwater, he grasped her knees and tried to pull her to him. He was amazed at her strength as she kicked hard and broke from his grasp. He rose up from the water which was now up over his shoulders. In the dark it was hard to see her. She sank once and then resurfaced, her face filled with mad determination.

Before she sank below the surface for the last time, he saw her smile. She called out over the rush of water, "Go save the mother! New life needs its mother!" He could do no more. Finally Alexander accepted that death was what she wanted.

He strained to see the top of her white-haired head in the gloom. He cried out in amazement. There it was—the cosmic egg, just as before, hovering over where she likely was. He was struck with awe at its sheer beauty and mysterious grace. A curious sense of joy and exhaustion infused every muscle and fibre of his body.

Behind him, Lia screamed out. "Help me! I can't hold on!"

Alex broke from his state of wonder. Energy hit in shock waves. With strong strokes, he swam to her. Gently he turned her onto her back and supported her neck. Holding her under her chin, he swam backwards toward the stairs holding her head above the water. When they reached the stairwell, she was strong enough to climb the stairs.

She clung to Alex's arm "My baby! Please! Where is Celestine?"

He said, "She's safe. I promise. She's in the lifeboat."

At last they were on the main deck. Lia sank against Alexander and he and another deck hand lifted her into the boat. When the other passengers handed the baby to her, Lia wept from joy and exhaustion.

"An elderly woman has drowned in the hold!" Alex shouted at the crew.

"Nothing we can do now, sir! What was her name?"

"Miss Maureen Trump."

Alexander was torn between elation and great sorrow. The child, the new life, would have her chance to grow in her mother's love and care. But the loss of Miss Trump filled him with desolation. He would not forget the determination in her eyes as she sank below the water. Only now did he have a chance to reflect on his vision of the cosmic egg in all its mysterious beauty and wonder. He could not conceive of where it came from or what it was. But he knew that all his efforts to find the artist, who had painted it, were essential. On to Paris to find Henri Dumont!

CAEN

CHAPTER 12

When the lifeboats arrived in Caen, a red dawn was breaking through the grey skies over the beaches. Bleary eyed, Alexander had surprisingly slept through much of the trip from the doomed ferry into port. Stiff and cold, he made his way slowly onto the dock. Lia handed the baby up to him and then got off. He gazed at the sleeping child in his arms, wondering at her peaceful expression. In the ferry terminal, they tried at least six hotels before finding one with two rooms near the beach. They left together.

For a moment, he stood on the steps and surveyed the beaches once blood soaked years ago from war. A sense of eternal loss, like heavy fog, hung in the air. White gulls dipped over the stony beaches and screamed in eerily human voices which could have been the agonized cries of fallen soldiers. Grey light spread out and seeped into the land and the water. But the sea was a glassy calm with no reminder of last night's turbulence.

Much further along stood a white building which he assumed was their hotel. *How many people drowned last night,* he wondered?

"Lia? Wait here a moment. I want to find out about the passenger list."

She nodded and sat on a bench to nurse her child.

Inside the terminal, he found the purser. "Did everyone get to shore safely?"

The man checked his list. "Yes, sir—except for one, Miss Maureen Trump."

"Has the body been brought ashore?"

"Yes, it has. Are you a relative, sir?"

Alex shook his head and heard himself say, "No but she was a friend, a very good friend."

The purser inclined his head. "Then please accept our condolences."

Alex nodded. "Did you find her passport?"

"No, but we have that information in our Portsmouth office. If you are not a relative, I do not believe they will give you much information."

Alex returned to Lia and got a cab for them to the *Hotel DuMaurier*. He would do what he could to take care of her and her child. Fortunately, he still had his wallet and passport.

The low-rise *Hotel DuMaurier* looked as if it had been built sometime in the nineteen sixties when the style was simple, if not strip-down and cheap. The basics were there—bed, shower, lamp and twenty-six inch TV which watched like an accusing eye from the corner of the room. The floors were linoleum with a rug or two scattered about. Alexander sighed and sank to his bed. *It doesn't matter. But in this depressing place, I'll have to*

*wait until I get information about Miss Trump. But thank God
Lia and the child are all right!*

The afternoon was pleasant enough under the circumstance.
Lia, the baby and he took a cab into town and bought clothing.
Everything had been lost—even his picture of the cosmic egg.
No trouble. He could get another copy by email.

For an instant, an image of the golden egg flashed before his
eyes and he remembered his awe when it appeared just above
Miss Trump and recalled some of her last words—*you have
much work to do.* But he had no idea what the work might be.

For the child, he bought diapers, nighties and a little dress.
And Lia—she chose what she needed. For himself, he bought
several pairs of trousers, two shirts, underwear, socks and a
jacket. For him it was all for *life—new life.* What better activity
could there be after a death!

At supper in the hotel that evening, Lia said, "Did you
know Miss Trump well?"

"No, I didn't. I only met her on the train coming down
from London to Portsmouth. "But…" He played with his fork.
"Within a space of only a few hours, I felt I had known her a
lifetime."

"Yes, I know what that's like. Sometimes a very special
person enters your life for a particular purpose and then they
are gone. She was most definitely one such person."

He looked at her carefully. "You understand then…?"

Lia nodded. Celestine stirred in her cot at their feet.

Alexander smiled. "Your daughter is so lovely. Where is
her father?"

Lia turned away. He thought he saw her eyes glistening as
she bent to tend to the baby. "He is dead, sir."

"I'm so *very* sorry, Lia."

Sadly she smiled up at him. "Thank you."

"How do you provide for her?"

"I have regular bookings on these ferry boats. I can bring her with me and I earn a little money from singing and playing the lute and also from the Tarot Cards."

They lingered over coffee.

"What will you do next?"

"I'll wait for the ferry. It will go back the day after tomorrow." She hesitated as if considering a question. "And you? Will you wait for Miss Trump?"

At first Alex was confused but then he said, "Yes, you're right. I do want to find out about her—see if I can do anything, try to reach relatives."

She smiled. "I thought you might."

Alex helped her with the child to her room. Outside her door, he said, "Perhaps we can help each other. I'll help you until you go back on the ferry and you can help me with Miss Trump."

She took his hand. "Yes. That's right. You are a most kind man."

Alex retired to his room and, after a hot shower, he switched on the TV and lay on the bed. When he tried to fall asleep, images of Miss Trump's last moments filled his mind along with the vision of the cosmic egg floating just above her head.

All day, questions had trailed through his mind. Now, lying in the dark, he felt almost pulled under by the weight of them. No matter how hard anyone tried they could not reason, imagine or feel what happened at death. Some gave the matter little thought as if to say—*don't bother me with questions which have no answers.* Others had no need to question anything— *The Lord has his mysterious ways. It is not ours to know.*

In awe of the mystery of life and death, he sought to find meaning, through speculation. Miss Trump had seemed to welcome it. In fact, her face was nearly beatific. Perhaps for her it was a release from some burdens of *this* world. Of course, she wanted him to save the child and not her. But then, in the darkness, he was haunted by a question—had he used that as an excuse not to try harder? Could he have saved them both? Not if she continued to resist him. At last he drifted off on the waves of sleep to a deep and dreamless six hours.

Next morning was colder, but sunny. A stiff breeze came from the sea and only a few stacks of clouds sat on the horizon. Alex decided to shave his beard which had grown considerably during the last few days.

Suddenly, as he was washing his razor, a feeling swept over him as if another very determined being had suddenly inhabited him. He could scarcely put into words the sense of another being, with its own thoughts and sensibilities, moving within him. Puzzled, he sank to the edge of the tub. Although he still felt very much himself, it was as if his own spirit had made room for another.

He *must* speak with Miss Trump's relatives. Didn't she say her deceased sister had four children all living in London? But she had not mentioned any names. He remembered that her sister had lived until the last year or so in Portsmouth. Her husband had died in the same year. But he could not remember their names. It made sense to inquire in Portsmouth. Surely, he could locate at least one of them! His feelings had grown to a compulsion.

Unable to tear himself away from his circuitous thoughts, he sought out Lia in the breakfast room. She was fixed in a study of a spread of her Tarot cards. He had little appetite and so ordered only coffee, juice and a warm biscuit. Lia was planning a stroll outside with Celestine.

Alex hurried along the pathway to the ferry terminal, infused with an unexpected, powerful energy. Bending into the wind, he drew his collar up to his chin. His spirit filled him to bursting as he marched on ever more quickly. The *other* spirit, he had felt earlier, seemed to have disappeared and he felt quite alone inside himself.

The ferry terminal was a low, squat brick building which at first appeared locked. He banged on the glass door and shielded his eyes to see inside. A man, wearing a green visor and suspenders, hobbled to the door and unlocked it. He motioned him in.

"Is the purser from the ship that sank here?" he asked.

The man nodded and pointed Alex down a hallway. He knocked at the door and a man with red-rimmed eyes poked his head out.

"You're the purser from the ferry which sank? I believe we spoke yesterday."

The man nodded and let him in. "Yes, sir. Please excuse me." He blew his nose and regarded Alex bleakly. "What can I do for you?"

"Do you have the names of Miss Trump's relatives yet?"

As if devoid of all energy, the purser retrieved a thin file folder and spread it on the desk revealing only one sheet of paper. "As you can see, she had no relatives."

Alexander examined the paper, a form for names of next of kin in case of accident. Apparently Miss Trump had written— *none.* He assumed it was her signature. She had given her address 45 Fortnum Road in London's East End.

"But she spoke of nieces or nephews in London."

The purser shrugged. "It is all we have. That is what she told us—*none.*"

"Do you have a copy of her passport?"

The man fussed with the few papers. "It seems, sir, that we don't have that documentation here. It must be at head office."

"May I have a copy of the sheet you do have?"

"Certainment, monsieur." The purser left and then returned with a copy. "Here you are. I hope you find someone."

Alex examined the paper carefully. What help could it be? It only had her signature and—*none.* But it had her home address, 45 Fortnum Road, London. "Will the company try to find next of kin?"

The man gave an elaborate shrug. "That is for head office to decide. Please tell no one I gave you a copy."

"Where is the body? What will be done with it?"

"It is at the morgue in Caen. If you can identify it, you should go there. They will hold it for seventy two hours and if no one claims it, it will be cremated and the ashes stored for one year."

Alex nodded and left. Although he was disappointed, he marched back to the hotel, his mind bristling with plans. *First to phone Jamie and get him working on it. Next, go to the morgue.*

When he arrived at the DuMaurier, he looked for Lia and the child but could not find them. After he returned to his room, he telephoned me.

"Jamie?"

"Yes, Alex. Where are you? I tried to reach you at the hotel in Paris but you hadn't checked in."

"It's terrible. The ferry almost sank and everyone survived except for one."

"Good Lord, Alex! Are you all right? Where are you?"

"I'm in Caen. I'm fine, but I need your help."

"Of course. Do you need money?"

"No. I need two things. First, I want you to find *anything* you can about a Maureen Trump. Unfortunately, she drowned." There was a pause. "I tried to save her but I couldn't..."

I knew how devastating that would be to Alex. He is extremely demanding of himself and undoubtedly would be harbouring all kinds of dark thoughts about his attempts.

I said, "I'm so very sorry, Alex. What can you tell me about Miss Trump?"

"Not very much. I met her on the train coming down and then again on the ferry. We got to talking—you know how it is."

Indeed I did know. Alex is a person whom people seek out especially when he travels.

"All I know," he continued, "is that her address is 45 Fortnum Road in London's East End. Apparently she has four nieces and nephews who live in London, but I don't have any names. Also she mentioned a deceased sister and brother in law who lived in Portsmouth. Unfortunately she didn't mention any names. Miss Trump was likely somewhere in her early seventies. Rather thin and frail and not terribly well dressed— decently but modestly."

"Hmmm... I'll pop around to the Fortnum Road address and see what I can find out."

"Thank you, Jamie. Call me on my mobile, please."

Alex has made many acquaintances on his travels. Although he would tell you his inspiration comes from his muse, I know he learns much from his travels and the people he meets. Some quality of mind or spirit within him causes people to tell him their stories *and* contemplate their lives—in fact, existence itself. In his presence, people experience a sense of wisdom but it is very much a two way street. Alex gains as much as they do and he comes away enriched by a profound respect for and love of the human spirit. Alex calls it *searching for his light*. I set about on my Miss Trump assignment with considerable interest.

After we hung up, Alex called the morgue in Caen. A severe looking gendarme picked him up at the hotel and delivered him to a redbrick building on the far side of town.

Alex had seen only a few corpses at funerals and so was unprepared. There lay the body, covered with a white sheet, lying on a slab just like in the films. The sheet was lowered. Alex jumped back as if shot through the heart with an electric shock.

Rigormortis had frozen Miss Trump's hands in ghastly, twisted shapes like broken twigs on a branch. Her lips were curled in a grimace of the cruellest pain. Her eyes remained stubbornly open staring out into empty space. Although her expression had been serene as she slipped under water, her death could not have been easy. One's spirit might welcome death—even court it—but her body had desperately fought it off. Where was she now and what was she seeing?

He turned away. "Yes...that is Miss Trump."

In an office upstairs, he signed some papers. A rather officious bureaucrat told him that, if next of kin did not claim the body within three days, it would be cremated and the ashes kept in a wooden box for a year.

In the cab back to the hotel, he thought it was odd. A dead body looked like an empty, discarded container whose contents had been drained out. Some invisible, animating element—the human spirit— was simply gone. Poor Miss Trump. What greater proof could there be of that invisible spirit's existence other than its absence?

I called Alex back at the hotel.

"Yes, Jamie. What did you find out?"

I sighed deeply. "Alex, I went to 45 Fortnum Road this afternoon only to find that it's a garage for servicing cars. Of course, I checked any houses in the vicinity and even spoke with the woman running the greengrocer's. No one's ever heard of a Maureen Trump. I gave everyone your description."

Alex groaned. "Thanks ever so much Jamie, but how can that be?"

"I also searched with information. There are about thirty *Trumps* in the book. Do you want me to call *all* of them?"

"No, of course not. That'll take days. Whatever we do, needs to be done quickly."

"What's the hurry?"

"They'll cremate the body in three days. I've already identified it, but I really just want any next of kin to have a say beforehand. Maybe they don't want cremation."

"Surely the police are trying to find someone."

"If they are, they're very secretive about it."

Alex sounded extremely tired but there was an underlying note of –what shall I say—*tenacity* or *resolve*? But no, those are inadequate words. My friend can be exceedingly stubborn, even pig-headed. But that is still not quite right either. Sometimes, Alex can become almost *possessed* with an idea or plan. At those times, he may depart from his usual calm, collected self. Now I sensed the stirring of some deeply felt passion within him, so strong it scarcely seemed his own.

I asked, "Alex? Are you all right? You seem deeply troubled."

When his voice thickened, I realized how upset he was.

"She was a person who walked into my life, Jamie. She seemed to know exactly why she was there and what she should be doing. Me? I have no clue whatsoever!"

I could think of nothing to say and so I said, "Tell me more?"

"Water rushed into the belly of the ship. I tried to rescue her but she pushed me away."

"Good Lord, Alex..." I gulped. "But you can't blame yourself. You think she wanted to drown?"

Alex didn't reply for some moments. At last he said, "No I don't. I did manage to save the mother and her baby. Miss Trump demanded I go to them."

"So, she wanted you to save a new life. You said she was old..." I knew I was grasping at straws. Alex would blame himself regardless of what I said.

"I guess it was something like that, Jamie." His voice had become a whisper.

"Who were the mother and child?" I asked.

"The Tarot card reader. She also played the lute and sang. Candle light danced in her presence…" Her daughter's name— *Celestine*. Her name is *Lia*."

Alex is a powerful creator of vivid images with only a word or two. Now they *danced* in *my* brain. I could see a hooded woman arranging cards on a table by candlelight. I saw torrents of water rushing down corridors at the deepest, darkest levels of the ship. *And*, I could see the serene face of an elderly woman slipping under the surface.

Alex broke the silence. "I have to do *something*, Jamie. I have to mark the life of Maureen Trump. This trip has just become a mess of loose ends. I've got to find her relatives or else take care of her remains myself. You know I'm not religious, but when the very first human being died, we've always had definite rituals—funerals, readings, a minister…and it somehow gives it importance and meaning even if we don't know what or whit is."

I listened carefully. There was such pain in my friend's voice and something *else* as well. He was grappling with the meaning of life—Miss Trump's, his own…all life. Anyone who thought he was insensitive to human concerns was utterly wrong.

I said, "Alex I could hire an investigator who might find somebody. Nowadays they have access to hundreds of searches performed at a click."

"All right. See what you can find. I've got at least another day before I have to do anything."

"Good. I'll get back to you by noon tomorrow." We rang off. I must have sat there for ten minutes just visualizing Tarot card spreads. I also knew I'd better hurry because Alex was torturing himself. Fortunately, I knew just the person to call— Dennis McLean, private investigator.

After I laid out the problem, Dennis called me back by the end of the day.

"Jamie!" Dennis has a strange voice for a private investigator. It booms.

He continued, "Your Miss Trump is nowhere to be found! I checked birth and marriage records…hospitals…tax department. There's just no record. It's like she never existed."

"Could you please phone the Trumps in the London phone book?"

"Already have, Jamie. Nothing!"

"Thanks so much for trying, Dennis. Anything more you can think of—anything?"

"Not with *some* more information. Any idea of where she grew up…went to school?"

I rang off and called Alex. His reaction was as I thought— flummoxed and depressed.

Alex had dinner with Lia at the hotel that evening. Celestine lay in her bassinette at her mother's feet.

"I've never seen such a happy and serene child." Alex beamed down on the baby. "May I hold her?"

"Of course," Lia said with a smile. She lifted Celestine up and settled her into Alex's arms.

Gazing at her, he marvelled at her perfection—every bit of her so tiny and yet complete! *Amazing that everything is there for her to grow into a child, an adult and then an old woman.* He admitted he knew little if anything about children and absolutely nothing about babies.

Celestine opened her eyes and studied Alex with such a look of grave intelligence that he nearly laughed aloud. Eagerly he asked Lia, "What do you think she is thinking?"

Lia smiled slowly. She reached over and smoothed her daughter's blanket. "She is thinking of many things. But right now, she is thinking that your face is very kind."

Alex chuckled. He found himself slipping further into a state of wonderment. *New life…new chances…the flow of life like an unending river.*

Although the baby obviously brought joy to Alex, Lia asked, "You seem very sad. May I ask why that is?"

"I didn't realize…"

"Are you a writer, Mr. Wainwright?"

He shook his head. "No...I'm a painter."

"I thought something like that…" she murmured.

He looked at her with curiosity.

"Sometimes I think of life as one long unbroken stream momentarily interrupted only by birth and death. Like your creative flow. Sometimes you paint with a driving passion and sometimes you can think of absolutely nothing to paint. Am I right?"

"Yes. That is very well put." The baby reached up and tugged on his collar. He beamed down upon her.

Lia spoke quietly. "A writer would say that— one lifetime is like a chapter in a book. Part of the story is told. The entire story is told in a novel or a trilogy of novels—even more." She touched Alex's hand and smiled. "Maybe even enough to fill a library with endless shelves!" She smiled up at him. "My husband wanted very much to be a writer."

Alex stared at her for long moments. At last he said quietly, "Lia! That is beautifully put. It contains all the wisdom there is! The creative flow is like the unending river of life."

When Alex returned to his room, he was planning an early night. I called just as he was snapping on the TV.

"Any luck, Jamie?" he asked.

"I'm afraid not. My man called any Trumps he could find in the phone book and did all sorts of searches with the government offices. She's left no trace."

"Damn it, Jamie. She *did* exist. I talked with her."

"I know...I know. If we had more time, we could delve deeper."

"Can your investigator think of anything else? If she weren't born in the UK, she might not show up. Or if she were, she might well have been receiving government benefits. Surely, there'd be a record of that or with the National Health Service. And then, maybe she was travelling under a different name."

"How far do you want to go with this, Alex?"

He sighed. "There's not much point after tomorrow, I suppose."

"True."

"Have him spend one more day on it, if he will."

"All right. I'll do that." I was concerned about Alex when we hung up. Usually, when he is obsessed with something, he is energized. Tonight he was in the slough of depression.

Alex was wakened at six-thirty the next morning by the telephone. Groggily, he muttered into it. "Yes?"

The voice on the other end was a high-pitched bark. "Monsieur Wainwright? It is Monsieur Colbert at the morgue. I wish to inform you that the remains of Miss Maureen Trump were cremated today at six am."

Alex swung his feet to the floor nearly leaping out of bed. "What in hell do you mean? You weren't going to cremate until tomorrow. I specifically asked you to wait so I could find any next of kin!"

"No monsieur! That is not correct. It is on my sheet right in front of me. Your initials are on it granting us the authority."

"No! There's a mistake. I never signed for anything!"

"It is done, monsieur. When do you wish to pick up the ashes?"

"Jesus Christ! I wanted to find her relatives. Put your supervisor on the line right now!"

Within a few minutes Monsieur Lavage said, "Oui monsieur? What may I assist you with this fine morning?"

Imbecile Alex muttered. "You've cremated the remains of my *friend* Miss Trump without any authority. What are you going to do about it?"

Monsieur Lavage's voice became oily and obsequious. "But of course, it is a great misfortune which has occurred through miscommunication, Monsieur Wainwright. But surely you must agree that nothing can be done about this regrettable turn of events which you apparently authorized. But in order to assist you in this predicament, we will prepare a letter to the next of kin giving a full apology—if you would be so kind as to give us their names and addresses."

"I don't know ..."

"Alas, monsieur."

"I'm coming to the morgue this morning."

"But we are not open to the public until ten o'clock—*je regrette.*"

"Fine!" Alex paused. He had no official standing with the staff at the morgue. They could disregard a *friend* of the deceased without fear of consequence. "All right. I'll be there at ten and will expect to see you, Monsieur Lavage."

Alexander could not remember such anger. *They won't get away trying to blame me!* Bile burned upward from his stomach and his chest grew painfully tight. To relax himself, he took a shower and found that he veered ridiculously between tears and shouts of laughter. It was the clash of comic darkness from the theatre of the absurd and ineffable frustration and sorrow arising from the mystery of death. As he examined his face in the mirror, he knew he was *driven.* But to do what and why? He wished Miss Trump had left a clue. After coffee and a bagel, Alex walked along the beach filling in time until he could go to the morgue.

At last, he called a cab which worked its way slowly through the morning traffic and drew up at nine forty-five in front of the morgue. It was a low-slung edifice of red brick sprawling on the outskirts of town between a railway track and an overpass. If he had not been so angry, the desolate tawdriness of the entire place would have driven him deeper into depression.

As soon as he stepped inside, it was obvious that they were ready for him. Apparently Monsieur Lavage was only a minor functionary. The Directeur M. Clemenceau awaited him in his office.

Clemenceau was a red-faced, corpulent man whose chins spilled out over his collar. Alex suspected a bottle of alcohol was never far away.

Clemenceau spoke sternly. "Are you a relative of the deceased?"

Alex shook his head, "No, Monsieur Directeur."

Clemenceau shuffled the two papers in the file and stabbed at the second one. "Then how is it that you signed for the cremation of the remains? Look at the signature right above the line marked *next of kin*."

"I didn't sign anything."

"Then you deny this is your signature? "He held it out for Alex who took it to study.

"No, I did not sign. It is not my signature."

Confusion spread over Clemenceau's face. "Then whose is it?"

"How would I know? Someone here must have..."

Clemenceau heaved himself up from his desk. "That would *never* happen here, but I will check with the proper persons immediately."

In the absence of the Director, Alex shuddered as he looked about the dingy room. On some makeshift shelves, there were five bottles filled with different coloured preservatives. White, brown and red blobs floated in the bottles. *God knows what's in them!*

Smiling, Clemenceau re-entered the room. "At this point, monsieur, as a practical matter, it is of no concern. Her remains have been cremated. You are free to take them at once after some paperwork."

"But that does not resolve the issue. I was told I had three days in which to locate her next of kin." Suddenly, Alex was swept with weariness. It was a pointless exercise. Nothing could reverse the cremation. "All right, but I want to leave my name so that if any next of kin inquire, they can reach me."

"Certainment! Leave your information at the front desk so that it will be available." Clemenceau sat back lacing his fingers over his stomach.

"May I take the ashes with me?"

"Where do you intend to take them?"

"I'm not sure…"

"Pardon?"

"I'm travelling on to Paris and so, I guess I'll have to take them with me."

"And after that?"

"Back to London."

"Oh no, Monsieur Wainwright. Je regrette! You are not allowed to take the ashes out of France without a special permit."

"You're joking! What sort of permit?"

"The government requires a certain fee if you wish to take the remains out of the country. It is quite a procedure lasting several weeks to obtain the permit and it is rather expensive."

According to Alex, all bureaucracies were specifically designed to frustrate him personally. Hoping to find *some* relatives, he had given little thought as to what to do with the ashes.

At last he said, "I'll take them with me to Paris. By the time I'm back, perhaps we'll have found some next of kin."

Clemenceau rubbed his hands together. "May I make a suggestion Mr. Wainwright in the interest of us all?"

"Yes?"

"We have a lovely little cemetery on our property. Many people find it convenient to bury the remains there. It is a simple and speedy solution to what can become difficult problems. *And* the fees and costs are not unreasonable."

Alex was revolted by the man. *Miss Trump will not be passed off with a simple and speedy solution! She deserves respect, some formalities and …* Alex's thinking stalled. How *should* he deal with the remains of someone of whom he knew almost nothing?

"My driver would be pleased to take you to the cemetery and show you all available plots."

Alex thought about the practicalities of the situation. How could he transport the ashes to Paris, find M. Dumont and then, hopefully, the painter of the cosmic egg? He said, "All right. I'll have a look. What are the charges?"

"I will give you our brochure." He heaved himself out of his chair. "It sets out all the costs and so you can peruse it at your leisure." He opened the door to show Alex out. "Bonne chance, Monsieur. My assistant will take you downstairs to the driver."

Alex glanced at the cover of the brochure displaying a charming and peaceful gravesite with well-tended shrubs and attractive flowerbeds.

Clemenceau held out his hand. "Monsieur, you may want to commit the ashes on this side of the Channel, given the bureaucratic pitfalls you may encounter. For a small additional charge we can include an officiate of any church or religion you like."

"I'd like to see the cemetery first. How far away is it?"

"Very close...five minutes by car. If you decide to use our services, we will be pleased to help."

In the car, the driver went around in what seemed to Alex dozens of circles. They raced past a post with a gerrymandered sign on which was written the word *indigents*. They drove up a narrow, winding track which looked as if it would end in a farmer's field but did not. One more twist and Alex saw the overpass, the railway track *and* two huge billboards—one advertising the services of a veterinary with a large poodle sniffing the air. The second one proclaimed—*Time to get your house in order. Jesus is coming.*

"Where are we?"

The driver said, "The cemetery, monsieur."

Wooden crosses marked the terrain of patchy yellowish-brown grass. When Alex kicked his toe into the ground dust rose everywhere. From where he stood, he could hear the hum of traffic on the road above and a noisy banging, snapping sound as vehicles passed overhead. The view was depressing. Only a few scrubby bushes growing from the stony ground surrounded the cemetery. Not a single flower much less a bed of them! Then, along the track, a freight train began to rumble.

"Jesus Christ! What kind of hell-hole is this?"

The driver did not reply.

Miss Trump would hate it here! Nobody should be here! Not even a dog. Energy sprang in him. "Take me back! This is disgusting."

Alex examined the brochure as they drove back to the morgue. *Good grief! Two thousand* euros! That only covered the burial rights in a tiny scrap of land under an overpass, beside a freight line adorned with advertising for poodles and the second coming. Perhaps they also buried the animals they put down at the vet.

Monsieur Clemenceau was waiting for Alex. "*Alors!* What do you think?

Alexander can be a very imposing figure when angered.

Clemenceau cringed as Alex stood ramrod straight with his face perfectly white. "How dare you even suggest ashes be buried beside an overpass and a railway track in a field more suited to a garbage dump! Have you no respect for the deceased?"

Clemenceau was foolish to grin. "Well...some people just want it done and over with."

"How dare you charge two thousand euros for such a place? Surely the departed deserve some care and consideration! Just give me the ashes and I'll be on my way."

"But there is paper-work, if you want to take them back to London."

Alex turned sharply back on him. "Just give me the ashes!"

"But of course, Monsieur. My staff will bring them to the reception desk. Good day, sir."

Without further word, Alex went downstairs. Most of all he was sickened by liveliness of such petty greed and avarice in a place where people were made vulnerable by grief. In fifteen minutes, Alex had the ashes of Miss Maureen Trump in a rough-hewn, plywood box resting in a paper bag. He got a cab back to the *Hotel DuMaurier*.

At first, he sat with the box squarely positioned on his knees so that it would not tip or spill. But soon he grew uncomfortable. He put it on the floor—no that was wrong. Perhaps, he should have put it in the boot. At last, he moved over to the right side of seat and placed the box carefully on the other side. *That feels right,* or so he thought. *As if she is travelling with me.*

In his room at the hotel, he had the same problem. At first, he placed the box on top of the TV. He sat on the bed and stared at the box. The TV stared bug-like back at him.

I could tell the minute I called that Alex was distraught.

"Jamie? Say you're not going to tell me she never existed?"

"What?"

"Because Miss Trump is sitting right across the room from me!"

"Alex! What on earth are you talking about? You said she was..."

There was a very long pause. Then he began to chuckle. "It doesn't matter whether we find any relatives because they've already cremated her. And the box containing her ashes is sitting on top of the telly in my room."

I was stunned. At last I said, "Why do *you* have the ashes?"

"Because they were going to dump them in a pauper's grave by a railway track! I couldn't let them do that."

"But what are *you* going to do with them?"

"I don't know. Apparently, I can't just take them back to London without a bunch of paperwork—at least according to the morgue people."

"Shouldn't you take the ashes back to the morgue, Alex? You were planning to go to Paris to find Dumont—the pianist."

"I think I'll take them to Paris with me."

Although it was his most positive statement yet, I said, "Alex, that's ridiculous. You can't carry them around with you. Think of the burden they'd be. *Besides* you might lose them."

Alex gave a disturbing laugh and said, "Despite your objections, Mr. Helmsworth, it'd be nice to have the company."

We sparred back and forth for several more minutes. Eventually Alex said, "Don't worry Jamie, I'll take good care but don't try to find any relatives before I get back."

Carrying the ashes of a woman he scarcely knew all over Paris! After we hung up, I had difficulty not chuckling at the absurdity of the situation myself.

For his part, Alex went to the mini-bar and toasted Miss Trump with a cognac. Just as he was finishing his drink, he noticed the red light on the telephone was flashing. He retrieved the message:

Monsieur Wainwright—please be advised that there is a letter awaiting you at reception.

Surely the morgue wasn't still trying to sell their services! Nonetheless, he went to the front desk and retrieved a pale blue envelope. He sat in the lobby and began to read.

Dear Mr. Wainwright,
I tried to find you to say goodbye before Celestine and I had to catch the ferry back to Portsmouth. Both of us have been deeply touched by knowing you and we are forever indebted to you for saving our lives and renewing our spirits. With all our hearts, we wish that you find what you seek.

Alex was greatly moved by Lia's words. Yet for the rest of the evening, he mulled over her last sentence. What was it he sought? He found himself staring at the plywood box on top of the telly. He was torn between leaving it there overnight and putting it in the back of the wardrobe. His last thought before he drifted off was that Miss Trump would not care for such confinement.

CHAPTER 13

Krysta, officially now Rinaldo's model, tossed her paintbrush down and found a cigarette. "Rinaldo's impossibly vain! A real old *fart*."

"Why did you want to meet with him?" Her friend Rene rubbed linseed oil on a rag and began cleaning the paint from her fingers.

Krysta laughed. "It's part of the conceptual art project— called *The Artistic Fart*. In fact, Rinaldo's perfect for it!"

"Why are you doing a conceptual art project?" Rene asked.

Krysta made a face. "It's for Randy's course work at the Slade. He's going to fail if he doesn't get some help and then his parents will cut him off."

Krysta and her friend Rene were both students at City and Guilds of London Art School where they and other students advocated a return to the more *traditional* forms of artistic expression. To them conceptual art was a *crock* for old geezers. Both of them ranked high in *fine art* painting and the craft of historic carving. They idolized the work of Alexander

Wainwright and were delighted when he won the Turner Prize with the *Hay Wagon.*

"But this conceptual art is really is kind of interesting, Rene. If you treat it as some weird joke, it might be fun."

"What kind of joke?"

"If I can get Rinaldo involved in it, it'd be like some kind of parody on that whole school of art."

"So what's the concept?"

"Rinaldo did some stupid *Rutting Fields* performance in Piccadilly Circus a few days ago and was arrested. He thinks that it's brilliant to contrast human and animal behaviour—animals are uninhibited about sex and humans are totally screwed up about it. So he had a bunch of cut-out animals set around the fountain and then brought in naked people who didn't move." Krysta sighed. "Actually, it's kind of sad…"

"So you parody that?"

Krysta grinned. "Yes, exactly! He wants me to be his model and cover me with papier-mache."

"What? How kinky is that!"

"I know it sounds stupid because it is."

"I've said he should paint the papier mache. Otherwise it'd be boring. Maybe something like Tarot cards." Krysta wrinkled her nose. "At least it'd be prettier don't you think?" She put out her cigarette. "But you know what he did then?"

Rene shook her head.

"He takes me by the wrist over to this beat up old bed and tries to come on to me."

Soon the two women were nearly collapsing with laughter.

Krysta struggled for breath. "But the old geezer couldn't get it up."

"Krysta! You didn't make fun of him! That'd be so cruel."

Laughing hard, Krysta gasped for air. "Yes! But stop! The way you're looking at me, you're going to make me feel sorry for him. What a fate for the creator of the *Rutting Fields!*"

CHAPTER 14

"Let's take a walk in Central Park this afternoon," Bradley Franks said on the phone.

To Daphne, her agency partner, sounded unaccountably nervous for a Sunday morning. Normally, he was cool and all business. She asked, "Where should we meet up?"

"How about at the Carousel at 66th Street."

"The carousel?" The carousel seemed an odd place especially on a cloudy, late autumn morning but she agreed.

Taking the subway, she reflected upon the two cities— London and New York, each with its own particular atmosphere. Nothing could compete with New York's explosive, edgy tempo even on a Sunday and nothing said London more than its stuffy reserve. But she was charmed by both of them and the idea of moving to London really appealed. Over the past twenty-four hours, her debate over Alex had not dissipated.

She first saw Brad, collar up against the sharp breeze, standing next to one of the horses on the ride. Seeing the stiffness in his frame, she thought—*what in hell has happened? Did we lose an important client?* But she also knew that whatever disaster might have occurred would be taken care of with Brad's usual professionalism and calm.

She waved and walked toward him. Two laughing children ran in circles chasing birds, their breath making clouds in the air. Their parents huddled on a nearby bench.

"So, what's up, Brad? You sounded so mysterious on the phone."

Smiling nervously, he hunched further down into his collar and grasped her arm. She winced for just a moment at his force. They walked past the fountain and into the park.

He faced her. "Daphne? I've been thinking about this all the time you've been gone."

"Jesus, Brad! What is it?"

He turned away and walked further along the path. "So, I'm just going to say it straight out." He grasped her shoulders and turned her to face him.

"What *is* it? You're scaring me half to death! We can't be bankrupt, surely."

He shook his head and looked off in the distance. "No, nothing like that." He grinned and blinked his eyes in the sun. "I've been thinking we should get married."

Daphne was stunned. Such a thought had never entered her mind. Brad was a good friend and business partner but that was it. She would never have imagined he might feel that way.

His face crinkled in horror. He spoke although his voice was scarcely more than a whisper. "Oh. God! I'm *so* sorry! This is a total shock for you."

"Brad?" She took his hand. He was a good and kind man— the last person in the world she would want to hurt. But he was like a brother to her. "Please! Don't think *that*. It's just that…"

He gulped for air like a man who had just been kicked in the gut.

"That we've been such amazing friends and business partners that…I just never thought that way…"

He waved her off. "Listen Daphne. Let's not talk anymore right now about it."

They walked further into the park in silence. He hunched his shoulders deep in his coat.

Daphne increased her pace to keep up with him. "Brad… stop." She didn't know what else to say. "Please, Brad." Suddenly an entirely new thought occurred to her. *But why not? He's wonderful in so many ways.*

He turned back to her. "Sorry, Daphne. I really blew it. I assumed way too much."

"But there's nothing to be upset about, Brad. Just because…"

He bit his lip and waited. His eyes flitted about and then bore into hers.

"It doesn't mean that I don't…I can't… Brad, this is such a shock…a surprise that I don't know what to say."

"You mean?"

She faced him straight on and heard herself say, "It means that I haven't thought that way before and maybe I just need time."

Again, he took her arm. She moved down the path with him thinking—*what have I just said?*

"So, I have reason to hope? I haven't just destroyed a great friendship?"

"No, of course you haven't. But I would need time...lots of time. And I just don't know...it might never happen."

He smiled. "Okay." He put his arm around her as they left the park "Let's have brunch at the Plaza."

Even though she felt her body tense at his embrace, she smiled and nodded.

PARIS

CHAPTER 15

Leaving Caen that morning, Alex had still been at a loss about Miss Trump's ashes kept only in a flimsy, plywood box. His hands trembled and his brow grew damp as he set the urn gently and respectfully on the bed in his hotel room. Then he carefully taped the lid and sides of the makeshift container and put it in a plastic bag.

Most of all, he feared spilling the contents. He had no connection with Miss Trump that would permit such intimate dealings as touching her ashes. It would be a violation of some deeply held primal taboo. His sense of common decency dictated he take the greatest care of her remains for he could not have buried them in that dismal excuse for a graveyard beside the railway tracks. At last, he simply packed the box in a separate section of his suitcase surrounded by his socks and hurried for his train.

The train from Caen took him directly into the Saint-Lazare Station in Paris. The tracks, trains and equipment in the darkened shed reminded him of the work of the French

Impressionist painter, Claude Monet, who created a series of paintings of this very railway station. Monet was best known for his ponds and lily pads bathed in exquisitely soft light. But in his paintings of railway stations, billowing blue, white and gray clouds of smoke nearly obscured the black iron horses as they chuffed and clanged along the tracks into Saint-Lazare.

Monet had created marvellously ambiguous swirls of light and shadow. What was solid? What was insubstantial? As if in a dream world, concrete shapes of heavy equipment melted into evocative, abstract forms.

Alex's teacher, Terrance Cuneo, whose statue graced Waterloo Station, had also been captivated by trains and machinery *and* so his pictures were much more solid and detailed. For Cuneo's art, it was essential to record the exterior world in all its glorious, physical detail. For Monet, it was all about the colour, light and shadow and the *impression* things in the physical world made upon his inner world.

Once again, Alex thought that art and life were intimately entwined. Why not? Art was the human expression of life. Did it matter whether his cosmic egg existed in the outer or inner world? Or, as some might argue, was there even an inner and outer world?

Leaving the station, he headed for the line of taxis. Only days ago, he had met Miss Trump. Since then life had become much more than ambiguous. In fact, his world and entire being seemed completely altered in ways he did not understand. He asked the driver to take him to the Hotel des Fleurs, Saint Germaine de Pres.

Now, in the cab from Saint-Lazare, he stared morosely out onto the streets of Paris and realized that his confusion was rapidly growing. That demanding, foreign spirit was rising within him again.

The taxi pulled up in front of the Hotel des Fleurs, an impressive five-storey edifice on the boulevard. The leaden cloud cover began to lift and rays of sun poked through. Nearby, a café was opening and outside a saxophone player was warming up. Alex determined to shake off his darkened state of mind. Checking in went smoothly and even his room was ready. All he wished to do was take a hot shower and relax for an hour or so.

"Damn!" He snapped his fingers in the lift. *Forgot to call Jamie. We have to locate this Henri Dumont, the Parisian Pianist.* He switched on the lights of his room and smiled. Before him lay a huge bed, a desk and comfortable armchair. From the window, he looked down onto an interior courtyard with arches adorning a garage, which must have served as stables more than a century ago. Easy to look back to other centuries and imagine the horses and carriages that had dropped off guests in their finery.

I was waiting to hear from Alex, when he called me from his room. I said, "Listen, Alex, this man is almost as hard to track down as your Maureen Trump."

"What? You can't find anything in this day and age where we're all supposed to be connected?"

I sighed. His tone was weary and frustrated. "Here's what we've got." I organized my meagre notes. "On the internet, we've traced him up to around ten years ago—under the name *Henri Dumont,* living on the *Ile de la Cite.*"

"What then? Did he just drop off the face of the earth?"

"Not entirely. He used to play at some very impressive places. Ten years ago he performed at a spectacular concert hall, Salle Gaveau and also at the Theatre du Chatelet. Both excellent venues! Rather like the Albert Hall."

"He must have had quite a reputation. Anything else on his career?"

"No…it just seems to end eight or ten years ago."

"No address or phone number?"

"I'm sorry to come up with so little, Alex."

There was a long pause, and then Alex asked, "Any particular composers he liked to play?"

"Very Baroque. You know Bach, Handel, and Vivaldi…"

"How old would he be?"

"Likely close to seventy by now."

"You're sure he's not dead?"

"No death certificate to be found." I was beginning to feel quite incompetent, but then my skills have never encompassed investigation beyond the world of art.

"So…ten years ago, the man was at the peak of his career and then he just dropped out of sight?"

"That's the way it looks, Alex. I'll keep trying if you like."

"It's hard to believe somebody can just *disappear* and leave no trace."

Alex is normally a fairly optimistic sort but I could hear the depression in his voice and in the silence which followed. At last he said, "No…don't bother, Jamie. I'll see what I can find here."

After we hung up, Alexander unpacked and set his computer on the desk. Without further thought, he removed

Miss Trump's makeshift urn and laid it on a side table. In the bathroom, he ran the shower as hot as he could and stepped in. Afterwards, he ordered coffee and croissants from the kitchen and turned on his computer.

The search for the elusive *H. Dumont, Parisian Pianist* began again. The food arrived and he ate hungrily. Although he did find some laudatory reviews of Dumont's performances at both Salle Gaveau and the Theatre du Chatelet that was it —*nothing more.* If he had died, surely such a concert pianist would have a lengthy obituary. He lay on the bed and drifted off. His last thought was—*how can there be no trace of the man after such grand performances?*

As he drifted deeper into his half sleep, a thought came into his mind. No, it was not a thought. It was a voice—almost as if someone were speaking in his room. What was it? *Dumont always carries with him…"* Alex's eyes flew open. Instantly, he knew he had read that somewhere on the internet, but *what* was it he always carried? Back at the desk, he reviewed his searches. But again—no luck.

In hopes of jogging his memory, he decided to go for a walk. Despite the late fall, it was a fine, mild afternoon. He decided to walk along St. Germaine toward the Louvre. Just as he was stepping off the curb, a car swerved around the corner. Swearing, he jumped back just avoiding his foot being run over. Persisting in his course, he turned the next corner. A flowerpot crashed from a balcony above down onto the sidewalk just grazing his shoulder.

Jesus! Alex turned abruptly and headed back toward the hotel. *Time for a different route! Something less dangerous.* He set off in the opposite direction for the Luxembourg Gardens.

Surely it would be safe to stroll through the Gardens which were a creation of Marie de Medici, widow of Henry IV in 1611 in imitation of the Pitti Palace in Florence. Among the sculpted greenery and statues, little touches of life and whimsy broke through the formality and even the late fall sterility of the park. The puppet theatre stood empty and the old-fashioned carousel with its horses was stilled in mid-air. Only a few children, nannies in tow, congregated about the pond for sailing miniature boats which had long since been put away.

Through the wooded area, he could see the café where he had spent a pleasant evening or two with friends drinking wine and listening to the violinists on the bandstand. Suddenly, his stomach began to growl loudly. *How can that be? I've eaten not an hour ago.* He veered from his path and headed for the café. Fortunately, it was open. In the large bay window stood a magnificent grand piano—far more elegant than he would have expected in such a café. He entered and found a table overlooking the bandstand.

The waitress approached with a menu in hand. Still ravenous, he ordered a glass of merlot and the beef bourguignon. On the far side of the café, a man and woman ate their sandwiches and tried to silence their two scuffling little boys. Alex frowned to see the father, a man with permanent rage etched on his face, jerk his elder son by the arm and growl at him. The little boy, holding back tears, struggled away to a corner and rubbed his arm.

From a darkened corridor near the bar crept a bent and frail figure. Not more than a shadow, it moved with such tentative motions that Alex immediately took notice. *Surely only serious ill health could produce such painful motions!* Alex expected that someone might help him to a table, but instead, the man proceeded to the piano.

Slowly, he removed his coat and folded it on the piano bench revealing a much worn tuxedo. Briefly he gave a ghastly smile to the few diners. The applause was sporadic but polite. He sat for some moments with his long neck bent down so far that his chin touched his collarbone. His shoulders rose and fell in a painful rhythm. His movements took on the ordered solemnity of a private ritual. From his bag, he withdrew a leather case, which he set carefully on the top of the piano.

Seated again, he closed his eyes. His lips moved rapidly seeming to repeat some incantation. Next, with studied movements, he opened his sheet music and adjusted his glasses on his nose.

Breathing deeply, the pianist began a Chopin *etude* which Alexander had heard many times before. But soon he realized this was no ordinary performance. To Alex's ear, the man coaxed the most mellow and meditative notes from the instrument that he had ever heard. The sweet expressions fleeting across the pianist's face fascinated him. The melody floated on the air straight from the performer's soul directly into the hearts of the audience. The two young boys sat motionless and peacefully together in one corner. Their mother appeared to have fallen into a trance and the father now sat motionless with his mouth hanging open as the notes cascaded about them.

For Alex, the old man was highly sensitive and skilled—no ordinary Sunday afternoon café player. In fact, as the pianist progressed through the familiar pieces, tears formed in Alex's eyes. After twenty minutes, the set ended. Sitting with his head bowed, the man scarcely acknowledged the applause.

Then he went outside onto the terrace, where he slowly smoked one cigarette. Alex could not help watching the sublime and sensuous pleasure he took from each meditative puff. When he had finished his smoke, a wry, twisting smile enlivened his features as he came inside.

Alex began to eat. The wine was excellent but the beef was of middling quality. By now, the family was preparing to leave. The boys had returned to their quarrelling. The father reached down and smacked the older one on the side of the head. Mother made no objection.

Poor kid, Alex thought! *The habitual, absent-mindedness of the father in slapping his son! No wonder the children bicker.* But Alexander knew he had little experience in such matters— never having raised a child himself.

The pianist moved in a curious, slumping fashion toward the piano. No longer did he convey *any* sense of *pleasure* and certainly no sense of the *sublime* so evident when he had played Chopin and smoked his cigarette. Again, the stilted, mysterious ritual took over. First, he made a curt bow toward the piano and approached it as though it were a respected foe. Arms rigid, he lifted the leather case from the top of the piano. He bowed once again to the audience and then sat down on the bench. With the case on his knees, he proceeded to unzip it.

He awkwardly withdrew a narrow pyramid shape which was, surprisingly, of incomparable beauty. It had a deep luster of gold which, in the light of the late afternoon café, took on a numinous sheen. The edges of the box appeared encrusted with diamonds. But when the pianist first held it up, his face sagged as if the life were being sucked from him. He slid a panel on the instrument aside and set it carefully on the piano. There it was—the most beautiful metronome ever seen. Immediately, Alex thought of his cosmic egg.

The pianist's face grew firm with determination. Alexander sensed the man was performing some sort of duty. He set the rod in motion. Alex caught his breath at the sharp, hectoring sound which filled the room as the rod clipped to and fro. The old man bowed deeply to the metronome and then took his place at the keyboard. After arranging his sheet music, he began to play one of Bach's Brandenburg concertos.

Such bold and disciplined music marched forth from the piano. Alex had always been stirred by these concertos, loving the rich, ordered sound which pictured for him the grandeur of Baroque cathedrals and palaces. Such vibrations surely must have come from on high!

Alex was fascinated to watch his face. Instead of the sweet expressions accompanying his playing of Chopin, angry furrows darted across his brow and his mouth tightened into a hard, unyielding line. With whom was the artist doing battle?

Upon completion of the set, the pianist sat with his head bent down to his collarbone. His meagre shoulders appeared to shudder briefly. Alex applauded enthusiastically and ordered another glass of wine. At last the old man stood up and stopped the metronome. Performing his ritual precisely in reverse, he put the instrument away in its case. Alex was impressed with smoothness and precision of the ceremony which he must have performed a hundred times over. To Alex's great surprise, the pianist gave him a mock salute and then proceeded down the darkened hall on the far side of the bar. Returning to his wine, Alex looked about the café to see that all the other patrons had left. He checked his watch and realized that he had wasted several hours with no progress toward finding *Henri Dumont*.

As Alex finished his beef dish, he mentally reviewed all the search efforts made to find the man. They had hunted through chat rooms for classical music aficionados where there were endless discussions of performances and innumerable blog posts. But nothing—not a mention of H. Dumont. *Someone can disappear if he wants.*

"You know, I really like Gershwin much better."

Alex looked up. There stood the pianist. His insubstantial body appeared to sway and waver in the light. Up close, his face was parched like a riverbed.

Surprised, Alex croaked, "You do?"

The old man nodded and smiled faintly. "May I sit down?"

"Yes, please do, sir."

He sat down across from Alex. "You enjoyed the performance? You watched so intently."

"Yes, I liked it very much. Do you play here often?"

The pianist gave a Gallic shrug. "Mais oui...here and there... wherever."

Alex held out his hand. "I'm Alexander Wainwright."

The man shook his hand. "A pleasure to meet you, sir."

"And you are?"

He smiled faintly and gave another shrug. "Are you a musician, Mr. Wainwright?"

"No. I'm a painter."

"Really? And what do you paint?"

"Landscapes."

"Marvellous!" He frowned in recollection. "Ah yes! Now I remember! You're the painter with the numinous light?"

Alexander smiled. "So they say..."

"Ah! A man of modesty as well." When the man smiled, his entire face crinkled.

It was Alex's turn to shrug. Then he continued, "I was very interested in your ritual with the metronome."

First, the old man's face paled and then it stiffened. His lips twisted sharply downward. Astonished, Alex sat back fearing a possible outburst. But no! The pianist spread out the fingers of both hands on the table, and sighing deeply, stared at them as if conjuring up a piece to play.

How odd, thought Alex! *The man is a bundle of contradictions. One moment he is completely relaxed and the very next he's wound up taut like a spring. And still, he hasn't said his name.*

The man spoke in low tones. "You see, Mr. Wainwright, I like to ensure that I'm fully prepared for *any* kind of performance."

"Of course! I hope my inquiry didn't offend you?"

Tossing back his head, he gave a mirthless laugh. "No one has ever asked me such a question. But I'll try to answer you."

"I'd like to hear. The creative process completely fascinates me."

"In that case, let me get my metronome." From his bag, he took out the leather case. "It's a *tragically* beautiful object, don't you think, Mr. Wainwright?"

Unsure of his meaning, Alex frowned but nodded his agreement.

"You see, this golden, bejewelled metronome was a gift from Father—a *very* great composer," he said softly.

"Really? How wonderful."

The pianist held up the metronome. "Although it has an incomparable richness of colour, I always sensed that a shadow lay underneath its surface." He smiled faintly. "Father taught me everything I know. But, sadly, he could not teach me the true art of composing."

"I'm sure you learned much from him." At Alex's first glance, the metronome had made him think of the cosmic egg. But then he suspected the old man was right. Something oddly *dark*—as if the instrument contained some spirit—negated his impression of unadulterated beauty.

"I did indeed, Mr. Wainwright." He examined his fingers for several moments as if attempting to judge their usefulness. "Father made a gift of this instrument to me on my tenth birthday." The old man slid the cover off the metronome and caressed the straight rod with his forefinger. Then, carefully, he adjusted the weight downward on the pendulum and set it in motion, producing an angry, staccato rhythm. "Father demanded I play at the swiftest, most disciplined pace."

"But doesn't all music have its own natural rhythm?" Alex asked.

The harsh, hectoring clacking was in perfect counterpoint to the pianist's oddly lilting voice. "Of course it does, Mr. Wainwright. But Father determined that music—really, all forms of art and most importantly, people— should be controlled by marking the passage of time." He gave a smirk. "Which really meant controlled by him." The pianist raised his finger and stilled the pendulum. Then he looked off in the distance, somewhere outside in the copse of trees surrounding the restaurant. "Such a Father. Such a teacher. Unsettling, isn't it?"

"Yes."

"Father was a great composer. The rhythm you just heard is *prestissimo.*" With his finger, he drew the weight up to the very highest point on the pendulum and let go. "This is *adagio*—for funeral marches."

"Yes."

"He was classically trained..."

"So you said."

Alex was aghast to see the contorted smile on the man's face. He marvelled that he still bled as if from fresh wounds administered by his father decades ago.

Moments later the old man smiled up at him. "Oh...it's not so bad. Father was only trying to help a rather dull student."

Alexander had to change the conversation immediately. He asked, "By the way, do you know any other musicians in town?"

"A few...not many." He shrugged amiably. "When you're old, you keep to yourself."

"I'm trying to locate a pianist by the name of *Henri Dumont.*"

Alexander was astonished. First, the pianist's eyes and the veins in his temples bulged. His hands clutched the metronome. Some black, formless dread began to stir in the back of Alexander's mind.

"Why do you want to find him?"

"It's a long story, sir." Alex said.

"If I am to help you, I must know the *why.*"

"So...you know him?"

"I ask again. *Why* do you want to know?"

"I have a painting with an inscription addressed to Henri Dumont, Pianist. I'm hoping he can tell me the name of the artist because I'd like to contact him."

The old man's eyes narrowed with suspicion. "Where did you get this painting?"

Vague perceptions, like storm clouds, were forming in Alex's mind. "It's a long story, but it belonged to a deceased collector. I'm responsible for his estate."

"Is it the Cosmic Egg?"

"How did you know?"

"Because it was given to me."

The circumstances of their meeting were so incredible, Alexander was truly shaken. But then he thought he might have guessed. "And so, *you* are *Henri Dumont?*"

"Yes. Now, perhaps we have something to discuss." Dumont sighed. "When I first saw you, I knew we must speak, but I didn't know why."

"What do you mean?"

With an insouciant smile and Gallic shrug, Henri said, "I do not know, sir. But tell me. Do you have the painting and the inscription here in Paris?"

"Not the original. But I can get a copy emailed by my art dealer."

"Did you know the painting was stolen from me?"

"No! Of course not." Inwardly, Alex sighed. He knew that the deceased art collector, Jonathan Pryde, might well have arranged a theft. "If you can establish yourself as the owner, then I shall return it to you."

"Then, Mr. Wainwright, I would like to invite you for dinner at my home tonight on the Ile de la Cite, Rue des Rennes, le numero trente-neuf." Henri Dumont zipped the metronome into its case. "Shall I see you then?"

"Yes. I will see you then. Thank you."

At the door of the café, the old man's face crinkled in a smile. "We shall have a fine evening of conversation."

Five minutes later, Alexander strolled back to the Hotel des Fleurs. Now he knew what Henri Dumont always carried with him—his father's metronome and his legacy of cruelty and scorn.

CHAPTER 16

Outside the Luxembourg café, Alexander momentarily stumbled in the surrounding dark woods. Reaching the sunlit, formal gardens and geometric paths, he became light-headed. Even in the now crisp fall day, he found it hard to breathe. Somewhat disoriented, he stopped in front of the imposing palace and then turned to follow the grand walkways past the pond, flowerbeds and statues. The sensation of floating outside his own body could only have been caused by the extraordinary happenings inside the café. He desperately wished to return to his hotel as quickly as possible.

He was both stunned and elated. A simple walk, with no particular purpose, had led him directly to the man. But then he frowned deeply at the remembrance of the crashing flower pot and the car. He had almost been forced to the Luxembourg Gardens. It was not the first time he had experienced such a coincidence—such a chance. In fact, he had lost count of the number of times such events had taken place in his life.

It made him think that there were *forces* at play in his life and in the lives of others, which somehow guided people in certain directions, making them feel that existence had purpose, meaning and significance. But his own life had told him that such guiding forces could not only lead to wonderful conclusions, but also be fraught with agonizing results. How could he tell which events should be embraced and followed or be heeded as a dire warnings? Everything depended on *interpretation.* Regardless, Alex was convinced that the world was far more than a meaningless dance of random energy as his friend Rinaldo would sometimes scoff.

When he opened his hotel room door, Alex stopped in his tracks. In the absolute middle of the bed sat the plywood box still carefully sealed in its plastic bag. Stunned, he approached it with care. He was sure he had left it in the desk drawer. Or had he? He could not imagine leaving it on the bed especially since he was so uncomfortable in its presence. Nothing else seemed out of place. He picked up the box and gave it a shake. Yes, the ashes were still inside. On the small table sat the tray with its cup and coffee pot. After the croissant and coffee, he'd taken a shower. *No...Damn! The other way around.* No one from the kitchen had been in the room to clean up.

Closing his eyes tightly, he tried to recall exactly what he had done in the room from check-in to going for the walk. In the dresser, his few clothes lay in neat piles in the top drawer. His toiletry case was where he'd left it in the bathroom. He thought he remembered putting the urn in the desk drawer at the same time as he'd set up his computer.

Then Alex began to laugh. At first, it came out hard and forced, but then he tossed back his head and gave a belly laugh so loud and long that tears ran down his cheeks. *This is ridiculous! Absurd and inexplicable!* Recovering, he took a deep breath and then carefully picked the box up and placed it in the drawer. *Perhaps I should lock it so she can't escape!* He lay down on the bed and, as his brain craved only oblivion, he immediately fell asleep for almost two hours.

He awoke to a pervading sense of gloom. Although he could not have said why, he did not really want to go to Henri's for dinner. He had not want to get involved with Henri's life problems. He just wanted to find the painter of the cosmic egg.

With great effort, he lurched upward and headed for the bathroom. He examined the face in the mirror which seemed to float separately from him. He studied his hands as he washed them in the sink. Yes, they were a part of him even though he felt as if he had no coherent centre—no point of attachment. After washing his face and brushing his teeth, he felt somewhat better but was still left with little energy.

He collected his wallet and keys and opened the desk drawer. *Best check on this urn to be sure I left it here. Just in case.* Of course it was right where he had left it. He shut the drawer, locked the room and set off.

Twilight crept through the Latin Quarter as Alexander walked its narrow streets with renewed energy suddenly eager to drink in the details of the passing street life. Since mediaeval times, the neighbourhood of the Sorbonne had been a lively centre of the arts and intellectual life in Paris. He strolled past shops, offices and squares with a casual, expectant energy he had not felt for some time. Cars zipped down one-way streets and people spilled out from shops and cafés onto the cobblestones. There were almost never any accidents. An unseen force seemed to guide all movement and so, he found himself falling naturally in step with it.

But he was troubled. He thought of Miss Trump and her last expression of peaceful determination as she slipped under the water for the last time. Just a day later in the *morgue*, her face was frozen with horror and her fingers were twisted like bare, broken twigs. And now, in his room, her ashes sat. He shook his head. *Will I simply have to scatter them somewhere?*

It seemed so wrong to him. Surely one who had sacrificed herself so that a child could live deserved a better burial! He was moved to do *something* but what he could not say.

Turning down the next street, Alex immediately recognized the church—*St. Julien le Pauvre* tucked in the shadows of Notre Dame. Next to that massive cathedral, the church was modest in every respect. Alex walked around Rene Viviani Square surrounding *St. Julien* to the west entrance of the church. For Alex, the Square had always been a place of calm reflection.

In the darkness of mediaeval times, this church with its small patch of land had provided a place of rest, sustenance and refreshment of body and spirit for thousands of pilgrims. Alex could visualize throngs of people, straggling out of the past, in dirty rags of clothing, broken sandals with bleeding, swollen feet. At *St. Julien* they would stop for respite on their way to the Camino Trail leading to Santiago, Spain. He would never comprehend pilgrims abasing the flesh or the spirit in search of other-worldly rewards.

But then, how different was he, who chased after *his* sense of the divine through his art? He, who was giving up on Daphne, himself and *love* all for his art! He stopped dead in his tracks. What had he just said about Daphne? The thought stunned him. Surely he hadn't already decided to devote himself exclusively to his art and spurn Daphne's love?

By this time he had reached the entrance to *St. Julien le Pauvre.* Faint, dying rays of sun palely illuminated the western wall protected by a small inner courtyard. An immense poster dominated the inner wall. Shocked, he gaped up at a large black and white image of a stark, tortured face. Could it be the ascetic—*St. Julien* himself? But then he read the name *Henri Dumont,* pianist, performing Chopin on Friday night. Dumont, in the café, had seemed a desperately wounded spirit. Here was that strange wound displayed for all to see on the poster.

St. Julien's tale was of extreme oedipal conflict. As a young man, Julien succumbed to blood lust in his hunting. He gained such great pleasure in his carnage that he could not stop murdering innocent creatures just for *fun.* In the legend, Julien had slaughtered a young deer for pleasure. The father of that deer placed a curse upon him that one day he would murder his own parents, which, in fact, he did. Gazing up into Henri's eyes, Alex sighed deeply. Could such a soul be haunted by unremitting pain caused by even greater heinous acts of his own father?

Inside the church, the nave lay before him. The ceiling, deeply ribbed and vaulted in Gothic style, enhanced the mystery and intimacy of the space. The impressive grand piano sat at the front surrounded by arches. Sinking to a pew, Alex was swept with the flow of time and history.

History and myth? What difference was there really? Alex fervently believed that humankind must have its stories— whether *true* or not. That was not the question. He liked to think that if a story, a painting or other work of art enhanced people's lives, then that made the art *true.* The poet Dante was said to have prayed and studied in this very building and that

St. Julien redeemed himself with good works performed right here. But it really didn't matter if those were historical facts or simply myth. If those stories comforted people and helped them live and love, then they had done their job. Art and life!

Alexander rose quickly and left the church. As he continued walking toward the Seine, he passed several florist shops. Suddenly, he stopped. Under one shop window, arrays of bouquets were laid out. Inside the shop, he paid for one and returned to St. Julien. Against an outside wall, he found a fountain, known in church lore as the miraculous healing waters. With great care, he bent down and placed the flowers beneath the fountain and thought—*In memory of Miss Maureen Trump.* He sat on a nearby bench and, after several moments, he left the Square and proceeded across the bridge to Île de la Cité and Henri Dumont's apartment.

CHAPTER 17

All the lamps of Paris were lit. The city spread before Alex as he strolled across the *Petit Pont* arching over the Seine and leading him into Île de la Cité. Alexander had read of the flaneur, who began strolling Paris almost a century ago observing the flow of life, simultaneously with engagement and detachment. All kinds of strolled throughout the city to experience it first-hand. He suddenly wondered why the urban landscape had not inspired him. But it was a highly personal matter. Each artist had to find his own source of inspiration.

On leaving the hotel, Alex had felt that eager excitement of the flaneur, but somewhere in the church, it had begun to slip away from him. The further he walked from *St. Julien le Pauvre,* the faster his pleasurable mood of detached and casual observation dissipated. Now, nearing Henri's, he walked with trepidation in his step.

Soon he was in a residential area where small shops— tobacconists, patisseries and libraries— lined the streets and housed apartments above them. Further on *Rue aux Fleurs* he traced the embankment of Île de la Cité. A light shower rained down making the cobblestones slick in the light of the street lamps. He walked up and down steps and pathways. Implacable wooden doorways were set at the sidewalk's edge announcing the grander residences. Other more modest entrances could only be glimpsed down narrow cul-de-sacs where simple iron gates and flower pots marked them. He strode more quickly now, looking for le numero trente-neuf.

Turning the corner, he saw the exterior of number thirty nine. Within moments, Alex stood in front of a green door. He grasped the brass ring which was clenched in the teeth of a gargoyle. After a moment, he let the ring drop several times. First he saw a shadow on the blind in the window. A finger pushed it back and Alex realized he was being studied. Finally, the door opened just a crack.

"Come in, Mr. Wainwright." The door did not open further and Alex was left to push on it himself.

Once inside the darkened vestibule, he could not see his host. When he opened the inner door, he saw the apartment was decorated like a dream of the French countryside cottage. So much *white* gave the impression of infinite space and the beginning of a headache. Through a window on one side of the apartment, there was Notre Dame floating in light outside. On the other, a grand piano dominated the darkened living room. Alexander scanned both sides but could not see his host.

"Hello?" he called.

There was no answer.

"M. Dumont, are you here?"

Silence. Then a tiny, gold lamp above the piano switched on. Henri's tortured face rose up from the dark just like in the poster at the church. Then he began to play. From that piano the most evocative notes Alexander had ever heard came to life and floated on the air. *Chopin? No. Beethoven? Likely. Who else could compose music that plucked every human heart string better than Beethoven? And who else can play like that—other than Henri Dumont?*

Alex crept to an armchair. For the next ten minutes, he sat motionless and listened to the clear, pure notes with rapt attention. He was fascinated to watch the swell and fall of every conceivable emotion across Henri's face—everything from the sweetness of the sublime to mad torrents of rage. Strangely, these changes of expression seemed dictated not by the music but by some inner dialogue of which Alex was becoming aware. At no time did his host speak.

Suddenly Henri banged and pounded up and down all eighty eight keys. Alex jumped from his chair overcome with the painful dissonance. After a last cacophonous roll, Henri sprang from the piano bench with a yelp and a laugh.

"Welcome Mr. Wainwright. Have you brought my painting?"

"Why yes…a copy that is. As I said I would this afternoon."

"May I see it?"

"Of course." Alexander opened the envelope and took out the copy of the cosmic egg painting.

"Ah…yes!" he breathed. "That is the painting."

Alexander turned the reverse side over. It read: *To my dearest friend, Henri Dumont—Parisian pianist and fine composer. May you step from the shadows and into the sunlight you so richly deserve!*

A thousand questions crowded into Alex's head, but Henri interrupted his thoughts.

"Mr. Wainwright, why are you returning it to me?" He gave a discrete cough. "I hope you are not hoping to sell it back to me!" He pursed his lips and then said, "It's really only of sentimental value."

"No. Actually, I want to meet the painter. That's why I'm here."

"But you *will* give me the painting? After all, my name really is on it."

"I'm responsible for the work. It was found in the estate of a collector and so, I don't quite know how to verify your claim."

"Whose estate?"

"Jonathan Pryde."

"Pryde? Good God! That man has stolen more art than the Nazis and the entire Russian army combined!"

Alexander did not want to offend the man. From what he knew of Pryde, it was entirely possible that the painting had been stolen. But there would have to be proof. He smiled and said, "M. Dumont, if what you say can be established, I will personally return the painting to you."

Dumont's entire body relaxed almost in one sensuous motion—as if a current of relief had flowed through him. "That is *most* satisfactory, Alexander." Then the man seemed momentarily confused. "I *did* invite you for dinner, didn't I?"

"Yes, you did. But if…"

Waving his hands in the air, he said, "No…no! Of course I did. I just wanted to be sure you still wanted to stay." He attempted a genial smile. "Some wine?" He went to the kitchen sideboard and held up a bottle. "I have a very smooth Malbec… such beautiful delicacy! Like a garden after a rain shower—dust, raspberry, flowers and herbs."

Alex nodded. "Thank you."

As he poured the wine, Henri called over his shoulder. "Please find a comfortable place to sit. I'm afraid I'm not much of a host. I rarely have visitors."

Alex sat down. For the first time since he had arrived Alex was suddenly and painfully aware of the clacking of clocks in the apartment. *How strange not to have noticed the God awful racket.* There must have been at least twenty large time pieces spread throughout the rooms. Now their ticking seemed enough to drive him mad. How could Henri stand it?

Henri handed him his glass. "You've just now noticed the infernal ticking in the place."

Alex smiled faintly. "I wouldn't say *infernal.*"

"Sometimes I think the noise will drive me mad."

"Then why do you have them?"

Henri gave an amiable shrug. "Not really sure. But they are Father's clocks and so I keep them in remembrance, I suppose."

He sat down across from Alex. "Now tell me please. Why do you want to meet the artist, the creator of the cosmic egg?"

"It's rather personal," said Alex.

Henri was not to be deterred. He simply stared at Alex and waited patiently.

Alex continued, "I wanted to speak with him about where he saw such an egg or whether it was simply his imagination."

"That sounds very normal, Mr. Wainwright. But it assumes a distinction which may not truly exist."

Alex waited for more. After a moment's silence, he said, "I'm not sure I understand."

"Really? It's simple. You seem to wonder whether such an image actually exists on the *outside* of oneself. Not simply something which has been produced *by and within* your mind, spirit or imagination. But I ask you if such a distinction actually exists? Is there really an *outside* or *inside?* Or is it just a matter of *flow* between various forces?"

Alex was pleased. Definitely Henri had spent much thought on art, creativity and inspiration. "Yes, I see you understand my questions well. In fact, I tend to agree with you. Perhaps there is no distinction."

"Yes, I suppose, but if there is no distinction, the world can be a rather confusing place." Henri, who had become more relaxed with his reflections, now sprang up. "Mr. Wainwright, I invited you for dinner and I sit here like a lazy lump. I must attend to the preparations."

Alex held up his hand. "Please! Don't make a fuss. It's very pleasant just to talk and sip wine here with you in this lovely setting."

"Ah! So you *do* like my place?"

"Very much."

"I thought perhaps you didn't."

"Really? Why?"

With another amiable shrug, the man grinned at him. "Can't say really. Just a feeling."

Alex wondered how many visages of Henri would appear before the night was out. At one moment, he was the young boy *fooling* around at the piano and at another, an old man withered by a domineering father. He tried to detect the smell of any cooking, but found none.

"Do you like eggs, Mr. Wainwright? I mean…to eat?"

"Yes, certainly."

"Then I shall prepare us an omelette and salad." With a burst of energy, Henri marched into the kitchen and took down a copper fry pan. From the top of the piano, he took the gold, bejeweled metronome and held it up. "All creative effort must be disciplined." He withdrew the cover, adjusted the weight on the pendulum and set it in motion. The harsh clacking of the device drowned out the ticking of some twenty clocks.

Alex winced.

Henri shrugged again. "I find it necessary to impose such a rhythm on all my creations. A sort of *forced march* pace. Father always said the very best creative work arose from the imposition of discipline. Without that ingredient, nothing of any value could be produced." Henri sighed as he broke six eggs in the bowl. "And so… I am bound…"

Alex wondered briefly if the metronome accompanied all Henri's actions—taking a shower…making the bed. Regardless, evidence of father was highly visible in every facet of Henri's life. But he found it hard to imagine creativity hand in hand with rigid discipline.

"Is your father still alive, Henri?"

"Oh no! He died almost ten years ago. February 19th. At four in the morning."

Henri, in perfect time to the metronome, whisked the eggs with milk and spices. Then he added cheese, onions and red peppers. Each step was attended by precise measurement. During this performance, Alex marvelled at the intense concentration on Henri's rigidly furrowed brow.

Soon, the supper was ready. Henri laid the omelette, steaming bread and spinach salad out on the harvest table.

"Is the Malbec satisfactory?" Henri asked holding up the bottle.

"Yes, it's perfect." The glasses were filled again and they began to eat.

"You are a painter, yourself, Alex. I greatly admire the quality of light you achieve in your work." Henri paused and dabbed his lips with a napkin. "How do you manage it? Do you have any rituals?"

"Rituals?"

"Yes. True artists so often do."

"I'm not sure I understand."

"How do you conjure up your muse?"

Alex chuckled. "I see! Yes, it's true. She is really quite faithless and must be courted every step of the way."

"Just like a woman!" Henri laughed.

Alex heard dark frustration in the musician's voice. "Yes. I suppose."

"When I look at your paintings, especially *The River of Remembrance,* I see the light of the sublime shining through not only the river and the rocks, but also the people. It's extraordinary that a painter can capture that light and express it through human form." His eyes took on a faraway cast. "I once knew someone just like that. She brought an other-worldly light into my life." He sighed.

Alex was unsure if he should inquire further about the woman's identity. He took another forkful of the omelette. Instead, he simply asked, "Which artist painted this cosmic egg?"

"Anton Chekhov."

"I beg your pardon?"

"I know it sounds absurd, but Anton is really a very fine painter and that is his name."

"Is he still alive? Where does he live?"

"St. Petersburg."

"Did he ever speak to you about his work—especially this one?"

"From time to time. Yes he did."

"I would really like to speak with him!"

Henri shrugged. "Why not? Anton is a great talker and has many opinions." His face became inscrutable. "Not all of which I agree with."

"Did he actually see this cosmic egg?"

Henri's face paled. His eyes took on a faraway look. "He said he did." He shrugged. "That's why he painted it, I suppose."

"Would you introduce me?"

"Of course."

Alexander sensed the mood had shifted. His curiosity overcame him and he said, "Tell me more about the influences on you and your superb artistry."

"Influences?"

"Yes, I find creativity an endlessly fascinating subject."

"Really just Father." A look of reverence slipped over the pianist's face. "Father was a great man—an amazing composer of music and a consummate performer! When I was just a little boy, I would climb up beside him on the piano bench and try to play along."

Alex just nodded. Henri gripped the stem of his wine glass so fiercely, Alex thought it might shatter.

"Father was classically trained, you see." Henri rose from the table holding a fork as if it were a baton. "He composed the most beautiful music rivaling Bach or Beethoven. His compositions were *always…*" He smacked the fork on the table. "*Always* created with the metronome ticking at his side. Father had the great gift of discipline. When I practiced, he would insist I use this metronome. If I did not, he would shout— *that's why you can't compose!*" His voice caught. "And then, Mr. Wainwright!" With his face knotted in fury, he spat out, "He would shove me off the bench and bang up and down the keyboard shouting —*Blah…blah…blah! You have no discipline in your little mewling romantic soul!*"

Alexander was at a loss for words. After the outburst, an eerie calm settled over the apartment.

At last Alex said, "I'm very sorry, Henri. That must be a terrible burden to carry."

Henri gave him a piercing look. "No, Mr. Wainwright. I was indeed fortunate. Father did his best to improve my musical talent—such as it was. Actually, I like to talk about him."

Unsure of what else to say, he asked, "Do you have any of his pieces here?"

Henri waved at the bookcase on the wall stuffed with folios. "Ah yes! On those shelves you will find Father's life work."

Alex contemplated the man, who was so terribly divided, as if his entire being was split by an endless, cavernous rift. He must be nearly seventy years of age, if not older, but still the ghost of father hovered over the little boy.

"But you must understand, Alex, Father was a genius and geniuses are rather hard to live with." For just a moment, his voice broke. "And, I am but a lowly hack! That's why I perform in bars and cafes—a little light entertainment for a Sunday afternoon."

"But you're performing at *St Julien le Pauvre* on Friday night!"

"Oh that! Anyone can play there."

Alex thought it was pointless to argue with the man.

"When I was little, we lived in an apartment right here in Paris overlooking the Champs Elysees. A very grand place. Ten rooms in all. Four of them were bedrooms. Father had an amazing piano, which I could not keep my hands off. Whenever he was out, which was often, I would try to play."

"Did you have lessons?"

"Yes, but not until I was eight. Father said there was no point until then."

Henri hung his head. "I wasn't very good at my lessons." He gave a hollow laugh. "I just wanted to bang away and fool around. No taste or aptitude for any kind of real work." He turned his head away. "No discipline." He gave a brilliant smile.

Alex decided just to listen.

Henri sounded as if he were talking to himself. "I sit here at the piano and play. Once, years ago, I was much in demand in the concert halls. But I am cursed and unable to create my own classical music or find my own voice. As soon as I try to create, Father's music simply rushes into my head and I must submit to it."

Alexander hated hearing an artist denigrate his own work. Every fibre in his body struggled against such a notion. *Take care of your art. It is your life and love,* he thought. But he could not spend the evening contradicting his host. *What does he want me to say?*

Suddenly, Henri jumped up from the table almost knocking over the bench. "So sorry Alex! I've entirely forgotten my manners. Would you like some coffee? I have a tarte for dessert too."

"I'll have coffee, please."

Henri cleared away the plates and made the coffee. "If you like, Alex, I'll tell you a little story. It's from that long lost time of childhood. I shouldn't trouble you with my *artistic* problems." He arranged the cups on the table. "I'll tell you the story of a little girl who used to visit us in Paris. Her name was Millie—pretty little thing! Although she was a few years my junior, I think I was in love at first sight. She is the one I mentioned earlier about the light of her soul shining through." Henri grinned mischievously at him. "Let me get the coffee first."

CHAPTER 18

When Henri returned with the tray of coffee, the atmosphere had changed—almost as if a sharp breeze had penetrated the apartment to waken them.

As Henri poured the coffee, his face altered as though a pale and rigid mask had been fit in place. "Do you know, Alex, how it feels when a sudden, horrible truth splits open your world? *Nothing* is as it was before. You find you've lived with the most absurdly wrong understanding of it." He hung his head and when he looked up again, he said, "But that horrible truth was not told until many years later."

Alex simply stared at his host for a long moment. Then he nodded slowly. "Yes, I know *exactly* what you mean."

Henry began his story. "There was a young girl named Millie who used to visit Father and me in his apartment each July. I was never entirely sure who she was. A relative, friend of the family—who knows? But she was *very* lovely. I was only twelve or thirteen and she couldn't have been more than eleven when she first came."

Alexander sipped the steaming coffee as Henri spoke with a strange spellbinding intensity. Obviously Henri had been awestruck by her.

She was fine featured and blonde with a calm which radiated from deep within and blossomed out into the world with every word, gesture or laugh. Millie was Henri's Beatrice as in Dante's *La Vita Nuova*. She brought the *sublime* and the *numinous* into the world through her very being. Every July 3rd, just before Bastille Day, she would simply appear in the apartment and stay for the month.

The summer Henri turned fifteen, Father took them to the amusement park, Bois de Bologne. At their ages, Henri and Millie longed to create their own myth of childhood by parceling up its last vestiges in a beautiful package. At the park, they watched the Punch and Judy show at the *Theatre du Marionettes* and Millie, laughing, rode the Carnival Carousel. Once inside the darkened entrance to the Hall of Mirrors, they danced about and made faces at their reflections. In the mirrors, they were either so squat they thought they'd been squished, or so long and tall they thought they'd been torn to shreds! Nothing seemed *real*.

That night, Henri lost track of Millie outside the aviary. He shouted for her at the top of stairs and at the ends of twisting hallways.

At last, he heard a voice. "It's all right. I found her." Father appeared out of the darkness with Millie in hand. Millie would not look up at Henri. "Why didn't you take better care of her, Henri?" father demanded.

Next summer Millie was given her own little suite of rooms at the far side of the apartment which overlooked the Élysées Palace. One afternoon, Henri walked down her corridor and saw his father leaving her room. Henri darted down another hall and was not noticed.

When Father was gone, Henri hesitated in front of the white double doors to her suite. At last, he let the gold knocker fall. A muffled shriek came from within.

"Millie? C'est moi, Henri. Let's go for a walk."

"Just a minute then!"

Henri waited patiently for several minutes. Cupping his ear against the door, he thought he heard her crying.

"Millie, let me come in. Please!" He opened the door. She was not in the bedroom. He knocked on the bathroom door. A white towel, spotted with blood, had been shoved under a chair. He picked it up.

"Millie!" He knocked more loudly. "What are you doing? This towel...!"

She opened the door. "Give me that!"

"But what are you doing?"

Her sleeve fell away and revealed a myriad of little slices up and down her left forearm.

"My God, Millie! Why are you cutting yourself?"

She gazed steadily at him. "I can't stop," she whispered.

Henri was alarmed but also fascinated. He guided her to a settee and sat her down. "But you mustn't! Why? Are you trying to kill yourself?"

She shook her head. "No, I don't think so. But I'm afraid."

"Of what?"

"Of me! I'm afraid," she said glancing down at her arm. "This won't be enough."

"What do you mean?"

"I want to hurt somebody and, if I do, I won't be able to stop!" She began to rock back and forth. "There is something very black inside me—like a horrible beast!"

Henri grasped her shoulders. "Stop, Millie! Don't say that!" He held her face in his hands and looked deeply into her eyes. "You are a *good* and *kind* person! You *must* believe that. Everything you do brings joy to everyone around you!"

She gave him such a look of despair that he nearly froze.

"No, Henri, you are wrong. *You* are the good and kind one in spite of your suffering! I'm sick and demented." She began to weep.

For the very first time, he cradled her in his arms tenderly. He stroked her lovely hair and touched her soft cheeks. "No! It is not true. When I first saw you, Millie, my heart stopped. The world stopped. And then there was such a deep and beautiful silence—more beautiful than any music ever written!"

The next evening, he found Millie crying again in her room. Father had just slammed the door of his study. When Henri entered, her bedroom was entirely dark. Once his eyes adjusted to the light, he saw her lying in bed with the covers pulled up to her chin. He turned on the lamp and sat down.

A violent, red hand-print had blossomed on her pale and sickly face.

"My God!" he whispered. "Who has done this to you?" She lowered the cover so that her shoulders were bared. An ugly, vicious looking welt was on her neck.

Henri was frantic. "Sweet Jesus! Has father done this to you? I heard him slam his study door."

She did not answer. He touched her shuddering shoulders for a moment and then he went to the door.

She called after him. "Please, Henri! There is nothing you can do."

Henri had never experienced such fury *and* fear. He did not think to confront Father immediately. He needed time to grasp the enormity of the man. He quaked and sweat poured off his entire body. He huddled beneath the covers as if exposed under an Arctic moon. By morning he had formed a plan.

Father, Henri explained, was a very tall man and probably sixty pounds heavier than him and if he were to fight him, he would have to be higher up than him. *But how? And* he would need a weapon—a hammer. Next morning in the garden shed, he chose a little ballpeen hammer which fit neatly into his pocket. He tried to deaden all thought and feeling.

Suddenly tears ran down his face. "What am I doing? I cannot kill Father!" For long moments, he debated whether to toss the hammer out. *Maybe I can drop it on his head from a window when he comes in.*

It did not occur to him to talk to Millie again. He did not think to *discuss* the matter with Father. *And so,* he waited for most of the afternoon sitting on the ladder in Father's study. *He is a disgustingly cruel animal and he must pay. I must protect Millie from him.*

At precisely four o'clock, the study door opened. Distracted, Father walked in carrying a drink and his evening newspaper. Henri was so high up on the ladder that he was obscured in shadow. Unaware, Father sat down in his easy chair directly underneath Henri.

Frozen in place, Henri peered down on the large, bald, boney head twelve feet below. *I could just drop the hammer and that would kill him.* He sat on top of the ladder for another ten minutes. *To murder my Father is surely unforgiveable but I will happily go to hell to preserve Millie's honour!*

Henri was ready. He did not hurl the hammer. He did not shout at father. He simply let go of the hammer's handle. It hit its mark directly.

Roaring, Father jumped from his chair shouting. "Putainde merdre! Foutre!" The little ballpeen hammer had merely bounced off the great bald head and landed on the floor.

Looking up, Father rubbed his head. "What in Christ do you think you're doing, Henri, you idiot! Have you gone out of your tiny, little brain?"

Henri was so frightened, he jumped from ten feet up and landed on the carpet beside Father. Father tried to grab his collar, but Henri was too fast. Skittering across the floor, he reached the door and was gone from the apartment. Father followed but he did not catch Henri.

Alex, astounded at the tale, poured himself more cognac. "Good Lord! What happened when he caught up with you?"

Henri smirked and raised his glass. "It was very fortunate. Father had to go on a five week tour the very next day—off to Vienna, Prague—you know, the usual haunts. By the time he returned home, the matter was forgotten. Or at least, it was never mentioned again.

"And what about Millie?" Alexander asked, spotting a flash of anger in Henri's eyes.

"Several days later, she returned to London, without a word."

"How did you live with your suspicions about your father and Millie?"

Henri's gaze softened. "Oh….I don't know. Father probably did nothing. He was always more bark than bite."

The two men sat for long moments in silence. Alex sipped his cognac.

"Did you ever try to find Millie?" Alex asked.

Henri just shook his head. "There seemed to be no point…"

The bleak, dispirited tone of Henri's voice made Alex desperate to change the topic. He wanted to tell him the rest of his own story about the cosmic egg. He said, "I should tell you why I want to meet Anton. Incredibly, just before I saw this painting, I had a *vision!*"

Henri grew completely still.

"A vision of the cosmic egg. It was exactly the same as the one Anton painted."

Henri appeared confused. "What? I don't understand. Where did you see it?"

"In my studio. It floated before me just before I began some abstract drawings. I'd been dissatisfied with my efforts of late and was trying to find something *new.*" He shrugged his shoulders and sighed. "Finding new kinds of light in new places."

"Anton claims he's seen it too. You will both have much to talk about."

"Have you seen it?"

Henri's face clouded over and he spoke softly. "Perhaps in a dream...perhaps." After a moment, Henri struggled up from his chair. "Let's get out of here!" His tone was plaintive. "I cannot bear sitting here a minute longer."

Alex set aside his newly poured cognac and prepared to leave.

"Sorry, Alex! When I think so much about Millie, I go a little *crazy*. I'll walk you back to the bridge."

Alex merely nodded and then followed in silence. The old man had become extraordinarily jittery almost dancing ahead of Alex in the narrow street winding around the embankment to Pont au Change. But soon he came to a stop at a bench beside lamppost.

More rain during their dinner had made the cobblestones slick and slippery in the gleaming light. Crouched beneath his umbrella, Henri made a lonely figure under the lamplight.

Who wouldn't feel sorry for a man who had lived his life under the thumb of a tyrannical father? But surely a sense of self-preservation alone would make him take refuge from such assaults. But he seemed to enjoy his abuse.

Now they were in sight of the Pont au Change. In the dark, lights from street lamps, cars and *les bateaux* on the Seine made shimmering, golden patterns on the water.

Henri seemed to have regained his energy and said, "If truth be known, Alex, I did try to reach Millie many times after she left for London that summer."

Alex wondered how many story versions he would he hear in one evening.

"You see, I had fallen deeply in love with her. It was her great *goodness* that captivated me." Henri stopped on the bridge.

NIGHT CROSSING — 185

"Don't you see, Alex? She was a sliver of eternity which so rarely shines on earth."

Alex did not know what to say.

"I could not get her out of my mind." He chuckled to himself. "She haunted me with her smile and soft voice."

Strangely embarrassed for the man, Alex remained silent. Henri sounded more like a love-struck teenager than a man of nearly seventy.

Henri pursed his lips and then said, "That is why I had to deal with Father so severely in the library."

Alex was just able to suppress his laughter. He could not imagine a less effective way of dealing with father. It was a very sad story in so many respects.

"Actually, I heard that she died not long afterwards," said Henri.

"What? But how could that be? How did you find out?"

"The following summer, I *did* ask Father when Millie was coming. He looked at me sadly and said, "I did not want to tell you, son, but Millie died last year—by her own hand.""

Alex stopped in his tracks. "Good God! What on earth happened?"

Henri shrugged again. "I never found out." He smiled a tight smile. "One of those mysteries of life, I suppose."

"You never asked?" Alex was aghast. *How on earth can one declare undying love for his Beatrice and dismiss her death as just a mystery?* He felt dizzy and sank to a bench facing Le Theatre du Chatelet.

Henri said, "I hope I haven't upset you too much, Alex. It's a terrible blow to lose such a love."

Alex closed his eyes.

"Have you ever been in Le Theatre du Chatelet?" Henri asked pointing at the building where entrances were mysteriously lost in arches and arcades. "Father performed there many times. A great honour for him! Tchaikovsky, Mahler and Strauss all performed there."

Alex frowned. For some reason, he knew he should ask more questions but something constrained him. He did not want to look too deeply. Some souls, he thought, are better viewed only from the safe surface. Undoubtedly, much lay unresolved within Henri, but he felt no need or duty to pry.

"Here is Anton's address and your instructions. I'll tell him you're coming." said Henri.

They shook hands at the apex of the Pont au Change. The old man turned and hobbled and hitched his way back toward his apartment.

Opening his hotel room door, Alex laughed at his foolishness. *Absurd! What did I expect? That Miss Trump's ashes would now be on the night table? Or that Miss Trump, herself, would be seated in the chair at the desk?* But still, he was relieved to find the container of ashes right where he'd left it in the desk drawer. In the midst of undressing, he stopped. *I wish I could have known her better.*

As he sat on the bed, a sense of her presence crept into his imagination. First and foremost, she had fought him off. *Save the mother and child! A tremendous sacrifice.* Why did he still feel guilty?

He thought about her sacrifice. He suspected it was simply that the *time* was right for her and who would not want to save a mother and child in those circumstances? To Alex, she had seemed complete, whole and at peace. But his vision of her in the morgue told a different story—one of desperately fighting at the very last moments.

Suddenly, he rose from the bed and took out the box of ashes. From the mini-bar he got a small bottle of cognac and poured the dark, golden liquid into a glass.

With a grin, he gave a short bow and held up the glass. "To you, Miss Trump! Shall I tell you about my very strange evening with a gentleman by the name of Henri Dumont?" *Here I am alone in a hotel room in Paris talking to the deceased Miss Trump as if she'd come for a visit.*

"You see, by great good fortune—actually, it was a truly incredible set of circumstances—I found the man I came to Paris to find." His tone was conversational. "This afternoon, I simply came upon Henri Dumont, the Parisian pianist, playing in the Luxembourg café. He claims that he can play all right, but cannot compose because of his father's overbearing influence. Henri prostrates himself before the mental shrine he has constructed of his father, a classically trained pianist."

Alex tossed up his hands in frustration. "He's allowed his father to dominate him and his art both in life and death. It's as if he's choked out any ability to live."

Deep in thought, Alex paced the room. Suddenly, a strident scream echoed up and down the hallway which was followed by slamming doors and another scream. Alex threw open his door expecting to see someone in trouble. But the corridor was empty and eerily still. He shook his head but waited a moment.

Then he turned back into the room and again raised his glass to Miss Trump.

Alex continued, "He talked about a young girl as if she were Dante's Beatrice. You know the story of that angel Beatrice—the one who, by her very existence, brought radiance into this world—at least for the poet Dante? That was the effect *his* Millie had on him. He fell deeply in love with her, or at least so he thought."

His mind returned to Daphne, whom he could see clearly but at a distance. There she was somewhere—waiting for him. She had come into his life only a few years ago. He poured another cognac. She wanted a real *here and now* relationship in *this* world—and who could blame her. Once, she had accused him of making love to her with his art. He could understand that was extremely unsatisfying to any *normal* human being.

He sat back down on the bed. He could well imagine her hair spread out on the pillow and the soft line of her shoulder. He thought of Rinaldo's scoffing at him and his insistence that all humans needed far more sex than they ever got.

But how could he separate art, life and creativity? No, that was not the real question. It was how to join all those wonderful aspects of life together with real love. He felt scattered all over the earth in little pieces. *How can I achieve all I want and need in my art and still have such love?* He felt as if his brain had become addled.

He addressed himself in the mirror on the far side of the room. "I just want to get the hell out of Paris and off to St. Petersburg to see—of all people, Anton Chekhov—the artist, not the writer." He laughed. "After all, I only wanted to find

Henri to find the painter. For God's sake! I never meant to get involved in his life and all his problems!"

Never mind! Tomorrow I'll be on the train to Berlin and then to St. Petersburg. Immediately, the infinitely vast steppes of Russia floated in his mind's eye. Then he realized that he'd had too much to drink. He fell upon the bed and did not wake until eight the next morning.

TO ST. PETERSBURG

CHAPTER 19

Although often inconvenient, Alex avoided flying whenever possible. His reluctance wasn't as simple as instinctive *fear*—nor nearly as powerful. Flight just seemed vaguely ominous, somewhat sterile and detached. Always *above* life never involved in it.

Of course, he loved taking the train because he could wander about the world and within himself. *Exploring* was a special pleasure for him which he could rarely describe in words. Sometimes, on his travels, that creative spark came to him like a brilliant shaft of sunlight piercing the clouds. Just like after meeting Daphne on the Orient Express.

He had time to ponder questions. Why was he possessed by images of the English country side when he had lived only in cities? He smiled to think of the city of his birth— Liverpool. Why was he not consumed with maritime images? He recalled walking along docks with freighters as tall as skyscrapers lined up from every country in the world. The sharp sunlight contrasted with the deep shadows of the ships and illuminated them as angular, distorted shapes. Liverpool had fine architecture and he remembered many outings with mother at first and then alone through churches, libraries and the city hall. Why not architecture? He supposed that the call of the *other, the foreign*—country landscapes— would always hold sway in his heart.

He purchased a ticket for the Train à Grande Vitesse to Berlin. After a night there, he would board the *Persephone,* for St. Petersburg. *Persephone!* He wondered who had chosen such a name—the goddess of the light and dark of the underworld. The goddess of *life and death!*

He tried to recall the story of Persephone—a tale of birth, death and regeneration. Persephone had been taken to the underworld by Hades and, because she had eaten a pomegranate seed, she had to live in the underworld for three quarters of the year and then blossom in *this* world for three months. He chuckled to himself. What other possible proof of life after death might one ask for? The tillers of the soil knew the score!

After buying several new sketch pads and a newspaper, Alexander settled into his seat on the TGV to Berlin. Staring out the window into the darkened station platform, he asked for inspiration. The train slid so quietly along the track that he did not notice until they were outside and into the glaring, grey light of a tired looking Paris.

Closing his eyes, he tried to visualize those drawings he had created just after the cosmic egg had floated before him. Energy had flowed within him and shot through his fingertips. Those lyrical shapes had grown angular edges and burst upon the page with no regard for boundaries. With larger sheets of paper, they would have grown without end—escaping from the tip of his pens in their raucous demands for freedom.

For Alex, inspiration could come from just the tiniest inkling of something *hidden*. That golden thread had to be teased up out of the depths of the unconscious. A scene suffused with meaning might appear just off to one side of his vision, his consciousness—like a dream. *And* he knew he must coax it into life. That, of course, was only the *recognition* of the inspiration. Next he had to decide what to make of it. He liked Miss Trump's question. What secrets did those empty spaces contain? It was the artist's job to find out.

But today, his hand hovered over the pack of charcoal sticks. At first, nothing stirred within him. He stared at the blank page. But then, with curious detachment, he watched his hand begin to draw with an unexpected energy. Windows? Tall leaded windows like in a library appeared on the sheet. Or were they the massive freighters at the Liverpool docks? He caught his breath. *Where is my light?* No light without darkness. As he worked his charcoal stick, shapes without name appeared upon sheet after sheet. *Are these the shapes to express the light?* After nearly an hour, he was exhausted and stopped. At his feet was a pile of drawings.

He walked two cars forward and bought a coffee and sandwich. Back at his seat, he stared out the window. The sandwich was dry and filled with some unidentifiable, pasty substance with little taste.

He checked his phone. *Good God!* A message from Daphne. *Arrived safely in New York. Hope you find your man in Paris. Have a wonderful time!*

Alex tried to respond, but could get no signal.

That's a relief. At least, she's sent a message!

Yes! He had stepped over some boundary the other night, indistinct at first, but glaringly obvious in retrospect. Her silence said so much. A brief, sad smile, followed by coolness, expressed far more than angry words or ultimatums. The temperature in the room just dropped and politeness reigned. He sighed deeply and set aside his drawing materials. *I won't be able to create while this is unresolved.* He shut his eyes and hoped the train would lull him to sleep.

Ten minutes later, he sat up straight unable to avoid thinking of their dinner. What a fool he was to let her think the Paris trip was a romantic adventure when really he was completely consumed with the need to find his damned cosmic egg painter!

That day in his studio, they had talked about her opening an office in London. Why not? Her business needed to expand into British and European markets. What had he done? Discussed the matter from a business perspective—not that he knew a thing about her business—when she was wanting him to say something quite simple. *That he loved her and wanted her in London where they could be together.* He ordered a scotch and shrank behind his newspaper. *People can be damned stupid about love!*

He tried to look at it from her perspective. Never once had he considered what it might be like to be an artist's muse. If one inspired the creation, how could you not want to have a part in it? Suddenly, he looked up. The train had pulled into the station in Berlin. After getting his luggage, he found a cab to his hotel where, within minutes, he was asleep until morning.

CHAPTER 20

Next day at three pm, Alexander boarded the *Persephone* and settled into his cabin. Although he had left messages for Daphne, he had been unable to speak with her. Since early morning, her presence had blossomed in his mind and now seemed to inhabit his very being with an uncharacteristic persistence.

Outside, the station was dark. Inside, his cabin was gloomy. Where was his light? He sighed and shoved his bag into a cubby-hole. The cabin was cramped but comfortable enough for two nights. Rushing for the train, he had missed lunch and now left his cabin to find the dining car. As the train pulled from the station, Alex studied the city drifting past. Dark, grey and dirty—or was that simply his *mood?*

When he entered the dining car, the waiter motioned him to a table at the far end of the car where two men were seated.

"Can I sit right up here? There's not much light back there," Alex said.

The waiter shook his head fiercely. His arm swept over the first part of the car. "No, mein Herr! No one is attending these tables." Ignoring Alex, the waiter busied himself with polishing the counter.

Alex shrugged and walked slowly along the car through a haze of grey, brown and charcoal. The further he progressed the fainter the light became until he nearly crept in the dark. The only two people in the dining car sat together at the farthest table. Nodding briefly at them, Alex sat down nearby and opened his newspaper.

The two men did not speak but, from the tension taut between them, Alex knew that much had already been said. The smaller man's frame was narrowly built and flattened rigidly against the wall. His face, etched with unforgiving lips, was implacable and disapproving. His glasses glinted in the light as racing clouds parted in the sky for just an instant. When he adjusted his coat, Alex saw the clerical collar.

Alex glanced at the other, younger man—a large, sprawling sort of bearded fellow—one who liked his comforts and pleasures, he concluded. As a pastime, Alex enjoyed inventing lives for the people he met on his travels. He imagined the man as some sort of farmer—at least one somehow connected to the earth.

In the dim light, dust motes floated in the air coating every particle of matter in the dining car. The windows were smeared with dirty brown grease. The tables were coated in a fine reddish powder. Alex sought the waiter, who was nowhere in sight.

Suddenly brilliant shafts of sunlight broke through the grimy glass. Obscuring fog no longer clung to every surface.

When Alex looked back at them, the priest waggled his finger angrily. The younger man persisted with his patient smile.

Instantly, he envisioned them in a sort of artist's tableau—a still scene which later he realized foretold coming questions. He saw colourful, contrasting shades of brown and orange, red and yellow—light and dark— just as if they existed deep within the eternity of an ancient, chiaroscuro painting. *Art and life together,* he thought.

The younger man threw back his head and brayed with laughter. He motioned Alexander. "Monsieur, I would like to introduce my friend M. Soutine. We have been having a most *interesting* discussion. I am Philippe Cendre. Please to tell me your name?"

Alex was immediately charmed by the man's openness and apparent lack of guile. As if playing a part assigned to him, he was drawn in. "My name is Alexander Wainwright. Glad to meet you." He shook hands with M. Cendre. Soutine did not extend his hand. A chilly smile was his only response.

Grinning, Cendre addressed both of them. "We have been debating whether there is life after death. Do you not find it ironic that we are on this train so aptly named *Persephone* and at the very same moment we are engaged in such a debate? Add to that, we are heading directly into St. Petersburg, home of the Russian soul." He gestured toward Soutine but spoke to Alex. "My friend, M. Soutine, is a priest. It is one of the favourite topics of his profession."

Soutine strove to remain aloof. Alex waited.

Cendre gestured expansively with his hands. "If you are up on your Greek mythology, gentlemen, you will know that *Persephone* is the goddess of the underworld—of life and death."

Caught up, Alexander smiled. "Conversation with such knowledgeable people is a pleasant way to pass time on a long journey."

The priest pursed his lips and gave an impatient wave. "M. Wainwright, the church and I will never see eye to eye with M. Cendre."

"But the exchange of ideas? Surely, there's no harm in that." Alexander said.

The corners of Soutine's lips turned down. He stabbed a rigid finger in the air but then stopped as if he thought it useless to argue.

Cendre smiled pleasantly at his companions. "I am a simple man, M. Wainwright. My friend, M. Soutine, is far more knowledgeable and educated than me. But we do have something important in common. Each and every day, both of us must deal with matters of *life* and *death*." After extracting a cigar from his vest pocket, he gave an insouciant shrug. "You see, in this life, I believe we must take our pleasures where and when we find them. Not *just* such matters as a good cigar or a glass of cognac, but the great and fundamental keys to life."

"And what, in your opinion, might they be?" asked Soutine stiffly.

Cendre flashed a smile. "The love of a good woman who will follow you to the ends of the earth. *And*, of course, you are desperate to do the same for her." Raising his arms, he looked heavenward, "The smile of a little child who looks at you with unfailing trust. The last touch of dying mother or father...." Again, he breathed deeply. "I could go on and on—of course, as could we all. I call them *moments of life!*"

Alex was overwhelmed. *To meet a savant on this train!* He said, "So eloquently spoken, sir! You've taken my breath away.

You mentioned a profession dealing with matters of life and death? What do you do—if I may ask?"

Cendre looked at him gravely. "I am a *mortician*. And you, sir?"

"I'm an artist…a painter…of landscapes. I see… Now I understand what you meant about yourself and M. Soutine." *A farmer,* he thought. *Not quite but—his work does involve the earth.*

The mortician's eyes grew limpid. "Ah…M. Wainwright! As an artist, you must have an opinion on the matter of life and death."

"Me?" Alex heard the surprise in his own voice. He had not expected to be drawn in so suddenly to a brewing argument.

Cendre nodded pleasantly. Soutine shot him a critical look.

"If pressed, I would have to say that I do not know and that no one has any reliable way of knowing. But, I do feel it is important to arrive at some conclusions."

"Really?" Cendre asked. "Why?"

"The very fact that we keep looking, searching and yearning for answers suggests that we *must* have a fundamental need to know." Alex felt that his answers seemed to please both men. Suddenly, he rose from his table. "Excuse me, gentlemen, but I want to find that waiter. I'm getting *very* hungry."

Alex advanced up the corridor between the tables and knocked loudly on the galley door. "Hello…hello? Can I get a sandwich or a bowl of soup?"

The waiter stuck his head out. "The kitchen is closed until five o'clock."

"But surely, there is something to eat!"

The waiter stared at him and then hurried back into the kitchen calling out over his shoulder. "All right, mien Herr. Sit down and I will bring to you a leg of chicken and salad. That is all I have."

"And a glass of white wine, if you would be so kind." The waiter grunted and Alex returned to his seat. He hoped M. Soutine and Cendre had ended their conversation in his absence, but it appeared they were just warming up. He slid into his seat.

"So M. *Artist!*" began the mortician, "Please tell us more of your views. Where does an artist, such as yourself, find inspiration?"

Alex mumbled, "In many places—many sources," Although his head had begun to ache, he brightened with a new thought. "We go through our lives with this sense of separation from ourselves, others and perhaps something which people might call God. I call it my *light.*" Alexander felt as if someone else were talking. "*And,* I admit that sometimes, I am desperate to find it. I seem to travel to distant places just for a glimpse." He surprised himself when he continued, "If I could overcome just one of those *divides* in my lifetime, I would consider it a life well lived."

The priest, Soutine, had paid rapt attention.

The mortician nodded sagely. "Is separation from your *light* more important than separation from other human beings?"

Alexander frowned. "Your question bears much thought…" His gaze shifted to the low hills and scrubby forests parading past the window of the train. He spoke quietly, as if only to himself. "My art—my painting—in fact my entire life is a constant search for something elusive which I cannot name. As for others, I assume you mean people one might *love?*"

With a twinkle in his eye, Philippe said softly, "That is indeed correct, sir."

Alexander examined his hands as if expecting to find a paint brush somewhere nearby. When he looked up again at his companions, a beatific smile graced his lips. At the same instant, both the mortician and the priest took deep breaths and exhaled in unison.

Alex shrugged. "But, gentlemen, I do know when I've found that light! *And* that is what I live for." In the same moment, he wondered at his ignoring the mortician's second question about people one loved. "It could be anywhere. In the ocean, on the shore!" He gave a short laugh. "Even under a rock or a piece of wood!"

Neither Cendre nor Soutine, seemingly arrested in space and time, responded.

Alexander gave an embarrassed laugh. "Perhaps that is what many call God. Whatever the name, I call it my *light*."

Cendre puffed on his cigar. "Splendidly said, M. Wainwright. Spoken as a true artist. I see you require more time to answer the other question about human beings?"

Alexander nodded. "I believe that is true." At last the chicken leg and salad were placed before him and he began to eat.

With a chuckle, Cendre slapped the table top. "Now my friend, we must continue our little debate with, of course, the greatest good will and respect." He lowered his eyes, but gave Alex a sideways glance and wink. "Just as we are speeding along the railway track to St. Petersburg whisked along by *Persephone* herself. You see, the priest and I differ on a fundamental view of the world. I, perhaps it is in the nature of my profession as a mortician, will believe to my dying day that there is no life beyond the *here and now*. We must enjoy it while we can because—ashes to ashes, dust to dust. Once the last breath is taken, we are at the end of our journey where only sweet oblivion and rest await us."

Obviously annoyed, Soutine sat motionless. He was not a man used to challenge or argument. Outwardly his body seemed coiled and ready to spring into action at the first opportunity. But he spoke in dry and weary tones. "The church has settled these matters over the centuries, M. Cendre. Great minds—far greater than ours—have given the question very serious consideration. The teaching is that—another world... Heaven, Hell and Purgatory exist and are very *real* places where we go after death." He punctuated his thoughts with another stab of his finger. "In our *physical* bodies." He sat back as if his words were all that were needed to settle the matter.

The mortician expressed only patience. "M. Soutine, I have only the greatest respect for the church and its teachings, but here, it seems to fly in the face of all observable fact and reason. Every day my little funeral home must deal with the bodies of the deceased with the utmost respect, of course. We perform the procedures and rites to prepare the body for either cremation or burial." Cendre paused to relight his cigar and then continued. "I don't like to be coarse but, we either burn or bury the corpse. Please explain—I am just a simple man— how can that body be resurrected to another place? It was but a mass of cells, which self-destructed. Daily, I see the evidence before my very eyes."

It was impossible for the priest to keep all arrogance from his voice. "My dear sir, Scripture teaches us that Our Lord Jesus Christ, who died for our sins, rose on the third day in his physical form, just as we will on death."

The mortician addressed Alex as he shook his head sadly. "It is not my friend's fault! It is a belief required by his profession.

I'm sure it is as heartfelt as mine. His church tells him he must believe that which is demonstrably *not so!* His church requires that heaven or hell await the deceased." He gave a little shrug. "And if he is to be tortured in hell, of course, I do see the need of a physical body." Cendre waved his arm in the air. "But, with the greatest respect, I must ask how such punishment of misguided souls *and* their bodies can be the act of an all knowing, all loving God?"

"My good man!" The priest's patience was fraying. "Scripture is the *word* of our Lord God Almighty! You either accept the teachings of the church or you don't." With a dark and canny look, he added, "But be reminded, son, that pride is a sin."

"But excuse me, sir, how can that be? You only answer my question by saying it is so and because others say it is so. I repeat, with the greatest deference, I have just destroyed that body in one of two ways. Either by fire or leaving it for the industry of the worm. It is lifeless! How can it go anywhere?" Cendre's voice flared up in frustration. "There is no life in ashes! That hard boney substance which remains is absolutely *lifeless.* It has no power here or anywhere else."

The priest's face froze. "Once again, I tell you. It is the word of God which must be accepted! We do not have the wit or understanding to comprehend."

Wanting only the peace and quiet of his cabin, Alex hurried to finish his meal. Oddly, he pictured the little make-shift urn—not more than a cardboard box—in his suitcase. *Miss Trump's ashes.* Suddenly, he became aware that the mortician was speaking to him.

"M. Wainwright? I want to tell you and my friend, M. Soutine, a little story."

About to be trapped, Alex tried to conceal his disappointment. Most men, he knew, would unceremoniously excuse themselves, but he found it hard to resist a story. "Really?" he croaked as he swallowed his last bite.

Cendre's tone was so charming and friendly that Alex felt gathered into a special aura of confidence. The ancient art of the storytelling had *great* power.

The mortician began with a question. "Do you know the little town of Vercel right near the border with Switzerland, close by Saint Croix?" He beamed at Alexander and the priest and then waved his hand distractedly in the air. "Ah…yes. There is no earthly reason why you should. It is the tiniest of specks on a most lovely landscape." He tapped Alexander on the arm. "You, a landscape painter, would love to visit. To see the sun rise upon the Alps from the town is breathtaking. It makes you love life, the world and all its beauty." Cendre spoke with a quiet passion which magically drew both listeners further into the story.

"It is true that I have one of the saddest professions on earth. I am this beautiful little town's mortician." He hung his head. "Fortunately, I am usually not terribly busy. After all, what man would want to be busy in that line of work? But still I provide an essential service and if regarded in the proper light, my job is to provide comfort, dignity and love to those who have lost a treasured soul. It is an ancient ritual helping us deal with such loss. If a man or woman is old, has loved ones and friends, it is only fitting that I give him the most respectful send-off. But what if the natural law has been contravened—for example, the departed has died in an accident at a young age?" Cendre spread out his hands and shrugged. "What can I, or *anyone* else, possibly say to give comfort?"

Neither the priest nor Alexander spoke. Tears glinted in Cendre's eyes. Unashamed, he took a snowy, white handkerchief and dabbed them. With great delicacy, he gently blew his nose. The priest compressed his lips and looked away. Alexander hung on the man's next words. Philippe began his tale in quiet, dream-like tones as if relating something eternally *true*, which cast a spell of ancient fables. Alex and the priest sat in rapt attention as Cendre began.

It was a sunny morning in late spring in the little town of Vercel, not twenty kilometers from the Swiss border and the town of Saint Croix. Nestled in the foothills of the Alps, Vercel has perhaps one thousand residents—une boulangerie, une bouchere and le bureau de poste. It was my habit to awaken at seven am. For a moment, I lay in bed enjoying the aroma of coffee and bacon and wondering what the day might bring. There was a funeral at two pm. for Mme. Larouse. It would definitely be a small gathering. Not many friends left and besides she had become more reclusive in recent years. It seems cruel to say so, but she would not be greatly missed *only* because there were so few left to miss her. Such is the fate of those living to a great age.

Everything in my life and that of my wife and children –even the entire town, seemed idyllic. No fear! I was not bored but perhaps I was a little complacent. Why should one man enjoy so many benefits and pleasures?

The wife called from downstairs. "Hurry, mon cherie! Your breakfast is on the table and your first appointment is in an hour."

In an hour? Good grief! True! M. Alain Flaubert with his smile and catalogue of caskets would be at the door of my establishment, Cendre and Sons, in hopes of a stack of orders. As I have said, fortunately, we are not that busy.

I was at the breakfast table within ten minutes. My dear wife sat with me but did not look up from the paper. Although both of us are getting older, she's still a beautiful woman. Sometimes, I wonder what she does all day in this sleepy little town. But I do not ask. I only smile and kiss her cheek as I start out the door.

Before arriving at the funeral parlour, I like to stroll along the main street of our little town. You know, just to say *hello*. Of course, like all avocats and morticians, we keep an eye on the obituaries. For a mortician, it is wise to present a calm, respectful but friendly demeanor. One does not wish to be *shunned* or *feared*.

That morning I stopped to buy some cigars at M. Lever's, the tobacconist. Although he puts on a brave front, I know he is worried. His wife has been in hospital for almost two weeks and so, he has been to our house for supper several times. The doctors cannot find what is wrong with her, what is causing her to faint at the drop of a hat—so to speak. Everyone, of course, arrives at my door eventually.

I turned up the next street and entered Cendre and Son, the funeral parlour. Cordelia, whom we used to call the blonde bombshell, sat at the reception desk. As we have for the past twenty years, we exchanged our *good mornings* and then began our daily tasks. She opens the mail—first the envelopes most likely to contain cheques. And I find some coffee and retreat to my office to examine the day's schedule. It never takes much time. I called Rene, my assistant on the night shift. *A quiet night*, he reports. *Everyone—that is M. Brasseur and Mme Touchard— slept soundly.* Each day has the same quiet rhythm which I find most pleasing.

When I gazed out the office window, I was filled with a sense of satisfaction. I could see shopkeepers sweeping their sidewalks and customers with their bags of cheese, loaves and milk chatting with one another. But I felt an unidentifiable restlessness stirring within me. It would be far too strong to describe this sensation as muffled panic.

Sirens blaring, two police cars roared around the corner. *Mon Dieu!* I jumped from my chair and raced to the window. I could see nothing for they were gone. But what I heard next would stay with me for the rest of my life. *Gun shots!* I was almost certain although I have only rarely heard a hunter discharge a rifle. No! This was different. Perhaps like in the war. Machine guns. An ugly, unremitting barrage of shots came from only several blocks away—down near the school. The horror of gunfire must have lasted more than a full minute but it seemed like hours. And then again, I could only think—*this is France—a civilized country. Not like the Americans who are accustomed to their guns and death. Does one ever simply accept evil in the midst of normalcy?* No one should ever witness what we saw that day.

Cordelia and I ran although neither of us had run for years. The sirens cut to a low, menacing growl. Dozens of townspeople crowded down the street to the school and church. Our tiny force of six gendarmes tried to reach the man standing on the front lawn of the school under the chestnut tree. A weapon lay at his feet. It was a military style machine gun, used for killing hundreds of people in seconds.

He held a hand gun high in the air. His expression was not mad, crazy or dangerous. In fact, he looked quite normal as if he had simply lost his way and hoped someone could give him directions. In truth, perhaps that's how he really felt. His eyes became dull and his movements slow.

A few in the crowd recognized him. *"That's Jacques!"* I heard someone whisper. In an instant, the man put the revolver in his mouth and pulled the trigger.

I am not the sort of person who takes pleasure in conveying ghoulish details. I have no such prurient interest. All I will say is that his head exploded and his body crashed to the ground. Inside, I raged at and cursed the heavens. But I had not yet seen or heard the worst.

When a gendarme opened the front door, he keeled over. The townspeople rushed to see. I am at a loss to describe the inhuman sound rising up from those who bore witness to the carnage. Like mortally wounded beasts, only incomprehensible gibberish gurgled from their throats. It was the wail of my town's collective soul being wrenched from its breast. Then screams flew upward piercing the hellishly beautiful, blue sky above. Even though nature had split nature asunder—forever—our surface world still looked the same. Our smugness was buried that day when we realized that the most dangerous of souls lived among us—and we *never* knew!

Inside the foyer of the school, twenty tiny bodies, riddled with bullets, were floating in seas of blood. Only moments ago, they had been lovely little school children. Now they were ravaged piles of flesh. The bodies of two teachers were slumped over some of the children in a valiant effort to protect them.

For days, we wept. We could not stop. The sun shone down as if to mock us. Endless tears rolled down our faces and dripped onto our hands and arms. I would sit at the breakfast table trying to read the newspaper—seeking normalcy in routine. But my vacant gaze would drift out the window trying to escape what my eyes had seen. The paper would become damp with tears. Knowing we could not stop, we did not try.

Twenty tiny bodies were delivered to Cendre and Son— twenty ripped apart by uncountable bullets sprayed into a school by a *mad* gunman.

The very worst part? The gunman looked just like us. Twenty minutes ago he might have been paying for his coffee at the boulangerie. Perhaps he gave the girl a wink. His normalcy haunted me.

I will not give you the terrible details of what morticians must do. *Mon Dieu!* Those little children went to school expecting to be home in time for lunch. That morning, their mothers had tidied the house and shopped and chatted with friends as usual. Just at 11:30 a man marched into the school with a gun and sprayed bullets everywhere in the front hallway. Then, standing under the chestnut tree, he shot himself. God help those children. And God help the man with the gun.

I had much time to think as I performed the grimmest of all possible tasks. The man with the gun, Jacques, gave us no warning. He was a garage mechanic who kept to himself but, when spoken to, was apparently agreeable enough. No trouble with the law at any time. How can anyone begin to understand? Many lives were destroyed that day. His mother, who never spoke again, sat in a corner of her cottage and never came out.

One evil act spreads far, wide and deep and no one is unaffected. Was he evil or mad? Or is there a difference? I do not know. I only have questions.

Arguments broke out in our town and revealed our darker side. What should be done with the mad gunman's body? Should he be given a Christian burial? Should his ashes be laid to rest in our cemetery? I tried to ascertain the mother's wishes but she was so affected that she simply gazed vacantly out the window when asked. The priest's view was that such a monster should not be permitted on hallowed ground. Many of the townspeople agreed.

One night, as I was closing up, a sharp rap came at the door. When I opened it, a dozen men demanded the body. Emile, a dear friend since childhood, was at the head of their delegation. The cold fury in their manner was very disturbing, but I think I was troubled most by the glint in their eyes which spoke of the kind of madness which must have afflicted the gunman Jacques.

"We are here for the body," said Emile.

"But why? It is forbidden by my profession to release it, Emile."

Emile moved toward me clenching his fists. Surely, my friend would not lose all sense and harm me! "Please Emile! If you persist, I will have to call les gendarmes."

The other men behind him pressed closer. They drew their strength from one another.

"Will it satisfy you if I promise not to deal with the body until the townspeople have agreed about its disposal?"

Emile turned to the men behind him. "What do you think?" Twelve eyes stared hard at me and then at him. They wanted the body. They lusted for revenge. God knows what unspeakable acts they had planned. I held my breath and waited. In the front row, one man rhythmical smacked a truncheon against his leg. Another shifted from one foot to another as if preparing for assault.

"Do you swear, Philippe?" Emile asked.

I nodded. "Yes, Emile. On the Bible."

The men muttered and grew more restless. There is something about crowds. Once I read in a magazine that people in crowds do things they would never do if they were alone. I waited.

Emile held up his hand and addressed the men. "I believe Philippe." He turned to me. "If you don't then we will be back some other night and you will wish…"

"Please Emile," I said. "You know I am a man of my word."

Of course, I was hurt by Emile's distrust of me. But I was relieved when the men grumbled for some moments but then left.

That evening, I realized the very same cruel brutality of the mad gunman lived within the men, whom I had known for many years. If it resided in my dear friend Emile then it resided in each and every one of us. Fortunately, I am respected in the town and I was able to dissuade them by appealing to their better natures. But that is so difficult when men thirst for revenge in their hearts.

I thought it wise to stand guard that night and so I went downstairs to the room where we prepare the bodies. On the stainless steel table lay poor Jacques. The small amount of his head which remained was covered with cloth. From the first moment I had seen Jacques, I had been impressed with his apparent normality. He did not look like a monster—just someone who had lost his way. Most certainly we never saw such carnage coming and I doubt that Jacques did either.

I know I drifted off several times, but most of the night I was awake contemplating the body laid before me. I am not a highly intelligent man. I do not have much education. But I like to think I have my share of common decency. And so, by dawn, I had reached only one conclusion. *The twelve men at the door did not look as if they had lost their way. They knew exactly what they were doing. Their hearts were shrunken and dried with no connection to their bodies. The gleam in their eyes was from a world of hatred and malice. Were they just like Jacques? Or were they worse?*

Philippe broke off with a sigh. Then he said, "Gentlemen that is only part of my story."

Alexander had been most impressed with Cendre's telling of the story. At last, he held out his hands in a gesture of frustration. "But why on earth would anyone do such a horrific thing? Little children!"

"I cannot answer your question, but I leave you with another thought. Whenever I passed by that school, I could almost *see* Jacques looking so sorrowful and lost endlessly torturing himself for committing such a heinous, inhuman act. Like a ghostly scar in the atmosphere. And, my friend, I was not the only one in town who had seen him wandering."

Philippe dabbed his eyes with his handkerchief. "I do not know, M. Wainwright. *C'est incroyable!* But that is not all, monsieur. Several days later, the priest held a funeral mass for the children. The parents of these little angels had been struck dumb with grief." Cendre puffed on his cigar. "Outside our little church, one mother caught up with the priest—I'm sorry to say— an abrupt, curt unpleasant sort of man." The mortician shook his head and looked out the window. "I will tell you the rest of the story."

The mother's twin daughters were dead. It was beyond any human ability to bear. The priest—a tense and rigid man, with a cruel straight mouth, had no intention of staying any longer than necessary. He rushed from the church steps in hopes of getting to his car. The woman was young—not yet thirty. Her daughters had been only five years old and now both were gone. She rushed after the priest and caught the sleeve of his robe.

"Please! Give us comfort, priest!" she begged.

Turning away, with an unctuous twist of his lips, the priest made the sign of the cross. But she marched after him. Her husband tried to hold her back.

"But you *must*, priest!" Her voice rose shrilly up an octave. "You must! You cannot leave us without *some* words of comfort!"

The priest made the sign of the cross again and reached for the door handle of his car.

The mother tore at his skirts. "Don't leave us!" she wailed. "Why did God let this happen to my children? Why did He not protect them? Is God so *evil* that he would kill my babies?"

Briefly, the priest looked skyward. "Child! Calm yourself. God did not cause this to happen."

"But God is all powerful—all seeing. Why did he let my babies be murdered?" Her eyes, devoured by a mad world of horror, glinted in the unremitting sunshine. Suddenly she screamed "God killed them!" Her entire body shuddered as she sank to her knees.

With tears staining his cheeks, her husband begged her. "Please! Come away, my darling." He caught her by the arm.

Transfixing the priest with her mad eyes, the mother nearly dragged him to the ground.

At first, the crowd thought the priest might relent, but he pushed her away and spat out, "Control yourself, child! God's ways are mysterious. It is a sin to question his will." He tore his cassock from her grasp. He turned his back on her, entered his car and drove away.

The mother sank to the hard scrabble ground and wept. The women closed in to comfort her. The men shook their fists at the departing black car.

Once she was helped up, the mother threw her head back. Arms thrust skyward and teeth bared, she shrieked. "I curse you, priest! May you die a miserable death within the month!" Then she collapsed in her husband's arms.

On the train, when the mortician had finished his tale, he shouted down the darkened car to the waiter. "Beer, sir! Bring us a pitcher of beer."

He did not speak until the pitcher and three glasses had been set upon the table. At last he said quietly, "That priest was found dead in his house on the thirtieth day of the month of May."

Astonished, Alex sat open-mouthed.

"Mon Dieu!" whispered the priest seated beside the mortician. "How did the poor man die? What happened?"

The mortician blinked in the last rays of sun lowering over the steppes. "No one ever knew, monsieur. I prepared the body, of course." He shook his head slowly in recollection. "It must have been a very unpleasant passing."

A look of alarm passed over M. Soutine's face. "What do you mean? You must have seen! How did it happen?"

"Monsieur, it looked like he had choked and drowned on his own bile." Again, he shook his head. "I've not seen the like of it in twenty years. As though he had died in his own poison."

Alex closed his eyes against the swimming light. When he opened them again, the priest stood stiffly before them.

"Good afternoon, gentlemen." He nodded curtly to the mortician. "I shall pray for you, my son." Then he turned to Alexander. "Although, he tells a moving story, I trust, sir that you will consider that the Scriptures are very clear on the matter. There *is* Heaven and there *is* Hell. Judgment comes to all of us." His lips tightened as he gave a small but dismissive wave and left.

Because they were lost in their own private thoughts, it was some moments before Alexander or Philippe spoke.

The mortician shook his head. "It is a real shame, my friend. Rigid minds have been robbed of their humanity. Don't you think?"

Alex sighed. "A dreadful story! I'm afraid you're right, Philippe. Such people have lost what it means to be human. But what on earth did you make of the woman's curse?"

In frustration, Philippe tossed up his hands. "I do not know. It is inexplicable." He paused as he searched for a new cigar. "Sometimes, at night, when I take the graveyard shift, I have sensed some very strange things. I say *sensed* because never have I actually seen anything at all. All a matter of impressions… interpretations, you see. Sometimes I feel as if there is *something* to this life after death business, but I could never say what. There seems to be mysterious forces at work which we cannot understand. But I have not been entirely truthful. I have seen something which causes me to wonder."

Puffing on his cigar, the mortician gazed out the window. "But I have no doubt—none whatsoever—about the power of that poor woman's curse. Not only was terrible physical violence done the day of the shooting, but great cruelty was inflicted upon that mother only days later. With her imprecations, she avenged the priest's callous inhumanity. It was as if a strange spiritual force had entered our town and we have never been the same since." Suddenly Philippe turned to Alex with a grin. "Never underestimate a mother's power!"

Alex smiled. "That much is definitely true! *And* I certainly agree with you about mysterious forces. Thank you for telling your story."

"I did say I have seen something. When I mentioned the school where the ghastly murders were committed, I said that it seemed to have left some sort of scar. The same is true of the church where the priest treated the mother so cruelly. I have seen the priest wandering through the church yard. Sometimes he paces, as if in anger, along the walkway to the cemetery, I fear he has learned nothing. That much I have seen and know with certainty. At least for those who have committed grave acts, there seems to be some sort of continued existence for a period of time."

Alex said, "Yes, I can understand that. It's as if a marker or stain has been left."

Philippe sighed deeply. "When I began my story, I painted my little town as idyllic. But that is only true on the surface."

The two men shook hands and parted. Alex returned to his cabin and lay down. It was impossible to drift off. Within ten minutes, he was seated upright. He switched on the light, took the urn from his case and stared at it. He could think of nothing to say and so, he put it away. Fortunately, he fell sound asleep until morning.

ST. PETERSBURG

CHAPTER 21

Grit burned Alex's eyes as he stepped into the darkness of the Vitebsky Station platform in St. Petersburg. Except for the passengers from his train, the main hall was nearly deserted at seven o'clock that evening. Here and there clusters of people milled about in the shadows at the foot of the marble staircase. As Alex passed by, they shuffled about and reluctantly made way for him. Climbing up the steps, he paused to check for the note Henri had scrawled for him. On the landing above, he set down his bag and opened the paper which read:

At Vitebsky, exit the main staircase and get a cab for the Marriott Hotel. Go directly there and don't let your driver suggest anything else. If he does, insist that you have a reservation and a party is waiting for you. They love to drive you around and charge unsuspecting tourists ridiculous sums. At the hotel, check in and wait to hear from Anton or someone else from the Les Cavalier Jaune—his artists' group. That will likely be within two days of your arrival. Good luck in your search. If you are in any difficulty, don't hesitate to call me. Anton should be most helpful.

Alex picked up his bag again. Why did he feel such confusion? Until now, he had been *driven* to meet with Anton without really understanding *why*. For Alex, visualizing the cosmic egg was a gift—a sign of creativity and success in his own work. With Anton claiming the vision, surely they must have much in common. Alex had also seen the egg just above Miss Trump in her final moments. Did that signify wholeness or completion? Sighing, he acknowledged he could only blame himself for his troubled search for his ineffable cosmic egg. To find *his* spiritual dimension in the midst of one of the most mysterious cities in the world—St. Petersburg— was no simple task.

A light rain spattered down on the line of cabs crawling up the drive and under the portico. Headlights made pools of light in the rain puddles. A light wind had picked up. He pulled his collar tighter and opened the rear door of the next cab which had just swerved into the line. Suddenly he realized that he had not one word of Russian at his command.

The bearded driver wore a woolen cap pulled down over his ears.

Alex leaned forward and shouted, "Marriott Hotel, please!"

The driver turned around. Headlights from other cabs fell full on his face revealing bulbous lips nearly overrun by a thick beard and immense eyebrows. He said sweetly, "You need not to shout. I am not deaf. Which Marriott Hotel, if you please?"

Alexander chuckled. "I *am* sorry! The one in the historic centre—Nevsky Prospect"

"This is St. Petersburg," the man smiled. "Everything is historic."

Alex nodded. "Do you know the one I mean?"

"Yes…yes. I will take you there." He roared the engine and started off lurching into low gear.

Alex jerked forward but then sat back and rearranged his belongings relieved that his driver spoke English.

At the next set of lights, the driver wrenched around. "My name is Fyodor. You are from?"

"Paris."

"And your name?"

Alex frowned. "Alex," he said. "Why?"

Fyodor shrugged his massive shoulders. Alex could see his broad grin in the rear-view mirror. "Always interested in visitors. We need more tourists. I want you to feel welcome in my city *and* my country."

"Thank you," Alex said slowly. Although he liked to talk with people on his travels, he felt oddly tired and uncomfortable. *It's just because I've never been here before.*

"You like St. Petersburg? Very beautiful city!" At the next light, Fyodor turned around and held up a bottle. "A drink for you, sir."

Alex shook his head. The man shrugged and took a swig.

Alex peered out the windows which were growing foggy. By now, he expected to see a grand avenue lined with churches and cathedrals. Where were the sumptuous hotels and the Gostiny Dvor and the massive department store he had always heard of? All he could see were rows of low-slung, dark buildings in a shabby industrial area. "Are we near Nevsky Prospect?"

Fyodor waved dismissively. "All in good time, sir. We are close by. You have nothing to worry about. I promise to get you there." He speeded up around the next corner.

Alex sat back and tried to relax, telling himself he knew nothing of St. Petersburg and the driver was all right. Very soon, he began to feel his eyelids closing. *I must be exhausted from my travels.*

"I am pleased to inform you, Alexander, that within ten short minutes, you will be at your destination. All will be well."

"How did you know my name? I didn't tell you."

"You are tired, sir, from your long trip." The driver winked at him in the mirror. "You told me your name when I told you mine."

Alex could not remember. *What the hell does it matter,* he thought? *I'm tired.* All he could think of was getting to his room *and* into bed. Briefly, he closed his eyes.

The cab braked hard. Alex shot forward smashing his head against the glass wall between the front and back seats.

"Jesus! What are you doing?" Alex shouted. Rubbing his head, he tried to see out the window. "Where the hell are we?"

Grinning, the driver turned around. "That'll be four hundred and sixty-six Russian Rubles, please."

"What? Four hundred and..."

Fyodor gave him a kindly smile. "Please! It is not so very much. In your country it would be only..." The driver looked at the ceiling. "About ten British Pounds. Plus tip, if you would be so kind, sir."

Alexander rubbed his head again. "But where are we?"

Again, the driver grinned. He rolled down the window. "You see, we have arrived. You drifted off and missed the most impressive parts of Nevsky Prospect. Now we are at the hotel to which you wished me to take you."

Suspiciously, Alex poked his head out and was relieved to see that the Marriott chain sign blinked in the night. He looked up and down the avenue and was pleased to see many cathedrals and businesses. "How long did I sleep? I don't remember."

"You slept for almost one half hour, sir."

Alex took the bills from his wallet and paid the driver. "Where is my bag?"

The driver jumped out and lumbered to the back of the cab. "Right here, sir."

"You seem to know me, sir." Alex spoke tentatively. "Are you connected with Anton Chekhov or his group *Les Cavaliers Jaune?*"

A shadow of confusion passed over Fyodor's face. He shrugged. "I do not know of what you speak. Anton Chekhov? Everyone knows him. He is our most famous writer…well next to Tolstoy or Dostoyevsky."

Alex handed him the money. "No, of course not. This is a different Chekhov. A painter." *It's stupid,* he thought. *This man has nothing to do with him. He picked me up by chance.*

Snatching off his wool cap, the driver gave a servile smile and a formal bow, "Should you require a driver or *any* other assistance during your stay, here is my card."

Alex shook his head. "No thank you. I'm meeting people here." But he took Fyodor's card.

Pulling on his cap, he replied, "Good evening, sir. Have a pleasant stay in our beautiful city." Then he was off.

For a moment, Alex gazed up at the Marriott Hotel which looked very grand and comfortable.

As he mounted the steps, a porter stepped forward to greet him. "Checking in, sir?"

Somewhat disoriented, Alex simply nodded. He climbed slowly up the steps. His arms and legs felt oddly heavy. The man took his luggage and held the door open for him.

When he entered the lobby, Alexander caught his breath. Before him lay a grand baroque theatre of voluptuous, curving space and breath-catching verticals! Richly coloured tapestries of braided gold, green and purple threads hung on the walls and marble expanses spread out before him. Although initially overwhelmed, Alex felt entirely at home. With life in his step, he approached the front desk and took out his reservation and passport.

The desk clerk reluctantly rose from a stool and pushed a lock of hair from his brow. "You are checking in, sir?"

"Yes. I have a reservation. Wainwright, Alexander Wainwright."

The clerk gave the keyboard a laconic tap and scanned the computer screen. He frowned. Weary, Alex let his eyes drift shut for a moment. He was surprised to feel his legs begin to buckle underneath him.

"Sorry sir, but there is no reservation under that name. Could it have been made under a different one?"

The clerk's face began to swim before Alex's eyes. "No, it could not." He thrust his reservation across to the clerk. "Look! Right here. It says three nights starting tonight."

The clerk spent a long moment examining the sheet of paper and then shook his head. "If it's not in our computer, Mr. Wainwright, then the reservation is not confirmed."

Alex's sharp tone filled the lobby. "What? But that's ridiculous! It says right here..." He grabbed the paper back and read, "One deluxe room, double bed, with en suite. October 28th to 30th. That's now, tonight!"

The clerk stared blankly at him. "But, as I have said, Mr. Wainwright, if it is not in the computer, then it is not confirmed."

Alex nearly shouted, "Where is your manager? Tell him I want my room."

The clerk stared at him. His face began to swim before Alex's eyes.

"Well? Where is the manager?" Alex demanded.

For the first time, the clerk blinked. "He'll be here in a moment, Mr. Wainwright. Now if you'll just step aside, I have to assist the next person."

Alex shifted along the counter. In moments, a very clean cut looking man, perhaps in his mid-thirties joined him at the counter. When the man roughly grasped his arm, Alex thought of the KGB.

"Are you the manager?" Alex asked, fishing out his reservation.

The KGB man did not answer. Instead, he ferried him toward the far end of the counter. "The clerk is correct, sir. If the booking is not in our system it is not confirmed."

"Then find me another room."

"We are sorry, but we are entirely filled up. We have no room whatsoever."

"Look! Your hotel sent this email confirming that a room was set aside for me for these three nights." Alex shook his head. The entire lobby and the people in it had acquired a distant, dream-like quality.

Not a wrinkle fleeted across the man's face. Not one muscle twitched. The eyes were ice cold.

"This is customer service?

"I tell you again, sir. We are fully booked."

"But it's almost eight o'clock. Make some calls. Find me another hotel."

"Certainly, sir. Please sit down over there." The man motioned to a straight backed chair in a far corner. "The desk clerk will inform you if we find anything for you."

"*If?* What do you mean *if?*"

"We will do our best, sir." The man clicked his heels sharply together and strode swiftly off.

Alex picked up several magazines and sat down. After leafing through the first one, he stood up slowly and checked his watch, the face of which seemed to waver before his eyes. Five minutes, he thought, had passed, The clerk had returned to lounging at his post.

He approached the desk. "Have you tried to find me a room at another hotel?"

"Sir? Someone else is making the calls. Please sit down and be patient."

"Was that the manager I spoke with?"

"Yes."

"This is ridiculous! Do you treat all your guests this way?"

Alexander brought his fist down on the counter. "I want to see the manager again!"

"Sir, I must advise you that I have been authorized to call security if you become…I'm sure that won't be necessary."

Alexander was stunned. He could think of no reason for such treatment. "Do you realize…"

When he felt a tug on his sleeve, he turned and looked into the heavy, bearded face of Fyodor, his cab driver.

"Alexander, you need my help. I will get you out of here and find you another hotel."

The desk clerk looked relieved and nodded at Fyodor. "Yes! For God's sake find him some place. We have nothing for him here."

Fyodor leaned close to Alex. "I will find you suitable accommodation, if you will come with me. I know of several hotels which have rooms. I will even carry your suitcase." Tossing his arm over Alex's shoulder, he beamed at him. "Is that not good?"

Once they were outside, Fyodor started at a jog down the street.

Alex shouted after him. "Where are you going? Why aren't we taking your cab?"

"No need, my friend! It is not far away from here."

Alex rushed after him only to be surprised when the man made a sharp left turn down the next block and into an intricate web of narrow streets and alleyways. When he thought of the contents of his bag, which Fyodor swung by its handle, he cared only for one item. Everything except Miss Trump's ashes was replaceable.

The alley was poorly lit and Alex stumbled in his hurry to keep up. Dark shadows fell across the cobblestoned street lined with strange buildings. At first the architecture seemed plain. There were broken staircases leading up to sagging verandahs on rudimentary hovels. Carts laden with barrels and tools were crammed in alleyways and doors hung open on their hinges.

Alex called up ahead. "Fyodor? Where are you going? Are there *really* hotels this way? He could no longer see the driver with his suitcase. He shouted. "Fyodor?"

Alex jumped when the driver stuck his face into his. He nearly gagged from the stench of the man's beard.

Fyodor's eyes shone brightly. "I am right here, my friend. I am showing you that part of St. Petersburg which few westerners ever get to see." He waved his arm in a circle above his head. "Tonight, sir, is your lucky night." Then he made a deep bow.

"But I need a hotel. I've been travelling for days." Alex was embarrassed by the whining in his voice.

Fyodor only grinned. "Come! Please. I will take you to highly suitable accommodations, Alexander. Did I not tell you so? There are many other hotels with many other rooms."

Alex looked about doubtfully. The buildings had grown more substantial even enough to support faux-Corinthian columns. But how could that be? He had not moved.

"Where are we, Fyodor?" he called out. The man, who was now at least twenty yards ahead of him, seemed to be dancing up the narrow street into the shadows. Stopping to wave at Alex, he turned down another, even darker laneway.

Although he could see no one, Alex heard muffled cries and shouts of laughter from the shack-like structures lining what had become a dirt lane. A bottle, flying from somewhere above, whizzed past his ear. *I must be in hell,* he thought. He drew his collar up around his chin and forged onward. *The worst would be to lose Fyodor and the ashes.* He hurried his pace.

From an upper window a woman's rough voice came. "You're fuckin' *are* gonna pay me, you son-of-a-bitch!" When she screamed and gave a drunken hoot of laughter, Alex cried out in surprise. Fyodor had disappeared in the mist.

Not ten yards ahead of him appeared two figures. He could see only the first one clearly. She wore a sleeveless, red-satin dress, which hitched up her thigh and spread tightly across her stomach and breasts. Red splotches dotted the greyish skin of her arms.

"Hey! Mister! Looking for some fun?" The woman slithered close to him and took his arm. In the yellow light from a window, her red mouth made a violent slash across her face.

"No! Please!" Alexander recoiled when she pulled him closer. He pushed her away. Tottering in her absurdly high heels, she stumbled backwards but regained her balance.

"What the fuck you doing to my friend?" shouted the other woman, who was dressed in an old fashioned coat which caught about her ankles. She gave Alex a push. "Who do you think you are? Mister high and mighty?" Then she opened her coat. With a sly smile she said, "Maybe you like me better."

Alex was aghast to see how ragged her scant clothing was underneath the coat. Her withered breasts were contained in a brassiere which was smeared with some brownish substance and her underpants, once silken, were ripped. "Please, ladies! My driver is taking me to my hotel." Instantly, he regretted his words.

The women's cackling was harsh and strident. They began to push him. "Aren't we high and mighty! My *driver* is it now? How many servants does he have, Rodya?"

Usually Alex had much sympathy for those less fortunate. But tonight, he was repulsed by the women and, actually frightened, he drew back from them.

"Ha!" shouted the one in the red dress. "He thinks he's above us! Look at him…the way he looks down on us …so *superior.*"

The foul stench of her breath and her chipped and yellowed teeth caused Alex to cover his nose and mouth.

"Listen! I will give you money but I don't want to go anywhere with you."

"See Lizabetta! He don't wanna dirty himself with the likes of us!" She grabbed his coat collar. "Scared ya might catch something?" He could see nothing but her huge red lips. "We don't want your money…least not without giving something in return. You insult us with your fine manners and high and mighty ways!"

Desperate to rid himself of the women, he struggled to escape. He turned down an alley way and was relieved to see Fyodor straight ahead.

Fyodor shook his head sadly. "Alexander! You surprise me. You will have to do much better than that."

Alex heard the smashing of glasses. *What kind of people live here? This is like from another century. A different place in time… What is happening to me?*

Fyodor took his arm. "Come. We are not in the finest of neighbourhoods, the privileged kind you are used to. Keep close to me, my friend."

Alex pushed him away. "Then why have you brought me here?"

"I am taking you to your hotel. Are you ill?" The driver looked at him with pity. "Are you always so forgetful? I should not have to keep repeating myself. My father is eighty years old and is *much* better than you."

"But where is this hotel?" Alex stopped up. He looked at Fyodor with suspicion. "If you've taken me here to rob me, you've wasted your time. I have only a few more rubles, which I'd gladly have given you."

Fyodor looked hurt. "Rob you? Of course not! Why would you think that? I am trying to help you. You have much to learn." He turned his back to him. "But if you think that, then perhaps we should go our separate ways."

Alex looked fearfully about him and then said, "No! Don't leave me here…please. Get me to this hotel. How far is it?"

Fyodor grinned. "Just a few more streets, friend. There is no reason to be frightened. If you have the right attitude, you will be entirely safe."

"Right attitude? What's wrong with my attitude?"

Fyodor waved as if to placate him. "Sometimes, I fear you do not understand much. Tell me, sir. You must live a life of comfort in London."

"How do you know I'm from London?"

The man tossed back his head and roared with laughter. He gasped and then said, "It's obvious Alex. *And* you are a very fine painter."

"How do you...?"

The driver waved dismissively. "Enough foolish questions! You are a well-to-do painter. Your art, your talent has made a rich man of you. Do you deny that?"

Alex shook his head.

"Then it cannot be helped. You know nothing of the people who live here. That is not your fault. They worry constantly of serious matters. Not the interesting little, esthetic and academic concerns that you play with."

"Such as?"

Fyodor furrowed his brow and did a fine imitation of Alex's solemnity. "What does the appearance of a cosmic egg mean to my art? Is this a random universe? Is there life after death—heaven or hell. These people want to know how to survive in *this* hell. It makes them like cockroaches—the best survivors in existence."

"How did you know about...?"

Fyodor gave an insouciant shrug.

"I'm not to blame for their condition!"

"Neither are they, my friend." He looked sadly at Alex. "You are isolated. Here you are in St. Petersburg, the heart and soul of Mother Russia, and you cannot see that your search for spiritual illumination can only start here in the lowest of the low parts of *this* world."

Alex was alarmed. "How do you know all this about me?" He backed away from the man. "Who *are* you?"

Fyodor shrugged. "Shall I leave you now?"

Alex grabbed the sleeve of his coat. "No, please don't!"

The man smiled gently. "All right. But you must remember that you have a *very* long journey ahead of you. And *much* to learn. You must do far better on your next test."

Alex stood stock still. He began to laugh. "Now I understand, Fyodor. You *are* a friend of Anton Chekhov. You are an artist—a member in good-standing of *Les Cavaliers Jaune.* No one else would know about my art, my struggles and the cosmic egg. Is this your idea of performance art? Where are your cameras?"

Fyodor's face darkened. "You are babbling, sir! I do not know of what you speak! I know no one named Anton Chekhov except the writer and this business about yellow horsemen is beyond belief. What are you talking about—*Les Cavaliers Jaune* and—what did you say—a cosmic egg?"

"Yes. You just spoke of it yourself!" Alexander was struck by the seriousness of the man. For just an instant, he wondered if he were telling the truth. *No! That is too far-fetched. This is all a very clever joke.*

"Are you ready, Alexander? I truly hope, for your sake, that you have understood me well." He set off down the narrow alleyway.

Alex followed. Soon they were passing several shops which were still open. Lights burned within. Out of the shadows came three men who surrounded Alex.

"Look at him!" one exclaimed.

"Such fine clothing he wears!" said the next.

"And see how he looks down his nose at us," said the third.

They moved in closer to Alex, who frantically sought his guide. "Fyodor," he called out.

One of the men jeered, "Smell the fear on him!"

The first man pressed something hard into Alex's shoulder.

The next shoved his face within an inch of Alex's face.

Alex tried not to breathe. The stench was foul.

The third said, "Look at the fine watch he has!" The first man reached out and tried to tear the bracelet from his wrist. Alex jerked back.

Someone placed his hands, almost gently, around his neck. "Look into my friend's eyes. What do you see?"

Alex was forced to look deep into the man's dark eyes. Oddly, he felt an objectivity descend upon him. Fear departed and he did his best to really *see* the man. *How often have I walked the streets of London crossing over to escape the accusing stare of a beggar?* This time he looked.

Alex whispered, "I see a man who has never had a chance. I see someone whose life has been stolen by circumstances he did not create." He realized that, although the man seemed ancient, with his scarred and worn face, he was really not more than thirty or forty at most. Life had indeed been brutal—and dangerous.

Alex continued, "Take my watch, sir. I have no need of it. In fact, I want to make you a gift of it." Carefully, he took off the gold watch and, with both hands outstretched, presented it to him. As if he were taking part in a ritual play, he said, "It would please me greatly, sir, if you would accept it." Alex felt as if some other person within him had spoken.

The man spoke earnestly. "Thank you, sir." The three of them doffed their caps, turned and walked away.

Within a few moments, Fyodor stepped out of the shadows. "I'm proud of you, my friend. You have done far better than I expected. Not only have you acted with compassion, you have also treated the man with the greatest respect even though he is but a poor vassal. I have a wonderful treat for you."

Alex felt so weak, he felt he might sink to the cobblestoned path. Fyodor held out his arm, which Alex took.

"Come. We are not quite done."

Without a word, Alex followed.

Just as they turned down yet another narrow passageway, Alex faltered. "Fyodor? Where are you taking me?"

"To your cosmic egg, my friend."

"But how can that be?"

"Did I not say your spiritual journey would be long?" Fyodor looked closely at him. "I am sorry it is so hard. But you are doing much better than I thought. At the end there will be a surprise for you—one that few ever see."

"All I really want is a place to sleep."

To Alex's left, a staircase wound upward to a door. At first, he did not see the dark form looming above but only saw it seconds before it landed upon him crushing him to the stones. Thick arms flailed at him and immense hands clutched his throat. Releasing his grip, the attacker shouted unintelligibly and brandished a knife. Frozen, as if in a nightmare, Alex could only gurgle when the cold steel of the knife tickled his throat.

Staring into the black eyes of his assailant, he managed to whisper, "What do you want? Please let me give you whatever I have."

He was a youngish man, painfully thin with a shabby coat wrapped around him. Suddenly, Alex saw him quite differently. His eyes were not those of a ferocious killer, but a frightened, wounded beast. Alex saw the burning pain and the deep ache of sorrow in the man and in his life. "If you need money, sir," he gasped. "Please. Let me give it to you."

The man's body went limp. Alex was amazed to see him wipe tears from his eyes. Slowly, he rose up from Alex. Covering his face, he gave an agonized cry, "Dear God! I am no killer!"

Alex sat up. "Why are you so desperate? Let me help you."

The man began to weep. "It is my son."

"What is wrong? Please tell me."

"He is sick. Very sick. He is only eight years old."

"What sickness does he have?"

"Tuberculosis. His coughing and retching goes on all night and day. His mother is exhausted from caring for him. We need medicine." He threw out his hands. "I have no money…at all." The man sank to the steps and cradled his head in his hands. "And…I am a terrible person."

"Whatever do you mean?" Alex had managed to get to his feet.

Burying his head in his hands, he groaned. "I am a cruel and selfish man. I hated my own son. I wanted him to die last night. I wanted to kill him."

The man's words ripped through Alexander's heart. Henri's face appeared in his mind—the one who had suffered so greatly at the hands of a cruel father. Alex said, "You and your family are in such pain. I'm sure you cannot think straight, sir."

"I hated the sound of my boy's coughing and retching..."

"No wonder! It would be terrible to bear such suffering."

"No! You do not understand. It...he disgusted me. It made me want to silence him forever."

Alex took a deep breath. "You must try to forgive yourself."

He reached for his wallet and took out his remaining money. "Please. Take this for your son. What is his name?"

"Vladimir." The man took the money and stuffed it in his pocket. Then he took both Alex's hands in his and kissed them. "Thank you. You have saved three lives." Then he was gone.

As if by magic, Fyodor appeared at his side. His smile was beatific. "Alexander! You have passed—how do you say— with flying colours. Your cosmic egg is not far off." Fyodor doffed his cap and bowed deeply. "Come my friend, you have earned the right to witness something very special."

Then as if unencumbered by physical form, Fyodor floated ahead of Alex and dissolved into shadow. Then, magically, he reappeared in the light, beckoning him to his side. Desperate not to lose his guide, Alex rushed after him. Once he stumbled against a cart blocking his passage. *Where am I,* he asked himself? Reaching out like a blind man, he sought to right his balance.

"Fyodor? Where are you?" he called out. Then he whispered, "Wait for me—please."

When Alexander drew to his side, Fyodor chided, "You must keep up. I cannot lose you—not here."

"What? Where are we? Are we in danger?" Alex's own timidity made him cringe.

Fyodor shook his head and turned down the next corner. Alex followed. Lights from the upper storeys flooded a laneway creating a magical, golden egg-shaped vision in his mind. The passageway was so narrow that Alex was certain, if he stretched out his arms, he would touch the walls of the buildings on either side. Suddenly, the alley was pitched into abysmal darkness. So disoriented was he, that he thought he would fall— without stopping— forever.

Alex staggered, but did not lose his footing. "Fyodor? What is happening?"

"*Nothing at all!* Take my arm. We are getting close."

"Close? To what?" He clutched the guide's arm.

"Our destination. This is the place which I said only a very few people get to see."

"The hotel?"

"Soon, my friend."

Sudden light made Alexander scrunch his eyes shut. But when he opened them, he saw many torches held by darkened figures crouched in shadow.

"Fyodor, who are these people? Are they from *now?*"

The guide looked worriedly at him. "From what other time could they possibly be?"

"But they look different. From at least a century ago."

"*Nyet!* Come with me." He grasped Alex's arm. "We are going in here." He pushed him roughly through a door.

Alex found himself on a low sort of balcony overlooking a room—more like a cave with a dirt floor. Four people were there. Nearby, an elderly man with a shock of white hair was crouched on a stool. Next to him sat a boy, not more than eight, wearing torn pants rolled up at the cuffs and a ragged shirt and vest. An old woman, dressed in a long black skirt, sat before the fireplace beside a young girl, perhaps five years old. *Frozen in time,* thought Alex. *This is not real!*

As if reading his mind, Fyodor said, "These ones," he gestured toward the four of them. "As you would say, they are *not* from right *now*. They are from *all time as in a myth or story*. They lived long ago, presently and will in any future time. Or so we believe. He pointed to the old couple, "They are the grandparents of the boy and girl and they are *all* grandparents of all time in this world.." He scrutinized Alex's face carefully. "Do you understand what I am saying?"

"I think so…" said Alex. From the balcony, he saw a set of wooden steps leading downward into the room. "Am I to go down?"

Fyodor nodded. "Yes, they cannot see you."

"What? Why not?"

Fyodor simply shrugged. "I cannot say with any certainty, but I think they are in some other timeless place."

"Why are we here?"

Fyodor smirked. "You have much to learn, my friend." He pointed to a bench along the wall. "Sit there, if you please."

Both men sat in silence for some moments.

"Why can't they see us?"

His guide looked at him with admiration. "You're questions show a certain perceptiveness, Alex. But I don't know if you can understand what I'm about to tell you."

"Try me."

"These people are here all the time. But what you are about to witness happened many years ago and, to this day, still continues."

"Like an eternal event, like a stain in the ether? Which never disappears?"

"Yes, something like that. How do you know of such things?"

"I must have read about it somewhere. Some physicists think time is like a sliced loaf of bread. Although you can't normally see them, the slices, or each moment in time, still exists—*somewhere.*"

"Hmmmh…I have not heard such an explanation before."

"Are all the houses here like this?"

"No. Just this one."

"Why do you think such scenes keep occurring?"

Fyodor shrugged. "I do not know, but maybe when something terrible has happened. Like sometimes a battlefield seems ghostly and you can almost smell the blood." His guide looked about doubtfully and then said, "Perhaps there is another place where such things remain?"

"Yes. It must be something like that." If he were to visit the places described by Cendre in fifty years' time, perhaps the infamy would be stained on the grass and the trees—and the sky above. You could feel it, sense it like an evil presence. Perhaps you might even *see* it just like he was seeing these people now.

Almost fearfully, Alex asked, "Fyodor, what happened here?"

His guide shook his head and said reassuringly, "Do not worry, my friend, you will not bear witness to some violent, bloody act. You will see that this is different. It is a scene of high emotion, but one of great compassion and love. So great that it is repeated time and again. Perhaps so that humanity will not forget."

"Really? It's wonderful to imagine that good, not just evil, acts can be recorded in such a fashion. When will we see this?"

"As soon as the father comes home. You can set your watch by it. In about ten minutes."

244 — M A R Y   E .   M A R T I N

Again, they sat in silence. Alex studied the children's faces. He was certain they knew the gnawing emptiness of chronic hunger. The boy was thin faced and wary. He sat on a stool as if he might need to run at any moment. Why so fearful? The little girl grew sleepy as the grandmother brushed her hair with slow and gentle strokes. Was she too young to share her brother's disquiet?

"Something good will happen?" Alex asked anxiously.

Fyodor smiled broadly. "Yes, my friend! Have no fear." He gave Alex a speculative look. "Do you believe in a life after this one?"

"I don't know, but I would certainly like to." He thought of the priest on the train and the one in Cendre's story. "But not in any conventional sense. I do not believe for a moment what religion teaches."

Fyodor nodded agreeably. "Indeed!" He reached into his coat pocket and took out a small, silver cigarette case. "Do you smoke, Alex?"

"They won't smell the smoke?"

Fyodor chuckled. "Of course not!" He opened the case and Alex took a cigarette. "We are both in very *different* worlds." A reflective mood came over them and they sat together for the next five minutes enjoying their cigarettes.

"Shall I tell you my theory?" Fyodor asked.

"Yes, of course."

"What we are about to witness is a sort of life after death. These people lived in this hovel more than a century ago. But, as you can see, they are—in a manner of speaking—still here. And so, all the events that have ever happened in a life are still *recorded* on your *slice of bread*. Surely, that is a form of life after death."

"Good God! Are we then doomed to endlessly repeat that one life?"

Fyodor grinned. "It sounds strange, but I can think of no other explanation for what we are about to see." He looked at his watch. "Oh, I'm sorry. I did not read my watch correctly. It will not be for another ten minutes."

Oddly, Alex found himself thinking of Rinaldo and his creation of ritual in his performances. With grudging respect, he wondered if the man had been onto something about the ambiguous nature of time.

By now, Alex's eyes had adjusted to the dim light and he was overcome with conflicting impressions of the entire room. It was a hodge-podge of confusion and yet there was an order which he knew he did not understand—but hoped would be revealed.

To one side of the fireplace was a huge box of wood, mostly kindling, all of which was neatly arranged according to length and thickness. They would not take long to burn, he thought. On the other side, lining the wall, were rows of shelves crammed full of pots, jars, spoons and knives along with rags stuffed into baskets for no apparent purpose.

Next to the shelves stood a rack from which hung the girl's clean dress, neatly pressed and a pair of trousers and starched shirt for the boy. Despite their poverty, the children were well cared for.

Alexander looked further into the room. At the back, he could see a kitchen table, a stove and sink almost hanging from the wall. Further back yet, he saw a double bed and three single ones shoved together.

Then his eyes fell upon a counter where neat rows of boots and shoes were arranged. Each one of the pairs was highly polished. Each one displayed a price tag. Red, blue and yellow women's hats, festooned with feathers and flowers, hung on pegs on the wall.

"Is this a store?" Alex asked.

Fyodor nodded. "But nobody ever buys anything."

"Why not?"

"Surely you can see, Alex. People are too poor. No money, little food."

Looking about, Alex said, "It's strange, but the whole place first seems an utter jumble. Chaos. Everything thrown together randomly. But if you look long enough, a sort of order emerges."

Fyodor smiled. "Much like life, I think, especially in retrospect."

"First you see only garbage." Alex continued. "Dirt and junk. But then you see what they consider vital and essential for their lives."

"It's not so easy, my friend, to distinguish what *is* and *is not* garbage."

Alex regarded at the man with great interest. *My driver is a guide and an intelligent philosopher.* "True. It is a matter of opinion and people are always making such judgments about people as well."

"It is always a question of judgment. What is good? What is bad? In my country, there is much cruelty arising from these judgments," said Fyodor.

Faces came to Alex's mind. Again, he saw Cendre's priest on the train with his visage as implacable as a locked church door. Such vivid images did the mortician create that Alex could see the cruel and cunning expressions on the faces of the townspeople when they demanded Jacques body. What horrible acts of vengeance did they lust for?

At last Alex said, "There's great cruelty in *every* country, Fyodor. Wherever human beings live."

"Yes, but here, I am thinking of the government. Faceless, petty bureaucrats wielding the small powers they possess. *And the church!* You must see the world as they do. If you do, then you are *good*. If you do not, then you are *evil*. They only want to protect themselves and their powers. But, my friend, it robs them of their humanity and turns them into monsters." He shook his head sadly. "These people here were considered garbage—the lowest of the low. Treated like rats in a sewer. Except they were not rats. They were human beings but treated like vermin. Yet, as you will see, they had the greatest gift of all."

"What was that?"

Fyodor gave him a knowing look. "Ah, my friend, do not be impatient. You will see soon enough." The man paused as if choosing his words carefully. He gave Alex a penetrating glance. "Then there is a man like you who has great understanding."

Alex bent closer to his driver. "What...?"

Fyodor waved him off and whispered harshly, "Quiet. The father will be here soon. Watch what happens."

Anticipation creeping over him, Alex leaned forward. He thought again of Rinaldo's *games* or *tricks*—perhaps not so silly after all. Perhaps there was a message that—his rituals actually helped us tell the difference between what people valued and what they scorned. We enshrined the really important *things* with rituals. Rinaldo's other message was that we must pay attention to our physical selves...our bodies and not get carried away with vague spiritual intangibles. Perhaps Rinaldo was onto something!

The stage was set. Players were in their places ready to come to life. As if animated by an unseen force, the little boy sprang from his stool.

"Grandfather? May we do it tonight—*please?*"

The old man looked puzzled. "Jacob?" He tousled the little boy's hair and then drew him closer. "I'm just a forgetful old man." He caught his wife's eye and winked. "Are you sure I said *tonight?*"

Jacob nodded enthusiastically. "Yes, Grandfather. You said it'd be tonight before Father gets home."

The little girl suddenly came to life. "Yes, Grandfather—*please!* You *did* say tonight."

The old man shook his head doubtfully. "Well, Sarah, if *both* of you say so…" He took a deep breath and slapped his knee. "Then it must be so!" He looked across at his wife, who smiled back. He waggled a finger at them. "But, children! There are certain conditions."

"Yes, Grandfather. Whatever you say."

"All right then, but it must be our little secret. You must not tell Father."

The children grinned in excitement. "Yes, Grandfather. We'll never tell. What else?"

"First, you must help Grandmother set the table. *And* we must set the food out on the plates so that all is ready when Father gets home."

Shaking her head, the old woman stood up. "There is only a little food, Sam. But we will make do. Come children."

Sarah and Jacob followed her to the kitchen where they got out the knives and forks.

The little girl asked, "Grandmother? Why do we lay out the knives and forks when there is nothing to cut?"

"You never know, dearie," she answered. "Your Father might bring something home tonight."

"Children, get the bread from the cupboard. Take out five plates," their Grandmother said. "I will find some cheese. So we'll have a real feast."

Jacob set the bread on the cutting board. "Will you cut the loaf, Grandfather?" he asked.

With practised strokes, Grandfather sliced the loaf thinly saying, "Now put the bread on the plates and be sure that Father has enough. He has worked very hard today, I am sure! Then you and your sister, who are growing so fast, will be next." He glanced at his wife. "Then Grandmother!" He made a show of jiggling his belly which hung just a little over his belt and laughed. "Just a sliver for me. I have stored plenty up."

Jacob followed his instructions. Grandmother brought a small chunk of cheese which she cut into pieces and set beside the bread on each plate.

"Wonderful! Little ones. Are you ready now?"

Sarah clapped her hands together and cried out. "Yes, Grandfather! We're all ready now."

Jacob, being older, was more serious and reserved. "Shall I get the magic jar, Grandfather?"

"Let us build the fire first, my dear one." Together they knelt before the grate and heaped the kindling up.

Frowning, the boy asked, "Should we use this much?"

"Yes, my darlings! Tonight is a special night. Remember? When we ask for good fortune, we must have a proper fire. Not too big. Not too little."

The grandmother looked worriedly at the remaining stack of wood. "Sam, be sure to save enough for tomorrow night."

He waved her off with a laugh. "Don't worry, my sweet. I will get more tomorrow morning."

"But where, Sam?"

"Do not trouble yourself with such details. I will fill the box...no trouble at all."

When he had finished building the fire, the Grandfather sighed with satisfaction and hugged his grandchildren. "We will have the finest conflagration St. Petersburg has ever seen!" Turning to his grandson, he said, "Jacob, now you will bring the magic jar. Take care and be sure not to drop it."

The boy hurried to the shelves at the far end of the room and took down a glass container which sparkled like crystal fine enough to grace the table of a palace. With solemn and measured pace, he approached the fireplace. When he reached his Grandfather, he sank to his knees careful not to spill the jar and its contents.

The crystal glass was filled with a sparkling purple grains which shone in the fire light.

"Who will do the honours tonight?" asked the old man.

"It's my turn," said Sarah.

Grandfather looked at her in surprise. "Why, I do believe you're right, dearie. That means Jacob will say the magic incantation. Do you remember it, my boy?"

Jacob nodded eagerly.

"Then please begin."

"Please help Father to help us and himself. Give him great strength so that he can return to us safe each night."

Removing the lid of the jar, the little girl reached in and took a small handful of the purple crystals. She held them up and asked, "Is this too much?"

"No, sweetheart," said Grandfather quietly. "It's just perfect."

She scattered the crystals on the fire. From the grate rose a sparkling, swirling cloud as if a genie had been released from captivity. Then thousands of tiny pinpoints of light danced and sparked.

The children's faces glowed with enchantment. Laughing, they clapped their hands together, gasping in delight as the kindling snapped and sparked. Grandfather and Grandmother looked with great love upon each other and their grandchildren.

"It is *so beautiful!*" the grandparents crooned. "And look at their smiles!"

Like an explosion, the front door banged open. At first they thought it was the wind, but it was not. Father, a gaunt figure huddled in a worn coat, towered at the door. He looked so weary they were amazed he could stand up.

"Why are you wasting precious wood on such nonsense? Do you not care that we will freeze in our beds tonight?"

Fearing the light in his son's eyes, Grandfather rose slowly and tentatively touched his coat sleeve. "Dmitri, do come in you must be exhausted. Come. Sit by the fire."

In bitter tones, Dmitri said, "Yes, Father. I *am* completely exhausted. How kind of you to notice."

The old man's heart sank when he saw his son's empty hands and nothing under his coat. "You have had a hard day, my son. Did you walk far?"

"All day…everywhere. And I found *nothing*! No work. No one has money to hire. No one has food." He hunched himself down by the fire to warm his hands.

"And here you waste the wood and money on those stupid crystals!"

The grandmother edged closer. "Dmitri, please understand. The children…"

Dmitri shot up shouting. "The children? The children will starve or freeze in their beds tonight! And what will they remember? Hunger gnawing out their guts. Their feet and hands growing numb! I pray they go quickly!" Tears glinted in his eyes. "But, of course, of course," he laughed shaking his head, "They will remember the beauty, the lovely beauty of the *fucking* crystals! How fortunate we are. No food, no life but our souls are *saved* by beauty and art!"

"Dmitri, please! You must not speak that way. The children…" The grandfather tried to embrace his son but was pushed away. "It is such a small price to pay for their smiles and laughter—their happiness—if only for a moment."

The more his father tried to placate him, the more enraged Dmitri became. "I have walked all day looking for work. Please God! Just a few kopeks to feed my family!" He nearly wept. "It is so *little* I ask for. But nothing anywhere!" He shook his fist at the ceiling. "Goddamn you! I curse you! How can you permit this hellishly slow suffering? Which will take us first—starvation or freezing to death?"

"Dmitri," the Grandmother said softly, trying to soothe her son. "Please. We have a little food. Come to the table. You will feel better if you eat a little. I have made a vegetable soup. We have some bread and cheese, too."

"Jesus Christ! Why prolong the agony? We are slowly dying just a little bit each day. I curse the day we were born!"

Terrified, the children with saucer eyes, had hidden under blankets in the beds. In silence, they watched Father permit his mother to guide him to the table.

She smiled at Sarah and Jacob. "Come children. You must not mind what your Father says. He is only tired and hungry."

Slowly, the family gathered at the table. Without the urgings of the Grandmother, the children would not have sat down. The old woman served the soup careful to give her son the fullest bowl. The Grandfather waved her off. "Give it to the children," he whispered.

The old man could not prevent himself. With only a mild degree of sternness, he began, "Son, you must not take the name of our Lord in vain. We may not understand his reasons, but it is not for us to question, especially not in the presence of the children."

A flush rose from Dmitri's collar. Arms outstretched, he leapt to his feet and grasped his father's throat. The old man gasped and his eyes bulged. But he struggled only slightly— almost as if he welcomed the end.

Gasping with fright, the old woman rushed to his side. "No, son!" Weeping, she grabbed at his hands and tried to peel back his fingers. The children cowered at the end of the table.

Dmitri released his grip and dumped his bowl of soup. He slammed the bowl hard upon his father's head. Instantly, the shock of white hair was covered with blood and the old man's eyes rolled back in his head as he slumped to one side.

"No!" the Grandmother screamed. "Do not kill him! He is your *Father!*"

Stricken, Dmitri sank to his knees. He held tightly to his Father's legs. "Dear God! What have I done? *Forgive* me Father!" He tried to staunch the blood now pouring down the old man's face. He kissed his father's hands and his wounds. "Please Father. I am so *sorry!*"

Fortunately, his Father's eyes opened. "I am all right." He shoved himself to his feet. "Get me a towel…something to stop the blood."

Holding out a towel, Jacob ran to his Grandfather's side. Carefully, he dabbed the old man's scalp with the motions of a skilled physician. He spoke gently. "Grandfather, please lie down. I think you will be all right. Father? Please get some hot water so we can clean his wound."

Tears ran down Dmitri's face. But he hurried to the stove and soaked another towel in hot water from a pot. Now his Father lay on the bed. Jacob, the young child sank to his knees beside his grandfather and with the help of his own father, cleaned and bandaged the wound which, fortunately, was quite superficial.

"Forgive me Father!" Dmitri continued to whisper as he worked. He stopped several times to look admiringly at his son who continued to dress the wound.

"He will be all right," said Jacob. "I am *so* sorry, Father. I know how hard you've tried."

With open-mouthed surprise, Dimitri asked Jacob, "How did you become such a fine young man? I must not have been paying attention." Then he spoke to his Father. "Forgive me, please."

The old man smiled weakly. "You have not lost your strength, Dmitri. I should not have criticized you—not my darling son— when I know how hard you work. It is *you* who must forgive me."

Father, son and grandson embraced.

Alex was shaken. His face was damp with tears. He stood outside the hovel with Fyodor at his side.

"Now I will take you to your hotel, Alexander. I hope I have given you much to think on."

Alexander still looked stunned. "Yes you have. And thank you." He paused and turned back. "Tell me, Fyodor…how…" Alexander broke into a grin and, shaking his head said, "Never mind! There is no answer!"

In front of the hotel, Fyodor said, "All I can tell you, my friend, is that the family's performance happens every night at nine o'clock. Anyone can come to watch and many do. It is a story which people everywhere need to hear time and again." Grinning, Fyodor grasped Alex's shoulder. "My friend, you have learned well! Far better than I ever expected." Then he was gone in his cab.

CHAPTER 22

$\overline{}$

Daphne took a cab from Madison Avenue down to Rembrandt Artists' Supplies in SOHO. It was a day on the cusp of late fall and early winter. Gusting winds drove clouds scudding across the sky. Moments later, sleet blanketed the streets and caused the taxi to skid through the lights.

Daphne was thrown against the door. "Be careful!" she shouted. "Damned careless," she muttered.

In meetings most of the day, she'd had little time to consider her situation which she described as caught between two men. Brad had stayed over at her apartment last night which had made for a pleasant enough evening. She reviewed the list of pros and cons in her head. Brad was a good friend and excellent business partner. Very reliable and fun. As a lover—something was missing.

This morning she had debated the practicalities of her situation at the age of thirty-six. While she never intended to *settle,* she was ready to make a few trades. It was easy to envision a very comfortable, enjoyable life together. She would always have Brad's attention and presence as he seemed to hang on her every word. With Alex and his art, she would never understand or feel entirely at ease in that place most important to him—his creative world. Perhaps if she tried her hand at art…

The cab pulled up in front of Rembrandt Artists. *I'll look around. Get a drawing pad and some charcoal. Maybe some pastels. This can't be too hard.* She had not questioned why she had decided to try to draw.

She paid the driver and entered the brightly lit store. To her left were rows upon rows of stretched canvases. To her right were shelves and bins of paints, pens and charcoal. Further along she found pads and various drafting supplies— protractors, compasses and knives. Where to start? She had never drawn before.

A store clerk, who reminded her of a very bushy Van Gogh, approached her. "Hey? Can I help?"

Daphne had hoped to be left alone to browse. "No, I'd really just like to look around." She started for the back of the store.

"Cool. Take your time." The clerk wandered off behind the counter.

Alex uses charcoal to sketch out his ideas. He goes off in his mind—alone. She picked out several drawing pads and boxes of charcoal and pastels.

At the counter, the clerk asked, "Do you paint, too? We got a sale on oil paints."

"Oh yes, I do!" Daphne said and then was shocked at her words. *Why did I say that? Why am I trying to impress anyone?*

"What kinda thing?"

"Landscapes."

"Really? Urban…country?"

"Both." *For God's sake! Why am I lying?*

"Fantastic! Do you exhibit?"

"Yes. I've had a few exhibitions. Not that many."

"Great! Where?"

"Oh here and there. Mostly at small galleries— all out of town."

"Terrific. Do you need any brushes or canvases? We can deliver."

She shook her head. "No. Just the pad and charcoal." She turned away afraid that she would make her story even more absurd. She had planned to get a book—drawing for beginners—but now she couldn't. No matter. How hard could drawing be? Just practise!

As she was leaving, a stack of books caught her eye. Leafing through the top one, she saw that it was especially designed as a planning diary for art projects. *Alex could use something like this to get him organized. What he really needs is someone to put some order in his life. Maybe then he'd have more time to spend here rather than there.*

Without further thought, she returned to the counter and bought the agenda. When she got up this morning, she was set on Brad. But now something tugged on her. She could always return to London.

Within moments she was out on the sidewalk hailing a cab. The driver sped up Broadway and onto Amsterdam Avenue where she lived at 73rd Street. The cabbie must have been almost seventy and was very talkative.

"Lady? Are you OK? Pretty lady like you shouldn't look so sad."

Daphne was annoyed. "Pardon? Why do you say I look sad?"

The cabbie shrugged his shoulders and grinned. "Sorry! No offence. But I thought you just looked kinda lonely."

"Well, I'm not!" *Good grief! Is it that obvious?* At first, Daphne just wanted to sit quietly and stare out the window, but she studied the man—a harmless, grandfatherly type!

The driver's eyebrows shot up. "A fella like me is never lonely. I've been married forty five years come next September and there's never been time to be lonely. Too damned busy!" He gave Daphne a charming smile. "You know—the wife, two kids and five grandkids—all needing something."

Daphne was drawn in. "I suppose…" Marriage had always been a touchy subject for her. On the one hand, she enjoyed her independence. But yes, sometimes she was lonely, but she knew how to handle it.

"You married, lady?"

At first Daphne was shocked at the familiarity. "No," she said.

"I gotta say I'm surprised!"

"Why?" Daphne reflected for only a moment on her participation in the conversation. She should have cut it off right at the start.

"I dunno. You look like the kinda person who'd get lots of proposals and would've accepted one."

In spite of herself, Daphne laughed and heard herself say, "I like being on my own. Running my own show."

The cabbie shrugged. "Well to each her own! For me, I wouldn't have had much of a life without the wife and kids. I think of all the times I was real down and Helen was always there to pick me up and give me a boot in the ass." He laughed and slapped the wheel. "Nothing like a woman to keep you in line!"

"Don't you miss being able to make up your own mind… decide for yourself your independence?"

"Sometimes, I guess. But that don't take the place of love. That's what it's all about."

"How do you know when it's real love?" Daphne was amazed. Here she was asking fundamental questions about life with a total stranger in a cab in New York City.

The driver chuckled. "That's the age old question, isn't it?" When he was stopped at the lights at Amsterdam and 50th, he turned around to look at her. His eyes twinkled as he said, "You never really do. It's not so important really. 'Cuz sometimes you'll be in love with her and some days you won't. But you gotta have someone you really like." He gave a merry shrug. "The sex stuff doesn't last forever anyway." He paused for a moment and then said quietly, "After all, what good is life without love? A little kindness goes a long way too."

The traffic started to move again. Daphne stared out the window. *He makes it all sound so simple.*

She had to give Brad an answer soon. Or did she? Why not wait and see? She could go back to Alex for a while just to see if they could get together. The man was a brilliant artist. He must have seen something important in her which would draw them together. If they could make it work, she would have an exciting, challenging life in the arts and the creative world. After all, her work was creative too. She knew she could organize him for more time here in this world.

The driver said, "Got a little story for you so you'll understand."

"Yes?"

"Everybody thinks love's gonna last forever and make life just grand from beginning to end, but they're wrong. It doesn't.

But it does a lot of important things. When our daughter, Katie, was only five, I took her to the park one Saturday morning. There I sat on the bench reading the paper and talking to the other guys. I didn't see that Katie and a little friend had gone outside the gates and were running into the street to get a ball. Then I heard tires screeching and brakes slamming. Horns. It was awful! I ran fast as I could—it seemed like forever— and there was my little darling lying on the road."

"Oh my God!" Daphne said. "Was she…?"

"Thank the Lord, no!" he breathed. "Only her ankle was broken, so it wasn't too bad. But you see, I could never forgive myself for being so stupid. Helen—that's my wife—she knew that. So every time I started to ask her forgiveness, she'd say *I know you'd take back the moment if you could, but you can't. Katie and I forgave you a long time ago. She only broke her ankle. But something much bigger—your spirit— broke inside you. The only one who needs to forgive you is yourself.*

"Lady! When she said that, I started to blubber just like a little kid. You see, that's what real love is all about. She knew how bad I was hurting and she made sure I could forgive myself. Love makes you grow…makes you a better person. That's why it's so important."

Daphne knew she would ponder the man's story for a long time. She said, "That's an incredibly beautiful story. I'm very glad you told me."

The driver pulled up to the curb. He turned around and smiled. "Think about it lady. I'm glad you liked the story. By the way, that'll be fifteen dollars, please."

"Pardon?"

The man pointed up to the building. "You're home now. And the meter says fifteen bucks."

"Yes, of course." She paid him and collected her parcels. She held his gaze. "Thank you again."

He grinned and said, "No problem, lady."

Lost in thought, Daphne slowly mounted the stairs of her brownstone and let herself in.

CHAPTER 23

Back in his London studio, Rinaldo lay collapsed on the bed next to Krysta. Usually, after sex, he would jump up and head for the bathroom to clean himself up. But now, gazing into her eyes, he reached out and stroked her hair. Her eyes frightened him. *Was this what everyone talked about—love?* He had to admit that Krysta was the best lay he'd had in years. But it wasn't just that. Something about her captivated him. She *had* to be his muse, because he didn't really believe in love.

He shook his head, rolled over and headed for the bathroom. Even so, as he scrubbed himself in the shower, he could not forget her slow caresses. It wasn't just technique either! When he tried to describe her touch, the only word which came to mind was *loving.* He stared at himself in the mirror and shrugged. Women could rarely resist him! *Probably I just really turned her on.*

As he dried himself off, curious words came to him— *sacred—profane!* He sank down to the toilet seat and stared at his feet. Images of policemen appeared before him. *What in hell is happening to me?* Then he chuckled. *Brilliant! When I went on that religious rant at the police station, it got me out of a lot of trouble.*

With a grin, Krysta rose from the bed and wrapped the robe around her. Men were ridiculously vain, but Rinaldo was exceptionally so. Easy to get him under her thumb. She walked about the stage examining some of the items which were, in her opinion, mostly garbage. At the back sat an old cardboard box into which he had tossed a huge assortment of felt pens. On the side of the box he had painted *The Art Project.* That was ridiculous! He had called it *art.* In admiring tones, she had asked him what concept lay behind the work. His answer was so stupid. *If you must ask, my dear, you'll never understand no matter what I say.*

Rinaldo came out of the bathroom entirely naked. She smiled appreciatively. He gave a deep bow. "So glad you were thrilled and satisfied my dear!"

"It was totally marvellous, Rinaldo. Now I understand your reputation."

Rinaldo grinned.

She came to him and caressed his shoulder and down his back. "Can I tell you about *The People's Art Project?* I just know an avant guard like you will be really interested."

Rinaldo had little interest in her project. Models and muses had to learn not only how to keep still but also silent. But she was a great lay and he wanted to repay her in some fashion. *Always keep the score even.* He sat down on the bed. "Go ahead, my dear. Tell me about your little idea. After that, we'll start the papier mache."

Krysta thought he was so old-fashioned—especially his idea of what constituted *art*. According to him, some concept—*any concept*— no matter how dim and badly expressed, could be brilliant simply because it came from him. Krysta respected craftsmanship and discipline, something totally lacking in Rinaldo's work.

"We…" she began.

"Who is 'we'?"

"The artist's group behind the movement."

"Oh *gawd!* Not a fucking collaboration!"

"Not in the way you think of it, Rinaldo. Our group stands for the democratization of art. Everyone has an equal voice. If they don't want to work within a group concept then they are perfectly free to go off and do their own thing."

Rinaldo was already bored. These young students had no experience…no talent. All their thinking was political. For him, politics and art had no common ground.

She grasped his hands and smiled brilliantly at him. "Just listen! You're going to love this. It's your kind of thing. I promise. I want to use your fantastic idea where we make papier mache, but they'd be Tarot card masks like the Tower, Death cards and the Fool."

"But I'm planning to cover the entire body with papier mache."

She shook her head. "We need to be practical. No one will be able to move so we want people to be free to run around Piccadilly Circus with these masks and confront people. And, we want you to have the most important role *The Fool.*

"Ha?"

Krysta laughed and kissed him. "Rinaldo, The Fool is very important. He's the savant, who travels the world. He has the highest intelligence and is open to life, love and learning. The great artist is *always* portrayed as The Fool, because he has the most original and creative spirit." She ran her fingers across his chest. "*And*, that is why our group *must* have you lead us through our very first conceptual art project."

"I don't know…" He ran his finger over her breast almost gently. "What's your plan?"

Eyes aglow, Krysta sat back and began. "We were inspired by your first event in Piccadilly which we all thought was truly brilliant."

His eyes narrowed. "I thought you didn't know about it."

"Oh, we saw it on You Tube when it went viral."

"It did?"

"You didn't know? I think it's had over a million hits."

"Really?" Despite his Piccadilly manifesto about sex, Rinaldo had not actually had many lovers. Consequently, he was easily flattered by a young woman who seemed to like him if not love him. So that he could have her as he wished, he decided to help with her group's little project.

"The Tarot card Fool is the one who travels through life learning from all the others he meets like the Magician and the Hierophant. We can go through the deck if you like, but you're the main character—The Fool. In Piccadilly, we'll have masks for the whole group and we will ad-lib a performance." She put her hand on his thigh and caressed him gently. "Please Rinaldo, we so need you. Say you'll come!"

Rinaldo slid on top of her. "All right, my lovely, I'll be there."

It was the first time Rinaldo had fallen under the spell of a woman. He worried that he had foolishly fallen in love with her. That could be the only reason for his lapse in judgment.

CHAPTER 24

Next morning, Alexander was awakened by the telephone.

"Hello?"

"Mr. Wainwright? It is Sergei Vladstock speaking. I am to take you to Anton Chekhov this morning."

Alex sat up and rubbed his face. "Where is Fyodor, my driver?"

"Fyodor? I know of no one by that name, sir."

Alex shook his head. "But he was with me last night." Then he remembered that Fyodor had denied any connection with Anton. "Are you a member of *Les Cavaliers Jaune?*"

"I work for them… sometimes."

"Where is Anton?"

"I will take you to him."

"Where are you now?"

"Downstairs."

Alex checked his watch—nine am. *Good grief. I certainly slept in.* "Give me twenty minutes and I'll be down."

268 — M A R Y   E .   M A R T I N

"Yes, sir."

Only when he headed for the bathroom, did Alex notice that his bed was immense. A king size! Only in North America—where the giants lived! What normal person could ever need such space? Acres of marble tile with yards upon yards of brass fittings stretched throughout the bathroom. No European or Russian hotel had such space. *How in hell did I get here? Wherever Fyodor took me last night, there'd be no hotel like this!*

His eyes fell upon the rack of towels all of which were embossed—*Marriott Hotel.*

Under the shower, he tried to remember last night. Of course, he could recall almost every detail of Fyodor's face—the bushy eyebrows, the beard and the piercing eyes. He dried off and began to dress. *They must have found a room and Fyodor brought me back but why don't I remember?* Like wisps of a dream, the hollow eyes of two little children lingered under the surface of his consciousness. As he dressed, only the sense of a dream—but no detail—flitted just beneath his perceptions. But as he rushed down the hall to the elevators, any dream was simply gone.

In the lobby, he passed the front desk.

"Good morning, Mr. Wainwright. I trust you had a pleasant night."

My God! It's the same desk clerk who threw me out. He stopped up. *But what really happened last night?*

He had no time for further thought. A short, rotund figure sidled toward him. Hair bristled out from underneath a Yankees baseball cap.

"Mr. Wainwright? I am Sergei. Please to come with me." His words were more a command than an invitation.

Alex followed him to his car parked in the driveway outside the front door. After a few minutes' drive, he could see the Winter Palace's coloured walls of blue and ochre. Peering beyond the gates, Alex easily imagined the fine carriages of the Tsars' pulling up into the forecourt beneath architecture, rich in historical fantasy. Under heavy cloud, they drove along boulevards flanked by low rise buildings interspersed with the occasional church or government building. With no breakfast, Alex found himself light headed.

Within forty minutes, they had come to a suburban area near the grand Peterhof Palace. With one turn down a street, they were in an entirely different *land*—a myriad of winding lanes all flanked with fine homes of brick and stucco. Alex was delighted to see columns, windows, ledges and doors laden with unusual touches of arabesque décor. *Anton Chekhov, must be a very successful artist to live here.*

Within moments, Sergei was holding the front door of number twenty-nine open for him. From the foyer, they proceeded off to the left.

Bumping against tables, boxes and stray chairs, Alex and Sergei edged through a darkened hallway to the rear of the house and, at last, into a large, perfectly proportioned room. Despite the riot of red and gold brocade coverings, the mismatched Baroque furniture and rich wall tapestries hanging askew, Alex knew that the room's entire structure and symmetry spoke of a deep, harmonious balance. Every artist, he thought, admired the harmony of the classical *golden rectangle*. The proportions of the space were based on an ancient but simple mathematical equation. The length of the room was twice its width and its height was the length plus the width divided in two. That *divine* equation had created peace and order in the human psyche since Pythagoras. Whatever clashing, warring decorative detail one might throw into such a room, nothing would disturb the underlying sense of calm and balance.

Much like a life one might hope to construct, he thought. Chaotic events might clutter the landscape but, with underlying stability, all might be well. *Art and life,* he mused. *In art, we hold a mirror up to satisfy our souls.*

So jumbled was the parlour, that Alex did not notice it was occupied until an extremely tall figure rose from a chair. The eyes first caught his attention. They burned fiercely and then were cast heavenward in a true Christ-like gaze focused on another world. *We poor mortals cannot see what this man sees.*

"Anton Chekhov?" Alex asked.

The man did not answer but kept his eyes cast *elsewhere.* Alex was not sure what to do next and so, he remained standing in the middle of the room until Sergei motioned him to sit down near the fire. When he did, the man resumed his seat and looked upon him with considerable interest.

"Yes, Mr. Wainwright, indeed, I am Anton Chekhov." His smile stretched his lips tightly over his skull. When his eyes focused on Alex, it was with such burning intensity, that Alex wondered if the man were ill. Although thin to the point of being skeletal, he exuded an aura of great energy. Alex could think of no other than the Russian, Rasputin, mystic incarnate to Catherine the Great.

"Henri said you wished to see me. What is your purpose, Mr. Wainwright? Is it about Henri?"

"No, not about Henri. I am interested in one of your paintings which has come into my hands via an estate. It's of a cosmic egg and on the back of the canvas I understand that you have inscribed it *to Henri Dumont, the Parisian pianist.*"

"Do you have it with you?"

"No, only a copy."

"Where is the original?"

"In London."

"And how did you come by it?"

"Last year, I became the executor of the estate of Jonathan Pryde, an art collector."

"I didn't know the bastard was dead! When did that happen?"

"Last autumn."

"Hmmh…" Anton rose up from his chair like an apparition. "And what is your interest in bringing it to me? Pryde stole it, you know."

"No…I didn't, not at least until Henri said the same. But if either of you can establish that, then I will most certainly return it to you or to Henri."

Anton seemed satisfied with Alex's response. "But what," he asked, "is your interest in the cosmic egg?"

"I wanted to know if you had actually seen the egg yourself or whether you imagined it." Alex averted his eyes. After all the travels he'd had to date, the reason he now gave sounded rather paltry, if not outright stupid. He looked up. Anton's eyes were aflame.

"Of course, I have seen it! I see it every day…around every corner. Always there but just out of sight! Why do you ask?"

"I wanted to know…" Never having considered his motivations, Alex shrugged in confusion. "What you made of it? What it means to you?"

Anton drew near, crowding over Alex. "Have you seen the cosmic egg?"

"Yes. And I have a very remarkable story about its appearance."

"Go on."

"I was working in my studio…I'm a representational painter."

For the first time, Anton smiled in delight. "You are *the* Alexander Wainwright?"

Alex nodded.

"I thought so. You are the one who sees the *light* and either *cannot* or *will not* express its purest form in your art. For God's sake man! Why ever not?"

"That's exactly what I'm trying to do!" Alex began to pace in frustration. "That day I'd been working with all sorts of abstract shapes in hopes of freeing myself from the concrete world. Right in my studio rose the most beautiful jewel encrusted cosmic egg. It just floated there spinning slowly. My God, it was beautiful. After it disappeared, I could feel right down to my fingertips something new was about to appear! I picked up my chalk and the most gorgeous shapes flowed onto the page. I, too, took it as a sign."

Alex sank back into his seat as if overcome with weariness. "But there's more!" His excitement grew. "The very next day, my art dealer invited me for lunch and showed me your painting of the cosmic egg. Amazing! My vision is *exactly* the same as the one you've painted."

Anton Chekhov took a sharp intake of breath. His eyes drifted heavenward. "Not everyone sees it, Mr. Wainwright. Only those who are *blessed*."

"Blessed?"

"You asked me the meaning of it. It's very simple. It is a clear sign that you are on the right track—with your *art*."

"And life?"

The artist gave a shrug. "I am no fortune teller, Mr. Wainwright. I do not speak of *life* as you might. You see the two as inseparable. I see art as the only aspect worth either striving or living for. Life? Who can say? Life must never be allowed to come between an artist and his art."

Just behind Anton, a heavy curtain parted and a trolley emerged. Upon it sat a large, silver samovar perhaps two feet in height. The bottom portion, shaped like a rotund vat, was ornately scrolled with delicate design. The sparkling upper portion was shaped like a very large teapot.

Within a moment a woman emerged. She did not speak but glanced shyly at Alex. He immediately thought her a pleasant, but plain looking woman. Anton's gaze was, once again, directed heavenward until she left.

He turned to Alex. "Is that not superb?"

Unsure whether he meant the teapot or the woman, Alex replied eagerly. "Absolutely! A true gem."

Anton said, "Oh…by the way…that woman was my wife Chloe. A fine woman, don't you think?"

Alex nodded his head in agreement. "Why yes, of course."

Anton took a teacup and placed his finger on the spigot of the samovar. "Alexander, do you have a woman?"

"Pardon? A woman?"

"Someone to satisfy whatever needs you might have?"

"I guess I don't really think of people that way…"

Anton laughed. "Don't be so pompous, old man. We all have needs…especially great artists such as you and me. Neither of us has much time to invest. We must always be striving, toiling for our art. Not out making serious commitments of time and emotion." He winked at Alex. "But still, we are burdened with our bodies and must satisfy their demands. I'm sure you understand me."

Suddenly, Anton's face flushed. He threw back the curtain and shouted, "Chloe! Get back in here, you stupid cow! Where is the milk and sugar?"

A frightened face appeared at the doorway. He grabbed her shoulder and pulled her into the room. "Look what you've forgotten, foolish woman! What about the milk and sugar?"

She spoke in real fear. "Yes, Anton, I'll bring them right now." Then she disappeared only to return within a moment. "Here they are. Shall I pour the tea?"

Anton looked upon her indulgently and spoke in a kindly manner as if to a treasured pet. "I'm glad you are quick to correct your error, Chloe. Yes, you may serve it now."

Alex was stunned into silence. *How can this man talk of art and life yet treat his wife in such a manner?* To him, it was madness.

Eyes cast down, Chloe served the tea according to some ill rehearsed ritual. At one point, she dropped a teaspoon and glanced furtively at her husband. Fortunately, his gaze was fixed *elsewhere*. When she had finished, she slipped from the parlour without a word.

Alex sipped his tea. Suddenly his host's attention focused upon him.

"When we've finished, I want to show you the work in my studio. I last saw the cosmic egg when I began working on this current project."

Alex nodded. For the next five minutes, they sat together— at least in physical proximity. Anton slurped his tea. Alex sipped his and wondered, with some annoyance, just what *dimension* Anton might be exploring. Not once did their eyes meet.

Cup and saucer rattling as he set it down, his host rose up swiftly. "Come this way, sir. You will find it most interesting."

He opened an outer door to the back garden where weeds poked through a cracked sidewalk. In moments, they were descending a narrow set of stairs to a basement door. After several attempts, Anton found the right key and opened it. The musty smell of mold nearly overcame Alex. It was pitch dark inside.

"Watch your step, Alexander. Put your hand on my shoulder and follow me in. We'll be in the dry studio in a minute."

When Alex felt something soft brush past his against leg, he cursed.

Anton shouted, "Goddamnit I thought all the rats in that tunnel had been killed! So sorry to frighten you Alexander."

Soon they were stepping onto what felt like a solid concrete floor.

"Now for the light!" Anton snapped on a switch.

As an artist, Alex had expected to enter a well-lit space with canvases, brushes and pots of paint set out in a comfortable, familiar scene. But that was *his* kind of studio designed for *his* kind of work.

In Anton's work space, two naked bulbs swaying from the ceiling cast off a meagre light and made shadows swing across the walls. The room was empty, except for two metal, folding chairs side by side in the middle of the studio. Upon entering, Anton appeared transformed. Moments ago the man had vehemently cursed his wife. Now lethargy had descended upon him.

In the studio, Alex had a curious sense—not claustrophobia—but of pressing deprivation. The parlour, more to his taste, had been crammed with scattered knick knacks—the dilapidated samovar, old tea cups, newspapers and piles of books. This space was devoid of any decoration or, thought Alex, of any life. A somewhat grubby sterility was the overriding impression which seemed odd for creative work. A puzzling loneliness and vague yearning fell upon him.

His host gestured him to take a seat and then, with a remote control in hand, sat down beside him. Two very large television screens were mounted on the far wall. A tune, played on a clarinet, slid out of nowhere, as if doing lazy cartwheels in the air. The notes circled upward and filled each and every bit of space of the studio. Alex smiled and began to relax.

"And, by the way," Anton whispered, "That's Roger, one of Henri's friends, playing the jazz score Henri composed. A sort of joyful, endless loop." Anton snapped off the ceiling lights.

"Really? But Henri told me he couldn't compose because of his father's influence."

Anton gave a mirthless laugh. "Henri is far too modest."

"So you and Henri collaborate on projects?"

"Sometimes we do. Did he entertain you with his life story?"

"Some of it."

Anton gave deep chuckle. "Later, I will give you the *true* version."

Alex said no more. An immense, oval shaped body of water floating in the cosmos, appeared on the screen. The shimmering, blue water was streaked with strings of tiny bubbles forming long, lacey patterns. Then a heavy, knotted rope swung lazily back and forth across the screen evoking a hot summer's day at a swimming hole.

Alex stood in awe. "Anton! It's a marvelous creation. So *dreamlike*. It's sublimely beautiful!" When viewing art, Alex liked to take his time to experience every aspect of the work.

After several moments, he murmured, "It's like sheer diamond surfaces constantly in motion— sparkling blues, whites and greens and delicate traces of lace extending forever."

The contrast between the water and the rope fascinated him. Water was elemental, eternal, yet alive and in constant motion. For all anyone knew, it might be found anywhere in the cosmos. By contrast, the rough texture of the knotted rope demanded he reach out and touch it as something very *real* in this here and now, present world of the senses.

Henri's now tranquil clarinet notes slid together in the composition with the yearning melody of a saxophone. Alex loved most music—especially jazz. To him, it felt like two o'clock in the morning at a jazz club in Chelsea where the musicians were just talking, joking and improvising. For Alex, when great music touched the heart strings, all the colours of the rainbow burst open and swirled before him like visions.

The screen continued to change. First he saw through the water as if looking up from the bottom of the sea. Soft light from above beckoned him. Sometimes the water was viewed from above or just under the surface and then from one side to another. At first, there was only water, but as he watched, rocks, fish and other wildly coloured sea creatures appeared and disappeared before his eyes.

Through the speakers came Anton's voice over. *Everything— all life—began here, in this water. And surely, all death takes place here, too. Life is but the briefest of interludes and we are tantalized by the prospect of what lies beyond.*

Alex glanced at his host. Although his prerecorded voice contained the energy of a preacher, now the man's form was slack as if his spirit could scarcely bother to inhabit its body. So detached was he from the world of the senses, he scarcely troubled himself to breathe. But his eyes, fixed on the screen, glowed with an intensity Alex had rarely seen.

Anton was a man who bristled with contradictions. One moment, he was attacking his wife's shortcomings and discussing his sexual needs and the next he was *elsewhere* without energy for *this* world. Alex could not say *why* but Anton seemed only to exist in some shadowy world of spirit which occasionally made dramatic forays into the here and now. He wondered if his dedication to art and creativity deprived him of something important.

Obviously, the artist drew his inspiration from the physical world. After all, where else could he find it? But did he ever take a moment to savour the taste of a peach or the smell of fresh bread?

Once again, the perspective on the screen changed. The viewer was diving to the bottom of the ocean past fish, which scarcely bothered to drift away. Tendrils of green and blue plant life waved lazily upward. The deeper the descent, the murkier the vision became until darkness was nearly total.

Anton's voice over filled the room with seductively spoken words. *Follow me to the source of all art and creativity—the watery depths of our minds and spirits.*

After a moment, a diffuse light illuminated the ocean floor and Alex bore witness. A dark, purplish mass, like a nascent clump of cells, formed into a bubble-like shape. With a great roar, it burst upward and shot skyward like an immense yellow sun.

Anton's voice came again against the insistent rhythm of the drums in Henri's music. *You have just witnessed the birth of a thought, the hallmark of mankind. Where did it come from and where does it go?*

When the first screen went black, the second one instantly lit up to reveal the sun streaking against a hard, brilliantly blue sky. Rapidly, it lost speed and drifted out of sight behind miles of sand dunes.

He heard Anton's voice over. *In the desert the spirit soars free of the dross, material world. It is every man's goal to free his spirit in the elusive beyond he yearns for.*

Now the music was a meditative piano piece Chopin might have composed. On the screen, a distant procession of dark-robed figures passed over a dune and toward a mountain of caves. Then the line of black figures halted and remained posted as if in prayer on the edge of a great precipice.

Anton touched Alex's arm. "That, too, is Henri playing one of his sonatas." He pointed the remote at the screen and darkened it.

Alexander was unsure of what to say. On the one hand, for him, the work was sublimely beautiful and yet he was puzzled. The tension between the man and his art nearly overwhelmed him! At times, Anton seemed bereft of life and yet he possessed and expressed his creative ideas with a terrible passion.

At last he said, "Anton! That is a wonderful creation. What was your inspiration for this work?"

Anton sat with his arms clasped tightly across his chest as if to protect himself against any potentially hostile forces. "My intent was to express what lies beneath or beyond the tangible world. A sort of field of energy which holds everything together."

Alex looked at his host with great respect.

"Fascinating! So, is this how you visualize what lies beyond?"

Anton spoke with slightly more energy. "Yes. Something like that. With the splitting of the atom, we learned much about ourselves and the universe, but we opened Pandora's Box. This world of solidity is but an illusion. If you continue to examine physical objects, you will soon find that there is nothing there except tiny particles—only little packets of energy. And so, Alex, you are quite correct to say that your best chance of expressing the beyond is by turning away from painting your fields and streams. You must simplify your existing forms into abstract shapes until you reach a state of nothingness." He gave Alex a wry smile. "But don't be distressed! At least you sense *something* underpins this cosmos"

"Why are you so sure about me? I've said almost nothing."

"It is in your work. Because your constant search is for your light—*the* light." He tossed his hands up in amazement. "Most people are completely unaware of it. But you are! And the reason I know that? Because the cosmic egg has driven you here on this most improbable journey from Paris to St. Petersburg." With great effort, his host brought himself to his feet. "I'm delighted you have come because I want to make you an offer."

"Really? What sort of offer?"

"I want you to work here….say for a year or so."

"But why? My studio is back in London."

"You, my friend, have seen the cosmic egg. That means we are on the same journey and, if we are to be successful, we must work together." He averted his eyes and spoke in quieter tones. "Henri is the only other one I personally know who has seen this marvelous symbol of life, art and creativity in a vision."

"Henri has? He didn't say anything…"

"Henri wouldn't." Anton leaned forward and spoke intensely. "Only here in St. Petersburg will you find your light which we could find together." He tugged Alex's sleeve. "You worry me, Alexander."

"What? Why?"

"You are a divided man—one who might split in two at any moment! As a great artist, you must never permit any *person* or any *circumstance* to come between you and your art, your creative spirit." Fixed by the fire in Anton's eye, Alex drew back slightly. "As great artists, we have this duty to search for the source." Almost in despair, Anton turned away. "I fear you may crumble and give into the demands of others. Please! Do not let that happen!"

Alex could not help but think of Daphne and how she might fit in his life. He said, "But you've only just met me. Why do you think you know so much about me?"

"As I said, it is in your work. One glance and…"

"I shall give your invitation serious consideration, Anton."

Anton shook his head fiercely. "No…no! It is urgent you decide. I worked so very hard to save Henri's art. And look what happened!"

"What does Henri have to do with this?"

Anton gave a glimmer of a smile. "Let us go for a walk, my friend and I will tell you a story which I expect you will find instructive."

Alex was glad to get outside where he might feel less cornered. When they had climbed the staircase, they were back in the untended garden. The grass was dirty brown and soaked. They stepped on flagstones and made their way to the gate.

CHAPTER 25

Suddenly Anton burst through the gate and marched across the roadway. On the other side, he cast a tall, almost skeletal figure against the grey sky. Clutching his long coat about him, he turned back and summoned Alexander. The man, so bereft of energy in the studio, had been replaced by one radiating an unsettling zeal.

"Come Alexander!" he shouted, "You must hear the *whole* story. Otherwise, you will understand absolutely *nothing*!" In the chill fall air, Alex's host clapped his arms about his chest for warmth. As if caught in a storm, he shouted, "You must remember that Henri, you and I are the ones who have seen this identical cosmic egg in a vision. That makes our relationship special." Beckoning Alex onward, Anton turned away and strode to an embankment which ran alongside the roadway. From there, he set out across a footbridge. The heels of his boots rang out with every urgent step on the iron footings. Alex hurried and caught up with him on the bridge.

Anton swung around. "Why would a father want to destroy his son?" he demanded.

Alex stood stock-still. "You mean Henri's father?"

Anton ignored him and continued marching across the bridge. Alex looked over the edge to the river below where water roiled and splashed over rocks.

"Yes!" Anton shouted back at him. Henri's father. The child was a supremely gifted musical prodigy at the very earliest stages."

"Yes, so I understand."

Anton fixed his gaze on the far riverbank. "He coaxed the most sublime music from that piano with extraordinary grace and emotion. Right away, you knew his *daemon* was in command and that there would be no denying its presence. His father also knew that right away."

Alexander chuckled. "Oh yes! The *daemon*! That demanding spirit which drives the artist to the heights and never gives any rest."

"Indeed. Anyone who creates *anything* good must have a hard task master."

By now, they had reached the centre of the footbridge. Both of them stared out onto the turgidly flowing river.

In dark tones, Anton said fiercely, "What I am about to tell you is a tale of *hatred, revenge* and *betrayal*. And, it all began when Henri was only three."

"Good Lord!"

"The man was desperate to destroy his only son. He began by ensuring he had control of him—that the child submitted to his will in every conceivable way."

"But why?"

"The man was vicious—like a mad dog! Jealousy, alone, would not account for such hatred and malice." Anton was close to tears. "It was like defacing the *Mona Lisa*."

Alex was mesmerized.

His host grasped his coat sleeve and drew him near. "The three of us—you, me and Henri—we are like brothers." His breath was harsh on Alex's cheek. "I say this because we share the vision. And so, you *must* hear the entire story."

"Of course, but…"

"Walk with me then!"

Suddenly, snowflakes began swirling down on them coating the wrought iron railing of the footbridge. They began the trek to the far side of the bridge. The sunlight broke through and streamed down through the layers of cloud and illuminated the riverbank in brilliant flashes of light.

Just under the bridge, Alex could see a deep indentation in the bank, which he realized was a cave or grotto. He was about to turn away when a quick movement drew his eye. At the entrance to the cave was a young, wobbly deer struggling to stand. Quickly it was joined by its mother which gently nosed it upward to its feet. Within a moment, the baby stood on its own, head held proudly in the air.

Alexander was ready to listen. "Please go on."

Anton motioned Alex to a bench where they sat down. His host offered him a cigarette, which he accepted. Anton began.

At the time, I was a permanent guest at the palace, which resembled a mini Versailles. In the music room was a strange collection of metronomes housed in two cabinets. They were absolutely beautiful! Just imagine layers of scrolled gold and silver. Obviously, the man was obsessed with time keeping and rhythm. What did this signify? *A refusal to permit one undisciplined breath of life!* It was as if he needed to buttress himself against threats of the creative spirit. The little boy hunched over the keyboard was just such a threat.

For martinets, not one note can be written next to another without the aid of the metronome! For those with a freer, flowing spirit, the use of it is akin to wearing handcuffs at the piano. You can guess into which camp each of them fell. That day, I was invited to sit through the lesson for poor little Henri.

As with any art, technical skill must be learned. But unremitting and cruel discipline will crush the life and joy out of any art. Father remained perched on a stool beside the piano. In his hand was a yard long pointer stick. On the piano sat two metronomes clacking away like angry ducks.

As Henri proceeded dutifully through yet another set of scales, Father tapped the pointer on his shoulder—gently enough at first— but as the notes rose higher, Father's motions grew harsher. After five minutes of practice, Henri's eyes were filled with tears and he stopped to rub his shoulder.

Father roared, "No progress without pain and effort young man!" He smacked the boy's head with the pointer. "You must discipline yourself."

Henri's eyes were filled with terror before an inexplicably wrathful god. No wonder he sought to please and placate! Next time the pointer was swifter. It made a sickening, singing noise in the air just before it struck Henri's knuckles. The child gave a shrill squeal but silenced himself almost at once.

"Wait!" I tried to intervene. "You must not!"

The Father silenced me with the iciest stare I have ever seen.

It was too much for Henri. His shoulders quaked and tears rolled unabated down his cheeks.

"Ah ha! More tears now, is it?" The man slid from the stool and, retrieving a plant from the windowsill, held it under Henri's face. "Don't waste those precious droppings. Water the plants with your tears. They are of no use to the development of your musical talent." That was too much for little Henri. With his chin on his chest, he could not prevent another sob as he fled the room.

Anton jumped from the bench and began to pace. During his telling of the story, he had smoked three cigarettes, violently sucking them down to the filter, throwing them on the ground and then grinding them out with his heel until they were in shreds. Now he stood at the railing and looked up and down the river as if searching for answers.

Then he turned on Alex and growled. "The Goddamned bastard! For years I have tried to understand the sickness of his mind." He marched toward Alex, shaking his fist in the air. "Henri could have been a truly *great* composer, but his father took pleasure in crushing his talent—his genius."

When he resumed his seat, Alex saw the tears in his eyes. An odd question struck him. *Was Anton more distraught from the destruction of artistic talent or the injury to the heart of a little boy?* But he only said, "Good God! That's a truly story of incredible cruelty!"

Anton laughed bitterly. "Oh, but wait. That's just the beginning. As Henri grew up, it became far worse." He continued his tale.

Henri must have been fifteen when he fell in love with Millie. At the time, Henri and I had the palace to ourselves. Father was performing in Prague and Millie had been sent back to London.

One hot, stifling afternoon, I went to the gardener's shed to find a ladder for hanging some pictures. When I entered, I shouted, "Sweet Jesus! Stop Henri!" Henri had tossed a heavy, knotted rope over a ceiling beam and was about to climb onto a stool.

A pallid look of terror was etched on his face. Shaking, he sank to the stool and buried his head in his hands.

"Henri, what is so terrible that you would think of such a thing?"

His voice choked. "Father is a monster!"

"I know, Henri. He has tried to destroy your artistry. But it's from jealousy."

"No! It's not that. It's about what he's done to Millie." He tried not to sob. "*And* I can't do *anything*. I want to kill him! I want to wrap my fingers around his throat and squeeze the life out of him! But I can't…"

Henri's suffering was so great that I feared for his sanity. "What in God's name has he done?"

Henri burst into tears and could not speak for some moments. At last he said, "Father did something to Millie and I failed to protect her. Then he sent her back to London."

"Mon Dieu! What did he do?" Of course, I envisioned the worst. Millie was a very attractive young woman. "Did he rape her?"

"I don't know, Anton," he cried out. "But he did something *terrible*." He chewed on his thumb. "Who would ever want to hurt her?" He looked up defiantly. "She's an angel. I love her so much." He grasped his stomach as if he were going to be ill.

"We must speak with *les gendarmes!*"

Henri jumped up. "No! No! We cannot!" He took a huge hammer from the workbench. "I *will* kill him!" He was a thin specimen of manhood and so, little threat to his father.

I grasped his forearm and held him fast. "You will *not* kill him because I will not let you throw your life away in jail."

Henri pitched the hammer to the floor. He sank onto a stool. "Millie's gone. There's no one to make the complaint and Father's on tour for five weeks. Besides no one will believe me."

The boy's reasoning made much sense. *Les gendarmes* would pay no attention— not when they learned it was Father whose influence was legendary. Henri gnawed on his thumb. His eyes ricocheted about the shed. I dared not leave him alone.

"Henri?" I sat him down. "Tell me what happened—exactly."

His lower lip trembled and his shoulders began to shake. In so many ways he was a mere child.

"You can tell me. I swear it will remain our secret."

He shook his head violently and turned his back. "No! I cannot."

"But why?"

"It is *too* vile!"

"Likely so, but it is *his* vileness not yours." I was completely shocked at his response which told me how troubled he was. Henri was bursting apart with so many painful contradictions about his father and his art.

"Father is a great man, Anton." He pulled himself up and turned to me. "It is *I* who have misunderstood. I am *stupid.* I know nothing of these things. I cannot betray him!"

Someone should have stopped Father from coming between Henri and his art. The child was utterly defenseless because he had been taught to worship Father ever since infancy. What chance did he have? I *did* try to save the boy's art but I could not.

I tried to be patient with him. "Henri, why don't you simply tell me what you saw or heard?"

"All right, Anton. I will try," he said.

Lined up on a shelf sat a dozen or more clay pots—the kind you grow young seedlings in. Casually, Henri retrieved the hammer and smashed it down on the first clay pot. A thousand shards flew across the shed.

"One night, I found Millie lying in bed, crying. Father had just slammed the door of his study downstairs. The covers were pulled up to her chin but I could see a violent, red hand print blossoming on her face. She refused to tell me who had struck her. But there was only one possibility—Father. There was a vicious red welt on her neck."

Henri's hammer bludgeoned down on another clay pot. "Her nightie was ripped and bloody," he shouted. Then he whispered, "I had to have a plan!"

"What kind of plan?" I asked.

Henri's shoulders slumped. "It was so stupid!" he said. He took a half-hearted swipe at the next clay pot. "The next day,

I tried to drop a ball-peen hammer on his head from a ladder in his library."

"What?" Such a hammer is ridiculously small and made only for the finest of jobs. I barely contained a laugh.

"It was like trying to kill a tiger with a pop gun." Henri hung his head. "It just bounced off his head and onto the floor. It only annoyed him."

I reached over and took the hammer from him. "I'm glad that's all, Henri. You *must not* try to kill your father. You have a marvellous life ahead of you and I will not let you destroy it."

Weary from his storytelling, Anton sank to the bench. "Alexander, I have only scraped the surface of this disastrous relationship between father and son which extended over the decades." Anton nearly began to weep. "So often, I have wondered if his father had cherished his son's gifts, what heights they would have reached. Because of his father, you can hear the note of a crippled soul in his music."

"Perhaps that isn't so terrible…"

His host nodded slowly. "Yes, you may be right, Alexander." He took another cigarette which he pressed between his lips but did not light. His eyes darkened. "Now I will speak of an event occurring many years ago."

Alex was riveted by Anton's dramatic story telling. After warming himself by stamping his feet, he sat down beside him on the bench. He asked, "Did Henri tell you what his father said about Millie?"

Anton took a sharp breath as if to ease a pain in his chest. "He said that Millie had committed suicide and that somehow it was Henri's fault."

Alex said, "He didn't mention that he was blamed in any way."

Anton gave a snort. "Years later I learned that Millie was alive but Henri simply refused to believe me. He could not believe that his father would tell such a grotesque lie." Anton lit another cigarette.

He continued with his story. I was in London at the Tate to see an exhibit by the sculptor Maureen Graves, who creates very beautiful, classical work with such haunting, empty spaces within her sculptures." He gave Alex a canny look. "Have you ever seen an adult whom you have known only as a child? You instantly recognize that essential self, that essence of the much younger version. Something, whether it's a smile, a glance or inflection of voice, resides like an indelible shadow in the adult and brings back the child just as surely as if the two stood together before you. I was *absolutely* certain Maureen Graves was Henri's Millie."

"When I introduced myself to her at the reception, I asked whether she knew Henri Dumont. She startled backwards as if I had given her an electric shock. Her eyes revealed a strange mixture of anger, fear and—a frisson of delight. When I asked if she were Millicent Trump, Henri Dumont's friend, she backed away saying—*No! I know of no one by that name!*

Even though she denied it, I have no doubt she was Millicent Trump— Henri's Millie."

Anton was alarmed at Alex's pallor. "What the devil is wrong, Alexander?"

My Miss Maureen Trump has the same last name as Henri's Millicent Trump?

Alex gasped. "Did you say *Trump—Millicent Trump?*

"Yes, of course. That was the name of Henri's Millie. Why?"

For Alex, it could be another twist in a tale so convoluted as to be absolutely incredible! Such a connection could not be possible! *But wait! My Miss Trump was Maureen. A sister? But it's Maureen Graves.*

"What year did this happen?"

Anton frowned. "I'd say about 1960…"

"And she'd be thirteen or fourteen then?"

"Yes…"

"Born around 1945 or 1946?"

"Yes, that's right."

"Dear God!' Alex sank to the bench. *Was the Maureen Trump I failed to save from drowning actually the famed sculptor Maureen Graves and Millicent Trump? How can this be?* He gaped up at Anton.

Anton's alarm was growing.

"Anton," Alex said at last, "I can hardly believe this!"

"It is true my friend. The man was capable of telling any number of hurtful lies to his son. To claim that Millie had committed suicide was terrible, but the real crime was the destruction of his art."

"However, one incident gave me some hope. He wrote to me saying that he had dreamed of the most beautiful egg shape, all encrusted with jewels. It was the same *cosmic egg* which you and I have seen. That is why I painted the one you now have in your possession. It was my fervent hope that I could convince him his dream was a significant *sign* and that he must follow his own art. But I'm afraid Henri was too far gone by then."

Alexander felt his head might burst with all Anton's revelations. He sought logic to help him absorb his disparate thoughts.

His Maureen Trump, whose ashes he carried, was now at least two people and maybe a third, all in one. Was the rather unkempt elderly woman who demanded he save the child, the world renowned sculptor, Maureen Graves *and* Henri's Millie. Appearances are not always as they seem, he thought. He had never even seen a picture of Graves and so he could not know if she resembled his Miss T. He shook his head as if to consolidate his thoughts.

Anton had been muttering and clenching his fists. He jumped up to pace. Throwing up his arms, he shouted, "I curse the name of the father—*Reginald Trump.*"

Hearing the name *Reginald Trump,* Alexander saw dark shadows forming on his peripheral vision. In moments, he could scarcely breathe as if he had been kicked in the gut. Then he was swept with enervating weakness throughout his entire body. He heard his own voice saying—*but I thought the father's name was Dumont!*

Alarmed, Anton saw his guest's eyes roll upward in his head as he sank to the stone pathway—unconscious.

Anton struggled to help Alex to his feet, but it was an impossible task. Rushing across the bridge, he shouted, "Hurry! Help! Come at once Vladimir!"

The gardener and his assistant ran across the bridge. Together, they raised Alex up and half carried, half dragged

294 — MARY E. MARTIN

him to the yard and into the house. In the parlour, they laid him on the sofa and stood, caps in hand, waiting for Anton Chekhov.

Alexander's legs dangled over the end of the couch. Every muscle of his body was slack. Chekhov stood over him shaking his shoulders and pinching his face until his eyes began to open.

"Good God, Alexander! Have you seen a ghost? Do you need a doctor?"

Alexander's eyes were unfocused. With great concentration, he tried to recall the face now hanging above him. Another face appeared—a woman's. *Who can she be? She looks so kind and so worried. How have I frightened them? Oh yes! That is Anton Chekhov.* He smiled faintly, amused at the absurdity of the name. *and that is his poor wife Chloe.*

His entire body tensed. Recollection was stealing back into his mind.

Anton shook his head. "You have had some shock, Alexander?"

When Alex had heard the name *Reginald Trump,* he could scarcely catch his breath. At first, he had tried to take short, shallow gulps and then gradually tried to breathe more deeply. But then darkness had rolled in and now, somehow, now he was back in the parlour.

When he tried to sit up, Anton held his shoulder. "No…do not try to move, sir."

Alex muttered, "I could not have heard you correctly."

"Heard? Heard what?"

"The name," he said faintly. "Did you say *Reginald Trump?*"

"Yes. That was Henri's father."

Alexander was staggered. Surely, his head would burst with the incomprehensible thoughts spinning in his brain. Some sense of reality, which glued him together at the centre, had violently departed. Surely Anton must be wrong.

A strange and new reality was pressing in on him with undeniable force. *Was Miss Trump really Henri's Millie—his Beatrice? How can that be? And now she's the famous sculptor, Maureen Graves. And each July she visited Reginald Trump, whom she called 'father.'*

His brain was suspended between *fear* and *wonderment—terror* and *awe*. His mind could scarcely bear to glimpse the implications of such a conflagration of events.

At last he eased himself to a sitting position and tried his best to reason. By chance, he had met Miss Trump on the train. Circumstance had called him to try to save her life but she had refused. *And* that is where his sense of obligation had begun. He had tried his best to find her relatives. When he was unsuccessful, he had borne her ashes from Caen to Paris with no clear plan—only a sense of obligation.

But no! It was *too fantastic!* According to Henri, hadn't his Millie committed suicide at a very early age? But no! According to Anton, she was not only alive but also the renowned artist Maureen Graves.

Anton grasped his hand. "Alexander! Speak to us. You look terribly ill."

Alexander's eyes took on a frightening gleam. "But you *said* that Millie committed suicide when she was young. So she couldn't be *my* Miss Trump!"

Anton glanced at Chloe and Vladimir and shook his head. "Is he not mad?" he asked them. "Please Alexander! I already told you I saw her at the Tate calling herself Maureen Graves."

Alex looked vacantly at him. "Oh yes. You did say that. Are you absolutely sure?"

"Yes. Henri's Millie was alive and well back then."

"So she did not die an early death?"

Frowning, Anton shook his head. "You must try to understand, sir."

Burying his face in his hands, Alexander slumped back down again. In a distant voice, he said, "It is too *incredible*, Anton!" Suddenly he jumped to his feet. "Simply unbelievable!" He began to march about the parlour in circles like a man gone mad. "I must tell you my fantastic story."

"Tell me, then. What is this story? Do not keep me waiting."

"You will not believe it." Alex gave an absurd laugh.

"You *must* tell me!"

"You must not think me mad."

Anton sat down. He crossed his legs and assumed a patient air. "I will not think you mad, sir."

"Well then…where do I begin?" said Alex. He took another turn about the room. "In my suitcase back at the hotel, I carry certain ashes from a cremation."

Anton remained attentive.

"They are the ashes of Miss Maureen Trump." Alexander then related all the details of his journey which were growing more incredible by the moment. Anton sat wide-eyed in silence at the description of Alex's attempting to save Miss Trump on the ferry and his coming upon Henri in the Luxembourg café. But it was Alex's overpowering sense of being possessed which made the greatest impression on Anton.

It took only a brief moment for the significance of Alex's words to dawn upon Chekhov. He spoke calmly. "You mean that Miss Trump's spirit guided you throughout."

"That fantastic conclusion to my story is why I fainted."

"Yes, I see." Anton examined the ceiling with care and then sighed heavily. "You, Henri and I are bound together by the vision of the cosmic egg. And so it is *you*, Alexander, who have been selected to resolve this terrible situation which has lasted throughout Henri's life."

"What? How can that be?" Alex asked.

Anton shrugged. "I haven't the slightest idea, my friend. But both of us know it is so."

"What am I to do now?"

"You must return to Paris, tell Henri absolutely *everything* and, of course, give him the ashes for a proper burial. Only then will he be convinced that Millie did not commit suicide."

"But what will be his reaction?"

"He will be shocked to the very core, but it will set him free. You saw Miss Trump on the ferryboat. That much alone will prove to Henri that his father's story of Millie's suicide was yet another terrible lie to undermine his art. And if he questions that your Maureen Trump is his Millie, you must tell him I saw Millie at the Tate as Maureen Graves."

"Will you come?" Alex asked.

Chekhov shook his head. "No, my friend, this is your task and yours alone. Alas! I am too old for travel."

Alexander nodded. "All right. I'd best get going. Will your driver take me back to my hotel?"

"Yes, of course."

The two men shook hands at the front door. Anton said reverentially, "My friend, some force has sent you to us. I do not know what it is but I know that it is very powerful."

Alexander was immediately uncomfortable. He knew all too well that he was just one man with all the usual foibles and weaknesses of any human being. He had no special power to accomplish what Anton clearly hoped for. After all, how could he, a new comer on the scene, possibly unravel a lifetime of injury done by father to son?

Anton patted his hand. "I know that you doubt your abilities, Alexander, but I have faith in you."

Alex smiled weakly. "I can only try. But tell me. What about Millie?"

Anton shrugged. "What about her?"

"Won't he be grief-stricken that the love of his life—Millie, his Beatrice was alive all this time? That if he had tried to find her he likely would have succeeded?"

A slow grin broke across Anton's face. His eyes twinkled. "He'll get over it. What is a woman—no matter how attractive— next to art?" He winked, patted Alex's shoulder and said, "Let me know how it turns out."

Within the hour, Alex was in his hotel and packing. Miss Trump's ashes were carefully placed in a separate compartment of his suitcase. He said, "Miss Trump, now I am taking you home."

He got the next flight from St. Petersburg to Paris.

CHAPTER 26

Daphne opened the front door of her flat in a brownstone on the Upper West Side just off Amsterdam Avenue. Before her lay the spacious living room with two bay windows at the far end. Rays of late afternoon sun filtered through the window curtains and made the mahogany floors gleam. High ceilings were capped off with moldings and cornices and a Persian rug in gold with exotic blue and green birds lay in front of a red bricked fireplace. The classical proportions of the room gave her a sense of calm and balance. *Everything I have, I've earned myself and here it is.*

Over the mantle-piece hung two delicate, charcoal sketches of her by Alex which he had drawn on the Orient Express. Although he had created them only hours after they'd met, he had captured her essence and she was startled to be known so well. Or so it seemed. How had he done that?

It was not simple technical skill. His genius lay in his exquisitely sensitive perceptions of people and his ability to express them on paper. After all, he had captured her vulnerability and sadness which she had sought to hide. He was far more than an immensely talented artist. He was an exceptionally attuned human being. Suddenly, she grew ashamed of her earlier accusations. *He is not someone with his head in the clouds—detached, self-absorbed and uncaring. Quite the opposite.*

Daphne set out her drawing materials on the kitchen table. The window looked down on a small playground of a neighbouring park. Swings and a roundabout were fenced in with a wrought iron gate. Her eye caught the deep shadows of a gargoyle set in the brickwork above the gate still illuminated in the cold light of late afternoon. No children were playing.

After she opened her pad, she stared at the blank page trying to imagine what she could draw. Her hand hovered nervously over the empty expanse of white spread before her. *Maybe I should try to draw Alex?* Drawing any human likeness would be challenge enough! She laughed out loud to think she might capture his *essence*—whatever that might be. After a long pause, she had to admit that she had no idea how to proceed. *I'll draw that gargoyle on the far wall.*

She returned to the window with her sketch book. Alex always developed a certain rhythm when he drew and so, holding her breath, she tried to imitate his motions with her hand. The gargoyle was oval shaped. She envisioned curving lines interspersed with a few angular ones. Then she would shade in parts to create depth. She knew what she should do, but doing it was an entirely different matter.

What appeared on the page bore no resemblance to what was in her mind. A black, ballooning circle occupied most of the page. A straight black line stood for the nose. *Good grief! A kindergarten child's effort!* Surely that was simply technical skill.

But how many hours of practice would it take to make a decent drawing—hundreds if not thousands? The *artist* would have to be obsessed and totally devoted to his *art*— just like Alex. And she had wondered why he stood her up or had forgotten to call.

Once again, she thought of Alex's drawings. When she considered his talent, she began to understand his distance— that he was looking at the world from a far different perspective than everyone else. Somehow Alex breathed life into the inanimate and created his numinous light in black and white with charcoal sticks. *How can that be?*

She thought she could try a street scene and turned the page. She imagined the corner of Amsterdam Avenue and 73rd with all the little flower shops and grocery stores. First, she tried to lay down the line of the curbs and fit in the shops and people. After ten minutes of intense work, she sighed deeply. It was ridiculous! She knew perspective was the invention of the human mind transferring the three dimensional world onto a two dimensional surface. But only now did she understand how daunting that was.

Perspective. An interesting word, she thought, to be used in different senses. Everyone saw the world differently and everyone had their own way of rendering their impressions of that world. Communication of that perspective from one dimension—the mind—to another—the world, whether in words, actions or music required consummate skill if it were to be considered art. While she could envision the concept of the street clearly in her mind, her renderings were absurd. Again, there had to be single-mindedness.

Her attempts at capturing even a straight line were embarrassingly child-like. At work, she would have simply said to the art department, *I want a drawing of a street corner with lots of shops and people. Cars too.* Within an hour it would be on her desk. The draughtsman would have magically captured the idea she had expressed.

Suddenly, Mr. Dodsbury appeared in her mind—that ridiculously unpleasant man who cornered her in London. For Daphne art and creativity were necessarily a collaborative effort requiring the input of many talents. Sounding almost narcissistic, Dodsbury had romanticized the creative act to envision a lone soul labouring in the dead of night, cut off from others who might help. *Like someone who can draw!* At the time she could neither understand the man's hostility nor her anger at his views. She bent to her work again.

Outside, she heard the shouts and laugher of children and then a frightened cry. Below, she could see three boys surrounding a fourth much smaller child. One held a rock. The little child was forced up against the brick wall just below the gargoyle.

One of the bigger boys laughed, "Look! He's so scared he's going to shit his pants!"

The child cowered against the wall trying not to cry. "Lemme go!" he wailed.

Damn kids! How cruel can they be?

To Daphne's great surprise, an image floated up in her mind's eye. She could see it in stark relief. It was that iconic painting by Pablo Picasso, *Guernica.* Unused to having pictures suddenly appear before her, she wondered at the connection with the boys now taunting the kid.

Picasso painted it in 1937 in protest against the bombardment of that small town of Guernica in his homeland, Spain, by German and Italian planes in support of the governing forces. Why did it appear to her at this moment? Of course! Beneath her, children were acting with great cruelty which could never be dismissed as just a kid's prank. But children were not alone in their guilt. Nations destroyed innocent civilians and their towns.

Daphne did not usually involve herself in the lives of strangers. But she threw open the window and shouted into the playground.

"Stop that right now! Leave that boy alone or I'll call the police."

The boys stopped and looked up. Daphne had feared her intervention might make matters worse but fortunately the biggest one shrugged and muttered, "Okay, lady!" Then the others sidled off.

She spoke kindly to the little boy. "Do you want to go out the front way so they don't see you?"

He nodded solemnly up at her.

"Wait there and I'll let you out to the street through the front gate."

Within minutes Daphne was downstairs and asked him, "What's your name? Are you okay? Do you want me to call your Mom?"

The little boy shook his head and darted down the laneway to the street.

Upstairs, Daphne put on a pot of coffee and closed up her sketch book. *Amazing! That is the first time I've actually had something like a vision. Is that what Alex is always talking about?* She felt oddly pleased but was not sure why.

Definitely, she was glad she had stepped in. The cruelty of children—no, the cruelty of human beings—was *ever* present. But kindness and compassion were also part of human nature. Why was one alive in a person and not the other? *And* she

was undoubtedly intrigued with her thought that linked art
to life—*her* life. It was a perspective that she had never before
considered. Is that, she wondered, what Alex experiences when
his head is in the clouds?

She looked down at her hands. "My God! They're all
blackened with charcoal!" She sighed and rubbed her nose.
Moments later, when washing her hands, she saw the black
smudges all over her face. *Why am I doing this? I can't draw!
And I don't want to try.*

In the kitchen she picked up the drawing sheets from the
floor and crumpled them up for the garbage. *I was his muse not
the artist!*

Suddenly, Daphne was overtaken with a yearning so strong
that she sank to the chair at the kitchen table. Staring out
the window, she realized how much she missed being the
inspiration for Alex's work. *If I can inspire him, why can't I be
a part of his work in some way?* She missed Alex terribly—even
just the part of him he chose to share.

She thought of her own world of advertising. *We sell the
illusion of happiness. Buy this or that and you will be happy.* But
it was more than that. It was the illusion that there was some
ideal life one could attain—one in which floors were always
sparkling and skin was always soft and wrinkle free. But that,
of course, was not reality yet it was the most powerful selling
tool on the planet. *How sad!* We are dream peddlers.

Daphne had always regarded advertising as an art form.
But when it had such a commercial purpose, how could it be?
With Alex she could be a part of a lifelong exploration of his
talents and art. For that to happen, she realized she would have
to share him with whomever was his current muse.

With Brad, she would spend her life engaged in the creating, packaging and selling of an *ideal* life which did not actually exist. The choice was between the excitement of the truly creative act and comfort and security

CHAPTER 27

That evening, Rinaldo mounted the steps of Piccadilly Tube station and, with a patronizing air, sauntered to the statue of *Anteros*. Glancing about furtively, he then donned his Fool's mask as instructed. After several moments, he tore it off. Too stuffy!

This People's Art group is strictly amateur. No concept has been stated. These kids know nothing about conceptual art.

He spied Krysta walking across the plaza toward him. He couldn't understand how she made him feel. Something about her pulled him in. Was it the way the corner of her mouth turned down when she smiled? When they lay in bed, she would curl around him while he stroked her hair. Was this love? It was fucking scary! He *never* let his guard down and now he felt naked. As she approached, he jumped up, grinned and waved.

She was followed by five other people whom she shouted at from time to time over her shoulder. Looking sombre and dedicated to their task, they encircled him.

"So, you came, Rinaldo! We thought you might chicken out." She grinned at him. "So where's your Fool's mask?"

He caught his breath. She was gorgeous—even when she yelled like a drill sergeant.

He reached for her hand. "I wouldn't miss a minute of your performance project," he said softly. When he looked deeply into her eyes, he felt his stomach sink and his heart thump. It was ridiculous, he thought. *Profane and sacred—all in one!*

"So…Rinaldo, what do you think we should be doing?" she asked.

"What? This is your project—not mine, my lovely."

Krysta gave a dramatic shrug. "Okay. So, where's your mask? Put it on."

Later, Rinaldo reflected that he should have sensed something. He would have been on his guard, if his mind hadn't been so clouded with *lust*. He acknowledged, with just touch of pride, that sexual prowess was his greatest, most vital attribute. But it could also be his downfall. He was blinded to her tone, which was almost a bark.

The others donned their masks. Rinaldo struggled with his so much that Krysta had to help him. He was encircled by the *King and Queen of Pentacles, Temperance and Death, The Tower and the Knight of Wands.*

Two of them grasped his arms and sat him down on the edge of the fountain. Just as the sun dropped behind the buildings, two men with camera equipment and lights appeared out of nowhere. They positioned themselves ten feet away and focused the lights on him.

Backing off, Krysta called out, "Darling, get your mask on and look over this way."

Somebody said, "So...we're about to interview the *Fool* of Piccadilly. Are you ready, Rinaldo?"

Rinaldo nodded. As an artist, he was used to at least a modicum of respect. Usually he was the *mocker*, the *inquisitor*. Consequently, he expected to be addressed in respectful tones.

The first question was shouted out at him. "Don't you think conceptual art is outdated, Rinaldo? A hang-over from the last century for old guys like you?"

Rinaldo's eyes nearly popped out from behind his mask. "What? Of course not! Conceptual art is in the vanguard. It is the representational painters who are stranded in the mists of time!"

"But *Fool* don't you realize that art is a living thing? It's grown and moved on from the nonsense of dressing up some ill thought out ideas and parading them about as the latest avant-guard thinking. Isn't most of it just silliness and cheap tricks?"

Rinaldo snatched off his mask. When he shielded his eyes against the camera lights, he acquired a cringing look for the internet's eternity.

Further back in the crowd, guffaws could be heard and then a voice rang out, "Who's the old fart anyway?"

Rinaldo strove to maintain his icy superiority. "Don't be ridiculous! Only the hopelessly old fashioned have failed to move beyond hanging pretty, bourgeois pictures on walls and calling them art." Focused close up on his face, the cameras caught the disturbingly feral look of a cornered animal.

"Why do you call your so-called performances art? What meaning did your Piccadilly Circus event have?"

Rinaldo was pleased. Now he had a chance to explain to these children what real art was all about. "It's all about— *fucking*," he began with a grin on his face.

The crowd broke into gales of laughter. "What? Has the old fart lost it? Is he demented, a senile old man?"

The word *demented* infuriated Rinaldo. He lurched forward to yank the camera away from the man. "You heard me, you little shit!"

Unfortunately, the lens captured Rinaldo's face in an explosion of furious red. It was the perfect image for a cartoon of an insane old man, which in seconds was launched into the twitterverse.

"Now in the twenty-first century, don't you think an artist must not only have a couple of ideas but also real craft and skill? How can you possibly describe your work as craft?"

Later, Rinaldo wondered—*why didn't I just get up and leave?* He had no answer. He had let them provoke him into lashing out. The last image on You Tube was his tearing off his mask to reveal a face consumed with rage.

"You fucking idiots!" he roared as he tried to wrest the camera from the stupid kid. "Concept in art is *everything*. Without that, you have *nothing!*"

Rinaldo should have known that models and muses were essentially stupid and should never be allowed to influence the artist. The fury now consuming him blotted any love he might have felt. And yet, as he hurried from Piccadilly, he looked over his shoulder. When he saw Krysta gently kissing the guy with the camera, memory of her soft hand on his dick sliced through his heart. In confusion, he ran for the tube station. Violent thoughts of sex inflamed him and yet—he could not forget the sweetness of her smile and soft laugh. *Jesus Christ, if this is love, I'm in hell!*

Within twenty four hours, the video had half a million hits on You Tube. The most memorable moment was when he punched the guy operating the camera lights. For another twenty four hours he laid low half expecting the cops at his door.

CHAPTER 28

During the flight from St. Petersburg, Alex had swung from a state of awe and elation to a murky, frightening sense that inexplicable forces had taken him over. So overwhelmed was he that he only dared glimpse the events which defied any rational explanation. Until speaking with Anton, he could not have guessed the ashes, he felt compelled to carry, were to be delivered to Henri. Miss Trump's presence in his life, while extremely unusual, had seemed completely unrelated to the main task with Anton, Henri and the cosmic egg. How could it have occurred to him that she was destined to return to Henri, her teenaged lover?

At seven pm. Alex posted himself at the baggage carousel in the great hall of Charles De Gaulle airport. It was now seven thirty and his luggage had not appeared. Dwarfed by the darkening, cavernous space, the remaining passengers floated about like disembodied spirits, watching the few unclaimed bags parade solemnly past. Alex's bag was charcoal gray and looked like any other. When the next one toppled onto the conveyor belt, he held his breath. It was not his. He waited five more minutes in hopes that another would drop onto the belt, but his bag did not appear. *Where in God's name are Miss Trump's ashes?*

As he strained to see his bag, suddenly he whispered, "*Jesus Christ!* I don't believe it! Another revelation!"

Millicent Trump most definitely regarded Reginald Trump as her father. *And* so did Henri!" His name *Dumont* must have come from the mistress Miss T mentioned. He sank to a nearby bench. His thoughts were so garbled that he had not taken it in. Henri and Millie were *half brother and sister!* Had Millie realized the relationship? Where did that leave Henri? Surely he must be told. Or should he?

In retrospect, it seemed as if he had been driven to accomplish a mystical purpose totally beyond his abilities. Now the return of the ashes might be thwarted by a mundane event—the loss of luggage. As if waking frozen from a nightmare, he could scarcely move. But then flames of panic shot through him and he tried to breathe.

The vast, nearly deserted concourse, was shrouded in evening gloom. If he squinted he could read a neon sign on a kiosk on the far side of the building marked *Baggage Claims.* He began his trek. Five minutes later, he stood in front of the counter to find no attendant in sight. After searching his pockets, he retrieved his claim ticket and rapped on the glass partition.

A thin-lipped bureaucrat stuck his head out from behind a door.

"Oui?"

Alex was not as fluent in French as he wished. However, once the clerk made his inquiries, Alex learned that his bag was still in St. Petersburg but would be on the first flight next day landing at eight am.

He began to relax a little. Surely in the morning he would have the ashes and would see Henri. There was no point going into Paris. He phoned the nearest airport hotel and got a room.

In the hotel, fumbling with his key card, he opened his door and entered. Immediately, the walls seemed to close in on him. The room wasn't *that* small, but a sense of claustrophobia swept over him. He sank to the bed. Fortunately, he had stopped at the store off the lobby and gotten toothpaste and a brush, a razor and shaving cream. After a hot shower, he realized he was hungry and ordered a sandwich and coffee from the kitchen.

He switched on the television but almost immediately turned it off. He wanted someone to talk to, not someone talking *at* him.

The leering face of Anton Chekhov floated into his mind. "*A woman?*" the man had crowed. "You must allow *no one* to come between you and your art. You, Alexander Wainwright, are on a spiritual journey of the greatest importance. You yearn to express your *light* through new, abstract forms of the greatest beauty. A *woman* will only distract you from the tasks demanded by your daemon."

Sadly, Alex reflected upon Daphne. What kind of fool was he? How could Anton be right? Must he set aside all human feeling to be an artist? It made no sense. Surely one could argue the reverse—that love enriched art and that one could not achieve greatness without the human aspect of true love.

He chuckled. "Where are you now, Miss Trump? Now that I need you?"

It was absurd, but throughout the trip, he had felt as if she were his stalwart companion, always by his side—guiding and giving advice. Now, she was back in St. Petersburg—alone and abandoned. And so was he. He wanted to ask her how Henri would react to the news and whether he should tell him of the relationship between them. Would she have told him? Apparently Henri did not know. Any reaction was possible.

He nearly laughed out loud. The situation was like a skit from the theatre of the absurd in which the main actor, Miss Trump, had wandered off stage, but somehow hovered in the background pulling the strings like a puppeteer. Although little time had been spent in conversation on the train or boat, he could hear each tone and inflection of her voice intimately in his ear. At first he had dismissed her as a rather dim and garrulous old woman, but soon realized her great contrasts. Thinking of the few details of her past, he concluded he could not possibly have guessed the connection. The more he thought about her, the lonelier he became.

Just as he began to pace the narrow confines of his room, he heard a gentle tap at the door. Expecting the waiter, he threw open the door.

She was not tall. She was not beautiful but there was an indefinable comeliness and courtesy to her.

Automatically, he took a deep breath. "Thank you. Please. You can set the tray on the night table."

She smiled a tentative smile.

He looked beyond her into the hall. There was no tray or food.

Confused, he asked, "May I help you?"

She walked past him into the room.

Although he was greatly surprised, he could not help being intrigued. Obviously it was foolhardy to let a stranger into his room, but her smile disarmed him and she was scarcely threatening in any way.

"Again, Miss? What can I do for you? Why are you here?"

She sat down on the bed. "Don't worry. I've been paid for."

"What?" The softness of her voice set him on edge. "This is ridiculous. You must have come to the wrong room. I didn't request…" He wondered just how old she was. He remained standing. "Listen, you really must leave. I'm expecting some dinner."

She shrugged. "It doesn't really matter, but I'd like to stay. I'm hungry too."

He looked more closely at her. She was rather thin. In fact, with closer attention, he saw that she was weary and perhaps a little frightened.

He shook his head. "I'm sorry but I still don't understand. Who sent you here?"

She shrugged again. "They make the arrangements downstairs. Then I just go to the room they tell me."

He put his hand on the doorknob. "There's obviously been a mistake. Please. You'd better go down and find out where you're supposed to be."

He caught the fear in her eyes.

"Please. They don't like it if I cause trouble." Her hands twisted in her lap.

"Trouble? But if they sent you to the wrong room, it's not your fault. Besides someone else will be expecting you."

A rap came at the door. She jumped up and ran into the bathroom. Alex opened the door. It was the food. The waiter set it out and Alex signed the bill.

After the waiter left, Alex knocked on the bathroom door. "You can come out now," he said.

She slipped out back into the room. Again, she sat on the bed and looked hungrily at the tray.

Alex sighed. "Would you like some coffee and part of the sandwich? It's tuna, I think."

She hesitated but then nodded eagerly.

He poured the coffee and gave her half the sandwich. "What's your name?"

"Liz."

"Do you have a last name?"

"Peacock."

"Hmmm."

They ate hungrily.

"Who are you so afraid of?" Alex was not sure he wanted to know.

"Oh, the manager and the desk clerk."

"You mean they sent you?"

She gave a brief nod. "This way," she pointed at the food, "I can at least get a break and..." She drank the coffee. "If you want, we can..."

Alex shook his head. "No, that's not necessary. But thank you, anyway." He was worried another person might come to the room looking for her. Suddenly, he smiled. "Actually, I was just thinking I could use someone to talk to."

"Really?" She looked at him with what he thought was genuine interest.

"Yes. I'm waiting for my bag, which is stuck in St. Petersburg. It's supposed to be on the first morning flight."

She nodded.

He heard himself say, "There's something very important in the bag. I simply can't afford to lose it."

"What is it?"

"Ashes."

Her eyes widened. "You mean a cremation?"

"Yes."

"A close relative?"

He shook his head. "No."

She tucked her feet underneath her and settled back on the bed. "So are you going to tell me the story or not?"

Alex was surprised to hear the words tumbling from his mouth. After five minutes of talking, he finally said, "I don't understand any of this. But I'm worried about Henri and how he'll react to it. *And* whether I should tell him the part about her being his half-sister?"

She spoke quietly. "It's such a *romantic* story!"

When she looked up at him, he saw the tears in her eyes.

"You never hear of love like that anymore. Not one that lasts for years and years. Everybody's out for what they can get for themselves and right now."

Alex was intrigued. "I suppose you're right…"

"Think about it. Henri's loved this woman his *whole, entire* life even though he's never had a chance to be with her because of that horrible father."

"True enough…"

"He's even given up his *music* because of that cruel man! His father has stolen his life!" She gnawed on a fingernail. "I'll bet he's overcome with *joy* when you tell him."

"Really? Why?"

"Sure! It shows she was finally coming back to him—even as an old woman. That's got to be the most romantic thing I've ever heard! Love that lasts a lifetime—against all odds. Nobody does that these days. It's *real* special." She slid off the bed. "Oh, and *no*. You shouldn't tell Henri she was his sister."

She bunched her hands together like a small child. "Look. I really gotta go. They'll be looking for me by now."

At the door, she offered her hand. "It's been a real pleasure listening to your story Mr. Wainwright."

Alex smiled. She wanted him to think well of her—that she was a person of breeding, intelligence and compassion—which she most definitely was. The importance to her of that nearly broke his heart. He watched her walk to the lift. He was sure she was right. Henri would be overjoyed as long as he didn't tell him everything.

Back in the concourse the following morning, Alex was relieved to see his bag tumble onto the carousel. He hurried to a corner and opened it. Yes, there it was! The rude little box with the ashes inside. Realizing he had never opened it before, he did so now. What had he expected? Certainly not fragments of bone. Still, he dared not reach out and touch them. Happily, he closed up the box and his case and found a taxi into Paris.

PARIS

CHAPTER 29

When he arrived at the Hotel des Fleurs, Alexander hoped he could reach Henri right away. But as he entered his room, he was suddenly swept with a wave of weariness, so strong it forced him onto the bed. His head pounded as he shut his eyes against the dull light seeping in through the curtains. He got up and closed them tightly. *This is not my light!*

On the periphery of his vision, he saw tiny stars of light. Dark, shifting shapes and shadows seemed to gather ominously at the corners of the room. *What is wrong with me?* Over the last week, he had slept poorly and now his travels were taking their toll. In addition, he could not escape Miss T who, having invaded him, now marched him about. *I must finish the job!*

He called Henri on his mobile. "Henri?"

"So! You're in Paris?" said Henri.

Alex was taken aback by the underlying hostility in his tone.

"Yes. And I need to see you."

"Just because you've seen Anton, I'm supposed to drop everything and run to hear his great thoughts and critical opinions?"

"But it's important, Henri." Alex hesitated. "You need to know what I've learned and I have something you *must* see."

From the other end of the line came grumbling and then a sigh. "All right. But I'm in rehearsal all day."

"Really? That's wonderful."

"You thought I'd just sit around until you and Anton figured out my life for me?" Henri gave a harsh laugh. "I leave those kinds of questions up to my analyst."

Alex frowned at his phone. This was not the Henri he had expected. He said, "No, of course not. But I'm happy to hear you're playing."

"Come over at five for drinks. We can talk then." Henri hung up.

Alex threw open the curtains. He stared at the box of ashes now sitting on the desk. "Well, Miss Trump, *that* was a surprise! I didn't know he was so angry with Anton." He sighed. "But don't worry! I'll take you to him." He longed to return to London.

Alex sat down on the bed and continued to address Miss Trump. "Remember how you said to look beneath the surface? That's what I've done and what I see is *very* ugly."

He got up to pace but stopped in mid-step. "How will Henri react to this news about his—*your* father?" Suddenly he realized that, until now, he had been thinking only of Henri. But Miss Trump had been violated as much, if not more, than Henri. As a young girl, poor Millie undoubtedly had suffered untold horrors at her father's hands. "I'm *so* sorry Miss T! Here I've been thinking only of Henri. You probably know better than anyone what an utter monster he was." He stared at the container as if expecting a response. Although the room remained silent, at that moment, he was swept with a sense of calm and renewed energy.

Even though it was well before lunch, he was hungry. He phoned the kitchen for sandwiches and a pot of tea.

For the next twenty minutes, he fiddled with his drawing materials and looked out the window. From his vantage point, he had a view of the streets running down to the Seine where Notre Dame stood off in the distance. The clouds had blown off and the streets were drenched in sun and shadow.

Once, in his youth, Alex had photographed Notre Dame and its reflection in the water. It was at six o'clock in the morning when the waters of the Seine were entirely still. Partygoers still lounged in gowns and tuxedos at a corner café. The church was perfectly mirrored in the shimmering light of the new dawn—as if an *ideal* image of all churches ever constructed by man had miraculously broken through from an unseen world to grace the river and all of Paris.

At that hour, no tourist craft plied the waters and so the clarity of the image remained perfect. But when the motors growled, breaking the silence of the city, the boats slipped from their moorings. In the early morning light, the flawless reflection of Notre Dame—insubstantial as a dream— wavered and then broke apart in the expanding ripples. Just as his cosmic egg had dissipated before his eyes, the daily activity on the river dissolved that perfect image into thousands of tiny pieces.

Alex opened the window. Like an explorer peering with his eyeglass from his ship, he whispered, "There must be an opening—a channel to that other place where I'll find my light. I *know* it's there!"

When there was knock at the door, Alex opened it. A white-coated waiter, frail and stooped, stood before him tray in hand. The man blinked his watery eyes and moved stiffly into the room as if his every joint and fibre screamed in pain. Near the door, a corner of the rug was curled up.

Alex hastened to help the man. "Let me take it, monsieur."

The waiter's jaw jutted out. Intent upon performing his duties, he veered away sharply. His shoe caught the corner of the rug. He began to stumble and the tray began to tip. The pot of tea and plate of sandwiches careened downward. Alex grabbed for them but was too late. The entire contents of the tray clattered to the floor and shards of china and glass exploded on the hardwood.

Amazing! One small pot of tea seemed to flood an entire hotel room floor. The smashed pieces and were now strewn across the carpet.

A look of abject horror came over the waiter's face. "Mon Dieu!" he whispered.

"It's only tea and sandwiches, monsieur," said Alex as he bent to gather the biggest pieces of the pot.

The waiter crouched down painfully. "I will lose my job!"

"Surely not!"

"Oui, monsieur...!" The man said no more but hastened to gather the stray pieces and pile them on the tray. He shook his head. "They are *most* severe about breakage in this hotel."

"But I'll tell no one. You needn't be frightened. I'll pay for this and another tray."

The waiter's eyes bulged as he gazed up at Alex. "It brings terrible luck, sir, when order turns to chaos. It foretells much!"

"What? Order to chaos?" Alex began to laugh. "Surely we can create some order by getting another tray!" But then he stopped as he saw the man's face turn white. He reached for his wallet. "Listen, you go down and get me more tea and sandwiches."

"Two trays?"

Alex laughed. "Yes! I'm very hungry! I'll clean this up and tell the front desk I knocked it over. They'll not charge a guest." He winked at the old man and said, "Go on now. More tea please."

Scarcely believing his luck, the old man scurried from the room.

Alexander stationed himself at the window with his sketchpad and charcoal sticks in hand. He reflected that he was viewing a picture postcard of Paris—an idealized image every tourist would carry within himself whenever he thought of the city. Cream coloured facades of hotels and shops were topped by green mansard roofs with dormer windows and every one of the buildings was decorated with faux balconies and flowerpots. The streets sloped gently downward to the Seine giving a view of kiosks and souvenir shops lining the walkway along the river.

Suddenly, he was filled with a sense of accomplishment. He turned back into the room. "Well, Miss Trump. Our journey is almost done. Tonight we will go to Henri's. Did you love him as much as he loved you? I'll be sad to be parted from you."

He looked out the window again and then blinked. The view of the Parisian streets was changing. He squinted. His street scene, which he had intended to sketch, seemed to melt before his very eyes like a clock in a Dali painting. *What is happening to my eyes?*

"My God!" he breathed. He reached for his sketchpad and then froze. The street scene had vanished. *I must be exhausted or is it some strange trick of light?* His head had begun to pound again.

No longer did he see Paris of just moments ago. The scene appeared to be dissolving into a grey *nothingness.* First he feared he might be losing his vision to stroke but he dismissed that possibility. He sat transfixed as if peering into Miss Trump's *empty spaces.* For a second he hoped his pure *light* might fill up the vista, but then a look of terror overtook his face.

"What is *happening?*" he called out in a querulous voice and then he trembled to see what was to be revealed. Order *was* turning to chaos—or so it seemed.

Beneath his window appeared, as far as the horizon, immeasurable miles of craters and canyons so broad and deep they had no end or bottom. Arid clouds of red dust rose up and nearly choked him. *No one has ever seen such a landscape.* At once he knew it was a vast and *empty* ocean where no light could ever penetrate the cavernous depths. "No! It is against nature!" he cried.

Struck with terror, his mind and spirit rebelled. "This cannot be!"

He saw ancient ruins from some age not remembered by humankind and made barren by foreign, hostile forces. Some animating spirit had been withdrawn from the world and now a greyish pall settled over his vision. He nearly wept in the knowledge he would not see his *light* appear before his eyes.

He turned back into the room and said to Miss Trump, "Can you see this? Please help me?" With a fearful shudder, he stuck his head out the window again to see anew. Soft *light*—it seemed to come from within himself— spread before him and filled the dark, unending craters. But then, he nearly laughed in delight to see new buds of greenery gracing the hollows and crevices of the canyons. He knew water would soon flow again. He sighed deeply in relief.

He sank to a chair to savour the knowledge that the light *did* come from within himself. Rinaldo was right. *My light does not come from behind or beneath my fields and streams. It comes only from within me. It is what I put into my art.*

At first Alexander grinned and then he laughed until he heard the knock at the door. In confusion, he answered. It was a much younger waiter who entered the room with tea and sandwiches. No words were spoken.

When he had left, Alex ate hungrily and poured the tea. He remembered to call the kitchen to ask them to clear away the broken teapot and plate. He closed the curtains of the room and fell onto the bed into a deep sleep for several hours.

When Alex did wake up, he addressed Miss Trump. "Did you know that Henri said you were that little shard of heavenly light piercing straight into his heart? You were his Beatrice." When he had spoken, that sense of calm descended upon him again.

For the rest of the day, Alex wandered the streets of Paris pondering this thought. *The most important ingredient in a work of art is what the artist puts in it—of himself.*

CHAPTER 30

J ust before five o'clock, Alexander entered the narrow streets of Île de la Cité on the way to Henri's apartment. At the door, Henri was distracted if not outright unfriendly.

After pouring the wine, he said, "So, Alex, what did my dear friend Anton tell you about me that made this meeting so urgent?"

Surprised at the tone, Alex decided to proceed with care. He had rehearsed the telling of his story and visualized presenting him with the box of ashes—almost as a great gift. But, not even having been offered a chair, he stood marooned in the middle of the living room. Something was very wrong. There had been no prior hint from Henri of any hostility between Anton and himself—at least none that he could think of.

He tried to frame an answer to the question. "About you? No, Henri. Nothing he said caused me to hurry back. Anton simply spoke of your very great talent and how it had been— what shall I say—derailed. And that both of you had seen the cosmic egg. That's what lay behind his gift of the painting to you.

Henri smiled bitterly. "Oh yes! And that I was a fool to allow another human being, namely Father, to come between me and my exalted musical talent! Did he send you to save my artistic soul?"

"Actually, he said that to me about my work." Alex, tired of standing, found a seat.

"What the *great* artist fails to realize is that not all of us are withered souls like he is. That it is perfectly normal for anyone to want and need love. If he had his way, we would be either monks or fucking our brains out without the slightest bit of love or care for anyone.

Alex could scarcely think of a response. He set his wine glass down with care. Indeed, Henri was right. That was exactly what Anton thought…what he preached in a sort of spiritual gospel. Not wishing to antagonize Henri, Alex spoke softly. "Henri, I agree with you and not Anton. But that's not why I've come in such a rush."

"No? What then?"

Alex had already decided to tell his story without mentioning Millicent Trump's name until near the end. That way he could place a hint here and there which might make Henri ask questions. He could always abort the telling if Henri reacted badly at any point.

"If you'll be patient with me," he said, "I have a rather long story to tell you, which I hope you'll benefit from hearing. You may scarcely believe me because it is so incredible."

Henri had already sat down. He looked up with mild interest. "Tell me then. What is so *incroyable?*"

"Henri, do you believe in the possibility of events coming together in a way that means something special, so special you might think there was a message of some kind? Or would you just write it off as—freak *chance?*"

Henri shrugged. "Depends. I haven't had that happen very much."

Alex was pleased. At least the man was not discounting the possibility of such events. "As I was coming by ferry from Portsmouth to Caen, I met an elderly woman who had not been in Paris for many years. Actually, she struck up a conversation with me on the train down from London. I didn't see her until later on board where she was having her fortune read by a woman with a small baby."

Henri had begun to fidget.

"Unfortunately, in the night the ship hit something, filled up with water and nearly keeled over. This elderly woman was in a cabin near me and, when I tried to save her in chest high water, she pushed me away and insisted that I save the fortune teller and her baby. It was very sad because she had told me she was returning to Paris to find an old love she had not seen for many years."

Henri glanced up at him sharply.

"I did manage to get the woman and her baby to safety, but when I came back for her, she fought me off again and drowned."

"I'm sorry Alex you weren't able to save her, but what on earth does this have to do with me?"

"Please? Just hear me out. It's important. I promise you'll see."

Henri nodded.

"In Caen, I felt responsible for her remains. In fact, I simply had to be sure proper arrangements were made for her. And so, I took her ashes with me," he whispered and then he shook his head. "There was absolutely no record of any next of kin."

Henri's eyebrows shot up. "I'm sorry, but still I don't see…"

"This woman said that, as a child, she visited Paris from London only in July."

Slowly, Henri turned his head toward the light from the window.

His face grew taught. He blinked as if trying to focus on something at a great distance. "How old was this woman?" he asked.

"Around seventy, I think."

Henri frowned in recollection. "Did she tell you her name?"

Catching the edge in Henri's voice, Alex slowed the telling of the story. "I think she used several names and so…"

Henri drummed his fingers impatiently. "I'm sorry Alex but I just don't…"

Alex held up his hand. "Please just listen." Henri's eyes had begun to dart about the room. Alex was unsure about continuing.

"Well? Go on!"

"On the train, she said her trip was to reunite with the once young man she stayed with back then on those visits."

Henri muttered a word or two. Alex strained to hear.

"It is not possible…" Henri whispered.

Alexander waited.

Henri jumped to his feet. His voice cracked. "What in hell is this about, Alex?"

"Please! I will tell you. But first, here's the strangest part. Although I've been compelled to carry these ashes from Caen

332 — M A R Y   E .   M A R T I N

to Paris and then to St. Petersburg, I hadn't the slightest idea why. But now I do."

"What names did this woman give you?" Looking sicker by the moment, Henri whispered, "Did she say where she stayed?"

Alexander nodded slowly. "She told me her name was Maureen Trump."

Henri shrank back as if struck by a hammer.

Alex hesitated, "Henri, I learned her other name was Millicent Trump—Millie."

Henri's face seemed to cave in upon itself. "Jesus…" he whispered.

"Anton told me she was Millicent Graves, the famous sculptor."

Henri seemed not to have heard him. A look of revulsion passed over his face. He rose from his chair and towered over Alex. "And why couldn't you save her? Dear God! If she was my Millie…"

Alex had always felt sick at failing to save her. "Henri, believe me I tried with all my might, but she demanded I go to the woman with the baby."

Henri sank to his chair. "No," he groaned. "Why do you torture me with this? It is not possible! I was told years ago that Millie committed suicide. Dead for years."

"Who told you that?"

With an agonized cry, Henri slammed his fist on the table. "Father! And he said I was to blame!"

It was worse than Alex could have imagined. The father had not only lied but had blamed the son for something that had never happened.

"Anton saw her as Millicent Graves at the Tate twenty years ago."

Tears streamed down Henri's face. "Where are the ashes now? Do you have them with you?"

Alexander nodded. He reached for his satchel. "Yes. They are here." He took out the rude wooden box and placed it on the table between them.

Stunned, Henri remained motionless for long moments not knowing what to do. Then weeping, he sank to his knees. With one tentative finger, he reached out and gently touched the box. A long groan escaped him as if his own soul had departed. He stroked the edge of the box and touched it to his cheek. "Millie!"

Alexander held his breath while Henri's became harsh. His eyes blazed insanely. He leapt to his feet. "Yes! Yes! He stole my art but he took something far more important." He looked at Alex in desperation as if he could provide answers. "He killed any chance of love in my life! When he said she was dead, he killed my Millie!"

Henri strode to the piano. His hands scrabbled across the surface until he grasped the metronome. In rage, he picked it up and flung it at the window overlooking Notre Dame and the Seine. Such force had overtaken him that the glass shattered and the metronome flew outside.

He was not finished. He ran to the floor to ceiling book shelves —the ones which contained his father's music folios. As if possessed by other worldly strength, he tried to rip those shelves from the wall. As he pulled at the wooden slats, he shook himself more than the shelves. Of course, he could not dislodge them.

Sobbing he pried each folio loose and, one by one, yanked them from the shelves. As he dumped the folios on the floor, he cried out, sometimes only great, guttural sounds and sometimes curses upon the head of the father. "Goddamn your soul to hell!"

His agony was excruciating. At last, his energy was spent and he collapsed onto the pile of folios.

Alexander sat quietly for long moments. The story explained a great deal about Henri Dumont, whom he had found at first so inexplicably contradictory. No wonder the son would rarely speak ill of a father who had terrorized him all his life and reduced him to a non-entity.

Henri stood up and kicked the folios away. "No, you do not understand, Alex. He waved his arm over the volumes tossed about him. "That is my work. Each and every goddamned note. Not his!"

"Really? But you said…"

Henri shook his head violently. "It was my penance! He cursed me—

his own son."

"Penance? For what?"

"For pushing him down the stairs and kicking his head. It was my penance! He cursed me—his own son."

Henri sank to a nearby chair. With supreme effort, he fought to regain some control of his torrent of emotion. "You do not understand, Alex! One night, in hopes of reconciliation with Father, I invited him to my apartment for dinner—a tiny place on the second floor of 41 Rue de Rivoli." A calm descended upon Henri.

After we had eaten I cleared away the plates. Father sat back and puffed on his cigar.

He asked, "Do you remember that pretty little girl who used to visit in July? What was her name?"

Trying to be non-committal and hide the depth of my passion, I said, "Millie? Yes, she was very nice. But I always wondered, Father, why you sent her back to London that summer when I was fifteen. You never told me why."

The lizard-like glimmer in his eye instantly confirmed all my worst suspicions.

"Did she do something? What went wrong?"

Suddenly, his face grew ashen and he trembled with rage. "What the hell did you think you were doing by dropping that fucking hammer on my head?" He reached up and felt his skull. *Stupide!*"

So, the question was out in the open. "What did you do to Millie? She was bruised and beaten when you had just left her room. What in hell were you doing there anyway?"

"*Merdre!* You little turd!" he bellowed. Then he drew himself up. "Are you accusing me of impropriety?"

I simply stared at him and then said, "What were you doing in her room? Why did you attack her?"

The monster hesitated. But, as usual, he was about to bully me into submission. Once again, I was astounded to witness that lizard-like glimmer. He could not hide his true *evil*. Then his face began to crinkle into something akin to smile—of a man about to take another man into his sly world of confidence.

He regarded me from beneath lowered lids and sighed. "Millie was a very beautiful young girl. You know, a real *woman!*"

He might as well have punched me in the gut. The periphery of my vision grew a violent red and I struggled for air.

I stood over Father. "Go on!" I shouted, even though I knew another word from him would push me into the abyss where I would have no control whatsoever. Because I am not a violent man, I wanted the provocation to justify what I did next.

Father grinned up at me. "Sometimes she invited me to her room."

Insane fury raced through my entire being. I shouted, "You vile, disgusting excuse for a human being! I should have beaten your fucking brains out with that hammer!" Father blanched. It was extremely gratifying to see real fear in his eyes.

Father is at least five inches taller than me and almost forty pounds heavier. I must have been fuelled with every ounce of adrenalin a human body can produce. He stood up. The dinner table was positioned not six feet from the staircase. I leaned back and then threw all my weight into his stomach. He staggered backwards.

I will always remember the shock in his eyes as if he believed me incapable of such an action. *No balls,* he was fond of saying. He tumbled backwards down all thirteen steps. His body, in flight, was like an awkward, graceless bird. He bounced and twisted his way down each step and lay in a still and silent heap at the bottom.

I raced to him torn between fear and hope that he was dead.

"Father! Are you all right." He lay perfectly still. His nose was bloodied. I could not tell if he were breathing.

"You little *motherfucker!*" he groaned.

Slowly I rose up. Deliberately and coldly, I administered two hard kicks to each side of his head—right at the temples.

Then I raised my boot and I stamped on both of his hands. I said, "The shove was for the music and the art but the kicks are for Millie."

Although I am not a violent man, I felt entirely justified in my actions. Throughout the years, Father had slowly and painfully castrated me. With my actions, retribution had been meted out. His hands and fingers were broken and twisted. Now his eyes were shut, but he was still breathing. When he opened his eyes, one at a time, some combination of hatred and fear shone through. But I like to think there was a new element—*respect*.

I called the ambulance and accompanied him to the hospital. Hours later the doctor spoke with me. Because he would never admit that I had beaten him, I thought Father would never accuse me publicly.

The doctor said, "He's had a very bad fall. There are breaks in the fingers of the right hand and his left wrist is shattered. Also, he may be concussed. We will observe him for a few days and then— if all goes well—he can go home."

When the doctor was about to leave, he turned back and asked, "Has your father ever fallen before?"

"No. Never once in his life."

Of course, it depends on what you mean by *fall*. Father had lived his professional life without a misstep, reigning from on high over his world, but in terms of his treatment of human beings he had fallen countless times.

Father remained in hospital for almost a week. On the day of his discharge, I came to pick him up. He was sitting on the edge of the bed with his packed bag at his feet.

His voice was steely-edged. "You dare to look at me after all you've done?"

I could no longer continue the pretense. "And after all you've done to me all my life?"

"You sniveling little bastard! You never had the guts for anything.

No discipline—only giving up at the slightest obstacle."

I was too tired to argue with him. I just waved and made ready to go.

"Don't turn your back on me!" He bellowed so loudly that a nurse rushed down the hall. "Sit down! You're going to listen to me. The doctors say that I will never play the piano or any other instrument again."

He held his hands up. It's true. They were mangled quite badly.

"I was a great, classically trained concert pianist. You have robbed me of my livelihood and any pleasure I might have left in life. They tell me I've had a very severe concussion. Because of that my sight is poor and I will not have the concentration to compose music again."

"So now we're even," I said. I had come into that room angry. Angry about everything from the time I was born. And why? Father had undermined every effort I ever made. He had belittled me and made me feel unworthy of any respect. In short, he despised his only son.

But he said something else—again— which brought me to my knees.

"Not only are you a cruel and heartless son, but you were so thoughtless, you caused poor little Millie to kill herself!"

"No Father! How can you say that?"

He only stared at me coldly. But as I looked into those eyes, I confess I became afraid. The little boy had returned and now he cringed before the great man.

"I'm sorry, Father," I heard myself say. He knew he had me now.

"You have a serious problem, son."

"What?"

"Your actions show that *blood lust* rages in your veins. That's the only rational conclusion from your actions which were those of a *mad dog*. I curse you, you miserable excuse for a son. Goddamn you to hell! I have given you everything a son could want and need and how do you repay me? The blood lust will consume you and blot out any good in your life. Once you act with such violence, you are forever doomed to repeat it. You will not be able to help yourself."

"But father, that's ridiculous. I was angry about Millie. Now you're trying to justify what you did to her by calling me a mad dog?"

"I'm pressing charges."

"What? But you can't…"

He grinned at me. "But I can and I will. No court will let you off. You are facing severe retribution. That is—unless we come to certain terms."

"What do you mean?"

"Since my fingers have been destroyed and I cannot compose…"

"But Father you don't know that yet—not for sure."

"It's in the hospital discharge papers. You're looking at years in prison. You do know what happens to men like you in there?"

Father's enmity knew no bounds. Now he was questioning my manhood. A moment of perverse pleasure crept through me that I could upset him so greatly. But I said, "What terms do you mean?"

"You will compose and record for me as I tell you under my name. I will use you for my own purposes. If you fail to do this, I will file charges against you."

I tried to breathe. Once again Father had bullied me into submission. You may wonder how easily he did this but I assure you he has many years of experience. It's like a waterfall. Torrents plunge over rocks constantly wearing them down. Eventually pieces break away and fall into the water. That was the effect Father's words had on me.

Throughout the telling of the story, Alex sat spellbound. Father had convinced Henri that the *blood lust* coursing in his veins would doom him to a life of senseless violence. Only the penance—and that's what it was— of composing and recording in father's name would save poor Henri from such a life. It was to be a complete erasing of the person of Henri Dumont. Son would be subsumed in the Father. Son's labours would become Father's magnificent accomplishments. A diabolical way to steal great artistry and wreak revenge!

The story also explained a great deal more about Henri whom Alex had found so inexplicably strange. Until now, he could not understand why Henri abased himself before his father, the great man, with such fulsome praise. At the same time he spoke of him with such blind fury. Father had stolen everything—his music, his natural voice and Millie, his love. He had reduced his son to a non-entity.

CHAPTER 31

"Henri...please answer! I really *am* worried about you."

It was the fifth time Alex had called Henri since their meeting two days ago when he had delivered the ashes. Each day he had walked the banks of the Seine and sat in cafés nursing glasses of wine. Although he did not stop to sketch, he spent hours visualizing his next painting—and then he worried more.

As he walked, he could not rid himself of the vision that had appeared outside his hotel window. What did it mean—if anything at all? Was he going mad? All of Paris had suddenly been swallowed up. The yawning space of an empty ocean struck terror in him. The cavernous depths made him gasp in awe. When he stopped for a crème glacée from a street vendor, he realized that his vision, like in a dream, told him that when death came, it was replaced by the new growth. *And* that his light came from within himself. A good message after all?

He crossed the Pont au Change and wandered past Henri's apartment wondering what he might say if he encountered him. Surely, he thought, the man can't have committed suicide. But how could one ever know about another's state of mind? He couldn't leave Paris until he was sure Henri was all right.

Alex's cell phone rang just as he was debating whether to take yet another ride on *La Mermaid,* one of the boats plowing its way up and down the river. He sighed in relief when he heard the voice.

"Alex! So sorry I've not answered your calls. I've been making all the arrangements for Millie. You'll come to the funeral service on Saturday, won't you? It's out in the country north of Paris. You can ride up with me."

His friend sounded entirely himself—actually better than Alex had ever heard him. "Of course, I'll come Henri. You're all right then?"

"Yes and I am *eternally* grateful to you for making this all possible. I'll pick you up at 9 am tomorrow." They hung up.

On Saturday, Alexander and Henri drove out of Paris toward Caen for the burial service of Millie's ashes. Henri had placed the simple box on a soft, pink blanket on the back seat of the little Renault. In the distance, clouds raced across the sky blotting out the sun and casting a greyish light on Henri's face. Momentarily, his energy seemed to fade as they drew closer to the cemetery but then it sprang forth.

"I really have to thank you, Alex. If you hadn't followed your instincts and carried the ashes, none of this would have happened." His voice was barely a croak. "*And,* it could not have been easy. A great personal sacrifice on your part."

Alex smiled. "You're more than welcome, Henri." It was at least the fourth time that morning, Henri had given his heartfelt thanks.

"I'm not very good at these ritualistic things." Gripping the steering wheel, Henri sighed deeply. "But actually, I'm surprised. I didn't know I had this need for *something*—to mark or recognize this..." He swallowed hard. "Remarkable event." He chuckled and gestured toward the back seat. "A pink blanket somehow seemed right."

Alex simply nodded and then said, "I understand." Alex *did* understand. The event was *so* remarkable it still took his breath away whenever he thought of it. Although he never thought he was *religious* in any sense, he shared Henri's compulsion to partake in some sort of ceremony which might express, in an orderly way, the riot of feeling within. It just didn't seem right—indecent, in fact—to fail in finding some *true* expression of loss.

Henri said, "I've arranged for a priest." He gave a nonchalant wave. "To say a few words at the graveside. And then I've invited him and a good friend of mine to come for lunch with us."

Alex was pleased he would not be the only one at the service. "Who's your friend?"

"Roger Townsend. He plays the clarinet."

"Really? Will he play today?"

Henri smiled warmly. "I hope so. I've asked him to."

Closer to the coast, the sky began to clear a little. But after passing through several towns, winds picked up and heavy raindrops smacked down on the windshield. Just outside the tiny town of Auton du Mer, they climbed steeply upward through narrow rock cuts until they reached a parking lot. An immense white church belfry dominated the skyline.

"The graveyard is just up that staircase, Alex."

Looking doubtfully at the sky, Alex asked, "Do you have any umbrellas?"

"Yes, of course, in the boot. I'll get the ashes." When he had retrieved the box, he cradled it against his chest and started for the staircase. Alexander tried to hold the umbrella over both of them.

For the past several days, Alexander had been debating a question, which he now felt compelled to answer. Only he knew that Miss Trump, Henri's Millie, regarded Reginald Trump as her father as did Henri. Of course, that would make Henri and Millie half brother and sister. Although Henri might suspect this, he had no way of knowing for certain.

From a cool, legalistic point of view, he felt he should tell Henri especially now that the burial of her ashes was about to take place. Shouldn't the true and complete identity of a person be known to all before any rites were performed? To Alex, such reasoning seemed right and yet so *very* wrong.

He glanced over at Henri, who was slowing on the climb up the staircase. Yet he still held the rude box of ashes close to his chest with loving care. Alex was caught by the quiet peace shining within his friend. He saw a frail man at the end of a lifelong path to some kind of truth which would give him solace for all his perceived losses. But didn't this man need the final truth even if it were painful? But to take away contentment at this moment, Alex thought, would be another cruelty heaped upon a man who had already borne too much. It was not such a hard decision after all. Alex smiled at Henri. *What good is the truth,* he thought *unless it helps you love and live?* Let Henri have his memory—unsullied—of Millie.

Puffing, they stopped for several moments on a landing and then resumed their upward trek. Suddenly, the skies brightened and shafts of sunlight penetrated the gloom below. Then, in a burst of sunshine, the entire church was revealed above them. At the same moment, the bells rang out in deep and sonorous peals reverberating over the countryside.

At the top, a lush green meadow surrounded the church and graveyard. A stiff breeze, sweeping across the fields, stirred the yellow and purple wild flowers to life. Both men stood quietly side-by-side for some moments before moving closer toward the gravesite.

The front door of the church flew open. Two figures appeared on the steps. The first was an exceedingly tall and bulky, black man who nearly blotted the other one out. A delicate, soprano clarinet was nestled in his huge fingers.

Behind him came a short, rotund man who wore a simple cassock. His grin was shy and merry and his stride was full of life. Alex thought that the redness of his bulbous nose suggested a passion for the grape and a love of life. Alex had met many severe men of the cloth and so was intrigued with this one.

Rushing toward them, Henri smiled and held out his hand. "Roger! Delighted you're here."

Roger threw his arms around his friend in a huge bear hug. "Wouldn't have missed this for the world, bro."

The priest stepped forward. "I'm Pere Germaine. We spoke on the phone."

"We did, Pere. I really appreciate you've come."

After introducing Alex, Henri said, "For me, this is a very special occasion." He caressed the box lovingly. "There is an inspiring—a truly amazing story—which I hope my friend, Alex, will tell you at lunch. I've made reservations at

La Chautresse down in the village." He nodded at the priest. "You'll join us, won't you Father?"

"Mais oui, Henri! I do hope I may call you by your Christian name."

"Of course, Father."

"I love to dine! I find that, after these rituals," he said, glancing at the rows of grave markers, "that it is important to restore our sense of life." He grinned impishly and patted his belly. "A fine meal with friends is one of life's greatest pleasures." The little man winked. "You will see that I have conducted a considerable number of such ceremonies." The priest glanced about to confirm his view that this funeral was to have its lively even lighter notes. "How would you like to proceed, Henri? The grave-digger is still here but has done his work—hopefully to your satisfaction."

"First, I'd like to say a few words about Millie and what she meant to me, my life and art. And then, I'm hoping my friend Roger will play for us. After all that, Father, please say what is normally said on these occasions." He became awkward. "You know better than I how these things go. Does the gravedigger bury…?"

The priest smiled and spoke gently. "Yes, my son. That's how it goes."

The clouds blew off and the sunlight swept across the landscape like an ocean wave. They walked up the grass to the gravesite, which overlooked a broad valley running down to the sea. In the light, the distant waters, although dark and rough, had a magical shimmer. At the grave, the wind picked up enough to cause a whistling in the air. Henri turned his head to one side and gazed out upon the sea for several moments.

Alex stood back slightly. *What is Henri thinking of right now? Perhaps he is hearing the voice of his love in that breeze? Just imagine all the years of love and inspiration even without her presence. How powerful Miss T must have been!*

Stiffly, Henri bent down and carefully placed the box beside the small but deep cut in the earth. Roger helped him straighten himself up as he rose.

Henri checked his pocket. "It seems I've come without my notes."

"Speak from the heart man! That's all you need to do," said Roger with a grin.

Taking a deep breath, Henri stared down at the box. "In so many ways, my story is an incredible love story. But only because my friend, Alexander, followed his heart could this have happened." Henri smiled up at Alex and shifted from one foot to another. "When I was fifteen, I met Millie at my father's home for the very first time. To say it was love at first sight does not capture the emotion and the significance of that meeting." He looked up to the sky as if hoping to find some written words.

"Her very being penetrated my soul and her essence has clung to me for my entire life. If you have heard of Dante's love for his Beatrice, you will understand how the world can stand still upon seeing such a person. Although she was gone from my life forever within just a few years, she never really left. In fact she is still with me and will always be with me. But in the time I knew her, she gave me everything I needed for my art, my music but not my life."

"Tragically, I could not have both." Again he bowed his head and regarded the box. "I had her inspiration for art but could never have her true love here in *this* world. I would have given anything for that! Even my art. To have had her spiritual presence and inspiration was truly wonderful. But I would have traded all of that for—just once—feeling the touch of her hand and hearing her soft voice saying the words—*I love you, Henri.*" Looking skyward, he struggled to continue. "For years, I thought she was dead, but only because of Alex's mad, driven *certainty*, have her ashes been brought back to me." Awkwardly, he patted Alex on the shoulder.

Alex was pleased to hear Henri's words. Not one mention of father. Perhaps the stranglehold was loosening. But Henri's words struck far deeper. How could he *not* think of Daphne upon hearing his words about love?

Henri had recovered sufficiently to signal to Roger. "Roger and I play together frequently—he the clarinet and I the piano. And sometimes, I write a few tunes for him to play, when he can't find anything better. I've asked him to play something sweet for us in honour of my Millie."

Roger gave his enormous grin. "You bet, Henri, my friend. I wrote a little tune naturally called *Millie.*" He gave a massive shrug. "So, here goes!"

Gently, Roger placed the mouthpiece to his lips and drew in his breath so that his cheeks puffed out like balloons. The sun glinted on the silver instrument held up to the sky. As if in prayer to all the gods of music ever conceived, Roger played his sweet elegy to *Millie.* Alex thought he could almost see the mellow and fulsome notes floating and swirling ever upward into the endless sky. It was a happy, hopeful melody which danced above them across the valley and down to the sea. Alex glanced at Henri who had closed his eyes in bliss.

When Roger lowered his clarinet, he grinned at Henri. "Wasn't that a good send-off, my friend, for your true love? She's gotta know that she lives on in your awesome music, man."

Henri opened his eyes. "It was the *best*, Roger—the *very* best. Thank you." He turned to Pere Germaine who nodded at the gravedigger. "Would you please do the committal?"

Germaine arched his eyebrow. "After your words, Henri and that *heavenly* music, I think you might prefer something a little different from the usual?"

"Yes, please, Father."

The gravedigger stepped forward. With great care, he lowered the little box downward into the grave. The priest closed his Prayer book.

Smiling, he began. "What is death, after all is said and done? Many think it's about going to Heaven, but as we stand on this hill overlooking this beautiful valley, we look to the sky and ask—just where could this place called Heaven be?"

The little man gave a shrug. "I've been a priest for more than forty years and I have no answer for you. We stand in absolute awe of the little we know of the universe. Physicists and theologians devote their lives to these questions. But curiously, the more we think we learn, the more awe struck we are. Everyone has their own ideas, but I like to think of the universe as a wondrous creation and a fabulous work of art in which each soul may find a place in love."

Pere Germaine gave a little smile. "Henri tells us his *Millie* never left his side and was the constant inspiration for his art. How can that be? If you answer—that is the power of love and love is all—then perhaps we understand something about the universe, Henri and Millie and love."

Alexander had never heard a priest speak so eloquently. The connection between love, life and art was right in front of him—under his nose. As he watched the gravedigger spade the earth onto the box, he thought that *his* Miss Trump, although she had found her resting place, still lived on. What could be the point of a purely spiritual existence—one which denied the pleasure and reality of the senses here? Henri had said there was no comparison between art and inspiration in some unseen spiritual place and real love in *this* world. Besides, how could art be *only* spiritual and have any meaning for us here?

Pere Germaine cradled his prayer book in his hands and spoke, "My dear friends, be comforted. This is all in the natural course of events on this earth. The dust returns to the ground it came from, and the spirit returns to God who gave it." The priest regarded Henri with a loving eye. "Henri? Many who grieve are comforted to hear these words which are—after all—*poetry*:

'In my Father's house are many mansions: if it were not so, I would have told you. I go to prepare a place for you.' It's from John 14:2. That tells me *something* lies beyond and that this life is only a pause." Again, the little priest gave a charming shrug and brief smile. "I think everyone is ready for lunch?"

Henri returned the smile and bowed his head to the grave for another moment.

Pere Germaine, Alexander and Roger started toward the staircase to allow Henri some time alone. Although he seemed unwilling simply to leave, Henri eventually did. Then they all drove down through the twisting, narrow rock cuts and on into the town for lunch.

As the party took the road winding through fields laid fallow, the bright, warm weather disoriented Alex. Even though it was early November, it felt like a promising, early spring day. Getting out of the car at the restaurant, he drew in the fragrant air. With his eyes closed he warmed in the sun and felt the breeze on his cheek. Opening his eyes, he gazed upon the last of the flowers withering in their beds. A sudden and powerful joy suffused him. The words—*new life* shot through him.

Four laughing children spilled out onto the wide, white verandah where an elderly couple rocked back and forth in their chairs. They regarded the children with dour expressions. Alex smiled. In France and England for that matter, many still believed that children should be seen but not heard.

The littlest child—a boy no more than two with fiery red hair—was bounced up and onto his father's shoulders and carried to their car. Twin girls, perhaps five years old, were identically dressed in white skirts and blue blouses. Innocent and free, they skipped down the path to the car park.

The other boy, perhaps nine, straggled behind. By nature, he seemed more reserved but had the look of the *dreamer.* Alexander saw himself in the child. *Always looking for the beyond,* he thought. On deeper reflection, he knew that one came into the world very much oneself and such qualities lasted a lifetime. Looking back on his life, he felt that his basic, central nature had changed little and he assumed that was true for everyone.

Pere Germaine touched his shoulder. "New life is always wonderful to see, isn't it Alex? Do you have children?"

Wondering what to answer, Alex stopped on the top step. "No, I'm sorry to say I don't, Father. It's one of life's pleasures that ..."

Germaine gave his impish smile and said, "Yes, I know what you mean. Neither do I!"

Alexander laughed and then nodded to the old couple seated close by. "Good afternoon. A lovely day. I hope you recommend the food here?"

Both the man and woman seemed not to hear him and only increased the velocity of their rocking.

Germaine chuckled. "Sadly, it would seem they're deaf to life, Alexander."

Alex held the screen door open for the little man. Henri and Roger followed closely behind.

As they entered, Alex blinked to adjust his eyes to the darkness of the foyer. The mahogany floors gleamed in the shafts of sunlight pouring in from far windows. Immense bouquets of flowers were set on a harvest table in the centre of the room. Off to the left of the reception area, they could see the dining room and the patio beyond.

A woman dressed in a floral skirt greeted them warmly. "Bonjour. Avez-vous une réservation?"

Henri stepped forward. "Oui Madame. Henri Dumont."

She checked the book. "Certainment!"

They were led to an oval table beside the window overlooking the garden. Once they were seated, the waiter came with the menus. Close by were the chalkboards listing all the wines, which Henri began to study with care.

He turned and spoke to Alexander. "I spent a lot of time deciding where Millie should be buried. At first, I thought we should see if she had any relatives in London, but she's been gone almost two weeks and no one's inquired after her."

Alex nodded quickly. "Quite so, Henri."

"And," he smiled, "she was coming to look for me, wasn't she?"

"She was indeed. No one else but you."

Henri's entire body seemed to relax. "You know why I chose this town and this graveyard?"

Alex shook his head.

"You'll think it silly. I chose it because of this inn."

"Really?"

"You see, it was a famous hang-out for jazz musicians coming to Paris. They'd stop here overnight and play before travelling on. Usually the concerts were given free in exchange for a meal and lodging, just like painters who gave now priceless works to restaurants which fed them in hard times. It's said John Coltrane played here." Henri's gaze shifted to the garden where the gnarled and twisted branches of a chestnut tree scraped and scratched the sky. He smiled brightly and said, "That was so many years ago and now I've gotten old. I thought Millie might like to be close to the music and so would I. I've made the necessary arrangements so that we can be buried together when the time comes."

Roger signalled for the sommelier. "I want to propose a toast, sir. Bring us a bottle of Dom Perignon, please."

Delighted, the sommelier snapped his fingers and another waiter hurried off for the bottle.

Germaine nodded approvingly. "It is the liquor of the gods!" His eyes twinkled. "Did you know it is named after its creator—a monk?"

Roger grinned. "No, I didn't but that monk had to be truly inspired to create it! I think it's like music—like *jazz!*"

"Really? That's interesting, Roger," said Alexander. "How so?"

Roger drew closer to Alex. "*All* music is an outpouring of the soul. But especially jazz, which comes from both the joy and suffering of people together." He held up his thumb and forefinger to show the distance of an inch. "Just a little string of notes has got the whole history of a people in it."

"I really like that thought, Roger," Alex said.

Both Germaine and Alex looked forward to an afternoon in the musician's company. The sommelier set the silver bucket at Roger's side and held up the bottle to show the label.

Henri turned back from his examination of the chalkboard and the wines to see the champagne. "Roger? Wonderful! What are we toasting?"

Roger clapped him on the shoulder. "You'll see, man. You'll see."

The cork exploded out of the bottle landing dead centre on the table next to the silver saltcellar. The champagne began to gush. The sommelier poured and passed the glasses.

Alexander took his with a smile thinking he must be at an Irish Wake. He couldn't recall ever toasting the deceased before. But for a much loved person, why not? His memory of funerals was dark and dour.

Once the glasses were filled, Roger stood and said, "You may be wondering why we're toasting with champagne." He stopped and gave a bow to Alex, Germaine and Henri. "You see, we're toasting someone nobody's ever met. But still…he's very famous. At least in some circles."

The other three at the table looked up attentively.

"So why such suspense? Tell us." Alexander began.

Roger grinned broadly. "Have you ever heard of JP Sealy?"

Henri took a deep breath and then chuckled. "Probably nobody has, Roger. Not as dramatic as one might think!"

Roger laughed. "Well, it's damn well time they did."

Alexander's mouth dropped open. "You mean *the* JP Sealy? The jazz musician? He's a genius. I'll toast him any time. But why here and now?"

"You're absolutely right, Alex. JP Sealy is a brilliant composer and player."

"But no one has ever seen him," Alex said.

Germaine leaned forward. "That's right…I'd forgotten. Why hasn't anyone ever seen him?"

"Some people think it's a made up name for someone big in jazz world. Like a *nom de plume,*" Alex added. Sensing a stirring at the table just over his shoulder, he turned to see an elderly couple listening intently. The man winked at Alex and then spoke almost reverentially, "I *love* jazz…it's almost like a religion for me." Then he gave an embarrassed shrug. "So sorry to intrude but I couldn't help myself."

Roger motioned the waiter to pour glasses for the couple at the next table. "Enjoy! Today you're going to meet Mr. JP Sealy!" He grinned and raised his glass to Alex and the couple. "Do you know *why* he's the greatest living jazz musician?" Roger's eyes grew distant and his voice softer. "Cuz…the man captures the *moment* in time without killing it. Each note of the melody is set down and played to make it *eternal and yet— alive.* Like a gorgeous butterfly landing on your finger and then flying away—alive, not dead and frozen under glass." He laughed and slapped his forehead. "How does the man do that?"

Alexander was astounded. Reflectively, he twirled the stem of his glass admiring the pale gold champagne and anticipating its cool crispness. *What a beautifully creative way to express such an idea! Does that apply to all art…to all creativity?* Ideas, new ways of looking at life and art excited Alex. He felt as if a cool and invigorating breeze had just blown through the corridors of his mind. *Ideas and creativity are living things. They have to be alive. They come from a living person. How to preserve the life and vitality of the thing once it's on the page or on the canvas. Day in and out, artists struggle with this task. How to keep the life in the art! That's a connection between the two—life and art.*

Alex was so wrapped up in this new thought that he did not hear Roger. Everyone had stood and held up their glasses for the toast. Only Henri remained seated as if he, too, had not heard. Alex rose and raised his glass.

Roger began, "I wish to toast the greatest living jazz composer, JP Sealy and to thank him for his great body of work which will live on forever." He turned and beamed at Henri. "My friend Henri Dumont has composed the greatest jazz for the past twenty years under the name JP Sealy."

Slowly and rather unsteadily, Henri Dumont rose and gave a formal bow first to his friend Roger and then to the tables. Smiling faintly, he said, "Thank you Roger. It's time I brought an end to this charade and stepped out from behind Father."

Roger applauded enthusiastically. *"All right*, man! How long have I waited for you to say that?" His broad, charming grin lit up the room. "Millie has made a new man of you!"

Alexander was delighted and applauded loudly. "Excellent, Henri or shall we say JP?" He thought back to his first conversations with the man at dinner in his apartment. It seemed like years ago, but really it was not much more than a week or so when every word Henri said was in false homage to the old man.

Henri continued, "Because Millie returned to me, she gave me the strength to break from Father—thanks, of course, to Alex for bringing this miracle about! It is such a sense of *freedom*."

Slightly embarrassed, Alex contemplated the bubbles rising to the top of his glass. He knew there were a great many stories behind Henri's heartfelt statement.

"To Alexander Wainwright!" said Henri quietly as he raised his glass. Everyone stood and toasted Alex.

Roger caressed his clarinet case and began. "Just another moment of your attention, please." Looking about the table, he held up his hand. "I've had the great privilege of collaborating with Henri. All the members of the band call him JP. Piano and clarinet together conjure some of the deepest and most soulful melodies imaginable." He lifted the clarinet from its case and held it lovingly in his huge hands. "Actually, JP is the one who rescued the poor little clarinet from obscurity. It was almost tossed on the garbage heap of musical history after the Second World War when be-bop took over. The clarinet was too *uncool* next to the saxophone. You see, they'd forgotten that the clarinet could sing the most lovely, lyrical melodies climbing and sliding straight up to *heaven*! And, without that voice, the world is a colder place."

Many people in the restaurant had stopped to listen to Roger. They sat in silence hoping he would continue. Then a buzz of voices rose up. *Play something!*

Roger smiled broadly and then bowed to them. As he raised the clarinet to his lips, he breathed, "Just like this…" From the instrument came clear, polished notes in a swirl of sound. Everyone took deep breaths of pleasure and began clapping.

When he finished Roger bowed deeply to Henri. "Sir, because of your great talent in composition and your piano performances, my little instrument has been saved and can now take its rightful place in the jazz world. All those so-called jazz aficionados think the music is for non-conformists. But that's not true. Just think of the tyranny of *cool*! Not everyone can swim up stream. But JP can because he's composed some of the most innovative music for piano and clarinet *ever* heard. It's only by being brave enough to go your own way that this has happened. And so, JP now you have that *freedom* to announce to the world who you really are and what you can *really* do."

A blush rose up from Henri's collar. "It's true. I can't live this false life any longer. So my friends, the band is performing at the Blue Stinger Jazz Club on the Left Bank a week tomorrow. And you're both invited. There Roger and the band will announce that I am JP Sealy, whom no one has ever met." He grinned at them mischievously. "What if they don't believe me—call me a fraud."

"Ha! That won't happen," Roger laughed. "Not when they hear you play!" But how will you explain about your father?"

Henri's face darkened. "I haven't decided about that yet, Roger."

When the waiter arrived with his jovial smile and enthusiastic recommendations, the reflective mood was shattered. It was almost like waking abruptly from a dream. Suddenly, the world of light, colour, texture and aromas flooded in upon Alex and he breathed in deep appreciation.

Everyone began examining their menus in earnest.

Pere Germaine was the first to speak. "I can scarcely believe, Henri, what glorious food they have! Just look! Foie Gras, rabbit seasoned with thyme, Boeuf Bourguinon." The little man sighed with pleasure and patted his stomach which was not really as large as he pretended. "Alex? Do you like lamb? There's a dish here for two—lamb stew with glazed carrots and baby parsnips." His eyes twinkled and then he gazed at the ceiling.

Alex smiled. "Actually, Pere, I do like lamb—very much. But I think I'm in the mood for something a little bit lighter."

The father gave him a mock look of disappointment. "A shame." He brightened. "But I do look forward to our chat at lunch." He cast a speculative glance at Alex. "I think we have many interesting questions to discuss. If I'm not being too bold…"

"No, of course not! What did you have in mind?"

"I'm absolutely intrigued by the force you have mentioned which *compelled* you to carry Miss Trump's ashes from Caen to Paris."

"Yes, I'm intrigued myself, but I'm not sure I have any answers."

Pere Germaine only smiled.

Henri said, "Roger, what are you going to order?"

Roger made a show of serious indecision. Grinning at Germaine, he said, "Oh my God! What do you do first when you're in heaven?" He studied the menu then spoke to the waiter. "Please friend! Two perfect poached eggs *faites simple* to start. Followed by *courgette and tomato bake*. And then…*the sole almandine, s'il vous plait, monsieur*. Dessert? Hmmm. I'll decide about that later."

The waiter described some of the dishes and cooking methods to Alex—*simmer, saute* and *glaze*. The lore of cooking! The delights of—*veal almandine, scallops and quail with figs*—suffused him with such pleasure he chuckled. The words alone brought aromas and tastes to Alex's mind. They must have been created for the sole purpose of making him ravenous.

For Alex, food had so many associations with the past and the people in his life and with the thousands of places he had been. At first, he was surprised to find Daphne creeping into his mind and the few nights they had spent in Venice at dinner. The brine of fish in barrels. The smoothness of the sea bass on the …Her soft voice and intriguing smile. That is where it all started. He ordered *vichyssoise* and the sea bass with citrus.

Pere placed his order next— an asparagus soup with crab and the coq au vin. Henri took his time and asked the waiter many questions. Finally he decided on the mussels followed by a simple cheese omelette.

After the waiter left, Roger said, "Alexander, I understand you have Anton's painting of the cosmic egg."

"Yes, I do. The whole point of my trip was to find the artist who had painted it. I didn't know where to start except that, on the back, it was dedicated to Henri. *And*, there's quite an amazing story about finding Henri playing the piano in the Luxembourg Café."

Henri only smiled rather sadly.

"Yes, it was quite a gift!" Roger said. "But why did you want to find the painter—Anton?"

Alex sighed. "That, too, is quite a story." Taking a sip of his champagne first, he began, "Just for some background, I need to tell you a little about my painting."

"No need to explain *art* in our company," said Henri.

Alex nodded. "No, of course not. But, as you may know, I'm a landscape painter and people like my work mainly for the light they see in it." Studying his fingers, he twirled the stem of his glass and spoke in reverential tones. "For them, *and* for me, that light promises there is *something* magnificent lying behind, beyond or within the people of this tattered world. If I used more abstract forms, I'd have greater freedom in creating that light in my painting. If I could eliminate the solidity of this world—the dross…"Alex gave an elaborate shrug. "So, one night in my studio, I felt as if—you know what it's like—that I might be making some progress."

Roger winked at Germaine. "Like when a melody rises up to the heavens."

"Yes, just like that." Alex paused and looked about the table. To him everyone seemed very interested and so he continued. "Out of the corner of my eye, I saw something stunningly *beautiful* rising up." As if to capture a thought or memory, Alex searched the ceiling. "It was egg shaped and studded with gold and jewels—rubies, emeralds and sapphires. That, of course, is hard and fixed material. But somehow, this *vision*, in all its glory, seemed *alive*! It moved and turned almost as if it were a living form exuding a marvellously exciting energy!"

"The cosmic egg!" breathed Henri.

Roger nodded excitedly. "Oh man!"

Germaine simply smiled. "A vision of the beyond, my friend. You are indeed *blessed*."

Glad to be in such company, Alex smiled in relief at their understanding.

"Don't stop, Alex! Tell us *everything* you can!" Roger said.

"I'm not sure…"

"What did it *mean* to you? How did you feel?" asked the priest.

"It made me feel that, somehow, I was on the right track. That it was the *thing* I wanted to create. And I was getting to see that *thing* which perhaps exists somewhere else. If others have seen it too, then maybe it wasn't just a fantasy of mine. With all my heart, I wanted to reach out and bring it into this world."

Henri and Roger nodded eagerly.

Germaine spoke. "It's a symbol of fertility which contains the whole universe within itself." His excitement rose. "Something about to be born in and through you!"

Roger said, "It's the creative spirit right there! Man! What a gift. No wonder you wanted to find the painter."

Germaine was pensive but then he spoke. "All those jewels, Alex! It's one of those images shared by everyone on the inside—in the depths—but rarely ever seen."

Alex was impressed. This priest had travelled many avenues of thought and feeling unencumbered by dogma.

"And you thought that Anton had seen this same egg?" asked Roger.

Alex nodded. "Yes, of course. That's why I set out to find him."

"You hoped you'd found a sympathetic spirit like you?"

Alex shrugged. "Yes, I did…."

Henri held up his hand. "Alex? This may be disappointing news, but Anton never once had such a vision. I described it to him in great detail and he worked from that. He *pretended* he had seen it. That's what he wanted his followers to think."

"Followers? Sounds like some sort of cult."

Roger and Henri laughed. "Nothing as serious as that!" said Roger. "He just wanted to give his career a little boost. The followers hadn't been buying for some time."

"I see…"

"I'm sure Anton had many stories for you, Alex," said Henri quietly, "but you must take them all with a grain of salt—especially about your art."

Alex nodded. He had little patience with artists who did not respect their own work. It called into question all of Anton's heartfelt advice about entering some spiritual dimension of creativity to the exclusion of the sensual joys and pleasures of this world. How could one appreciate either without both?

Giving a short laugh, Roger hastened to add, "Anton's not exactly the most straight-up sort of guy!"

"Then, Henri, you've seen the cosmic egg?" Alex asked.

"Yes but rarely though. Just like you, it came at times, after a long period of doubt. It signalled a breakthrough in my composition. When I described the *egg* to Anton, he wrote it all down and then turned it into his own." In silence, Henri stared at his glass for a moment and then he smiled broadly. He patted Roger on the back. "The only other person, we know— until you— to have seen the *egg,* is this wonderful clarinetist, Roger."

Grinning Roger said, "It's only happened to me once, but— oh man—when it does, it is so *right.* You just know where you're headed."

The swing door to the kitchen flew open and aromas of fresh garlic, chives and splendid sauces for fish and meat, wafted outward to the tables. The waiters advanced with their steaming dishes covered with silver lids.

"My God isn't it glorious?" said Pere. His face lit up when his soup arrived. "A dream!" Gently, he poked the little pieces of crab about with the asparagus and then began to eat.

"Perfect eggs!" With a malicious grin on his face, Roger speared the yolk of one and watched it spill onto the toast.

Nearly overcome by the aroma of the warm, French stick, Alexander took a piece and began to spoon the chilled *vichyssoises.* Why, he wondered, was such sublime pleasure to be found in the simplest ingredients? Cooking was *art* of course, just as much as any painting in the National Gallery. It was *art,* just as much as any sonata or poem, mysteriously created by the human mind. All of it—life and art—was to be savoured together as part of one grand experiment in human creativity—finding what is within the empty spaces.

He was amazed at the simplicity of the meal now laid before him and presented as art. Perhaps simplicity was the bedrock for all art. Wherein lay the difference? As always, it was that indefinable ingredient—the skill and artistry of the creator. Art was composed of not only the *idea,* but the skilled *execution* of it and—*inspiration* and *light* from within the artist which would feed the body and the spirit with pleasure. Trying to identify each spice, Alexander inhaled the fragrances from the sea bass—orange, lemon, basil and dill.

Germaine set down his fork and turned to Alex. "I'm *so* interested in your experiences with so-called *chance.* What can you tell me?"

Alex smiled. "Some call it *chance.* I think it's probably the opposite of that."

Pere's eyes sparkled. "So…we understand each other, my friend. Not everyone appreciates that such amazing co-incidences *mean* something important. But to receive them as the gifts they really are, we must be truly open and watching for them." With an endearing passion mounting in his voice, he continued, "When two unrelated events cosmically collide—kaboom! — We think "Ah yes! There is a *message* for me." Rubbing his hands together, he chuckled. "And there is, but only if one is attentive!"

Watching the dancing eyebrows of the little man as he expounded, Alexander was encouraged. "I'm awestruck at the presence of the ashes. They came into my life completely unexpectedly. Miss Trump fought me off when I tried to save her. Because of a mix up at the cemetery, she was cremated and that made me feel responsible." He paused for a sip of his champagne. "Next I felt that I simply *had to* take them with me although I had no idea why. After all, I was occupied by another matter—finding Henri as I searched for this cosmic egg. Next, I came upon Henri purely by *chance*—and he happens to be the one she was going to visit in the first place. Who would ever think these two separate strands would meet for such a purpose?"

The priest nodded solemnly. "It's more than that. It's almost as if Henri has been re-born because of what was happening in you."

"I suppose… There had to be a connection not just between the events but also between Henri and me though Miss Trump."

"How do you think it happens?"

Alexander shrugged. "Hard to say but there must be another *place* where things happen because they just *need* to happen. I'm convinced there's an order here, not just chaos."

The priest smiled meditatively. "Such an interesting thought, Alex! Sometimes I think that's the job of human beings—to create order out of chaos." He gave an impish grin. "A tough job since nature is always wanting to slide back into the muck."

Alex laughed appreciatively. "There has to be some order! Somehow, it's beyond here but I don't know where. That belief is what's driven my art throughout my life."

"And, I venture to say—your very life itself. Perhaps you've been searching a very long time for something within you."

At the priest's words, Alexander sensed relief flooding his body like warm waves of water. It was true. His life and his art had been devoted to this sometimes painful search for *light* and meaning.

366 — MARY E. MARTIN

Philippe Cendre, the philosopher-mortician, flashed before Alex's eyes and he heard his voice. *The mother had only asked the priest how a loving, all-powerful God could have let her babies be murdered. When the priest turned his back on her, she cursed him and he was dead within the month.*

To Alex, such thinking led to making endless excuses for this all-powerful God. But how much better was his own thinking? Unable to visualize a god in human form, he babbled on about mysterious forces or energies governing the world.

The church's thinking was clearer than that. They could easily visualize a kindly face smiling down upon the world and all its people. On the other hand, his talk of mysterious forces made no judgment about whether those energies were *good* or *bad*. They just *were* like a part of nature we had yet to understand—like rain or tides or thunderstorm. That way, he did not have to make endless excuses for his god's action or inaction.

But how much more sense did he, Alexander Wainwright, make by insisting that vague, mysterious forces governed the universe? He pictured nameless, faceless and unpredictable powers. How did that help anyone find comfort? Despite his beliefs, he yearned to think of some *being* with intelligent and creative intent—a sort of master designer because it *humanized* the universe and the people in it.

The priest broke into Alexander's reverie. "I've spent a lot of time thinking about what makes for a good life."

"I can tell from your comments. You think quite differently from any priest I've met," Alex said.

The little man gave a merry smile. "I shall take that as a great compliment, Alex, as I'm sure it was meant. So many in the church are rigid fossils. They have not lived fully and yet they presume to offer advice on the topic of *life*." He leaned forward, eager to continue his thought. "After long struggles, I like to think I've reached a few tentative conclusions."

"And?"

"Regardless of whether a god of any kind exists, it seems we must look to ourselves right in the here and now. To me the real question is this: *What are the two best things a person can do in life? Maybe even three, if we're lucky.* As I see it, they are to become truly one with another person and to create something new—add something of value. On one level, a priest, by the calling of his profession, denies himself access to at least one of those opportunities. Obviously, we cannot marry but we are supposed to find our *oneness* with God. True, there is no law against a priest's being creative, but you'd be surprised, with all the dogmatic thinking, how rarely the opportunity arises. We are supposed to find our release in devotional study."

"Why did you join the church then?"

His face clouded and he spoke rather wistfully. "I'm not really sure, Alex…But," he continued, "If you can have those two aspects in your life, then I think you've done quite well."

The priest's words brought Daphne to mind. "You don't think that one excludes the other?"

Germaine looked slightly startled. "How so?"

Alexander shrugged. "I don't know. Perhaps if a person is devoted to creating his art, he cannot be very good at loving? I know it sounds rather silly, but…"

"No, I understand what you're saying. You're afraid that, because your art requires so much of you, that you have nothing else to give."

"Yes…"

Germaine smiled broadly. "Alexander, I think a man such as you should never fear that. You obviously have a very great deal to give and, indeed, your nature demands that of you."

Alex sat in silence for some moments. It was no idle question and it went straight to the heart of the matter. He loved Daphne, but he wondered if he had the capacity to divide himself between art and love. But what if both art and love were essential to each other? Did love in *this* world with all its wonderful pleasures, heartaches and obligations not stimulate the passions and the imagination to reach the other world in his art? How could he possibly create something new in any other world but this one?

When the priest had finished his coq au vin, he sat back and gave his belly a little pat. He said, "Our desire to love and create is part of our ongoing struggle against *chaos*. We are always seeking to push back the darkness and create the light."

Roger smiled broadly at Germaine. "Well said, my friend. It's just like music—just like *jazz*! We got all this fantastic energy dancing around inside us and it just *has* to happen and come out. Like we're all tuned in and pulsing together to the same *beat*! Sometimes, we slip back down, but we always keep trying to get into that beat and harmony." He opened up his clarinet case. "Hey man! That's human nature!" He sat back and gently drew his finger across the mouthpiece of the instrument. Reflectively, he said, "That way we shine a little light in all the dark places." He held up his clarinet. "This little lady has the sweetest sound of all. But somehow all of them sing the song of life even though they have different tones. Just like people's voices." Grinning, he looked about the table.

Henri said, "Roger's absolutely right. We all want to get in synch with one another. That's what I strive for in my composition—getting in synch with Roger and his clarinet and the rest of the band. If we do, we've created something beautiful. And if not, then it's *dead*." His eyes took on a faraway look. "I think that's how Millie has helped me all these years. She taught me how to fall in love and be in unison with someone. Same thing for creating art. She's been my constant inspiration and I know she'll continue."

Roger and Henri's words struck Alex as deeply true. Through love you synchronized with others and created. As he sat there, he felt as if he had found *some* answers.

As they left the restaurant, Germaine pointed out a poster on the wall near the reception desk. He spoke to the other three. "Did you know there's quite a ghost story attached to this place?"

They all stopped to look at the darkly coloured poster showing a willowy, faded figure in a long white dress. As she wandered through a woods to a lake, her hair was blown about so wildly that she resembled a desperate waif. Behind her was a pale and rakish looking man dressed in a formal morning coat who called out to her.

"It's great folk lore in this neighbourhood that one night, a young man and his newly wed spent their honeymoon right at this inn. It was a real tragedy of Romeo and Juliette proportions! On the second night of their honeymoon, Yvette, only twenty-two years old, decided to play a seductive game with her new husband, Richard. She left her shawl he had given her at the bottom of a shallow gully. She was hiding behind a tree on the far side of the ravine hoping she could lead him in a chase." Germaine smiled sadly. "Unfortunately, when he saw it, he thought she'd come to harm. So he rushed down, past rocks and roots, to rescue her. Close to the bottom, he tripped and smashed his head on a rock. He died instantly. When she saw him fall, she ran screaming to him." Germaine sighed deeply. "But her fate was to join him. She fell into the deep, roiling creek. The currents were far too strong for her and she was swept down into a whirlpool. Sadly she came up only once and then was carried off. They found her body several days later almost a mile away.

Roger set down his case and folded his arms across his chest. "Oh man! That's one sad story!"

"They say they've been seen every so often at night wandering through the woods hand in hand," Germaine continued.

The party moved out to the verandah. Alexander breathed deeply taking in the fragrance of orchids. He thought of the night with Fyodor in St. Petersburg and the whole family he had seen—people from some other time who somehow still existed *somewhere*.

Henri asked, "Pere? When did that happen?"

"From the way they are dressed, it would seem at least a century back."

"There's thousands of stories like that. It really makes you wonder," Alex said.

Germaine shrugged and pulled a face. "I think it happens. No one really knows what happens when you die. How can we? But as far as I can tell life goes on—perhaps in a different way or form. But still it continues and perhaps we leave our mark behind here on the atmosphere."

With a wry smile, Alex said, "It adds significance to the things we do and the choices we make." To himself, he thought—again the wonder of love that lasts a lifetime.

They got into the cars and headed back to Paris.

CHAPTER 32

A week later, Paris was layered in thick, fluffy snow so light you could blow it away. By ten that evening, a few fat, lacey flakes still floated down covering the railings and lamps on Rue de Tocqville on the Left Bank. A line of at least sixty people stood stamping their feet on the sidewalk waiting to enter the Blue Stinger Jazz Club for the first show. Rumour that JP Sealy would appear that night had swept through the crowd.

Inside the club, Henri and Roger were reviewing the programme. Frank Hawkins would be on drums, Pierre Juvet on bass and Stephan Orly on trumpet. They planned to start with Henri's jazz arrangement of a Bach piece which seemed to bridge his two worlds.

"Are you gonna tell them who you really are tonight, Henri?" Roger asked.

"I think so… I promised myself I'd claim my freedom from Father this evening."

Roger clapped him on the shoulder. "Good man! It's time."

"But how should I do it? Even though father's been dead a long time, it's still hard to betray his legacy even though it's a complete lie."

"All you gotta do is speak from the heart man! You don't have to destroy him." He laughed. "Oh…and leave the rest to me. I'll be right behind you backing you up."

At ten o'clock, the doors were thrown open and the crowd surged into the concert hall which doubled as a bar. Chairs were pulled up to tables as closely as possible. In the next fifteen minutes drinks orders were taken and served.

Roger peeked out from behind the stage curtain and nodded approvingly. It looked like a good crowd—a full house. These were the *aficionados* of jazz, all in a fine mood for music. Here and there he heard a ripple of questions. *Is JP Sealy really going to appear tonight?* At Henri's request, Roger polished the golden, bejeweled metronome and set it on top of the grand piano. This object, he knew, was fraught with meaning and ritual but now was the moment to change old habits!

Within five minutes, the audience had settled and was now looking expectantly at the stage. The curtains were drawn back and Roger took the microphone.

Grinning broadly, he began, "Ladies and gentlemen. Thanks for coming out on this wintry night. We're going to warm this place up with some *hot* jazz. Many of you know JP Sealy and his music, the one who's been giving the world the most beautiful, innovative jazz compositions ever heard. But no one has ever seen the man."

Ripples of interest shot through the audience. Maybe the rumours were true.

"Tonight we are truly honoured to witness the very first public appearance of JP Sealy who's been giving us all this great music for so many years. First, he's gonna play for you his very own arrangement of Bach's Prelude in C Minor. If you've never heard classical music set to jazz, you don't know what you're missing. So, I'll shut up now, introduce Mr. JP Sealy and get out of his way 'cuz you're in for a treat."

Applause and cheers filled the room. Strobe lighting swept across the stage. Henri made a slight and rather bent figure creeping toward the grand piano. At first he gave a tentative bow to the audience and blinked in the lights. When he stepped forward, Roger threw his arm over his shoulder.

"Ladies and gentlemen, it is my great pleasure to introduce Henri Dumont who has doubled as JP Sealy all these years and given us the greatest jazz compositions. You've all heard his music but this is the first time anyone's actual seen him!" Roger laughed. "Kinda *weird* isn't it?"

As soon as Henri sat down at the piano, he seemed taller. His demeanor suggested total command of the performance. His rolled up sleeves and open collar spoke of his complete relaxation. When he faced the audience, excited whispers rose up from the tables.

"Hey! That's the old guy who plays at the Luxembourg Café."

"Wow! And at St. Julien. All the Chopin on Friday nights"

"He's *really* JP Sealy?"

From his table near the stage, Alexander could see Henri's face. Gone was the tortured visage of a divided soul so evident on his poster at the church. Instead, Alex saw an expression, not only of peacefulness and serenity but also one of supreme confidence—of the true artist about to create something amazing from deep within. The bass player and drummer took their places and Roger played a few notes on his clarinet.

Roger said, "Here's Bach's Prelude in C Minor."

Henri bent to the keyboard. He began playing the music as Bach had written it at a driving rhythm. The bass player followed adding warmth and richness to the sound. Some of the melody came from Roger's clarinet. Alex had the sense of water rippling over rocks.

Then, like shifting gears, the rhythm changed and they were driving in the world of jazz. With the drummer joining in, the beat became a new pulse of energy. Alex caught his breath. That rippling water had grown into a driving torrent smashing its way over rock. When Roger came in with his clarinet, the melody bounced back and forth between Henri and himself like a meaningful conversation between two instruments—two artists.

As if to join in making the music, the audience cheered and clapped. Some leaned forward smiling in delight. As if in meditation of great truths, others sat with eyes closed and heads nodding in time. When Henri finished the piece, he bowed to the audience which leapt to its feet and applauded.

As soon as the audience had quieted, Roger stepped forward. "Thanks everybody for the great welcome! This is a real party! We want JP to stay with us and not go into hiding for another twenty years, so keep sending him your love and welcoming thoughts! Actually, by last count, in those years he's written probably thousands of pieces. Between sets, we're gonna sit down and talk with JP and have him tell us what's been up all this time. But now were going to play for you one of his latest compositions entitled *Fathers and Sons,* especially written for me 'cuz it features the clarinet." With a wink, Roger held up his clarinet and bowed toward Henri.

Alexander winced. He hoped the piece was not revealing of all the enmity between Henri and his father.

Roger tapped his foot. "One...two...three!" From his clarinet came a strong, silver- sweet melody floating out over the audience. JP began following him on piano gradually weaving his tune with the clarinet's. It wasn't cacophonous as Alex had feared. The melody was delicate and sweetly evocative of a yearning for love and connection. The tension mounted to near unbearable heights and then fell twisting this way and that throughout the entire piece. Entranced by the ebb and flow of emotion, no one in the audience moved or spoke.

After applause and cheers lasting several minutes, Roger spoke. "Man! That was incredible. There's gotta be a whole lifetime of stories behind that. After this set, JP, I'd like to talk on stage with you about what led up to that piece. Is that okay?"

Henri took a deep breath then smiled. "Sure Roger. I could go on and on but we haven't got the whole night."

"All right!" Let's play a few more pieces and then we'll talk."

JP began an intricate prelude. "This one is basically blues." He smiled at the audience. "It asks life's unanswerable questions."

The song entitled *Millie's Still Here,* began to waft through the concert hall like a soft breeze in spring. New growth. New life. Roger joined in with soaring energy building on JP's delicate prelude. Further in, dissonant notes brought doubt, confusion and darkness to the music. But toward the end, harmony and light was restored like sun breaking through cloud.

After forty minutes of playing, the set ended. The crowd broke off for drinks and conversation. Alexander wandered to the bar where he ordered a beer.

Until Henri explained about father's *curse,* the story had been confusing. Why would a grown man swing from ill-disguised hatred of his father to absolute obeisance? How could a father be so monstrous as to revile such a child and seek to undermine all his efforts to please? The lights dimmed and the curtain rose. Alex returned to his seat. Henri sat at the piano and Roger was perched on a stool, clarinet in hand.

Roger began. "So, JP I wanted to ask you about two of the pieces you played tonight—*Fathers and Sons* and *Millie's Still Here.* Somehow they've got that little *extra* quality in them that *real* artists like you somehow get in there. Something so meaningful from life. What can you tell us about that?"

Alex held his breath.

Smiling, Henri picked up the metronome. "I think everyone would say that this is one of the most beautiful metronomes in the world." He held it up to the audience which murmured appreciatively. "But for me, it represents hell on earth and tonight I'm going to free myself from it—at last. You see, it was a gift from my father—he was classically trained—and he hoped I would follow in his footsteps." He gave a short uncomfortable laugh.

Roger shook his head only slightly.

"To him, I was an undisciplined wretch…"

The audience squirmed and Henri, sensing their embarrassment, changed course.

Alex sighed deeply.

With a broad smile, Henri said, "But then, I found the world of jazz! How different! How exciting! Right away, I knew I had found my *true* home. So, I began to compose on my own, in secret, under the name JP Sealy." Henri looked out over the crowd which sat breathless, hanging on his words. "So, that's what's behind the song *Fathers and Sons*. Too bad I couldn't share my love of jazz with my father because he missed out on a whole new world of music." He nodded at Roger, saying, "I think that's what you mean by that *extra*—that yearning for something you know can never be."

Roger leaned over and clapped him on the shoulder. "Well said, man! That's exactly what it is! So, tell us about *Millie*. Where did the inspiration for that song come from?"

"*Millie* was the inspiration. I met her when I was only fifteen. Beautiful soul." His voice softened. "You know what it's like when the *divine* just shines through someone and out into the world? Although I haven't seen her for fifty years or more, she's never left my side. Always the inspiration for my music and my life."

"Hey! You know how lucky you are to have that? Amazing!" Roger said.

Throughout his speaking, Henri had been holding the metronome. Now he opened it and set it in motion at the fastest speed. Harsh clacking filled the hall. He grinned at Roger. "God awful sound isn't it? No place for it in the world of jazz where there's such an easy flow all in the key of love." He stopped the metronome and handed it to Roger. "Take this, my friend, and bury it somewhere, please!"

The crowd leapt to its feet in applause. Henri and Roger stood up and threw their arms around each other.

Roger took the microphone. "Ladies and gentleman, now for some more music from JP Sealy!"

Henri rubbed his hands together and sat at the piano. Both the bassist and the drummer took their places and Roger led with swirling notes from his clarinet.

Alexander thought about *habit*. Henri had always paid homage to Father, an angry, vengeful god. The public disposal of the metronome was a sort of ritual designed to set him free. He spent the rest of the evening listening to the music and playing with shapes and colours in his mind.

LONDON

CHAPTER 33

Back in London, Alexander, as he walked, ruminated over his trip. In retrospect, the events in Paris and St. Petersburg grew more rich and vivid. It seemed as if a story, filled with drama and intrigue, had been written by an invisible writer looking over his shoulder. He was no closer to understanding *how* it had all occurred and so he tried to draw lessons or guidance from it.

He had to decide about Daphne. He promised himself he would call her tonight. During his trip, he had almost convinced himself their relationship could not work—not with his need to follow his muse. He could hear Anton's whose words he now discounted—*never let a woman come between you and your art.* And then, there was Henri saying the exact opposite—*what is life and art without love?* Nothing!

A longing crept over him and he knew they *must* talk. After all, he could easily catch a flight to New York. Remembering her attempts at organizing him, he gave a slight shiver. He could get his head out of the clouds and be present for her. But he knew he could not adjust to any interference in his work.

He entered Piccadilly Circus and smiled up at the Anteros statue. Suddenly, six policemen ran past him. From near the statue, he heard shouts and cursing. He drew closer to see the police wrestling a small man to the ground.

"Oh my God!" whispered Alex. By now he was close enough to see that Rinaldo was at the centre of the disturbance. He rushed to his side to see him now on his feet.

Rinaldo's face was twisted with rage as he shouted, "Those women are vile, dishonest, traitorous whores…each and every one of them! Never let one of them come between you and your art!"

Immediately, Alex saw the pain in his eyes and he feared he was not lucid. This time Rinaldo could really be sentenced to jail. *After all, how many public disturbances can one make before the magistrate loses patience?*

He stepped forward and touched the sleeve of the sergeant. "Sir? My friend is terribly upset by a woman. I'll take him away from here so he won't cause trouble."

The officer looked carefully at Alex. "What is *wrong* with this bloke? He was here a week ago with some crazy demonstration. Then he was part of some other so-called *artistic* event here where he nearly destroyed someone's camera equipment."

"I'm dreadfully sorry, officer. I'm sure he'll settle down once he sees I'm here."

"Right then! If you can get him to leave quietly, there'll be no charges *this* time."

"Thank you, officer." Alex pushed through the crowd and stood before Rinaldo. "Rinaldo! How wonderful to run into you here! Come on. Let's get some lunch."

Rinaldo, ferret-like, grinned up at Alex. "Alexander! My saviour! Of course, let's have lunch." At the sergeant's nod the policemen released Rinaldo with a shove.

Rinaldo pivoted about and growled, "See here, officer, you can't treat the citizenry in such a brutal manner." With great care, he proceeded to brush off his jacket. Alex grabbed his arm and ferried him off toward Regent Street in search of a sandwich shop which they found nearby. He was shocked by the scrawniness of his friend's arm.

Once seated inside, Alex looked hard at him. He saw an intense combination of anger and sorrow. He could not recall such depths of fury ever so exposed in the man.

He tried to speak kindly. "What is wrong, Rinaldo? You look—I don't know— devastated. Have you gone mad? What has happened to you that you'd shout in Piccadilly about a muse?"

Rinaldo's eyes gleamed with fury. "The God damned bitch nearly castrated me!"

"What? Who?"

"Krysta!"

"Who's she?"

The waiter came with menus. Both of them ordered sandwiches and soup.

Rinaldo smirked. "Awfully good of you, Alex, to feed me again. You're a true friend."

"To say nothing of keeping you out of the hands of the police."

"That too…"

"Tell me about this Krysta."

Alex was shocked. Rinaldo looked as if he might cry. He hung his head down and played with his napkin.

At last he spoke. "Krysta was to be my model for my papier mache performance project."

"What is that?"

Rinaldo shrugged. "Just an idea where I would cover a person in papier mache like a mummy."

"Why?"

"I wanted to make a statement about the kinds of lives we all live. That we all go along dead to the world living unauthentic lives. We've been all hollowed out and have no reality other than the most superficial."

Alex frowned. "What would this papier mache person do?"

"I don't know. March around stiffly like a robot."

To Alex, Rinaldo's conceptual art projects seemed faintly ridiculous. Sighing, he remembered Rinaldo had tried to bridge the profane and the sacred in his last Piccadilly performance. "Did she agree to let you cover her in papier mache?"

"No. She took over the whole project. She's part of an artistic group called the People's Art and she talked me into participating." Rinaldo hung his head again. "I was *so* stupid! She imposed her ideas and talked me into being the—if you can believe it—the *grandfather*— of conceptual art. I thought they were trying to honour me, but when it was performed in Piccadilly Circus, they just laughed at me...my ideas... everything."

Alex immediately understood the pain of public humiliation. Ironically, the man who sat before him had tried to destroy him and his art several years ago, on the Williamsburg Bridge in New York City.

"I want to kill the fuckers!" Rinaldo nearly sobbed. "Just you watch out, Alex! You get a woman as a model and you think she's inspiring you to greatness in your art. But she's really screwing with you. Wants to take over, run the show and destroy your art." He banged his fist on the table, nearly upsetting the coffee, and hissed, "I'm telling you man to man. You just watch out for those bitches!"

Alex drew back. Never had he seen anyone so distressed about *art*—or women. Usually, Rinaldo always had a cutting comment ready to inflict on anyone criticizing his work. Something lay deeper. He asked, "Tell me more about Krysta."

For an instant, Rinaldo's eyes softened. Below the surface, Alex could see great sadness. *My God,* he thought. *This is Rinaldo in love?*

Rinaldo's insouciant grin appeared. "Alex, she was a great lay! Absolutely fantastic! But a complete bitch." He looked away. "You see, I need her to retract some of the statements she made about my art."

"Will she do that?"

"She won't even talk to me." He looked up at Alex brightly. "But I bet she'd talk to you!"

"Me? Why on earth would she do that?"

"She *loves* your work! She's part of a counter-revolution demanding a return to representational art and craftsmanship. And so, you see, she simply *adores* your fields and streams..." Rinaldo bit his lip suddenly remembering he shouldn't poke fun when asking a favour.

Alexander sighed deeply. The man sitting across from him had fundamentally changed in some undefined way. Apparently he had been touched by love, probably for the first time in his life. He debated whether to probe further about Krysta but decided it would be cruel to poke at an open, bleeding wound. Although he was not keen on speaking to the woman he was intrigued to meet the one who had brought Rinaldo to his knees.

"What on earth could I say to her?"

"Tell her that you greatly admire her work and you're delighted that she advocates the return to traditional forms of art." Warming to his topic, he sat forward and grasped Alex's sleeve. "But you must tell her that conceptual art has great value. You must say that we cannot make fun of other forms of art and that you, as an artist, have only the greatest respect for my work."

For Alex, it was a tall order. How many times had Rinaldo scoffed at his work and virtually everything else? But a strange feeling of pity came over him. Here sat one of the least deserving people on the planet of compassion. And yet, Alex felt compelled to act.

"All right, Rinaldo. I'll try but I can't promise anything at all."

"You're such a good chap! I knew a gentleman such as yourself would agree to call her."

"Give me her number and I'll call her tonight."

"From the bottom of my heart, I thank you kind sir!" Rinaldo grinned. "And you'll tell me what the lady says?"

"Of course."

Alex was troubled by Rinaldo's views of the *muse*. Obviously he had been seriously wounded by whatever Krysta had done, but he also knew that Rinaldo was having difficulty in coping with the emotion—new to him—of love.

Alex paid for lunch and headed back for his studio. Despite the highly emotional tirade, Rinaldo had made some points worth considering. He had never seriously thought Daphne might intentionally interfere in his work and certainly not with ill will. Yet the question was at the root of their relationship. Did she want to be a force in his creative life? That could spell trouble unless some limits were set. It was only sensible to discuss the question with her in an open and free manner. *Surely two intelligent people can talk about potential problems in a relationship.*

Alex smiled to think of Rinaldo's ghostly papier mache mummies dancing about stiff-legged as if risen from the dead. He gazed onto Trafalgar Square where thousands of pigeons were flocking about thousands of people. He realized that, on his travels, he had thought much about life—something after all of this—some form of existence. Where might Millicent Trump be? If anywhere at all? Sometimes she seemed right beside or inside him and at others extinguished, body, mind and spirit forever from this world.

Remembering that a few of her sculptures might still be on display at the National Gallery on the north side of the Square, he changed his course and mounted the steps to it. The concierge directed him to a far gallery on the second floor. As he walked, his footsteps echoed along darkened corridors and among the columns and arches. He saw no other visitors. As soon as he entered the gallery, he caught his breath.

Seven of her sleek and elegant marble pieces were on display. The marble formed not one but two shapes—the marble sculpture itself and the empty space within. One was three times the size of a human head. Its white marble was marked with little ripples of blue and tiny traces of red and gold. The marble formed the positive shapes. The negative empty shapes were so powerful that it seemed they had created the positive marble shapes by thrusting them into being.

A group of bored school children straggled into the gallery. When they saw the sculptures, their faces lit up.

"Look!" A little girl pointed at the sculpture. "That looks like somebody's Mummy!"

"Where?" asked the teacher. "What do you mean, Sophie?"

The little girl pointed again at the sculpture. "Right there… but she looks so sad."

Alex looked again carefully. The shape of the marble could really be a human head and the empty shapes carved in it were reminiscent of teardrops. Alex could see what the child saw. It might well be any mother, whose eyes contained the sorrow of all the mothers who had ever lived. And so Millie had insisted Lia and Celestine be saved. He left the gallery and returned to his studio. Several hours later, he had a strange sense that he might be able, at last, to paint. After all, perhaps it was true—that those empty spaces *really did* contain the stuff of all creation.

CHAPTER 34

Alexander had called earlier wanting my advice on a *personal* matter. Although he did not say so, I suspected it involved Daphne. Although I had spoken with him briefly, I had not seen him since his return from Paris. Now he was in a cab on his way to my gallery in Chelsea when his mobile rang.

"Hello?"

"Hi. It's me."

"Daphne! Are you in New York?"

"No. Actually I'm here in London."

"That's wonderful! I was just about to call you."

"Would you like to have dinner some time?"

"Of course! Tonight?"

"Sure. Where shall we go?"

"I'll pick you up at your hotel. Where are you staying?"

"Hayden House in the Strand."

Alex arranged to pick her up at seven and, after hanging up, he became nervous. *She didn't sound angry or cool.* He could not face another evening of a cold war between them. At the same time, he could not define *exactly* how he felt or what he wanted.

Some would say I do not appreciate the complexities of love and that my advice is far too simple. Although I am unused to giving advice to the love-struck, nevertheless, I am a practical man with a measure of clear-sightedness.

Alex arrived at my gallery door and entered with a tentative step.

"Wonderful to see you, Alex!"

We shook hands heartily and then, when I sat down at my desk, he began to pace back and forth.

"How was your trip?" I asked.

"Fine. Fine…"

"From the little you said on the phone, it sounded quite amazing."

He nodded and sat down abruptly across from me. "I've been debating, Jamie. Daphne is back in London."

"Wonderful…"

"Yes, but… All the time I was away I've been thinking things through—or at least trying to. I know that Daphne wants a more solid relationship…"

"That's not good?"

"I just don't know if I can give her what she wants or needs. She says I go off with my head in the clouds. That I'm not there for her." He gave a dramatic shrug. "She deserves better than…"

I held up my hand. "Stop right there, Alex. Aren't you *really* saying that you're afraid she'll keep you from your work—somehow impede your creativity? That's what you've said before."

"I don't know…"

"Come with me." We went to the next room where his painting *The River of Remembrance* hung. "Look at this masterful work. How and when did you come to paint this?"

Alex had painted it several years ago when he was trying to make the human figure the portal for his magical light. Each figure was sublimely beautiful, evincing the greatest depths and variety of emotion.

The focal point of it was a beautiful woman who looked from the canvas with a soft smile and unfathomable regret in her eyes—Daphne when he first saw her that morning on the Orient Express. Every bit of his skill was used to create that composition, which would include all those he met on his journey. Not only had he infused his landscape—the river, the rocks and the sky with that miraculous light, but he had also made it shine through each and every human figure in his painting. His creation throbbed with life.

He shoved his hands into his pockets and mumbled, "I painted it after the trip to Venice, and New York."

"And look at all the people in it. Where did they come from?"

"I met them on that trip."

"Who was the first one you met?"

"I know…Daphne."

"And you called her your muse, didn't you? *And* she forms the focal point of the entire work. She is at the centre of your art and wants a place at the centre of your life."

"But Jamie…"

"You cannot be serious, Alex! Love adds to life and art. It does not subtract. Without my wife of thirty years, I would be a far lesser man."

"You think she still wants me?"

"What did she do? She came to London and called you." I grasped his elbow and ferried him back to my office where we sat down. "Alex, if you are seriously worried about interference with your work, why don't you talk to her about it? Surely, as adults, you can resolve something as simple as that!"

He gave me a long and serious look. Then a slow smile slid over his face. "Thank you, Jamie. That's exactly what I'll do."

I was greatly pleased. Sometimes practical, straightforward advice can win the day.

As he stood out on the sidewalk, he said, "Do you know why we could find no record of Maureen Trump?"

I shook my head.

"She was actually the renowned sculptor, Maureen Graves. That was her real name or one of her names."

"What? How did you learn that?"

"Anton Chekhov told me."

"What? You're joking!"

"Not the writer Anton Chekhov…the Russian painter."

"Maureen Graves's work is gorgeous…the power of the empty space creating so many shapes and suggesting so much."

"That's exactly right. And I have an empty space to fill." He winked and hailed a cab. "Thanks Jamie. I'll be talking to you soon."

CHAPTER 35

Mobile in hand, Alex stood on the street corner after leaving my gallery in Chelsea.

"Krysta? "Alex said, "You don't know me but I'm a friend of Rinaldo's."

"So…What's your name?"

"Alexander Wainwright."

There was a choking sound on the other end. "You're joking, man!"

"Uh…no, I'm not."

"The painter?"

"Yes, I do paint." Alex could hear some muttering as if Krysta were talking to someone else in the background.

"You're not joking are you?" She was almost breathless. "I just so…admire your work."

"Thank you. I want to speak to you about Rinaldo. May I come see you? Where do you live?"

"Near the art school. But I can meet you at the café just outside the school."

"Excellent. When?"

"Half an hour?"

"Good I'll be there."

Thirty minutes later Alex walked into the *Artists' Haven*, a brightly lit space resembling an airport cafeteria. In the far corner sat a red haired young woman with a girlfriend beside her.

When she saw him, she grinned broadly and waved. "Mr. Wainwright…sir! It really is you! I thought Rinaldo was getting me back with some sort of trick."

"Really? Why would he do that?"

She lowered her eyes. "We were just joking around. Having some fun…"

"I ran into Rinaldo in Piccadilly today. "Alex smiled gently. "He was shouting about being betrayed by whores, Krysta." He chuckled. "I know that Rinaldo tends to get carried away but there did seem to be something in what he said."

"I'm really sorry. It was just some silly art project I was helping a friend with…"

Alex waved as if to dismiss her concerns. "It's not all that important. Rinaldo's done his share of tricks and probably deserved a taste of it himself." Alex ordered tea for the three of them and then, giving her a meaningful glance, said, "But I do think it's unwise for an artist to make enemies—especially of Rinaldo."

When the tea arrived, they sat in silence for several minutes. "You see, people like Rinaldo can always outdo just about anyone in nastiness—and I know personally."

Krysta bit her lip. Her friend still stared wide-eyed at Alex, probably still amazed at his presence.

Alex smiled broadly. "I'm sure you know he's completely and utterly in love with you. I've never once seen him like this!"

"Come on! That man's had just about every woman on the planet!"

Alex shrugged. "He begged me to speak with you and so I have. Perhaps you could smooth it over with him. Let him down gently. You seem far too nice a person to be an enemy."

Krysta nodded. "It's really great of you to speak up for someone like Rinaldo. Do you think we could visit your studio some time?"

Again, Alex smiled gently. "No. That wouldn't be a good idea." He stood up. "But I'll be on the lookout for your work." He gave a quick bow. "Thank you ladies. I'll tell Rinaldo we've spoken."

CHAPTER 36

That evening, Alexander rushed up the stairs of Piccadilly Station. Crowds jostled downward past him for the trains. On the street, people marched past with their heads down against the cold. Shivering, he strode to Hayden House Hotel in the Strand.

Throughout the entire day, he had wandered about London—along the Embankment where he gazed upon boats churning up and down the steel-grey waters of the Thames. Then he haunted Trafalgar Square and estimated the number of pigeons nesting beneath Nelson's Column. He was entirely at loose ends.

Images of Daphne crowded into his brain. There she was in the dining car on the Orient Express. Her vulnerability had nearly broken his heart. He saw her in Venice weaving her way past hawkers on the Rialto Bridge and then reaching for his hand. It was her soft smile, he thought, that drew him in. His rational side fought back. *I must approach this rationally. My*

*art is of the greatest importance to me. All else must come second.
But…how can I be so alone.*

As he sat in a tearoom near Canada House in Trafalgar
Square, he thought of his painting *The River of Remembrance.*
He had completed that huge canvas almost in a trance. The
focal point—no matter how many preliminary drawings of the
painting he made— was Daphne.

He remembered his first night on the train speeding toward
Venice. After dinner with Daphne, he had rushed to his cabin
and, with great passion, drawn twelve sketches of her. Then he
had hurried to her compartment to show them to her. In Venice,
although they had made love, they had parted in disappointed
silence. He had never stopped to consider *why.* And, of course,
it had happened again in London when he left for Paris. *What
dissatisfaction am I causing?* If he were truthful, he would know.

Despite his fears of her *distractions,* he knew that she was
much more than a muse—a passing inspiration. She embodied
all that he cherished in the world. Surely they could sort
things out!

From the tearoom, he had a view of the National Gallery
which dominated the Square with its broad staircases and
fluted columns. He remembered the words of the child who
saw a mother in Maureen Graves' sculpture. All the events
surrounding his Miss T which flowed from his meeting
Maureen Trump on the train seemed orchestrated by some
magical force. Indeed, he had felt inhabited by a purposeful,
alien spirit forcing him onward. If that god-awful morgue had
not mistakenly cremated her remains and if he had not insisted
on taking her ashes, Henri would never have had his Beatrice.
If he had not gone to Anton, he would not have learned the

true identity or identities of Miss Trump. All of it must contain some meaning—some purpose for *him*.

Since leaving my gallery, he had thought about Henri and the artist Anton Chekhov. Henri had his Millie, his Beatrice. But she was never really a part of his life. Millie was his love and inspiration, but even he admitted that it was a disembodied sort of love. What if he had lived with her—made accommodations as all relationships require? Would he have created his beautifully inspired music? Or would their love have been such a distraction making his art impossible. However he could not forget Henri's plaintive words—*I would have exchanged it all for just one kiss from her and to hear the words "I love you, Henri."*

As to Anton Chekhov, Alex was initially unsure what opinion he should form. The man was—probably like most human beings—a bundle of contradictions and contrariness. Most definitely he was a skilled and creative artist. But he was adamant that no *real* artist should ever permit any *woman* to come between him and his art. Alex suspected the man was an inveterate misogynist because of his shabby treatment of his poor, submissive wife, who clearly lived in terror of him. Why, Alex concluded, should he take any advice from him?

According to Rinaldo, women were a sort of sub-species of the human race and never to be trusted. Alex, having far more humanity and love in him than most men, vehemently disagreed with him. On the question of combining devotion to art and love, he had to consider Rinaldo's thoughts along with Anton's. I like to think even my few words had an impact on his thinking.

In her room at the Hayden House Hotel, Daphne rang housekeeping.

"Could you please send the chamber maid to the room to tidy up and give me some more towels?" She glanced at the table at the window. *Champagne? No. Over the top. Too overtly seductive.* "Also, would you have the sommelier choose a bottle of Merlot and have it delivered?" Not ostentatious, she thought. It could be in the room for any reason.

Standing before the full length mirror, she checked her skirt, blouse and jacket. Just the right touch of casual elegance. She sighed and made a face. Her stomach had been churning most of the afternoon. *Why so nervous?*

She slid a gold ring rimmed with tiny rubies and diamonds onto her finger. It had belonged to her mother, a fiercely independent woman, who had entered the practice of law at a time when women were distinctly unwelcome. She was a trailblazer. Daphne did not wear the ring often but only when she needed her mother's strength which tonight, she did. For her, the ring was a sort of talisman to ward off ill luck. *If all goes well, we can come back here. If not, we can both make a dignified retreat.*

Although she prized her independence, she felt a gaping hole within. The yearning sometimes became so strong that she feared all her accomplishments amounted to little more than a dry pile of dust. Where was the energy for life and love?

She was drawn to him in myriad ways. One glance from him could ignite her. He had a mystical, magical—some would say innocent or child-like—way of seeing the world and everything in it. The *light* in his paintings was the proof of that. How she longed to cast off her cynicism and suspicion hard earned from years in the world of advertising and see with his eyes for just a moment! That was the greatest quality Alex possessed which Brad, jaded himself, did not. She sat down to wait for the phone call from the front desk.

Alexander spun through the revolving doors of Hayden House. He requested the clerk call Daphne's room. Unaccountably nervous, he stood drumming his fingers on the counter so loudly that several guests looked up at him. He glowered at the rich tapestry of red, gold and blue birds and flowers hung on the wall behind the front desk. The clerk phoned up to Daphne's room.

"She'll be down shortly, sir."

Alex took a seat not far from the front desk in plain view of the elevators. He checked his watch. Five minutes had passed. He got up to pace back and forth in front of the reception desk.

At their last dinner, they had silently argued over his insensitivity. His remoteness—except when he wanted to talk about his art. He grimaced and took a deep breath resolving to do better. *She can't still be angry, not if she wants to have dinner—unless...*

His heart leapt when the elevator doors slid open and there she was. He grinned at her. When she saw him, she smiled broadly and quickened her pace. The tension in his chest eased somewhat. *It doesn't look like an argument tonight. In fact...*

He stepped forward and took her in his arms and gave her a lingering kiss.

"I made reservations for the dining room here. Is that all right?"

"Of course. That's perfectly fine."

"If you'd prefer elsewhere, we can..."

"No...no, not at all. I'm sure it's excellent here."

Because it was early, the dining room had few guests. Once seated in a bay window overlooking the square the waiter came with menus and gave a recitation of the specials.

An oddly awkward quiet fell over them. Something was different, he thought. Suddenly, he became aware that he had been staring at her left hand. He frowned.

"How was your trip to Paris?" she asked.

"Fine…very interesting in fact…I did find Henri Dumont. He was the one, if you remember…"

"Yes. I do remember." She smiled encouragingly. "Did you find the painter?"

"Yes, but he was in St. Petersburg and so I went there."

"Really? So you've been travelling all over."

To Alex, the conversation was painfully stilted. Why was he so chary of his words and thoughts? Suddenly he realized it was the ring she was wearing—a gold band rimmed with tiny rubies and diamonds. He was sure he had never seen it before.

He cleared his throat. "A very unfortunate incident occurred on the way over to Paris. I went by ferry from Portsmouth."

"Ferry? Surely there must be easier ways to get to Paris."

"Yes, but I just felt like going that way," he said in a mildly stubborn tone. He played with the edges of his menu. "But the ferry nearly sank and a woman, whom I'd just met, drowned. Even though I tried to save her…"

Daphne sat open mouthed. "Alex? What a story! Tell me more."

He shrugged. "Not much more to tell. She…I took her ashes with me to Paris and St. Petersburg."

"Did you know her well?"

"No. As I said, I'd only just met her." He knew he was sounding like a recalcitrant school boy, but each word seemed to stick in his throat. "She was quite old…in her seventies at least." His eye fell upon the ring again which sparkled in the candlelight. *What does it mean?*

They fell silent when the waiter came with bread and sparkling water.

"Would you care for wine, sir?" the waiter asked.

He gave Daphne a questioning glance. She nodded. "Yes. Bring us, please, a bottle of the Beaujolais," he said. The waiter bowed and disappeared.

"So," asked Alex. "How is New York? I wasn't sure you'd be back this soon."

She shrugged. "Can't stay away from London. I had a number of meetings back in New York with Brad and our accountants…"

"Brad? Who's he?"

"My business partner. I've mentioned him before. Remember?" Daphne gave a casual wave of her hand making her diamonds flash in the candlelight.

He could not take his eyes away from the band. *Damn! What sort of ring is this?*

"Everyone thinks the time is right for expansion into the UK and Europe."

"I suppose. Would you live here?"

"Probably, but I'd be going back and forth. Brad is excellent." Her face lit up. "He's more than capable of running the New York office on his own."

"Yes, you've always spoken well of him as I recall."

"He's a great partner. We complement each other and he's *very* reliable. I'd trust him completely. First rate judgment too. Besides, these days it's so easy to keep in touch."

Alexander was unused to the feeling growing in the pit of his stomach. A sort of burning tension, the cause of which, he couldn't immediately identify. The question exploded in his mind—*is that his ring?*

He tried to sound casual. "How long have you been in business together?"

"Five years as partners. Before that, he was my employee."

Over the last few days, Daphne had almost made up her mind. If things couldn't be worked out with Alex—and it didn't look promising at the moment—she could visualize a life with Brad. She had promised him an answer when she returned to New York.

The waiter came and they placed their orders. Alex had little interest in food.

"I suppose he's got a family?" he asked.

"Not really. Just his mother. She lives out in Long Island."

Alexander felt his gut contract. *So! I do have a rival.* He couldn't ask about the ring, not without looking ridiculous. *Best wait for her to tell me.*

Why is he so remote? Daphne wondered. *So wooden!*

The appetizers arrived. Daphne stirred her soup and Alex poked at his salad.

"Are you going to look for office space on this trip?"

She smiled brightly. "Yes. I think somewhere in Chelsea."

"Why Chelsea? I thought you were interested in the Embankment area."

"I don't know. Chelsea has lots to do with the arts." In fact, she had decided to establish her office some distance from the Embankment. *Don't crowd him.*

"True. Jamie might be able to help. That's where his gallery is."

Her cell phone vibrated. She frowned when she glanced down at it. "Sorry Alex. It's Brad. I need to take this call because we have contract negotiations underway." She answered. "Hi Brad. What's happening?"

Alex was slightly relieved at the business-like tone in her voice. She rose and went out to the lobby. Alex sipped his wine. Within moments, the dinner was delivered but Alex sent it back to keep it hot. Ten minutes later, he was pouring another glass of wine.

She appeared and sat down. Alex thought, even in the candlelight, that her cheeks were flushed.

"Everything all right?" he asked.

"Yes, of course." She smiled brightly. "Brad's extremely capable but we keep each other posted." She was upset. It wasn't a business call at all. Brad had been checking up on her.

Alex did not miss that she twisted the ring on her finger. He decided to change the subject. "Where would you live in London?"

His question disappointed her. Shouldn't he bring up the possibility of living together?

"I don't really know London well enough to decide. Do you have any suggestions?"

"Central London is very expensive, but you need to be close to your work." To him, they sounded like two reasonably friendly acquaintances.

At last their meals arrived. Alex had lost his appetite but tried to eat. Daphne pushed her food about on the plate. Alex called the waiter for another bottle of wine.

"Your trip sounds very interesting, Alex. Did you find what you hoped for?"

"I suppose," he muttered. "But I'm still not entirely sure." He felt sapped of energy and could scarcely turn his mind to understanding all that had occurred. "It was rather confusing, I'm afraid."

She gave him a quizzical look. "You sound so mysterious."

He shrugged. "Not really, Daphne. There were so many strange occurrences which I'm not sure how to interpret." With each word, he felt more tired.

Daphne felt shut out. "Sounds as if you don't really want to talk about it."

"It's not that. I'm just not sure what to say."

Her hopes for an evening in which they could speak heart to heart were crumbling. "Were you disappointed with the trip?"

He shook his head. "No, not really."

Daphne had too much wine and felt extremely tired herself. She could only think of getting upstairs and soaking in the tub. She could scarcely keep prying about the trip or anything else."

They sat in silence as they finished dinner with coffee.

She smiled brightly. "Alex, I have an early morning and so I should call it a night."

He tossed down his napkin and signaled the waiter for the bill. Once he had paid, they rose and returned to the lobby.

They stood near the lounge area and could hear a jazz trio in the bar. The light, complex tune was familiar to Alex. *That's Henri's music!* For Alex, it seemed that his friend Henri was standing next to him. *What a lovely co-incidence.*

He could tell from the line of her neck and shoulder that Daphne was tense and rigid. *I'm a fool. But what can I do? She's going to walk away and that will be it.*

He took her hand and bent to kiss her cheek. "How long will you be in London?"

"Probably just a few days. I have to get back soon."

"Perhaps we can have dinner again before you go."

"Yes. That would be nice, Alex. Give me a call." She smiled bravely. "Good night."

She turned from him and began to walk to the elevators.

Just then the door to the bar flew open and more melodies of Henri's floated out to the lobby. Alex could see Henri's face, twisted in pain as he said— *I would have given it all just to hear the words, "I love you, Henri."*

The elevator doors were opening. Daphne turned back to wave.

Alex rushed across the lobby and caught the doors. He grasped her hands like a drowning man. Breathless, he said, "Please Daphne! I don't want it to be this way! Please…"

Her eyes widened in surprise. When he took her in his arms, he felt her trembling.

Like a small child, she seemed ready to cry. She buried her face in his collar. "I don't either, Alex."

Someone behind them cleared his throat. "Excuse us, please!"

Alex turned about to see four people waiting to get on.

"Oh, excuse us. So sorry," Alex said as he took Daphne's hand and led her back to the lobby. They sat down next to each other on a couch.

"Daphne? Please. We have so much to talk about!"

"Of course. Let's have some more coffee in the bar."

Suddenly a voice boomed from behind them in the lobby.

"Why it's Ms. Daphne Bersault." A professorial looking man in a tweed jacket approached and extended his hand.

Alex thought he might be drunk. "Surely you remember our little tete a tete on the panel at the London School. Geoffrey Dodsbury."

Daphne's heart sank but she shook his hand. He continued to hold it and then grasped her forearm so forcefully she instinctively backed away.

"Yes, I do remember Mr. Dodsbury. I'd like to introduce my friend, Alexander Wainwright, the painter."

Alex shook his hand.

"Well now! What a great pleasure to actually meet you Mr. Wainwright." He turned to Daphne and stroked her arm. "I'm sure your friend would agree with me about the creative act and the long night of the soul." He stood so close to Daphne that she was repelled by the liquor on his breath.

She had to get rid of the obnoxious jerk as quickly as possible. "So nice to see you again, Geoffrey. Perhaps we can chat another time."

"Mr. Wainwright," the man persisted. "What do you think? Is the creative act a sole, lonely one or, as Ms. Bersault insists, collaborative."

Alexander was also hit by the overpowering smell liquor on the man's breath. "Probably a bit of both." Knowing such a person might turn ugly at any moment, he took Daphne's arm and turned to go.

"But as such a great painter with your magnificent light, don't you agree that..."

Alexander saw the man leering at Daphne. "Mr. Dodsbury, to tell the truth, the question is inane. Everyone creates in his or her own fashion. The process is entirely personal and dependent upon the objective, the nature of the work and materials." He stared coldly at Dodsbury. "Only a person with very limited understanding of art and the creative process would ask such a ridiculous question."

Dodsbury's face turned an ugly red. "Now you listen here… you son of a…!"

"Good evening, sir!" Alex ferried Daphne into the bar leaving Dodsbury clenching his fists and nearly spluttering.

"Nicely done, Alex." Daphne laughed. "He's been so intent on getting back at me for something."

"What?"

"I have absolutely no idea. But thank you for rescuing me from his clutches!"

He laughed and gave a mock bow. "Most welcome, Ma'am! Pleasure to serve!"

"Let's go into the bar."

Once they were seated she said, "What on earth has been bothering you all evening? I haven't been able to drag more than a few words out of you."

He looked straight at her hand. "It's that ring."

"Ring? What about it?"

"Who is it from? I've never seen it before. Does it mean I've lost you?"

"Oh my God! No. It's my mother's ring. Were you thinking it was…?"

"Yes. That's what I was afraid of."

Daphne sank with relief. "My mother was a very strong woman. She entered law practice when the men in the profession did everything they could to make life difficult for women lawyers. She hoped they'd think she was already married and had a protector."

"And so you wear it like a talisman for her strength?"

"Exactly. I was afraid I'd lose you too."

The waiter came with coffee.

Daphne sipped her cup. "Alex, I think we need to talk about some things."

"Of course. What are you thinking of?"

"Actually, Dodsbury has done us a favour by bringing up art and creativity."

"How so?"

"I think you're afraid that I might harm your creativity and your art.

I don't want to interfere at all. I know that I'm always saying you have your head in the clouds—and you do. But that's what's so special about you. It's so amazing the way you see the world that I just want to be able to see it as you do. I'd never try to takeover. After all, I do have my own work which is really important to me."

Alex sat very still. At last he said, "Today, I thought about when I painted the River of Remembrance and how you were always at the very centre of the painting and all the preliminary drawings. That's your place in my life and in my art—right at the very centre. *And* I hope I have the same place in yours."

She answered quietly. "That's exactly where I want to be. And you will always have that place with me."

Alex rose from his seat and bent over her. He touched her cheek gently and kissed her.

She smiled brightly. "Will you help me find office space tomorrow?"

"Yes. I'd *love* to."

"Great! I have appointments starting at eleven with a broker."

"Would you like to come to my flat for dinner tomorrow? If you like it and are comfortable there, you can stay for as long as you want."

She nodded. They sat close to each other holding hands. Alex felt that he had just completed yet another stage in his long journey.

"Would you like to come upstairs, Alex?"

"Yes." They left the bar.

Unfortunately Dodsbury was lurking near the newsstand. When Daphne saw him, she took Alex's arm. "Why is that awful man still there?" She was only half joking when she said, "Do you think he's spying on me?"

Alex stopped up. "You're right. It's odd. Shall I ask him?"

"No, of course not."

Dodsbury approached the desk. "Do you have an Alexander Wainwright registered here?" he asked the clerk.

The clerk checked the computer and then shook his head. "No sir, not that I can see."

Dodsbury returned to his post at the newsstand.

"What do you think he's up to?" Alex asked.

"You don't know him at all, do you Alex?" she asked.

He shook his head. "Why don't we ask him what he's doing?"

Daphne groaned. "Wait a minute. I'm *sure* he's spying on me!"

"Dodsbury? Whatever for?"

"I've been suspicious about something for a while." She took Alex by the arm to a nearby couch and sat down. Then she pulled him close and kissed him deeply and with such passion that passerbys stopped and grinned. Alex, of course, was delighted.

"See!" she whispered in his ear. "He's taking photos." They kissed again. "Let's give him a good one!" This time she encircled his neck with both arms. Then she rose swiftly and marched toward Dodsbury who hastily tried to cram his mobile phone into his pocket.

"So you're the one spying on me and taking pictures!" she demanded.

Dodsbury blanched and tried to hurry off. But Daphne grabbed his phone.

"How many photos have you taken? You're sending them to Brad, aren't you?"

"Listen, sweetie, I'm not surprised he wants to know what you're up to."

"So you're the one who's been following me all over New York and London!"

Dodsbury almost cringed in the face of her fury.

Daphne moved in closer. Her voice was low and threatening. "Since you're in such close touch with Mr. Franks, you tell him that there is no way I'd marry him—not when he's spying on me." Just as she was about to leave, she turned back. "And you can also tell him I'll be emailing him my buy-out proposal of his interest in the firm tomorrow morning."

"Now little lady…" Dodsbury was foolish to smirk.

Daphne was about to throw the mobile phone across the lobby.

Alex stepped in. "I think, Mr. Dodsbury, that it's time you left. You don't want to anger Daphne any more than she already is."

"And here's your phone back. I *do* want you to send those photos to Mr. Franks right away, especially the ones you've just taken."

As they got into the elevator, Alex reflected that the few steps across the lobby and into the lift represented the results of his entire trip from London to Paris and to St. Petersburg. As they rose up in the car, he thought of Miss Trump again as the sculptor, Maureen Graves. He had a sense that somehow her work would inspire the next stage in his art. But—as yet—he did not know how. But there were always empty spaces to fill. He felt in his breast pocket. *Good! My sketch notebook is there. I need to jot down just a few ideas.*

CHAPTER 37

The following week, Daphne returned to New York where she met with her lawyers to buy Brad out. Before she left, she signed an agreement to rent premises for her new office space. I think she also wanted to give Alexander time on his own for his next painting. I was greatly pleased because they seemed to have worked out their problems. She did, in fact, return two weeks later on a more or less permanent basis. No mention of Bradley Franks was ever made.

Alex felt that he had achieved a sort of balance in his life between his two worlds—art and love in his personal life. And why not? I had said to him earlier that most of us must strike such a balance. For example, my wife is constantly asking me to make time for her, the family and myself—away from work. But when one is so engaged in one's profession, it can be quite difficult. If you love your work, then it is not work. Why would you ever want to stop? But I expect it is much harder for Alex. He has been given a great and demanding gift and sees the world through inspired eyes.

Once I stood at the top of the steps of the National Gallery overlooking Trafalgar Square at dusk. Usually I would have only seen the cars, the people and the pigeons each as separate *things* as they appear to most of us. I believe Alex sees the same scene as if it were meshed together like a beautifully intricate patterned web, one part inextricably linked to another. I've heard him speak of a *silken web of meaning!* Where there are blank, empty spaces, he sees the potential for *something.* Or possibly, he would see that the emptiness is no different from the solid forms and that we just cannot see what occupies that empty space. In one sense it is the future for us to create right in front of us.

If my explanation is confusing, it is only because I lack the right words to express something I have only rarely experienced which I did for just an instant that day. For Alex, it is a daily occurrence which contributes mightily to his art. Consequently, for those with such powerful gifts, I think it must be much more difficult to find a balance in life. His *daemon* is an extremely hard and demanding task master.

For much of the first week, Alex simply wandered about London without any particular destination in mind. First it was along the Embankment back and forth from Westminster to Tower Bridge. Next it was into Kensington and around the palace grounds. I think he found the rhythm of walking conducive to his creative process. Then, one day, he simply stopped his walking and took a cab to his studio. He was ready.

He began with dozens upon dozens of sketches. Just out of the corner of his eye, he could catch the form he wanted to draw. But it was elusive. He watched his hand move across the page in new and different rhythms, as if guided by another being.

When he set out his drawings from the morning's work, he saw that one shape frequently reappeared—a curved cylindrical form, somewhat like an egg.

As he gazed at his work, he felt himself sliding downward into a dark and different place beneath deep waters. As if drowning, he struggled to stand up. He might have been back on the ferry. Greedily he took great lungful's of air and felt himself shooting upward just as if he were breaking through the surface of an endless ocean.

He thought of Maureen Graves the sculptor—Millicent Trump in another form. *And then,* he was back in his studio and ready to paint. He simply knew that his forms would be some combination of the cosmic egg and lyrical positive and negative shapes of her beautiful sculpture.

On the canvas, he sketched the beginnings of an egg shape segmented into its various parts—a little like a Cubist painting. He had a full palette of paints and so he was able to use every colour imaginable. The more he worked the broader his smile grew.

He saw the swirls of light and colour shimmer and sing a kind of joyful tune. Henri always maintained that his music was partly shaped by the silences between the bars of notes. Alex thought that must be true of painting. The empty spaces shaped the forms in some sort of thrilling collaboration.

Standing in the middle of his studio, he said matter of factly, "It is in those empty spaces that I will find my light." Then he worked non-stop on the canvas.

I tried to contact Alex over the next few days without success. Finally I went to his studio and knocked. He flung open the door.

"Ah, it's you Jamie. You've come at a perfect time. I am now done my work!' Although a joyful smile lit up his face, he was hollow-eyed and worn.

"How long have you been working?" I asked.

He rumpled his hair and looked toward the garbage can. "Hmmm... let me think. Six take-away cartons represent one lunch and one dinner over three days. Yes. That's it. Just three days."

I was breathless with excitement. "May I see it?"

"Of course." He guided me to the far end of the studio where a curtain was drawn across an easel. Slowly he pulled it back.

I stood, open-mouthed, before the painting as if I were viewing the Mona Lisa for the very first time. Of course, the subject matter was entirely different but his work had that certain elusive, timeless quality signifying great art—art which would be gazed at centuries from now.

"Alex! I have no words!"

He grinned at me.

How can I describe the work? Throughout the composition were egg shapes in various states of segmentation. The colours red, green, blue and yellow were at once vivid and intense yet soft and subtle. Together they seemed to shimmer and swirl in a delicate dance as if magically enlivened by some deeply buried force. Somehow he had found the way to combine his *light* with the *energy* which created that light and express it on the canvas.

But the most striking feature was the apparent contrast between form and empty space. It made me think that the source of Alex's creativity was found in those empty spaces so well placed in the composition that they were the source of his magical light shining through. In brief, the painting was sublime.

"Do you like it, Jamie?" he asked.

With tears in my eyes I said, "It is absolutely magnificent, my friend. You have created something which is truly *new— original.* I swear people will line up in the National Gallery hundreds of years from now to see this painting. You have truly outdone yourself."

"Good! There were times when I was about to trash it."

"Thank God, you didn't! You've brought another gift to the world. What was your inspiration?"

"Inspiration? I don't know—just a sense of what is so elusive in this world." He went to his kitchen. "I'm going to make us some tea and then I'll tell you about everyone I met on my trip. After all, you've done such a wonderful job of recording my other travels."

As he put the kettle on to boil, he gazed toward the windows. A slow, sweet smile spread across his face. I did not know at the time, but his *cosmic egg* had just floated past in a lovely, lyrical dance.

Just around dinner time, Daphne appeared at the door. She sat before Alex's painting for at least twenty minutes with him crouched down beside her.

"Do you like it, Daphne?" he asked taking her hand in his. "Again, you have been a great inspiration—along with my friend, Miss Trump."

"Who is she?"

"She has at least two names but one spirit. She is also the sculptor Maureen Graves, the woman I tried to save on the ferry."

She was at a loss for words. And so, she just smiled with tears in her eyes. At last she said, "Alex! It is sublimely beautiful. Please *always* show us what you find in your clouds."

CPSIA information can be obtained at www.ICGtesting.com
Printed in the USA
LVOW13s0519090714

393433LV00001B/2/P